TRIAL OF THE INNOCENT

TRIAL
OF THE
INNOCENT

SARA MITCHELL

BETHANY HOUSE PUBLISHERS
MINNEAPOLIS, MINNESOTA 55438

Cover illustration by Wes Lowe.

Published by Bethany House Publishers
A Ministry of Bethany Fellowship, Inc.
11300 Hampshire Avenue South
Minneapolis, Minnesota 55438

Printed in the United States of America.

Library of Congress Cataloging-in-Publication Data

Mitchell, Sara.
    Trial of the innocent / Sara Mitchell.
        p.   cm. — (Shadowcatchers)

    I. Title. II. Series: Mitchell, Sara. Shadowcatchers.
PS3563.I823T78   1995
813'.54—dc20   95–468
ISBN 1–55661–497–7   CIP

For my husband, and
our two daughters—
Because. . . .

SARA MITCHELL is the author of numerous popular novels published in the CBA market, as well as several musical dramas and skits. The wife of a retired U.S. Air Force officer, Sara spent twenty-two years traveling, visiting, and living in diverse locations from Colorado to England. This wealth of cultural experience finds its way into all her works. She and her husband and their two daughters now live in northern Virginia. She enjoys hearing from her readers. You may write to her at the following address:

Sara Mitchell
%Bethany House Publishers
11300 Hampshire Ave. South
Minneapolis, MN 55438

Contents

If the scourge slay suddenly,
he will laugh at the trial of the innocent.

Job 9:23 KJV

Prologue

Rhode Island Royal Hotel
December 1891

THE LETTER ARRIVED AFTER dinner, while Dexter was enjoying his favorite Cuban cigar in the quiet elegance of the Rhode Island Royal Hotel. Only two individuals knew of his whereabouts, so he opened the single sheet of paper with some curiosity. It was two days past Christmas, but he knew this was not likely to contain belated greetings of the season.

After reading it twice, a speculative smile gradually spread across his face. He leaned back in his chair, cigar clamped between his teeth, while he pondered whether to follow up on the letter's request.

So. A brief association he had enjoyed some two years ago might bear fruit after all. Folding the letter decisively, he gestured for one of the bellboys standing at attention near the doorway.

"Have my bags packed immediately. I'm afraid I've received some distressing news and must check out as soon as possible." He handed the startled boy a coin. "I'll need a hack within the hour."

Two hours later, comfortably arranged in a southbound Pullman Palace sleeping car, he set himself to the task of selecting his next identity. Something British, he decided, chuckling at an irony only he could appreciate. Something . . . aristocratic. Perhaps even a title. Southerners still doted on the English, probably because most southerners still lived as though the Civil War had ended the previous week instead of almost thirty years ago.

He must remember to refer to it as The War Between the States. He had almost ruined six months of careful wooing in Georgia over a little lapse like that. His thumb and finger idly caressed the twin clefts that ran down both cheeks, more visible now without the beard and moustache. Maybe he would grow whiskers back—his sojourn in Georgia had also taught him that southern women still preferred gentlemen with beards.

At least, the late Mrs. Dexter Greaves had.

Later that evening he ripped some pages out of a notebook, carefully burned them to ash, and prepared for bed. He never had trouble sleeping, even on a train, and functioned well with a mere four hours of rest. He never suffered from nightmares or any other annoying pricks of a conscience smitten by remorse.

Women were gullible and deserved their fate. It was his duty and privilege to mete out that fate in whatever fashion he selected, and to enjoy the benefits. Lulled by the rocking motion of the car, he drifted off to sleep with a smile as he contemplated the demise of his next bride.

PART ONE

———

TREACHERY

June–November 1893

1

THE MORNING STARTED LIKE ANY other lazy summer day.

Covered mule-drawn market wagons rumbled through the Richmond streets, bound for the crowded markets. Downtown, shopkeepers unrolled awnings over their store entrances and swept the sidewalks clean. Along the wide, tree-lined avenues, ice and milk wagons delivered their goods to the doors of stately homes.

By eight o'clock, houses teemed with the same bustling activity as the city. Housekeepers prepared lists of daily chores while domestics kneaded dough for the day's bread. Businessmen in dark suits and bowler hats tapped their canes along the sidewalk as they hurried to catch the corner trolley into town.

Normally Eve Sheridan embraced such summer mornings, reveling in the beauty of God's creation, arranged so delightfully in the backyard for her enjoyment. But not today—and she hadn't for many weeks.

Though the air teased her senses with the fragrance of roses and honeysuckle, her nose didn't even twitch. Sunbeams streaked through the eighty-year-old hardwoods shading the Sheridans' backyard, but Eve didn't stop to admire the dappled patterns. Instead, she walked down the well-worn path with the soundless step of a cat on the prowl.

This mental image of herself startled Eve. She despised cats. They preferred birds for breakfast, while Eve provided breakfast *for* the birds. A black-capped chickadee darted about the trees, waiting for her approach. Eve envied its playful freedom, the plucky indifference to danger.

She reached the last of the bird feeders scattered all over the yard—her favorite one near the back wall, tucked among the drooping branches of a dogwood—and she filled the little glass feeder. "Breakfast time," she murmured aloud, and was taken aback by the strain she could hear in her voice.

A chickadee darted down, lighting inches away on the replenished feeder. Motionless, Eve waited until the bird flew back to a branch. Then she scooped out a handful of seed and held her arm up. A second chickadee, watching with a bright black eye from another branch, flew down to perch in the palm of her hand. Their trust never failed to awe—and humble—Eve.

"Did you know," she murmured, her smile as strained as her voice, "that your Latin name weighs more than you do? And in case you didn't know, that's *Parus atri*—"

"Eve? Where are you?"

With a scolding chitter the tiny bird shot up into the tree.

"Sorry." Eve spread her fingers to let the rest of the seed fall. "My sister has no sense of avian mealtime decorum."

She closed her eyes and forced her countenance to relax. It wouldn't do to let Rebecca see her anxiety. Eve smiled a little grimly at the irony. Growing up, she and Rebecca had shared everything.

Now Rebecca was so caught up in wedding plans that she couldn't see anything else. Yet Eve didn't *want* her sister to perceive what she was feeling; it would only hurt

Rebecca and could not possibly remedy the situation. But Eve felt lonely, nevertheless, because for weeks—no, months now, she had been compelled to practice a charade, a soul-shriveling duplicity. *Four more days,* she breathed, almost as a prayer. She only had to pretend cheerfulness four more days.

"Who on earth are you talking to—or do I need to ask?" Rebecca Sheridan wound her way down the path and ducked beneath the sheltering dogwood branches. In the sun-dappled shade she looked as fresh and lovely as a Gainesborough painting, with her rich brown hair and butter yellow gown. The noose about Eve's heart constricted even tighter.

Mouth pursed, hands on her hips, Rebecca surveyed her sister. "Eve, you look like a guttersnipe in those old clothes, with your hair all over the place. And tell me that apron isn't one of Maggie's—" Suddenly she grinned, her hazel eyes sparkling. Eve knew that look, and she braced herself.

"Never mind," Rebecca waved her hand, "we won't start another squabble over your clothing, your red hair—or your birds. I've far more important matters to discuss." She thrust a letter in front of Eve's nose. "Jane Renfrow has invited me to be a bridesmaid in *her* wedding, but it's in September, and Giles and I will still be on our bridal trip in England, so of course I won't be able to attend. I want you to go in my place." She said it more as statement of fact than request. "Not as a bridesmaid, of course—just as a guest. It will be good for you; you and Mother can take the train."

Eve absently smoothed her disordered hair while she surveyed her younger sister, love and pain twining about her heart like thorny vines. It had been like this ever since the New Year's Ball, when Giles Dawson was introduced to Rebecca.

It wasn't jealousy. Rebecca had always glowed with vitality and life, and Eve had always been content to let her younger sister take center stage. Even when they were

15

children, Rebecca had attracted more attention than Eve by sheer force of personality.

The two were as different as sugar and salt. Outgoing and vibrant, Rebecca thrived on attention. Introspective, intelligent, and whimsical, Eve flourished in solitude, so she never begrudged her sister the extra attention. Sighing, she pushed back a rising flood of memories and smiled at Becca. "You know Mother and I can't be in the same room longer than ten minutes before she feels compelled to lecture, and I feel compelled to flee."

Rebecca's mouth drooped, and the teasing twinkle faded from her eyes. "I know, Eve—but this would mean so much to me. Jane will be dreadfully hurt if no one from the family attends."

Eve ducked her head, wiping her hands on the faded gingham apron. "All right," she finally agreed, her voice quiet. "For you, Rebecca, I'll go."

She watched Rebecca, with petticoats flying, dash back up to the house, as excited and exuberant as the blue jays who loved to swoop about the hedge. Rebecca's view of life was uncomplicated: she lived to enjoy it.

Eve shivered in spite of the morning sun, her own mood diametrically opposite her sister's. Rebecca's personality might resemble the rascally jays, but Giles Dawson reminded Eve of a hawk. Twice in the last six months she had glimpsed a fierce, predatory gleam in his amber brown eyes when he watched Rebecca—the focused gaze of the raptor hovering over its prey. Both times the look vanished within seconds, but Eve knew she had not misinterpreted it. She held a degree in ornithology, and she was trained to be observant.

But though uneasiness over her sister's betrothal lingered, Eve held her tongue. One could not, after all, object to a man because of a few elusive facial expressions.

A vivid male cardinal flew down and perched in a cluster of dogwood flowers, chirping an unmistakable demand. Eve grabbed the bucket of seed and finished making her rounds. What good would it do to burden Rebecca with groundless apprehensions about Giles, the man Rebecca would be marrying in four days?

Regardless of Eve's misgivings, her younger sister was about to become a wife. The most loving gift Eve could present would be an offering of continued silence and support—not a fanciful comparison of Giles Dawson to a bird of prey.

2

WITH A JAUNTY TAP OF HIS WALKING stick, Avery Paxton stepped through the doors of his favorite New York club, nodding to a couple of men on their way out. He paused at the top of the stairs leading down into the crowded bar area, scanned the dimly lit, smoke-laden room, then made his way over to the bartender.

"Evenin', Mr. Paxton. The usual?"

"Thank you, Eddie. That will be fine." The barkeep poured his drink, and Avery turned, resting his elbows on the bar behind him. He sipped from the tumbler as he watched the men filling the room. He liked coming here, liked both the familiarity and the anonymity the place afforded. He also liked the luxury. Avery found nothing vulgar in the crystal chandeliers, the wine-colored velvet drapes and matching carpet, or the carefully arranged greenery that afforded the privacy so valued by every member of this Sixth Avenue establishment.

He took another sip of his drink and watched the shuffling approach of one of his more recent "associates." Balding, with old-fashioned dundreary sideburns, Horace Topper tended toward portliness and always

18

managed to look slightly less than well-groomed. Avery inclined his head. "Topper."

"Mr. Paxton." Topper gratefully accepted a drink and downed it in one gulp. Avery frowned. "I've established contacts with several individuals who might prove to be of benefit in our—ah—latest business venture," Topper said, exhaling loudly.

Avery took a discreet, noiseless swallow, his gaze never leaving Topper. "Very good." He lifted his monocle and fitted it in place, then meticulously adjusted his snowy white collar and cuffs. "I need to have a brief word with Shiver, then perhaps you'll join me for dinner, and we can discuss the details. Shiver, of course, will be joining us."

Topper shifted nervously, his face flushing. He set the glass back down on the bar, then cleared his throat. "Yes, sir. Your private table?"

"Even surrounded by friends, one can never be too careful." Avery nodded to the barkeep, then led the way toward a door at the back of the room, behind a Chinese trifold screen. "By the way, Topper . . . have you heard from Gambrielli lately?"

"Not since his cable two weeks ago. You made the arrangements yourself, I was given to understand, and I cabled that information back to him the very same day I received it."

The pathetic little man looked even more nervous, and Avery laughed, pleased with himself. "Don't croak, Tops. You're still one of my favorite friends. I was merely inquiring." He produced a key from his vest pocket and opened the door, gesturing the other man through. "I think you'll be especially delighted by the progress of my latest plans for our—'business venture,' I believe you called it?"

"So, is old Mealymouth Muttonchops here tonight?"

Avery leaned against the bar and lifted a mildly rebuking brow at Joe Leoni, usually called Shiver. Avery indulged Shiver more than most because his particular specialty was vital to the well-being of Avery's organization. "Topper is quite well. He's waiting in the back room. But first, I have a job to discuss with you." He glanced about. "I received a most unusual letter—from the older Sheridan girl. Goes by the name of Eve." He began fiddling with his monocle, stroking it with caressing fingers. "I didn't care for the girl's tone, Shiver. She knows too much about my associations. Therefore I have formulated a plan." A slow smile spread across his face as he fit the monocle in place. "A plan I think you'll find most enjoyable, as it will allow us some entertainment, while removing potential trouble."

"You can depend on me, Mr. Paxton."

Avery clasped his hands, the smile deepening. "I need for you to secure the services of a particular female, one who meets my rather . . . ah . . . *specific* qualifications."

"I understand—" Shiver began, but his smirk faded when Avery, no longer smiling, cut him off with a look.

"The qualifications," he finished acidly, "entail the ability to keep her mouth shut, to follow orders without question . . . and to maintain a healthy respect for my power." He shoved away from the bar, a glint of humor returning to his eyes. "She will also need to wear a wig. A *red* wig."

After consulting his watch, Avery motioned Shiver through the door into his private dining room. Topper sat alone at the table, looking awkward and out-of-place. "I'll tell you all about it, after dinner. . . ."

3

A KNIFING WIND FLATTENED THE grasses on either side of the canal banks. Rebecca hunched her shoulders, shivering, clutching her coat as she walked. The housekeeper had warned about a storm brewing farther north, on the coast, but Rebecca needed fresh air—and escape from the stifling quiet of the cottage.

Giles had been gone four days this time. "I have to," he had told her, that look in his eyes again. It was a penetrating stare, which turned the warm brown eyes as hard and unyielding as the polished onyx handle of his cane. When Rebecca saw that look, she knew further pleading was useless.

She lifted her head now, biting her lip at the pewter sky and line of black clouds spreading like spilled ink on the horizon. Autumn arrived much earlier here than in Virginia. There wouldn't be much time. She sat down in her favorite spot—a private haven protected on three sides by thick bushes—and arranged her writing materials. She ignored the damp, prickling grass as well as the malicious tugs of the wind.

Dear Eve, she wrote haltingly, her fingers clutching the

fountain pen in a death grip. *I haven't wanted to further worry you, but I have no one else with whom I can share my apprehensions.*

A wood pigeon exploded from the bushes in a flurry of feathers. Rebecca jerked, then stared down at the ugly blob of ink smeared across the paper. It looked as ominous as the swelling clouds.

She was behaving like a timid, spineless mouse. Eve would never have allowed *her* imagination to run away with her like this, and most likely would have scolded Rebecca for reading too many dime novels. Rebecca took a deep breath and resumed writing. *I'm even more concerned now about Giles. Do you remember the letter I wrote you from New York? I've been thinking about what I told you, and am convinced that there must be something wrong with—*

A man's voice called her name, the syllables windblown but resonant, commanding. Her hands trembling, Rebecca hurriedly stuffed everything away and rose. "Giles!" she called, waving her arm to the hatless man striding down the bank toward her.

He was smiling—the boyish, carefree smile she loved. But the cold gleam in his eyes froze her more than the frigid wind blowing off the North Sea.

4

New York
September

"MAKE SURE IT LOOKS LIKE A robbery—not an assault. Remember, I want the incident linked to a series of burglaries visited upon lone women in hotels." Paxton stopped filing his nails to examine the man lounging in a chair opposite. "My sources indicate that the authorities there are most concerned about the safety of their gentle female citizens." He chuckled. "More likely they're concerned over their own public image. Of course, the Pinks won't know whether her demise is a haphazard one—or deliberately arranged." He rubbed his hands together, then laughed. "Yes, I do enjoy playing with puppets."

Shiver twirled a letter opener in his hands, then drew it across his throat. "Do you have a preference on the manner in which she's dispatched . . . or can I have some fun as long as the bluecoats don't know?"

"Spare me the details." Avery shuddered, rising to his feet and walking over to the window. Behind him, he heard the disgusting sound of Leoni's sadistic laugh. "You know better—" he began, his throat muscles tight.

Shiver interrupted with the familiarity Avery allowed no other man. "So I do, so I do. That's why you trust me more than the others, isn't it?"

Avery turned back around, meeting the thin-lipped smile with a calculated grin of his own. "I trust you, my friend . . . but remember that *I'm* not wanted for murder. You may be the best at what *you* do—but don't forget that *I'm* the best at everything else." He picked up an envelope and extracted a ticket. "By the way . . . this is for you. It's passage to England—since the worm is trying to wriggle off the hook. Do you comprehend?"

Shiver shrugged. "England's a cold, gloomy country, but if that's the way you want it—"

"Oh, it will be the way I want it," Avery promised quietly. He looked down at the ticket, running a thumb along the edge. "No matter what my friend Dante Gambrielli thinks—no matter how he chooses to scheme otherwise—it *will* be the way I want it." He held out the ticket.

Shiver tucked it away with a dismissive shrug and headed through the door. Avery called a final warning: "Watch out for the Pinks, remember. They've been very useful for this little caper . . . but they're too dangerous to discount."

Shiver mouthed an obscenity to show what he felt about Pinkerton's National Detective Agency and its operatives. Avery laughed. "I agree. But let's not risk pulling the tiger's tail too often, my friend. I can keep them caged—but they still have claws."

Lucy slipped her arm through that of the slight little man she had met at a backwater saloon in Manhattan. "Watch it, dearie." She giggled, reaching with her other hand to adjust one of the red curls she had carefully arranged. "You wouldn't be wantin' to muss the hair, now."

"That wouldn't do," Joey agreed in a nasal growl. He patted her hand, letting her arm stay hooked in his.

Lucy knew his friends called him Shiver. It was a joke, she had learned, spawned from Joey's fondness for knives—someone had told her that "shiv" was a British word for a knife. "You call me Joey," he had ordered, and the look in his dark, close-set eyes revealed to Lucy another reason people called him "Shiver."

He was real edgy tonight; the muscles Lucy felt beneath her hand were hard as a bed slat. She normally didn't treat him like one of her customers, but since they had met here . . . well, she had always known things might change. And she was willing to do whatever she had to for the two hundred dollars Joey paid at every meeting. So far all she'd had to do was deliver messages to the address Joey supplied. She weren't no fool, so she followed orders . . . and grew rich.

"What's the message for me tonight, dearie?" she purred, pressing closer to signal her willingness for something more than passing along some note. Her fingers stroked the strange tattoo on the back of his hand.

Joey jerked his chin, gesturing in the direction of the door. "Outside."

Maybe she was mistaken. Shrugging, Lucy followed, holding her underskirt up so the garbage wouldn't soil the flounces. Joey led her a short distance down an alley next to the saloon and stopped, turning to her with an unpleasant, thin-lipped smile barely visible in the foul-smelling darkness. Lucy experienced the first trickling of uneasiness. "So, what's the message?" she repeated, her voice a shade higher than usual.

When Joey finally spoke, his voice was flat, emotionless. "You won't be taking any more messages."

Smiling, he looked down at the crumpled form in the gutter. She had served her purpose for Paxton and associates, but now that Topper was in North Carolina, putting the Pinks onto the *real* prey, she wasn't needed anymore. He, for one, was glad to be rid of the loudmouthed, clinging wench.

Avery Paxton might suffer from the delusion that money and fear could keep a broad's mouth shut, but Joe Leoni knew better. He knew what had to be done to silence a skirt like this one—and whether or not Paxton approved, Joe Leoni intended to keep himself out of trouble. The girl knew too much; she would have put the finger on him in a second. And he couldn't take that chance.

He slipped out of the alley and tossed the bloodspattered red wig into the nearest sewer drain. Then, whistling, he stuck his hands in his pockets and sauntered casually up the street in the direction of Grand Central Station.

Another bird was waiting, as dumb and unsuspecting as the loudmouthed Lucy. It was going to be easy, so very easy.

Joe Leoni hastened his steps as he drew near the station. There was no time to waste. He had a train to catch . . . a southbound train.

5

North Carolina
September

THE WEDDING OF JANE RENFROW and David
Grey included six bridesmaids and six groomsmen, four
flower girls, two ring bearers, and several hundred guests.
Proclaimed by the Wilmington paper as the social function of the season, guests from as far away as Atlanta and
Richmond, Virginia, were expected to attend the gala
event. A reception, the paper's account continued, would
be held on the extensive back lawn of the Renfrow estate.

At the reception, some two hours after the ceremony,
Eve stood beneath the branches of a sycamore tree. Fan-
ning herself to relieve the humidity, she watched with ill-
concealed amusement as one of the ring bearers gathered
a pile of sycamore balls from another tree and began pelt-
ing the hapless flower girls with them.

Although her name and her mother's had appeared in
the paper as the guests from Richmond, Eve didn't know
anybody else here other than Jane; at the last moment her
mother had been unable to attend. After an hour of stiff
smiles and even stiffer conversation, Eve had found this
shady spot off to the side where—happily unnoticed—she
could observe to her heart's content.

At that moment a prickly green sycamore projectile

smacked a little girl's cherubic cheek and tangled in her orange-blossom head wreath. Several ladies rushed to attend the resulting howls, and Eve held the fan over her mouth to hide her smile. If *she'd* been over there, she'd be running off to hide like the guilty ring bearer. . . .

Becca, only for you would I be down here all alone in a crowd of strangers, Eve thought. Her own social ineptitude irritated her. She wished just this once she had yielded to Mother's bullying and telegraphed *her* regrets as well.

The flower girl's howls dwindled to sniffs, the lazy humming of hundreds of conversations resumed, and Eve abruptly decided she had fulfilled her promise to Rebecca. Lifting her skirt, she marched down the brick pathway, eager to leave the noise and crowd behind. First, unfortunately, she had to pay her respects to Jane and her new husband, who were surrounded by several laughing couples on the other side of the grounds.

There was no help for it. Eve joined the sea of chattering, laughing guests, a polite smile plastered on her face. She slipped past clusters of distinguished men and elegantly clad ladies, feeling overwhelmed by waves of satin, chiffon, and silk. The crush was unbearable, and one portly gentleman almost tripped her with his cane. Eve kept her eye focused on Jane's tulle veil, which was the only part of the bride she could see.

Strong fingers abruptly clamped around her arm, jerking her to a halt. A guttural, masculine voice hissed into her ear. "Here." Something was pressed into her gloved hand. "Whatever happens, don't lose it," the low voice commanded urgently.

Astonished, Eve stared down at a folded piece of paper, then lifted her gaze to search the crowd. Her only clue, beyond his hoarsely spoken words, was the blurred impression of a heavyset man whose grip would probably leave bruises. "Wait . . ." she began, then shook her head.

The man—whoever he was—had disappeared.

For over an hour Alexander MacKay had discreetly played the role of wedding guest, moving about the crowd, all the while keeping a sharp eye on the woman. In his ten years as a Pinkerton operative, he had never worked a case in the midst of such a fancy wedding. For these past several minutes, he had been chatting with an elegantly dressed matron seated on a wrought-iron bench, whose knowledge of horticulture was both immense and surprisingly interesting.

"The overly dry summer might have affected the taste of the Beurre Bosc pears," she concluded now, smiling up at Alex as if he were some blasted English earl. It remained a ceaseless wonder how ladies responded to the lilting brogue he exaggerated on occasions such as this.

In truth, he felt like Little Lord Fauntleroy, trussed up in the frock coat and striped pants he had worn for his youngest sister's wedding last year. "I quite agree, madam," he concurred now, smiling courteously at the matron while he watched the young, red-haired woman beneath the sycamore. A baffling sequence of emotions chased across her face when she caught sight of a mischievous boy throwing something at a group of identically clad young girls. Laughter, then wistfulness—was it?—followed by boredom and impatience. The latter two emotions Alex would have expected from that sort of female, but—

Without warning she abandoned her vigil beneath the tree and headed down the path, straight into a throng of people. If Alex didn't untangle his wits as well as his big feet, he'd lose her—which of course he suspected was the canny woman's strategy.

"Madam, this has been delightful—" He touched the brim of his top hat to the matron. "But I've just spotted an acquaintance I've been trying to locate all afternoon. With your kind permission?"

He headed briskly down the path. As he passed by one

of the pear trees they'd been discussing, he reached and snagged a ripe pear; turning back, he winked, and the aging dowager responded with an unexpectedly youthful smile. Alex grinned back, then hurriedly searched out Paxton's courier.

She moved through the crowd without pause, and Alex was forced to admire her style, especially when she almost lost him twice. From the corner of his eye, he caught sight of Topper, moving in from the woman's left.

The exchange lasted less than five seconds. Paxton knew how to pick his associates, right enough—though from her startled expression, the folded note hadn't been what the courier was anticipating.

Alex made it to the front of the house in time to observe the red-haired woman being helped into a hack. Tossing the pear up and down, he casually approached the next coach in the long row of carriages and liveries lining the sweeping circular drive. "The lady in that hackney was supposed to leave something with me, but we were separated," he told the indifferent driver. "Can you follow along, and we'll meet up there?" Alex didn't know where "there" was yet, but he would soon find out. He hopped onto the sagging seat and slammed the door shut, settling back as the driver jiggled the reins and snapped the whip.

It had been a neat, smoothly coordinated exchange. Alex bit a huge chunk out of the pear. He would have given a week's pay to know the contents of that note, but he had taken enough of a risk just showing up at the reception. He tugged his gloves off and tossed them into the crown of his top hat, and the gesture reminded him of the red-haired courier's hat. Alex shook his head. That hat!

The homburg style with its simple blue velvet bow *was* worn by many women these days—but for sporting activities like hunting or hiking. *Not* for a formal society wedding. Alex had four younger sisters, so he figured he knew nearly everything there was to know of girls and their fripperies.

30

Finishing the pear, he leaned back against the seat to ponder his next move, ignoring the jarring ride with the ease of long practice.

The telegram had arrived only two nights ago, alerting the Richmond office that one of Paxton's associates planned to attend a society wedding in North Carolina. He was expected to make contact with a new female courier. Their only information about her was that she had red hair and would arrive independently. Within an hour Alex had turned over a forgery case to a fellow operative and caught a ride in the mail car of a southbound train. He hooked up with Sam Pagett, an operative from Raleigh, early the next morning.

Alex grinned wryly. Charming rogue that he was, he had informed Pagett that *he* would shadow the red-haired courier. "Never could resist trailing a lass," he'd joked, though Pagett had turned out to be a stodgy sort with little humor.

Alex wasn't sure what he had expected of Paxton's new courier, but this woman wasn't it. Such people were typically chosen for their ability to blend into a crowd, but this one did the exact opposite—especially with her flaming hair and that ridiculous hat.

Still, she was professional enough. She had left the reception without even glancing at the note. That could mean several things, few of them good. Fighting the frustration of delay, he tugged out his watch, then glanced out the window when he heard a train whistle. So, it looked as though the pigeon would be flying back to the roost— and Alex might be heading for New York.

The hack with the red-haired courier stopped, and the woman hurried into the station. As Alex's driver pulled up behind, Alex quickly paid him and descended to follow leisurely, wandering over to read the notices posted on one of the walls. A line had formed at the ticket counter; he watched from the corner of his eye, and as the courier stepped up to talk to the stationmaster, Alex strolled closer.

"Can you tell me what time the *Florida Special* is scheduled to arrive in Richmond?" she asked. Alex almost stumbled.

Richmond? And why would she be wanting to know the time to Richmond? None of the answers that sprang immediately to mind promised anything honorable; Alex waited until she disappeared inside the ladies' lounge, then approached the counter.

"I need to send a telegram," he said.

6

Florida Special

AFTER THE LONG HOURS SPENT at the reception, Eve was relieved to find an empty seat on the train. Crowded with families, businessmen, and several rows of fresh-faced girls dressed in commencement gowns, the day coach vibrated with noise and movement in spite of the lateness of the hour.

Eve repressed a wistful yearning for a berth in one of the sleeping cars, where she could have enjoyed a modicum of privacy and a bed. She ignored the casually interested glances of two men, placed her traveling satchel on the seat beside her, and gratefully tugged out the boxed meal that Maggie, the Sheridans' aging Irish housekeeper, had prepared for her. Two cars ahead was a diner, but Eve would have sooner attended a fancy dress ball looking like a guttersnipe than eat in the dining car by herself.

"You got no business traveling that far all alone, miss," Maggie had grumped two days earlier as she carefully packed enough food for a family of six. "Sure, and it's asking for nothing but trouble."

"That may be, but there's nobody else available or willing," Eve had calmly returned. "And Becca would be hurt if I didn't."

A wave of utter loneliness swamped her. Eve had always been the family oddity, loved but often misunderstood. Rebecca, though two years younger, had been so much more than a sister. She was Eve's best friend, confidante, and buffer. Perhaps that was why Eve closed her eyes to her sister's streak of selfishness. Rebecca had always been tolerant of Eve's idiosyncrasies—largely, Eve admitted, because of Rebecca's consuming self-absorption.

But now Rebecca had Giles—a charming, cultured man everyone but Maggie adored, because he so obviously adored Rebecca. Or so it seemed.

The whistle of the train wailed mournfully in the darkness. And like its warning shriek, Eve's conscience warned her that her discomfiture with Giles ran deeper than twinges of jealousy and pain at the loss of her sister's affections. Something was wrong there—she could just feel it. Somehow, Giles Dawson was not the man her family believed him to be.

Take care of them both, Eve prayed silently, fighting back the inner sense of hopelessness. With despair—and little expectation—she also prayed for her unsettled state of mind. Then, determined to get her mind off Rebecca, she picked up a day-old newspaper left on the seat. Few of the articles uplifted her mood: a report on the hordes of people at the World's Columbian Exposition, recently opened in Chicago; some possible clues in an ongoing case involving the murders of several young married women; a great deal of political rhetoric about the financial panic; a grisly murder in Georgia; a robbery in New Jersey. . . .

"Sometimes Maggie's right about the world," Eve muttered. "It *is* full of brigands and fiends." She stuffed the paper behind her bag and dug out an apple to eat. Life was enough of a struggle without having to wallow in the wickedness and misery of others.

Not until the conductor had punched her ticket did Eve recall the note in her pocket. Sighing, groggy from fatigue and the train's motion, she almost didn't bother. On the other hand, it was going to be a long, uncomfortable night, and now that she *had* remembered, curiosity stirred her to action.

She rummaged in her pocket for the paper, then smoothed it open. *American Hotel, Richmond. This Friday noon, Main Street entrance. A matter of utmost gravity. Am depending on your absolute discretion—many lives will be adversely affected otherwise.* There was no signature.

Eve read it three times. Logic dictated that it was merely a nasty prank—rather like the ring bearer throwing sycamore balls. The man must have indiscriminately grabbed a hand out of the crowd. And yet—the American Hotel, Richmond—plainly indicated that the note *must* have been intended for Eve; to her knowledge she had been the only guest present from Richmond.

She stared absently at the slipping turban of a stout matron asleep in the chair ahead of her. For a few minutes she mulled over the matter, then her head dropped to rest against the pulled-down window shade. She dozed off, the note held loosely in her lap.

Eight rows behind, Alex toyed with the idea of slipping the note free just long enough to read it; the girl would never be the wiser, as long as he hadn't lost his touch. Unfortunately, there were too many witnesses about. The last thing he needed was a public scene that could unmask him, not to mention earning himself a scalding tirade from his superintendent.

He shifted to find a more comfortable position and jostled the dozing man next to him. "Sorry," Alex grimaced as he muttered the gruff apology. Why were train seats designed for midgets? More to the point, why had he been cursed with a pair of legs that stretched from Edinburgh to John O'Groats?

Trying to stay awake, he gazed out the window, seeing

nothing but a vague impression of his own reflection. Shaggy brown hair, bushy moustache . . . too dark to tell that his eyes were blue. His appearance was nothing unique. He was just one of thousands—men so alike they left little impression in people's minds. That, of course, was one of the reasons he made a good operative. . . .

I need a haircut, he realized glumly, and shifted his gaze to the front of the car. He passed the time reflecting over several cases, relieved that the woman had boarded a through train with few stops. It certainly made his job a lot easier.

Alex smiled to himself. *Aye, Lord, I thank You for that part of it. Now—could You help me understand why Avery Paxton makes use of a courier who stands out like a redbird in a flock of sparrows?* Abruptly his smile vanished, because for once God seemed to honor him with an immediate answer.

Instead of a red*bird*—she could be a red *herring,* deliberately fluttering across the trail as a diversion.

Alex sat up so fast that the sleeping man beside him snorted, opening his eyes to blink in bewilderment for a moment before he sank back into oblivion. Alex barely noticed. If that were the case, no wonder she hadn't made any effort to determine if she were being shadowed, much less any attempt to elude and confuse him. Her behavior at the party—standing apart, not mingling at all— must have been designed to keep attention focused on that out-of-the-way spot. And on *her,* of course. Meanwhile, the real courier—and thanks to Alex they might never discover an identity—had blithely wandered among the guests and was now enjoying a peaceful slumber somewhere.

He was a chump. Operative Alexander MacKay—the fearless and feared agent whose reputation spread from Virginia to the Rockies—was a *chump.*

At least—he hoped—they still had Topper, whom Pagett had been following. Since Alex had only met the Raleigh operative that morning, he wasn't sure of the man's abilities. He grinned sheepishly at the thought. Right now, any criticism Alex might bring against Pagett was a case of the pot calling the kettle black.

He may have been deluded, but now Alex had no choice except to follow the woman and learn what he could. If she were a decoy, he might still pick up some valuable information that could lead back to Paxton. She was still on Paxton's payroll, after all.

Maybe by the time the train stopped in Richmond, Hostler would have heard something from the other operative. At this point, *any* information would be welcome.

This Paxton case was the devil's own. Alex felt as if he had spent his entire life tearing up and down the East Coast like a pup who'd lost the scent, sniffing fruitlessly about in search of cast-iron evidence to put not only Topper but Avery Paxton and every last one of his infamous cohorts behind bars. Permanently. Robbery and embezzlement, forgery and fraud . . . and a string of murders with such scant evidence that the police threw up their hands. Nothing was too low for Paxton and associates.

If it weren't for private individuals and businesses demanding recompense and justice—sometimes only recompense, he acknowledged ruefully—Alex would be out of a job. At times it was frustrating and tedious work, but nonetheless the pursuit of justice was his calling. Pinkerton's National Detective Agency provided the means for him publicly to fulfill that calling and privately to serve His Maker.

His mouth tight and unsmiling, Alex stroked his moustache and reminded himself that Pinkerton's never gave up, no matter how many years or men it took. If "the real MacKay" didn't break open the case, so be it—another operative would. The Pinkerton Agency, "The Eye That Never Sleeps," deserved its reputation.

From the opposite end of the car a man appeared, dressed in dark, loose clothes, face partially concealed by a hat pulled low over his forehead. Swaying with the movement of the train, he used the back of the seats for balance. Still aggravated with himself, Alex almost missed the exchange.

The train rounded a curve just as the man drew alongside the seat where the red-haired woman slept, or pretended to, and the man lost his balance. Pitching forward, he stumbled toward the woman so that their faces were only inches apart. The woman never moved—Alex gave her full marks for that. The man regained his balance, continuing down the aisle. As he passed by, Alex memorized every detail, though lowered lights and the man's dark clothes prevented him from discerning if he was someone Alex knew. Slouched in the seat, eyes barely slitted, he watched. The train swung into another curve, and the man's hand braced on the chair in front of Alex, displaying for the space of a heartbeat an elaborate tattoo, right behind the knuckles. *Right-o, lad.* Now *I'll be recognizing you again.*

A little past midnight the train made a brief stop, and Alex saw that the red-haired woman was awake. He watched her surreptitiously looking about, and he tensed. Then she lifted her arms and began pulling pins from her hair. The tumbling mass spilled down her back, its color visible even in the dimly lighted coach. Alex wondered with a cynical grin how many men had been lured to their doom by that hair.

Oblivious to his hostility, the woman massaged her neck, then methodically rearranged everything in a tidy little knot. In that unguarded moment, the neat and efficient movement of her ungloved hands struck Alex as somehow young and vulnerable.

With a sigh he settled back, crossing his arms and scowling at the ceiling. There was, he conceded grudgingly, something about her that didn't quite fit with Paxton and his "associates." Even when she thought nobody was watching, her movements remained graceful. He remembered the way she walked at the reception—back straight as a broom handle. Long, determined strides,

with nothing of the seductive sway of an experienced limmer out to snare an unwary male.

And yet—none of his sisters had ever traveled unac-
companied on a train, though in this day and age he *had*
observed ladies going places and doing things that were
unheard of just a decade earlier. What had brought the
redbird to this point? Why sacrifice virtue for venality?

Paxton? He had always been something of a ladies'
man, with his impeccable sense of style and love of re-
fined things. Alex, of course, privately considered the fellow a little popinjay with an ego to rival Napoleon's. Paxton reminded Alex of Dante Gambrielli, another
sophisticated swine with more fake identities than fleas
on a dog. Alex had no hard evidence, but he was convinced that there was some kind of connection between
Paxton and Gambrielli. Gambrielli's fiendish specialty
was marrying—then murdering—his wives. He had been
a thorn in the side of insurance companies and the
Agency for over five years now. Alex had almost caught
the blighter down in Georgia two years ago. But, like Paxton, Gambrielli possessed both the luck and charm of Lu-
cifer himself.

Unlike Paxton, Gambrielli seemed to enjoy killing.
Paxton always hired others to do his dirty work. Alex despised both men, not so much because they broke the law
as because they lacked even a snippet of moral conscience. He always found it difficult to comprehend how
a woman would deliberately continue any affiliation with
such vermin.

He ran over in his mind the information he had received from the New York office about Paxton's new female courier. Paxton had first utilized her two months
earlier, to the best of their knowledge, and her function
so far seemed to consist solely of passing messages.

Average height and figure, red hair. Alone both before
and after message is passed, on previous sightings. For
clothing she favors fancy duds with a Parisian look. Seems
to enjoy attention, and makes no overt effort to elude de-

tection. Ach, but the only real similarity to this redbird was the hair color. More and more, this situation looked to be a deliberate design to bamboozle police—and Pinkerton operatives.

A gaggle of young ladies came whispering and scurrying down the aisle to their seats. Alex hid a smile beneath his hand. *Finishing school girls, obviously.* They did remind him of goslings trying their wings. Earlier they had packed off to the dining car, every one of them flirting madly with Alex as they passed, blushing and batting eyelashes and encouraging with coy smiles. Alex played along, enjoying their response to the approval he knew they could see in his eyes.

He suddenly felt decades older, more like a jaded old coot than a man in his prime who enjoyed bringing a smile to a young girl's face. Doubtless he had seen a deal too much in his ten years with Pinkerton's.

As always, the questions and frustrations that made his faith a constant struggle churned about in Alex's mind. He closed his eyes, feigning sleep as the train jerked forward. He silently prayed that nothing would ever intrude into the lives of those young girls to crush their spirits and destroy their innocence. That no Dante Gambrielli or Avery Paxton would entice them to join the unfortunate sorority of women like the one sitting eight rows up, whose moral fiber had been corrupted by greed, or fleshly pleasure—or both.

Why, he agonized again. *Why do they do it?*

7

Richmond

THE TRAIN PULLED INTO BYRD Street Station just before dawn. Exhausted and grimy, Eve stepped onto the platform, sighing in relief. Only a few other passengers disembarked in Richmond; most were northerners returning home after vacations in Florida. *Yankees,* Eve thought, smiling a little. She left off the accompanying adjective old-timers still applied with unforgiving scorn.

A family of four trooped past, the two young children trailing behind their parents and a stolid porter like the drooping tail of a tired puppy. A lone man lingered on the platform behind the family. Eve hesitated, but when he didn't precede her, she clasped the handle of her case in a firmer grip and headed for the entrance. She hoped her father hadn't been delayed. Usually he met her the moment she stepped off the train.

An uncomfortable tingling crept down the back of her neck—the unnerving sensation she experienced when someone was staring. Eve whirled sharply. Both the family and solitary man had disappeared. The only person left on the platform was the conductor. He waved his lantern to signal the engineer, and leaping shadows danced back and forth in the predawn mist.

With a rush of escaping steam, the wheels began to turn. An echoing "Bo-oarrd!" sounded almost simultaneously with the whistle, and the *Florida Special* rolled smoothly out of the station. With a last frowning look, Eve turned and went inside to search for her father. She was exhausted, and these ridiculous jitters deserved only to be ignored. They doubtless sprang from that note.

The note! *American Hotel, Richmond . . . Friday noon . . . utmost gravity. . . .*

Eve swiftly searched her pocket with her free hand. No note. She dropped her traveling case on a nearby bench and searched through it as well—but there was no sign of the single slip of paper. Thoroughly annoyed, Eve muttered the Latin name of every bird species she could recall—her method of coping with irritation.

With the note gone, prudence dictated that she refrain from mentioning the puzzling incident at all. Father would worry. Mother would nag. Friday morning, Eve would simply take the trolley downtown to the American Hotel and search for answers herself. If the note had been designed as a cruel prank, she could keep the humiliation to herself. If not . . . well, she would wait and see.

Letitia and William Sheridan had fretted over Eve's independent ways for years, but since Becca's wedding, her mother especially had grown more caustic. *"Must you always behave like an uninhibited bluestocking?"* she fumed when Eve insisted on attending Jane's wedding alone. Eve dropped her head and closed her eyes for a moment, willing away the memory.

Mother had been frustrated, lonely, and grieving for Becca. Relating tales of strangers and mysterious notes would doubtless prompt another wearying harangue, and Eve tried to avoid such scenes at all costs. Not for the first time, she considered the wisdom of moving out of her parents' house, perhaps even out of Richmond.

Outside, her father burst from a hack, his coat flapping, cane swinging as he strode into the depot. Relieved,

Eve grabbed her bag and started across the deserted room to meet him.

Alex moved from a concealing shadow near the end of the building. The door of the hack slammed shut behind the redbird and the older man who had met her, then the vehicle started down the street.

So . . . Paxton's new courier *had* planned to disembark here in Richmond, Alex's home base, instead of continuing on to New York. She had, in fact, been meeting someone. *Another Paxton associate?* Maybe Paxton had decided to move his operation south, since his people seemed to be sprouting at every station like poison ivy vines.

He had contacted Hostler from North Carolina. Why hadn't someone been waiting to follow them? Frustrated and angry, Alex slipped out into the open, so intent on the departing buggy that he failed to detect a nearby movement.

"Mr. MacKay." John Hostler stepped out from behind a post, looking as if he hadn't slept all night.

Hostler's appearance didn't surprise Alex. A large man whose bulk consisted of more muscle than fat, Hostler ran the Richmond office with ruthless efficiency—and blistering censure over displays of ineptitude or stupidity. *So why had he deliberately foiled Alex's movement?* Muscles clenched with frustration, Alex shifted his gaze from the retreating hackney.

"An hour ago a couple of hoodlums snatched forty thousand from the Adams Express Car coming out of Philadelphia," John rapped out with staccato speed. "I think it's those no-count Yancey brothers again. They jumped train near Fredericksburg, so I telegraphed the Philadelphia office that we'll handle it."

Alex barely hung on to his temper. "If I don't follow that hack, I'll lose one of our best leads to Paxton in eight months. I told you that in my wire."

Hostler pinched the bridge of his bulbous nose. In the

graying light Alex could see that it was turning red—not a good sign. "Pinkerton's maintains a longstanding agreement with the express company that *I* don't want to lose. You know the habit patterns of the Yanceys better than any operative in three states, so you catch the next train up to Fredericksburg and lead the posse." He paused, thick brows drawing together, and Alex knew his boss had almost reached boiling point. Angry himself, Alex didn't care.

"Someone else can do the Fredericksburg job," he protested. "I've got to follow—" He jammed his fists in his pockets and watched the hackney until it turned a corner and disappeared.

"You'll do what I tell you!" John exploded at last. "You're wasting valuable time—mine as well as that of thirty men in Fredericksburg!" Hostler scowled at Alex. "You're also a pigheaded, insubordinate Scotsman, and I don't know why I put up with you."

"Nor I you," Alex shot back, but mildly. One by one he relaxed his fingers, then withdrew his hands from his pockets. The redbird had flown, along with the opportunity; no sense resisting now. He cocked his head toward the super. "Am I allowed a change of clothes and some sleep, or is that the unreasonable request of a pigheaded Scot?"

John glared at him for one more furious second. Then he threw up his hands and shook his head. "Blast you, MacKay—one day I'm going to really lose my temper and have you transferred to a whistle-stop in Santa Fe."

"Yes, sir."

Hostler clapped him on the back and dug out his pipe. "You know you're the best operative I've ever had, you sorry scoundrel, and that's too bad." He lit the pipe and clamped it between his teeth, then winked. "Means I can't scare the pants off you to bring you in line."

"No, sir," Alex responded, solemn as a preacher.

"Bring in the Yanceys, son—and I'll make it up to you, starting now." He grinned, stroking his full black beard and looking for all the world like a conniving politician. "That hack you watched leaving just now—well, the driver's Simon Kincaid. Feel better?"

"You're as devious as old Scratch himself, sir," Alex retorted, feeling a wave of relief. "Thanks." Simon Kincaid was his friend, and one of the best undercover operatives around.

"If you hadn't been so blasted touchy, I also would have told you that last night I received a letter from the New York office. There seems to be a possibility that Paxton is testing the waters down south." He ignored Alex's disgruntled snort. "Topper, however, appears to be returning to New York. I received word from Pagett just before I left to meet you here. It's under control, Mr. MacKay. Just get those Yanceys for me. They've thumbed their noses up and down the line one too many times."

"You can depend on it."

"And, MacKay?"

"Sir?"

"You can fetch a change of clothes, but sleep can wait. There's a freight heading north in an hour. Be on it."

Alex heaved an inward sigh. "Next time," he tossed over his shoulder as he headed for the line of hackneys, "I'll no' be so efficient about telegraphing my whereabouts."

Behind him John hooted with deep-throated laughter.

8

Nettlesby
Lincolnshire, England

DANTE GAMBRIELLI WATCHED his plump little wife bustling about the parlor, setting up the tea trolley, fluffing cushions, readying the footstool. She was a homey creature, his Priscilla. Her devotion to him shone out of every glance from those myopic eyes. But then, he was not fool enough to treat her in a manner that would make her look at him any other way.

"Stop fussing, my dear," he instructed, smiling a little. "Pour the tea for both of us. I have a present for you."

Priscilla smiled sweetly. "Having you home is present enough. I do wish you didn't have to be away so much." She popped the tea cozy back over the pot, handed Dante his cup, then joined him on the settee. "*Unless* your present is a promise that you won't be traveling about so much anymore." She lowered her eyes, a faint blush staining the dimpled cheeks.

He curbed the instinct to lash out. He would not spoil the mood; it made the outcome so much more delectable. "Perhaps this will make up for my neglect," he murmured, withdrawing a long, thin box from his pocket. "*Necessary* neglect," he added, though lightly. Leaning forward, he brushed his lips across hers. "You know I adore you."

Moist-eyed and blushing, Priscilla opened the box, gaping at the diamond necklace and matching eardrops. "Oh, my goodness! I've never seen anything so grand in my entire life." Fat, trembling fingers lifted the necklace, then gently laid it back on the black velvet. "Mr. Gambrielli—Dante . . . you shouldn't spend—"

"Hush." His finger on her lips stilled her protest. "The sparkle in the stones reminds me of the way you sparkle when I return home." He took the cups and set them aside, then fastened the necklace about her neck. "There. Beautiful adornment for my beautiful wife." *But not for long. . . .*

Priscilla simpered, her eyelashes fluttering. It was an annoying habit, but Dante's smile didn't slip until her next words. "You didn't—" She hesitated, then blurted out, "You *didn't* buy these with the money Grandfather bequeathed to me when we married, did you? That's for our children . . . that is, when we have—"

"As a matter of fact, I did." The anger, unleashed like the swift strike of an adder, stopped her fluttering lashes. She stared at him, round-eyed and uncertain. Dante smiled. "But then, it's *my* money now, is it not?" He wrapped his fingers about her forearm. "Come. Let's take a walk down the lane."

"But, my dear . . . it's dark."

"I know."

An hour later Dante returned to the cottage. He changed clothes, then with swift, thorough movements tidied the parlor. He was a careful planner—and extraordinarily lucky. It would be days before someone noticed that the cottage was uninhabited.

A little before midnight, he slipped out the door, his Gladstone bag bulging. It would take three hours on foot to reach a village serviced by the railway, where he would purchase a ticket to London on the first train available. Before breakfast he would be miles down the road, on the way to his—

He smiled slowly. To his next wife.

9

Richmond

FRIDAY MORNING EVE DRESSED carefully. The
American Hotel was not as popular or as well-known as
the Ballard and Exchange Hotel, but it had a reputation
for being respectable and clean. Although families occa-
sionally stayed there, the hotel served primarily as a stop-
over for commercial travelers and businessmen.

All this Eve had learned from the trolley conductor the
previous day. He had told her that the name of the hotel
had recently been changed from the American to the Lexington. Whoever had written that note, Eve surmised,
must not have visited Richmond in a while.

In her bedroom now, she examined first a lace collar,
then an embroidered tie, trying to decide which to wear
with her plain white shirtwaist. Becca—if she were
here—would have roasted Eve about this uncharacteris-
tic dithering over her clothing. After all, it wasn't as if she
were attending a soiree or dance, or one of their mother's
insufferable benevolent society meetings. The unaccustomed indecision, she realized suddenly, masked a growing apprehension. Disgusted with herself, Eve snatched
up the lawn tie and fastened it about her neck in a neat,
uncluttered bow. As she pinned on the delicate enamel

brooch Rebecca had given her, she noticed that her fingers were unsteady. *Becca*, she thought, *how I miss you.*

She hadn't received a letter from her sister in weeks now. Eve glanced at the boudoir clock on her dressing table, then retrieved her Bible, opening it to the place where she had tucked the few letters Becca had written from England.

They were chatty, written with the same careless spontaneity with which Becca spoke. "You have dreadful penmanship," Eve murmured, smiling at the large loops and hurried, slanting letters that seemed to run together. As always, her sister ended with, *Don't forget to talk to God for me, Evie.* Rebecca was the only one Eve tolerated using the despised nickname.

Maggie's spare-framed body appeared in the doorway. "Miss Eve, I've finished checking the linens and—" Her sharp gaze moved from Eve's attire to the hat and cloak draped across the bed. "And where might you be off to this time?" She crossed her thin arms and raised her chin. "I was expecting some assistance with planning the accounts today—since you saw fit to disappear yesterday as well."

"I have to go downtown. I should be back by early afternoon." Eve couldn't beguile Maggie like Becca used to. "I'll help when I come home. Sophie can fill in until then." Sophie was the hired girl Eve's mother used on a more or less permanent basis, though—unlike Maggie—she lived in a boardinghouse. Eve fastened the cloak and picked up her hat.

"Sophie's as useful with the household accounts as a brainless chicken." Maggie scowled at the hat Eve was pinning in place. "But as usual, you'll be never-no-minding an old Irish biddy with too much to do, what with all your wanderings, and Miss Rebecca gone and hitched to that high-nose swell."

Once the housekeeper started in on Giles, it would be a good ten minutes before the diatribe wound down. Eve didn't have time to listen. "You're absolutely right, as always, Maggie." Eve fled downstairs and out the door into a chill, gray morning. The wind stung her cheeks; the air smelled of dying leaves and rain, and Eve suppressed a shiver of foreboding.

A little before eleven o'clock on Friday morning, Alex bounded up the stairs of the discreet brownstone which housed the Richmond branch of Pinkerton's. "Morning, Fred," he greeted a fellow operative, who was busily scribbling away at his desk.

"Mr. MacKay! Congratulations on catching the Yancey boys. I must say you made quick work of that case."

"Thanks, Fred. Any news on the Paxton case?"

"Mr. MacKay!" John yelled. "Quit wasting time and present yourself in here!" John's office was surrounded on three sides by waist-high windows, offering him a gold-fish-bowl view of all activities. When he wanted privacy, he simply pulled down the shades and shut the door. Few people risked their necks by knocking on the door when it was closed and the shades drawn.

"He was just over to the Third Street police station," Fred clued Alex with a grimace. "Last night they pinched the guy Kincaid's been shadowing all week."

"Mmmph." Alex tossed his hat on the rack and headed for the super's office. "He hates losing a collar to the police. No wonder he's in such a foul mood."

"MR. MACKAY!"

"Coming, sir." With a mocking salute to Fred, he entered the lion's den.

"Congratulations on the Yanceys," Hostler growled as if he hadn't been bellowing like an angry bull seconds earlier. Above the beard his lips twitched in a smirk. "Guess the Almighty you set such store by answered your prayers." He lifted a hand before Alex could respond to the jibe. "This malefactor the police nabbed last night matches one of our file cards on a vicious little mug out of New York. Goes by various monikers and is wanted for murder in at least four states." He paused, puffing on his favorite pipe and eyeing Alex with a shrewd intensity that lifted the hairs on the back of Alex's neck. "Kincaid thinks this Joe Leoni might be one of Paxton's stooges. Kincaid spotted him the night after you got back from North Carolina."

Leaning forward, Hostler steepled his fingers. "Near as Kincaid could figure it, this Joe Leoni was shadowing your bird, who by-the-by is staying at a house on East Franklin." He lifted a brow. "I thought you might like to trot down to the city jail and have a chat. Sergeant Johnson will be glad to fill you in."

"How was Leoni arrested?" Alex asked. "And what about Paxton's courier?"

John leveled a stare at him, which Alex stoically returned until the super growled something beneath his breath and answered, "A fairly well-heeled family by the name of Sheridan lives in the house on East Franklin. William Sheridan is an investment banker—solid reputation even with the Panic still fresh in everyone's minds. His wife has a managing hand in nearly every charitable organization in the city. That's all we know right now. It's possible Paxton is using the courier to attract Sheridan. I leave it to you to uncover the particulars."

Alex felt as if something vile had been shoved under his nose, though from long habit he kept his expression impassive. "As for Joe Leoni," John finished, "there was a fracas of some sort at a livery stable. Leoni knifed a hackman. Kincaid wasn't close enough to help, but he yelled and a patrolman on his beat gave chase. They caught Leoni at the corner of Twelfth and Main."

"I'm on my way." Alex headed for the door.

"Mr. MacKay. . . ."

Alex almost ignored the summons, then turned. Hostler surged to his feet, slamming his pipe down on the desk hard enough to snap the stem. "Mr. MacKay, you're not the only one with a fanatical desire to bring criminals

51

to justice. Kindly remember that—or I *will* arrange for you to be sent to Santa Fe." Hostler's words rumbled out in the tone of voice that sent grown men scurrying for cover. "Keep me informed."

"If I can, sir." Alex tossed him a cheeky grin and left on the run.

To save time, he grabbed a trolley. He walked into the city jail at twenty minutes past eleven—ten minutes after Joe Leoni had choked a guard, escaped from his cell, and disappeared.

10

Richmond

THE LOBBY WASN'T CROWDED, but a steady stream of guests, mostly male, occupied the desk clerk and kept his attention from dwelling overmuch on Eve. She arrived early, a little past eleven-thirty, and stationed herself off to the side where she could watch the entrance without being immediately noticed.

Twice she was approached by men whose speculative gazes repelled her; Eve dispatched both with the firm explanation that her escort would be arriving shortly. Inside her gloves, her palms grew damp, and as the minute hand on the large clock above the front desk ticked closer to noon, Eve wondered if she had committed a monstrous error in judgment.

At ten past twelve she stood, unable to sit in the uncomfortable chair a minute longer. A family of eight had just spilled into the lobby. The children talked and pointed, jostling one another while the scowling father approached the desk and the red-faced mother attempted to quiet the children. Shoulders stiff, Eve edged past. She wanted to peek inside the bar down the hall, just to be sure. With all the turmoil in the lobby, nobody would notice her movements, and she could be on her way home within five minutes. An entire morning had been wasted, and Maggie would scold—but at least Eve could finally put the whole uncomfortable episode out of her mind.

Several gentlemen lounged at the bar, their backs to Eve. Three men at one of the small tables glanced up, but none of them rose to approach her. Eve released a pent-up breath and started back down the dimly lit hallway, thinking only of catching the next trolley home.

A door opened, and a man slipped into the hall in front of Eve, blocking her way. "Knew you'd come."

Disconcerted, Eve's gaze swept over the nondescript figure. He was slight, clean shaven, and extremely disheveled. She had never seen him before. "Did you write that note?" she demanded, irritated with herself because suddenly her mouth was dry, and the words came out breathless instead of firm.

His mouth curled in an unpleasant smile, revealing a gap where one of his front teeth should have been. A trickle of blood seeped from the corner, as if the loss of the tooth was recent. "Not me. He's outside."

The man's proximity made Eve uncomfortable, and she backed up, hugging her umbrella beneath the folds of her full-length cloak. She was relieved that an explanation was forthcoming, but she had not expected such a . . . *ruffian*.

He gestured with his chin. "Let's go. He doesn't like to be kept waiting."

"Then you must extend my regrets," Eve retorted. Did he think her a loose woman as well as a gullible one? "I won't be going anywhere with a strange man, especially one who looks like he's the loser in a round of fisticuffs." She advanced toward him, her gaze unswerving. "If you don't let me pass, I'll scream . . . loudly enough to pierce your eardrums."

The vein at his temple suddenly pulsed outward. Quick as a snake, he grabbed her arm, jerked her through the doorway, and slammed it behind them in a blur of motion so swift Eve had no time to react. "Scream—and I'll slit your gullet open like gutting a fish." His voice was low, strangely calm.

The sour odor of sweat and putrid breath filled Eve's nostrils, choking her. She was blind and disoriented in the dark, airless room, and her stomach churned in mounting terror. Where was he taking her? His arm coiled about her waist, trapping her inside the cloak as he began dragging her forward. Eve stumbled, her feet tangling in the umbrella and folds of her cloak, her hat slipping sideways. Something sharp prodded her side. She managed to keep from struggling, knowing instinctively that it would only make matters worse.

"Don't move."

The bone-crushing clasp on her wrist lifted momentarily and she heard another door opening. Gray light spilled into the room, along with the muted noise of street traffic and the smell of rotting food. He was taking her to an alley.

A horrifying realization leaped into her brain. He was going to kill her. She knew it with soul-deep agony. She had been lured to her death . . . and she would never know why. A hopeless prayer died on her lips as a lifetime of questioning about sin and forgiveness yielded to a despairing conclusion. God hadn't answered her other prayers; how could she expect a response to this one? Somehow she must deserve this, for God to allow it.

"I've never killed me a *real* red-haired female," the nasal, emotionless voice mused aloud, taunting Eve. He forced her outside, demonically strong despite his slight stature. "But I *have* snuffed plenty of mouthy wenches as tart-tongued as you."

Was he trying to goad her into some sort of hysterical action? Eve felt as if she were somehow separated from herself, watching the scene like a silent, motionless spectator. A terrible coldness spread through her, numbing her hands and feet.

If she remained passive, would he kill her more quickly . . . or could she perhaps provoke him into making a mistake? A flicker of outrage kindled deep in her soul. God might not rescue her, but she would *not* meekly submit to such a degrading end. Determination sent strength into her watery limbs. While her mind scrambled for something to say, she kept quiet and did not resist.

"That's better," the voice murmured. "Cowed and quiet, like a lamb."

Something cold brushed the back of her neck, and in spite of herself Eve cringed, flesh quivering. Her hat tumbled off. She tightened her grip on the umbrella, still hidden inside her cloak.

"Now . . . I can't decide exactly how to finish you off," the man mused aloud. A rustling chuckle whispered in Eve's ear like the sound of a rattlesnake's tail. "He doesn't care, you know. Just as long as I don't share the details." He paused, fingering the vivid curls that had escaped the confining pins and now spilled about her face. "Too bad I can't take the time, since I was delayed. So . . ."

His hold about her middle slackened and he lifted the other arm. Without warning, Eve wrenched herself free and flung aside her cape, lifting the umbrella just as the man lunged. The blunt steel point caught him deep in the midriff and stopped him cold. He grunted and staggered back, a look of undisguised bloodlust blazing from his eyes.

"You'll be sorry for that, wench!" He hurled curses at her and gasped for breath.

Eve held the umbrella in front of her, pointed like a sword at her assailant. Step by step she edged backward, praying she wouldn't trip, her gaze fixed on the now ominously quiet man. He stalked her, wheezing, one hand clutching his middle, the other hand still holding the knife.

If she turned and ran he might catch her. She had not incapacitated him, only surprised him, and her flight would be hampered by her skirt and petticoats. Yet to stay meant certain death.

Suddenly he leaped, feinting to one side to avoid the umbrella. His knife sliced through the air in a vicious arc. Acting on blind instinct, Eve flung open the umbrella, rammed it against his thighs, then lifted her skirts to run. Her cloak billowed; she heard the sound of ripping cloth and felt a fierce tug that almost pulled her off balance. Sobbing, she threw off the cloak, then hurtled down the alley toward the street.

"Help!" She tried to scream, but fright had clenched her throat muscles and the plea emerged as a reedy gasp.

A man appeared in the entrance of the alley.

"Please!" Eve tried again, her voice stronger this time. "Help!" She stumbled, and the man swiftly caught her and thrust her behind him.

"Stay here. Don't move." He sprinted down the alley.

Eve took two wobbling steps to the side of the building and leaned against the cool masonry. Somehow, miraculously, she was still alive. Her eyes drifted shut.

When a hand closed over her elbow, she started violently. "It's all right," came a mellow, soothing voice. "I won't hurt you. I thought you were swooning."

Eve fought against panic but finally succumbed to the tremors that seized her. Her voice, when she spoke, was a pitiful croak. "I don't swoon. . . ." Her head twisted, a frightened gaze searching the alley. "Where—"

"He's escaped, I'm sorry to say."

Eve mustered enough courage to stiffen her spine and look up at her rescuer. Still shaken, her normal powers of observation deserted her, leaving her with only a blurred impression of tousled brown hair and intense blue eyes. He was much taller than Eve, and radiated strength and reassurance; but even in her present state Eve also sensed a frightening coiled power.

His voice, however, disarmed her with a lilting undertone that almost, but not quite, reminded her of Maggie. Eve had never felt such gratitude toward a strange man in all her twenty-three years. "Thank you." She clasped her trembling hands together and lifted her chin. "You saved my life."

"I think you saved your own," the man returned. "I found the remains of a woman's umbrella, a hat—and your cape." He handed Eve her hat, then held out the cloak, revealing a slash in the fabric. Eve swayed, and he wrapped the ruined cape about her shoulders. "Perhaps we should go inside."

"No. Not in there," Eve refuted strongly. She attempted a weak smile. "Thank you. . . ."

"Mmm. Well, you see, I need to try and track the blighter before the trail is cold, and I wouldn't think you'd care to be alone." He searched her features, and a shuttered expression behind the blue eyes alarmed Eve. "Beyond that," he murmured, almost to himself, "I'm afraid I don't want to be losing sight of you, either."

The way he spoke, coupled with the sudden lack of expression, jarred Eve back to full awareness. She studied the man more closely. On the surface, there was nothing alarming about his appearance . . . except for the blue eyes. Eve looked away quickly from those eyes. Cottonmouthed, she took a surreptitious step toward the street. "I think," she began, "that it would be best if you told me who you are. Most passersby would not deliberately risk chasing down a murderous cutthroat unless—" She stopped, alarm coursing through her. "Are *you* the man?"

"What man?" he repeated, too quietly.

She wouldn't be getting away from *this* fellow so easily—he didn't look as if anyone could ever outwit him for long. Eve edged a little farther into the street. A covered market wagon was approaching, and if she screamed and ran . . . perhaps . . .

Without further thought she gathered hat and skirts in her hands and bolted toward the curb. "Help!" she cried, this time with satisfying volume. From behind her she heard the man's startled exclamation, sensed his pursuit.

The colored driver of the wagon glanced over, looking

alarmed. Then came the shriek of a policeman's whistle from the other side of the street. Hope rekindled, filling Eve with a burst of extraordinary strength. She dashed toward the wagon, dropping her skirts to wave her hat. "Here! Help me!" she called.

One of the horses half reared, squealing. The other animal jerked sideways, yanking the reins from the driver's hands. Both horses lunged forward, straight toward Eve.

A hard arm whipped around her waist, hauling her up and back, inches from the clattering hooves and iron wheels. He dragged her, squirming and protesting, back onto the sidewalk. "Cease your struggles, woman!"

Red-faced and breathless, the policeman puffed down the walk, skidding to a stop in front of them. "What's this all about?" His sharp eye went first to Eve, then widened on the man subduing her with infuriating ease. "Why . . . it's MacKay, isn't it?"

Light-headed, her heart racing, Eve paid scant attention. When the arms holding her loosened, she tore herself free, her only thought to flee.

Then abruptly the policeman's words registered. She gaped at both men. "You know this man?" she asked the policeman, dazed.

"I do, right enough, ma'am." His voice was clipped, suspicious, one hand at the ready on his billy club.

"It's all right," Mr. MacKay interjected, a smile tugging at his lips. "I was only trying to save her, Officer Dawes—not apprehend her. Joe Leoni just tried to dispatch her, you see, and for some reason she thought *I* was an accomplice." He tilted his head, the smile disappearing as he subjected Eve to a look she hadn't received since she was nine years old. "But I wouldn't try running from me again. I'd no' be so gentle the second time."

Eve swiped tumbling hair out of her face and clumsily positioned her hat. "Stay away from me," she demanded. Without warning, tears rose to her eyes. She lowered her head, blinking rapidly.

A man's handkerchief appeared beneath her nose.

"Here." Numbly Eve accepted the handkerchief. It smelled faintly of cedar.

"Mr. Mackay, explanations are in order here," the policeman commanded. "You're mistaken about Leoni. He was arrested last night. Doubtless this woman is another victim of the cutthroat who's been preying on women in hotels lately." He frowned at Eve.

"Joe Leoni escaped a little over an hour ago," Mr. MacKay stated flatly. "I just came from the livery where he knifed the stableman. That's how I knew to come here." There was a pause, then the sound of rustling paper. A dark premonition shot down Eve's spine. "I found this in the dirt. Appears he must have dropped it in the scuffle when he was arrested."

Eve lifted her head, ignoring her dishevelment.

The policeman read the note. When he returned it to Mr. MacKay, Mr. MacKay then held it out to Eve. She didn't need to see the crumpled scrap of paper; she already knew what it said.

The color left her face, and for a moment she was afraid she really might faint. "I don't understand," she whispered.

Mr. MacKay's blue eyes were cold, assessing. "Well, now," he returned, his voice light and smooth, "I happen to think you might be understanding quite a bit. But perhaps it would be better to have a little talk down at the station."

11

Richmond

JOE LEONI SLIPPED DOWN THE FIRE escape into another alley. Hands clenched, blood pounding, he almost yielded to the urge to throttle the first passerby he encountered, just to relieve some of the pent-up fury.

He had been duped by a helpless woman. A skirt who should have been quivering and helpless, begging for her life. He wiped the sweat from his forehead and sidled up to the entrance of the street, but he stayed close to the building's wall, alert to every movement.

She would pay. He was not going to England until he had made her suffer; suffer and die a slow, agonizing death. Avery Paxton wanted her out of the way, but from this point on, Shiver knew his motives had nothing to do with Paxton, or Paxton's blackmailing of Dante Gambrielli.

He would kill Eve Sheridan because *nobody* made a fool of Joe Leoni—and lived.

Alex studied the redbird, who claimed she was Eve Sheridan, *daughter* of William Sheridan—and she had no idea why someone would try to kill her. Alex was inches

61

away from actually believing her. *This is what happens,* he chided himself grimly, *when you're a softie with the lasses.* Especially hurting, helpless ones.

They were on their way to the police station in the hotel's rattletrap depot wagon. Alex hadn't wanted the exposure of a trolley. A pale and trembling Miss Sheridan sat beside him, trying to stuff trailing tendrils of red hair back under her hat. She had removed her gloves and her left wrist was discolored, swollen.

Alex gritted his teeth. She might be a gifted liar—and a few other things besides—but she was still a brutalized young woman who had barely escaped a shocking murder. She was also one of the most self-possessed individuals Alex had ever encountered. No hysterics, no fainting away. He opened his mouth to inquire about her wrist, but she spoke first.

"Do you deal with wicked cutthroats like Joe Leoni all the time, Mr. MacKay?"

Alex stared down at her. "Why do you ask?" he countered, watching her fingers twining together in her lap. Her hands were still shaking.

She shot him a swift glance, and her dark brown eyes were so full of torment that Alex was taken aback.

"Never mind." She studied her wrist, grimacing as she turned it about. Obviously, she didn't want to continue.

Alex shifted, crowding her just enough to force her attention. "Tell me," he insisted, softening his voice. His sisters never had been able to resist that tone, nor had many other women. Fortunately, Miss Sheridan was no exception. After another wary, shamefaced look, she shrugged a little and complied.

"I've been puzzled about your attitude toward me. I'm used to being thought of as an oddity," she admitted with matter-of-fact indifference. "But I've never been treated like a criminal."

"If I had treated you like a criminal, we'd be heading for the station in a Black Maria," Alex muttered. He felt distinctly uncomfortable with her interpretation of his actions.

She slanted him another look. "Yes . . . well, I'm phrasing this poorly." The half-smile died before it was born. "I've never been confronted with wickedness before, either. It was . . . terrifying. I don't know how you—" She stopped, fighting for control of her voice before continuing. "That horrid man was terrible enough, but your attitude makes it worse. I don't know how to convince you that I'm not who you think I am. That's why I asked the question. If you spend most of your days associating with cutthroats and liars, it might have become difficult to distinguish the innocent from them."

" 'Satan himself transformed into an angel of light,' " Alex quoted beneath his breath, stunned both by her candidness and the articulate analysis of her thought processes. Already intrigued, he found himself wanting to understand this unusual creature—and not only for his job. There *had* to be more to the young woman than they had originally thought. Nobody was that accomplished an actress. He had steeled himself for a number of approaches, from the flirting of a shameless vamp to the cunning slyness of an alley cat. A philosophical discussion left him floundering.

"Until today, I've never had a problem," Alex said curtly. He found himself reluctant to elaborate. No matter what approach he offered to justify himself, either he would sound the pompous fool, or Miss Sheridan's observation might be proven correct. Alex suppressed a grim smile. Here he'd thought *he* was the only tortured soul who spent hours counting angels on the head of a penny nail. "I've learned that people are not always as they appear to be." *And you're taking the lesson one step further, Eve Sheridan . . . or whoever you turn out to be.*

He glanced across at the girl, then out the filthy window of the depot wagon. "Only God knows a person's heart, Miss Sheridan. Plain mortals such as myself muddle along as best we can. Of course, the Almighty and I enjoy a fair working relationship," he offered, hoping to lighten things a bit. "I badger Him with a lot of questions, and He listens." He smiled a little. "So far, my Superintendent seems to feel I've done fairly well at separating the sheep from the goats."

The girl gaped as if he had sprouted two heads.

Stung, Alex's temper slipped. "That surprises you? Well, I confess you surprise me as well. I wouldn't have expected one of Paxton's limmers to be worrying over wickedness and its attendant companions."

Her head jerked up. "*What* do you think I am?" she demanded, her voice incredulous.

Alex grinned. That had provoked her right enough, as he had meant to. "I wouldn't be thinking you're merely Eve Sheridan, innocent young lady living in a fancy home on East Franklin. We know you're one of Paxton's couriers, and have been for the past six weeks or more. You met Horace Topper at the wedding in North Carolina. Unfortunately, we *didn't* know that the contrived purpose of your meeting there was a devious method to arrange for the . . . ah . . . 'termination' of your employment. Perhaps Paxton thought—"

"You've been *spying* on me!" Miss Sheridan interrupted, fury fairly spitting from her eyes. She jerked back into the corner of the seat, tucking her skirt close, as far away from Alex as possible. He lifted his chin, casually stroking his moustache, and waited to see what her indignation would reveal. "I'll report you to the police myself. There's a law—"

"As you saw, the Richmond office of Pinkerton's happens to enjoy a good relationship with the local police, because we help them uphold the law."

"It's unconscionable that you harass and hound innocent citizens. . . ."

"You had no idea I was even there, so how could I have harassed you?"

"I demand to see your superior!"

"He yells a lot louder than you."

For some reason this last exchange unnerved Miss Sheridan completely. She looked as if he'd struck her, and the magnificent temper that had taken the place of shock and pallor disappeared as suddenly as if he'd blown out a candle.

"I—I beg your pardon. I don't know what came over me," she apologized stiffly, looking everywhere but at Alex. "I've never behaved like this before."

"Mmm. How do you usually behave, then? Do you normally inquire of strangers as to their astuteness in character judgment?"

"I don't *normally* talk to anybody," Miss Sheridan snapped, revealing more than perhaps she intended.

Alex allowed her to cloak herself in icy silence the rest of the ride. He tried to convince his uncomfortably noisy conscience that his motives were driven by necessity, grounded in the noble pursuit of justice—but he knew it was a lie, and he despised himself for it. Eve Sheridan had caught him off guard, and he didn't like it. But regardless of who or what she was, the girl had needed a gentle voice—not a whip.

Over the next few hours, he learned to despise himself even more.

"If she'd had that umbrella, she doubtless would have brained *me* like she tried to do to Joe Leoni." Alex eyed his friend Holt Taylor. They had met at Alex's favorite downtown restaurant for an early supper, and Alex had shared an expurgated version of the day's events. Holt had retired from active detective work two years earlier, when he married. He and Alex still met often whenever Alex was in town, and Alex felt free to confide in him.

"You don't usually make a mistake of that magnitude," Holt observed with a faintly wicked grin. "You'll be fortunate if her father doesn't demand your head on a platter. I've heard of William Sheridan. He's well thought of at City Hall, as they say. Saved a number of hides when the bottom dropped out of the silver market."

Alex wiped his mouth with a napkin and laid it aside. "Perhaps. But I have my doubts about Miss Sheridan hiding behind her father. She threatened all manner of reprisals if I so much as breathe a word of the incident to either of her parents. She wouldn't even allow anyone to escort her home—and this after an attempted murder. A very independent-minded female, she is." He scowled at the table.

Holt stroked the side of his face, looking thoughtful. "What's bothering you, Alex? You're worrying over the woman like a bad tooth. So you made a mistake about Eve Sheridan—you still saved her life, no matter what you claim. Give yourself credit for that, my friend."

"Ach—it's not my stupidity," Alex said. He shook his head. "It's the *feel* of this. I don't like it."

"Your fey grandmother's influence again?"

Alex ignored the jibe. "It doesn't fit," he insisted, staring across the table at Holt without seeing him. "We had the confirmed report of a red-haired female courier six weeks ago from a reliable, trusted operative who's worked New York for twenty years. But the woman he spotted was *not* Eve Sheridan. *Who was it?* And if—as I'm beginning to suspect—Paxton has been manipulating all of us like a ruddy bunch of marionettes—why use Eve Sheridan to do it? She's lived here in Richmond her entire life. She has a degree, if you can grasp this, in ornithology."

Holt sputtered. "Birds?" He began to laugh. "You've been shadowing a bird-watching spinster who—"

"Aye, the joke's on me," Alex agreed, interrupting with a tired grin. "Who would believe she'd look and behave like she does, hmm? The girl has backbone; I'll give her credit for that—although I'm wondering if it might be a streak of recklessness instead. She's also hiding something. I *know* I'm not wrong about that. She claims she's never heard of Avery Paxton—but she's lying." Alex stroked his moustache and smiled. "Contrary to what I believed earlier, she's actually a very poor liar."

" 'The real MacKay' shouldn't have any trouble—um—*persuading* her to tell the truth."

Alex stroked his moustache with his fingers. "It's difficult," he confessed at last, "to manipulate a girl whose great brown doe eyes stare at you like you're a hunter sighting her with a shotgun."

Holt lifted a hand, summoning the waitress. "Ach, I can see as how that would make matters a wee bit difficult."

Alex smiled, but it was an effort. "You still don't have the vowel tones right, much less the brogue."

They chatted of other matters as they left the restaurant and walked slowly down the sidewalk. Both seemed reluctant to end the evening. "You're gone too much, my friend," Holt reproached him. "When are you going to marry and settle down? Say, that reminds me!" He snapped his fingers. "I meant to suggest it earlier, but I got sidetracked. About the Sheridans—there's another daughter. She married this past summer; I remember reading the account in the paper." He laughed at Alex's snort. "Alice has thoroughly domesticated me, I know. At any rate, you might try reading up on last summer's society columns in the local papers for accounts of that wedding."

"They often list names of guests, don't they?" Alex clapped his friend's back. "Holt, you're a fine friend, even tethered and domesticated. I'll be in touch. Send Alice my regards."

Weddings.

For some reason, the word lifted fine hairs at the back of his neck.

Avery Paxton usually confined his murderous activities to robberies, extortions, and grand larceny. The class of women surrounding him would *not* be expecting marriage proposals. However, former Paxton associate Dante Gambrielli—last known alias Dexter Greaves—had "lost" his last wife two years ago, in Georgia.

Weddings. North Carolina. The reception where Paxton's associates had met. The groom's name, he suddenly remembered, had been *David Grey*.

Alex broke into a run.

12

New York

AVERY PAXTON CRUSHED THE UNLIT cigar and
threw it in the spittoon. "You take the first train to Richmond. It's been more than a week since he left New York.
Find him. Tell him if he does not immediately proceed to
England, I'll arrange it so he'll be looking over his shoulder the rest of his life." He began pacing back and forth,
paying no heed to Topper's pallid, sweating face.

"Mr. Paxton . . . I don't think—I mean, how would I
find him?"

Avery stopped in front of the quivering man. "That, I
believe, is what I just ordered you to do." His voice was
quiet, and he began twirling his ring, examining Topper
as if he were a piece of rancid meat. "Are you trying to tell
me you're unable to carry out my wishes?"

"N-no, sir. But—it's Shiver, sir."

"Ah. Yes. He *is* my most trusted, my most valuable as-
sistant, isn't he? And he might not take kindly to an associate"—he directed a scathing glance at Topper—"an
associate of somewhat lesser importance giving him orders." He paused, turning the ring so the afternoon sun
glinted off the tiger's-eye stone at its center. "Shiver does
have a propensity for violence, doesn't he? Most distaste-

ful, but necessary upon occasion."

"Couldn't you send Louie, or maybe Tony? I'm sure they would better know how to find him—sir." Topper looked like a fat turtle trying to disappear inside his shell.

Avery returned behind his desk and sat down, picked up an elaborately carved letter opener, and began to clean his nails. "I'm asking *you*," he repeated mildly. "Two days, Topper. I expect a telegram from you in two days, informing me that Shiver has accomplished his mission and is on his way to England." He put down the opener and fixed his gaze on Topper. "And if for some reason he is still there—remind him, please, about my feelings on insubordination?"

Topper rose, shoulders slumped. "I'll do my best, Mr. Paxton."

"Of course you will, Tops. And—might I suggest the American Hotel? I understand their rooms are quite nice."

13

GILES DAWSON RETURNED HOME just before dusk, wet and chilled from the soaking rains that had blanketed England for a week. He stood in the entrance to the parlor, watching his wife. A fire crackled in the grate, its warmth reaching across the room toward him. Still, he hesitated, savoring the cozy domestic scene with an intensity that bordered on pain.

Rebecca was unaware of his presence. From where he stood, Giles could see only the back of her head above the rocking chair where she sat, close to the fire. Wavering firelight glinted off her neatly coiled hair. His wife.

Silently Giles hung his ulster and top hat on the hall tree. His hands clenched in fists at his sides. Still moving soundlessly, he crossed the room until he stood just behind her. She was writing in that blasted journal again. "Good evening, my dear."

She jumped, book and pen flying. "Giles!" she gasped, leaping up—not to embrace her husband, but to grab the journal and stuff it inside her embroidery basket. "You're home! I didn't hear you."

"I see that." His glance went from the basket to her

70

flushed, guilty face. "Has the bloom of marriage faded so swiftly? You used to greet me with a kiss." Her growing reticence around him enraged Giles. He knew she was beginning to be suspicious, and he didn't like it.

"Lately your absence has been felt more than your presence," Rebecca retorted. She dutifully pecked his cheek. "There. I'm glad you're home."

"This childish petulance does not become you."

Her eyes flashed with temper, quickly hidden by the screen of her lashes. Giles' whole body tightened with need. "Sneaking about, deliberately trying to scare me, does not become *you*." She stepped around him. "I'll warm a kettle for you. I'm sure you'll want tea."

His hand closed over her arm, and he pulled her into a tight embrace. "What I want is *you*," he muttered fiercely, his mouth moving across her cheek to her lips. He could feel her resistance. "Rebecca . . . don't shut me out. I love you desperately." The words tore from his throat.

Her hands lifted to cup his face. "Do you?" she asked, a sheen of tears suddenly filling her eyes. "Do you really, Giles?"

They kissed, and then Giles released his wife so she could make the tea. After she disappeared into the kitchen, he withdrew the cablegram from his pocket and read it one last time. Then he shredded the paper into confetti-sized pieces and scattered them in the fire.

14

Richmond

TOPPER GLANCED AROUND THE shabby, soot-covered platform, clutching his small overnighter with sweaty fingers. People brushed past him, hurrying on their way; nobody noticed Topper at all. Filled with trepidation, he joined the crowd streaming into the depot, swallowing past the lump lodged in his throat. Inside, he looked furtively about. Sadly, Shiver was unlikely to be watching for him. Topper had sent a telegram to the hotel, but with little hope that Shiver would read it, much less respond to its message. Why couldn't Mr. Paxton have sent someone else?

A shoeshine boy sidled up, his voice shrill in its begging. Topper irritably dismissed the urchin and made his way through the milling crowd over to an empty bench. His feet hurt and his head ached. He passed a palm over his clammy brow, then tugged on the constricting collar.

Why *had* Mr. Paxton insisted that he come after Shiver?

Two important-looking businessmen strode by, one of them consulting his watch. Topper tugged out his own solid gold watch, fumbling with the clasp. September was gone, along with the last of lingering summer. It would be dark soon; he might as well go to the hotel.

He struggled to his feet, feeling a burning sensation gnawing in his abdomen. He didn't know how to track anybody down. He was a forger, approached by Mr. Paxton himself almost two years ago now. *I saw some of the twenties you did for Jarvis Radburn. I'm impressed,* Mr. Paxton had complimented in that friendly, confiding voice few people could resist. Topper had been disarmed, flattered; when Mr. Paxton offered him the security of full-time employment, Topper hadn't hesitated.

He hadn't known that his job would entail a confrontation with Shiver. At this moment as he started on the short, jolting ride to the hotel, Horace Topper wondered if perhaps the goat had been set after the lion.

Simon Kincaid knocked on Alex's door late one evening a little over a week after the attack on Eve Sheridan. The cold night air had a bite to it, alive with the scent of woodsmoke and the chill of approaching winter. Jack-o'-lanterns dotted porches and windows, and a cold white moon cast shards of light through the tree branches. Drifts of fallen leaves—courtesy of a hard rain the previous night—coated the front porch of the double residence where Alex lived.

"Think we need to talk," Simon announced, sauntering with noiseless tread past Alex, into the hall. "I don't suppose you've anything to eat?"

Alex eyed the operative. Lithe, intense, Simon lived the life of an alley cat: wild, solitary, and smart. Alex himself was considered an expert at shadowing, but he had no desire to match wits with Simon. "What's troubling you?" Alex queried, shutting the door. "And, yes, I can feed you. Mrs. Detweiler fixed a rump steak, and there's plenty left."

Simon glanced around. "She has gone, though?"

"It's almost ten o'clock, Simon." Alex led his friend

down the hall to the kitchen.

Mrs. Detweiler had adjusted the damper on the stove to keep the food warm, well knowing Alex's odd hours. Simon held his hands over the warming shelf as Alex cut hefty slices of the roast and heaped a generous portion of baked tomatoes on a plate. He set everything down on the kitchen table and gestured to Simon. "Here. Eat, and unburden yourself."

For the next hour they talked, sitting at the table long after Simon had finished eating. Finally, with a regretful sigh, his friend and fellow operative pushed back the chair and stood. Alex followed Simon's glance around the warm kitchen, bathed in the soft glow of the single gas lamp burning on the wall. "I like coming here," Simon said, half under his breath. "It's very . . . welcoming, somehow."

Alex had been deep in thought—all of it unpleasant—but at Simon's words the grim line of his mouth softened. "You're welcome to stop by anytime," he promised gently. He followed his friend down the hall to the door.

Simon crammed a worn fedora over his head and stepped out onto the porch. "Thanks for the meal. I'd best be off. Topper may have bedded down for the night, but I doubt Joe Leoni has such harmless plans." He gazed out into the night, then glanced over his shoulder at Alex. "And that being the case, I wouldn't bet on Eve Sheridan seeing her next birthday."

He vaulted down the steps and disappeared. Leaves rustled, then settled in slow swirls in his wake. For a long moment Alex stood, listening to the rising wind, feeling its bite. Then, shivering from more than the chill, he went back inside.

15

Richmond

EVE DRUMMED RESTLESS FINGERS on her walnut writing desk, her attention frayed. Books and papers cluttered the desk surface, the floor, and the window seat in the upstairs library of their home, where Eve had spent most of the past week. One chewed pencil was stuck in her hair, and four different ink pens lay scattered amid the books and papers.

Research for her second book—a discussion of birds in the New Testament—was not going well. The previous year Eve had had her first book published, a small and scholarly study of birds in the Old Testament. The work was recognized largely among academic circles, and few people outside the family knew of Eve's success.

Eve preferred it that way. She wrote because she loved birds, and because she had turned out to be a passably respectable writer. She was also writing for a very private reason, one which she had not even been able to share with Pastor Sidney, though sometimes she wondered if the wise old minister knew anyway.

Sidney Jamison was an old family friend who had greatly contributed to Eve's efforts, and she really needed to pay him a visit. Retired, a widower, Pastor Jamison suffered from crippling arthritis and was now confined to a wheelchair. If any consultation was to be done, Eve would have to go to him—which would require leaving the house.

Sighing, Eve flipped through several pages of the book in front of her—a dry, thoroughly enervating work with little to recommend it beyond some scanty references to further sources. She slammed the tome shut, stood, then walked over to the window seat. It was late afternoon, and through the lace curtain panels she could see shadows lengthening, stretching across the backyard in geometric patterns of mauve and gray. As dusk approached, any outdoor movement would be difficult to detect.

And behind the live oak at the corner of the house, or the bushes shielding the back wall—maybe even the elm below the library window—someone was watching. Watching and waiting, Eve knew, for her to . . . to *what*? If her suspicions were correct, she was being stalked. At first Eve had been angry: did he think her a featherhead because she had so easily flown into the web he had first woven with that note? But the relentless, eerie sensation of those stone-dead eyes watching, always watching, *was* wearing her down. Today, with each tick of the clock, her anger crumbled into apprehension.

"Eve? Are you in here?" Eve's mother poked her head through the doorway. The strong, blunt features of her face mirrored both irritation and concern. "Sophie's spilled glycerole shoe dressing on the rug, and Maggie hasn't returned from mass." She swept into the room, cloak over her arm, hat and gloves in hand. "I don't know *why* she can't go on Sundays like we do. . . ." She jerked on her gloves. "I promised to deliver the baskets of preserves that the Benevolence Society provided for the Home for Incurables and . . ." Her voice trailed off, eyes widening as she focused on the untidy library. Her gaze lifted to Eve, standing motionless by the window. For a moment neither of them spoke. Then her mother's lips firmed and she tucked her chin. "I wondered," she finished in a carefully neutral tone, "if you would see to Sophie for me. I know how difficult it is when you're in the middle—"

"I'll take care of it, Mother." Eve's mouth twitched at her mother's astonishment. "I've been having a bit of trouble collecting my thoughts, so perhaps a diversion will help. And Sophie's mishaps certainly provide a diversion."

"Well, then. Thank you." The snapping brown eyes softened a bit. "Eve? Is anything . . . what I mean to say is . . . are you ailing? You haven't left the house all week." Two spots of color tinted her lightly powdered cheekbones. She turned, reaching to rearrange a porcelain bust on the parlor table at her side. "I know my attitude is . . . overbearing at times. But I'm not the only one who has noticed that, for the past several days, you haven't been yourself at all." She quit fiddling with the statuette and glanced at Eve. "Maggie tells me you haven't even been out in the backyard, except to feed the birds. And she claims you practically *throw* the seed, then rush back indoors."

Eve turned back to gaze out the window, wondering what to do. Like Rebecca, her mother confronted life with the confidence of a general charging into battle. Brisk and managerial in her dealings with people, she simply would not understand Eve's growing fear, much less the need for caution. *"Nonsense,"* Mother would scoff. *"I thought you had long outgrown this childish preoccupation with imaginary goblins and phantasms. If you think someone is skulking about the bushes, for heaven's sake set the gardener after him."*

Eve shuddered at the prospect. Not for the first time, it occurred to her that perhaps she had clung a little too stubbornly to her independence. She really *should* have allowed that officious Pinkerton operative to escort her home last week and explain the situation to her father. William Sheridan might have the gentle soul of a saint, but he was an intelligent man. He at least would have lis-

tened to Mr. MacKay, even if he refused to believe someone really had tried to harm his daughter.

Beyond that, Eve herself should have broached the
matter before her father left on a trip to New York; he
wouldn't be home for three more days. And the very *last*
person in whom Eve would confide was her mother.

Her fingers stroked one of the drapery tassels while
she prepared to somehow pacify her mother. Then,
through the sheer lace panels, she caught sight of an
amorphous shape emerging beside the trunk of the elm
tree. A gust of wind sifted through the branches, rustling
the dying leaves, and the shadow disappeared.

Three quarters of an hour later, Eve slipped out the
front door. Upstairs in the library, a solitary lamp burned
on the desk. She had sent Sophie up on a mindless er-
rand, which—with Sophie—would entail at least ten minutes. The ploy was flimsy, but it was all Eve could contrive
on the spur of the moment. If that . . . that *churl* stayed
camped beneath the library window, hopefully he would
see Sophie's silhouette and be fooled long enough for Eve
to escape.

The street was quiet, deserted save for some children
playing Giant Steps. Glancing quickly about, Eve gathered up her skirts, then headed down the walk.

His face lit up with curiosity, but the streetcar conductor supplied the address for the Pinkerton Detective
Agency's offices without comment. Eve felt his gaze following her as she stepped down, and she suppressed the
urge to whirl and shake her finger at him. She *hated* people staring.

It was almost five, but lights still burned behind the
double glass-topped doors. A young man wearing a
striped shirt, matching suspenders, and a plain bow tie
looked up, then hastily donned the coat draped across the
back of his chair. "May I help you?" He listened to her
request, not hiding his astonishment. "You're MacKay's
redbird!" he exclaimed. A nameplate on the desk read

78

R. Peabody. Eve noted it, then fixed her eye upon the young man, who coughed, shuffling his feet. "Um . . . you're lucky—he's been out all day but came in a little while ago." He glanced to the right, where a closed door and drawn blinds concealed the interior of another office. "But I'm afraid he's busy right now."

"I'll wait," Eve walked over to a couple of hardback chairs shoved against the wall and sat down, prepared to camp there until midnight if necessary. Regardless of the consequences, she refused to return home after dark, alone.

A loud voice echoed through the other side of the closed door, words muffled but rife with irritation. Mr. Peabody glanced at Eve, then at the door; with a look of profound reluctance he stood and crossed the room.

"Not now!" a baritone roar answered the timid knock.

Mr. Peabody stood his ground and knocked again, this time three firm raps. The door jerked open, and a huge, barrel-chested man with a red face and imposing beard glared down at the hapless messenger. "Your pension just might be at stake if it's not important!" he boomed. Then he caught sight of Eve. "Who the devil is this?"

Eve stood. "Miss Eve Sheridan," she introduced herself, ignoring both propriety and his rudeness. She wished she had taken more care with her appearance. "You would be Mr. MacKay's superintendent, I imagine."

From behind the large man she heard a startled exclamation; seconds later Alexander MacKay elbowed his way out of the office. "Miss Sheridan." He reached her in three long strides. His intense blue eyes glittered with satisfaction as much as surprise. Energy crackled through him so powerfully that Eve stepped back. His thick, windblown hair and casual attire lent him a rakish, dangerous aura that dominated even the much larger superintendent.

If Eve hadn't been desperate, she would have marched back out the door. Annoyed, off balance, she folded her hands, staring at Mr. MacKay's unbuttoned collar. "I need help," she admitted after sifting through and discarding several polite *non sequiturs*. "I believe the man who accosted me last week is hiding somewhere outside my home. I've only glimpsed him twice," she finished hurriedly. "The last time just an hour or so ago." Her voice trembled a bit at the end. "That was when I decided to come here. I slipped out, and as far as I know, I wasn't followed."

The superintendent loudly—and rudely—cleared his throat. Eve stiffened even more. "I'm *not* imagining this, and as you can plainly see, neither am I on the verge of hysterics."

"I see very well," Mr. MacKay observed, leaving a disgruntled Eve to wonder at the many different shades of meaning invested in the evenly spoken words. "As it happens, Mr. Hostler and I have just been discussing you and your family. You perhaps noticed my surprise at your timely appearance?"

Color seeped beneath Eve's skin. "Is that so? Perhaps now that I'm here, you could share what you were discussing."

"Secure some refreshments for the lady, Mr. Peabody," Mr. Hostler ordered. He winked at Mr. MacKay. "Once again, Mr. MacKay, your instincts have been confirmed. Miss Sheridan, come into my office, and we'll discuss this . . . beginning with your reason for coming *here*, instead of contacting the Detective Bureau."

Mr. MacKay gestured toward the enclosed office. "After you, Miss Sheridan, if you please."

The superintendent followed, shutting the door. Trying to conceal the attack of nerves that assaulted her, Eve looked around the office. She was impressed by its well-organized arrangement, though the distinctly masculine aura intimidated her as much as its tidiness. Piles of folders were neatly arranged on the massive rolltop desk, whose top displayed a collection of ornately framed photographs. Matching oak file cabinets lined one wall, and the wooden floor was covered with a faded oriental carpet. Mr. MacKay led her to a leather straight-backed office chair that dwarfed her feminine stature.

"Don't be frightened," he said. "Evidence to the contrary, you haven't breached the gates of hell."

Eve darted him a quick look, relaxing at the note of dry humor. "That, Mr. MacKay, remains to be seen."

With another loud chuckle, Mr. Hostler settled behind his desk, the chair creaking beneath his weight as he reached for his pipe. After several puffs he leaned forward, all levity gone. "Miss Sheridan, your request presents us with a delicate dilemma. Pinkerton's agreements with its clients are always confidential, and it has not been our policy to permit, much less encourage, contact between client and operatives." He studied her a moment longer. "However . . . I will allow for the somewhat unique circumstances surrounding this particular case.

"Now—I've little use for dithering, over-imaginative ladies, and less for fools, Miss Sheridan. Mr. MacKay here assures me that you're not a fool, and you don't dither."

The prickling discomfort intensified, and Eve shot Alexander MacKay a barbed glare at Mr. Hostler's deliberate omission. Mr. MacKay deflected the glare with a bland smile.

"So," the superintendent went on, removing the pipe and pointing the stem at Eve, "for the time being I'll permit this conversation to continue. Tell me, if you please, exactly why you're convinced there is an unknown person purportedly spying upon your household, and that he is the same individual who attacked you in the alley behind the American—" He scowled. "The *Lexington* Hotel."

"It was referred to by the old name in the note," Eve pointed out, although doubtless he already knew that. She sat all the way back in the chair, holding herself very still, and tried to pretend she was sitting on a bench in Monroe Park. She wished Mr. Peabody would hurry with the refreshments. "I was hoping Mr. MacKay—or perhaps you—could do the explaining. That's why I came here.

You already have some knowledge of this . . . this cut-throat."

The two men exchanged glances. After an uncomfortable pause, Mr. Hostler leaned back, puffing his pipe and waiting, while Mr. MacKay gracefully sat down in a matching chair opposite Eve's. Ill at ease, flustered by the operative's proximity, Eve discreetly shifted so that her feet weren't in danger of brushing Mr. MacKay's. When she glanced up, she was surprised by the flicker of kindness on his face.

"Perhaps," she offered stiffly, "there is a need to secure the services of Pinkerton's National Detective Agency before—"

"Don't worry over that right now," Mr. MacKay interrupted, overriding Mr. Hostler as well. It was obvious the two men both possessed strong opinions, but of the two, Eve would far rather lock horns with the blustering superintendent. "Miss Sheridan," Alexander MacKay said, "we believe the name of the man who attacked you is Joe Leoni, a villainous cur wanted for murder in several states. Ah . . . it would be far more . . . appropriate . . . if we discussed these threats with the police, and your father. You *have* enlightened him about your assault?"

"He's been in New York all week," Eve hedged. "There was no opportunity. I certainly didn't want to worry my mother or the household servants, but I—I couldn't depend on my own counsel any longer. Not after—" She stopped, unprepared to admit her own foolishness and tell the whole story.

MacKay looked up abruptly and peered at Eve as if he knew exactly what she had been about to say. But he didn't press the issue. "Never mind. We'll see to it later. Actually, it's the man who *hired* Leoni whose identity is producing a certain . . . ah . . . difference of opinion between Mr. Hostler and myself as to how to discuss the matter with you."

"Mr. MacKay, this is precisely why I counseled waiting," Mr. Hostler snapped. The reprimand, ostensibly,

was directed at MacKay, but the superintendent was looking directly at Eve. "Now the girl's to be even more frightened out of her wits, but I don't suppose there's any help
for it. Ask her, MacKay—or I will."

Eve sighed, toying with the buttons on her gloves a
minute. Then she admitted with a wry smile, "Mr.
MacKay, whatever you tell me cannot possibly be any
worse than what I've endured this past week." Mentally
she added a prayer for affirmation of that bold pronouncement.

Again, she was disappointed.

Alexander MacKay rose to stand directly in front of
her. Eve gripped her hands so tightly together that her fingers ached from the tension. "We need," he pronounced,
"for you to tell us everything you know about Avery Paxton." The crisp Scottish brogue intensified when he added
with quiet menace, "And I wouldn't trouble myself with
lying again. If you want the help of this Agency—only the
truth will serve."

16

Richmond

HIS VEILED THREAT HOVERED IN the room. Alex let the heavy silence linger while he studied the young woman sitting in front of him with her hands so tightly intertwined. Her severe navy worsted suit might have been deliberately chosen to project an aura of control and self-possession, but he could tell Miss Sheridan was rattled.

Alex suppressed a smile. One of her gloves was beige, the other light gray; she had missed three buttonholes when she fastened the waist of her suit, and beneath her slipping hat several strands of gleaming red hair trailed unnoticed down the back of her neck.

It would seem the girl was hanging on to her self-possession by a thread—and Alex was about to snip it. The indomitable Miss Eve Sheridan, he had discovered, revealed a lot more when she *lost* that admirable quality. "I see you do have more than one hat," he observed, eyeing the object with just enough of a smile to provoke. "I was beginning to wonder. That's another bit of information I can add to your file card. The hat, by the way, is very attractive. I like the use of ribbons instead of bird feathers, which I'm sure is why you purchased it. Now, Miss Sheridan—about Avery Paxton. Where did you first meet him?"

Her hands flew automatically to her head. "My hat?" she repeated, trying in vain to reattach it more securely. "My card . . . you have a *file*? On *me*?"

Alex nodded.

Shock, confusion, and embarrassment paraded across her features. *Don't ever try to hide anything,* he told her silently, wondering with a stab of bitterness how long, in a world of deceit, cynicism, and lies, her face would continue to mirror her feelings so transparently.

As if he had spoken the thoughts aloud, Eve Sheridan lowered her head; when she raised it a moment later, Alex almost lost his balance. Was the girl *laughing* at him, then? "Mr. MacKay has a devious turn of mind," she said to John. "I would imagine him to be one of your better operatives because of it?"

"He's stubborn, opinionated, and bedevils the starch out of my collars," Hostler returned, equally dry. "And at least once a week I threaten to transfer him to Santa Fe. But yes, Miss Sheridan, Mr. MacKay's one of the best. It's equally plain, however, that you're a young lady who refuses to cower *or* bridle at his rather impertinent inquisition."

"I, too, commend your fortitude," Alex added. He sat back down, moving the chair closer to Eve Sheridan's. "And freely confess to being dangerously undone. Few people recognize my tactics quite so readily. My apologies—and admiration, Miss Sheridan."

He lapsed into silence, remembering both her guileless honesty in the depot wagon—and her poor attempt to lie about Paxton later. "Let me try again," he murmured, looking directly into the wary brown eyes. "Miss Sheridan, for several years Pinkerton's has been trying to secure enough evidence to prove that Avery Paxton is guilty of"—he paused, then finished carefully—"a number of crimes. I won't elaborate on that." *Nor will I,* he decided, *on a few other suspicions.* "It would be very helpful, perhaps crucial, if you would tell us what you know."

The immense brown eyes blinked twice, then shifted to inspect the print of an old map hanging on the wall behind Alex. "I only met Mr. Paxton a few times," she admitted slowly. "He was . . . very kind to me."

Alex kept his face impassive. "Why did you lie about it?"

The mismatched gloved hands separated, then dropped to her lap. "I'm not sure. You talked about him as if he were some despicable criminal, and I thought perhaps you were considering him in the same light you did—" She paused, then amended, "Or still do, me. I didn't feel it was right, and at the time I didn't think the matter was any of your business." She finally transferred her gaze from the map to Alex. "I shouldn't have lied, especially for such trivial reasons. Or at least, one of them is trivial. I suppose, though, it's still a sin, isn't it, since—" As if she realized she was rambling, the girl took a deep breath, and Alex watched her lips soundlessly forming words. She cleared her throat.

Alex waited, sensing her struggle, respecting her effort to remain calm.

"I met Mr. Paxton the first of the year, at a charity ball," she said in a forthright manner. "I believe he and my father share some business interests, though I don't know if he had come to Richmond other than to attend the ball. My father introduced him to both my sister and me. Then, later in the evening, Mr. Paxton introduced us to Mr. Giles Dawson—the man who ultimately married my sister. When they . . . when I saw that . . . ." Her color rose. "Mr. Paxton was very nice to me."

Alex could imagine the little snake-oil charmer mesmerizing the innocent in front of him. *God, why do You allow this?* He was both elated and enraged, because all the pieces of this extraordinarily difficult puzzle were fitting together at last . . . but the pattern forming chilled his blood.

"That would have been the Annual New Year's Ball—

the social event of the season?" John clarified, leaning forward, his own excitement barely restrained. "Held in The Grays Armory?"

Miss Sheridan shuddered. "Yes. My mother is one of the organizers. A lot of people attend. We go every year."

"You, I surmise, somewhat reluctantly?" Alex suggested.

"I'm afraid so," Miss Sheridan confessed. She lifted her hands, studying them with a rueful smile. "Things like this always seem to happen."

"Very awkward for you, to be sure." Alex managed to produce a smile and forced his voice to lightness. "I'm not fond of such social daffing myself. I always feel like a trained monkey at the circus, dressed as one is expected to be at those affairs." Alex paused, then returned to the subject at hand. "Now, you say Mr. Paxton introduced a Mr. Giles Dawson?" He exchanged a quick look with John. Giles Dawson bore a closer examination.

"I don't know why *that* could possibly interest you," Eve retorted. "Apparently you suspect everybody of having ulterior and nefarious motives, Mr. MacKay."

Well, there was no help for it now, Alex realized. But then, the disillusionment of the innocent was always painful. "Unfortunately, in this business you tend to discover that most people *do* have ulterior and nefarious motives, Miss Sheridan. In this particular case we have sufficient evidence to deduce that it is Avery Paxton who hired the man who tried to kill you. The note you received was a deliberate scheme to place you at the hotel at a time when your 'unfortunate demise' could be attributed— wrongly, of course—to a troublesome robber who has been assaulting women in hotels. Unfortunately, we haven't yet determined *why* Avery Paxton wants you out of his way. He has a passion for planning complicated, challenging jobs, and he loves to thumb his nose at the law. But he avoids indiscriminate violence, and as far as we know refuses to involve himself personally."

"It offends his sensibilities," John snarled, his voice

grating. "So he hires someone else to do the dirty work."

The door opened and Raymond entered, balancing a tray laden with steaming mugs of coffee and a plateful of sweet buns. And not a moment too soon, Alex saw. Raymond set the tray down, leaving with a concerned backward look. Alex handed a mug of hot coffee to the dumbfounded young woman. "Our very efficient Mr. Peabody has made a trip to the corner cafe. Drink it up, Miss Sheridan, and have a sweet roll. It will help."

"Thank you." She sipped, then grimaced, but after a few moments a hint of color seeped back into the chalk white skin. She did not, however, touch the sticky bun. To Alex's utter astonishment, she neither protested nor scoffed at his brutal revelation. "Why would Mr. Paxton want to hire someone to . . . to kill me? Why would *anyone?*"

"We don't know," John repeated, his frustration evident. "I was hoping to wait until we could provide some more definitive information, but Mr. MacKay here had to jump in with his two big feet."

Alex inclined his head. He was accustomed to functioning as John's favorite scapegoat. "They are that," he intoned, earning himself another livid glare. "I may have jumped in," he conceded, "but Miss Sheridan's arrival was so fortuitous as to be divinely arranged. And while Mr. Hostler scoffs at such, I'm sure you, Miss Sheridan, can appreciate my relief that your movements *are* being monitored at the highest level." He smiled at her, employing all his renowned charm to coax a bit of life back into the girl. He had to do something to compensate for his earlier treatment of her.

But for some reason she bit her lip, looking more uncertain than ever. "I wouldn't know about that," she whispered. "Mr. MacKay . . . it's obvious you have some ideas about—about all this. I'd appreciate hearing them, no matter how . . . distasteful they may be." Something dark and fearful flickered in her eyes for a second, then vanished. "I've discovered in the past few months that I have more to fear from unknown shadows than from unpalatable truth."

Months? Alex wondered, but he nodded. "The truth," he reminded her, "*will* set you free, Miss Sheridan—no matter how painful the process, as you say." He tilted his head and felt in his pocket. His fingers closed around his grandfather Dom's chamois pouch, with its wooden puzzle pieces. For as long as he could remember, he had carried such a puzzle so he would have something to do with his hands. It helped him think, helped him sort out the pieces of less tangible problems. But he didn't bring the puzzle out tonight. He didn't want to take the chance of distracting Eve Sheridan from what she had to say—or to hear.

He sensed—even though he wouldn't have been able to explain why—that Eve Sheridan would neither be placated nor satisfied with vague generalities. Of course, to proceed further he *would* have to secure John's agreement. "With your permission, Miss Sheridan, before I oblige I need to confer with Mr. Hostler here. No—don't get up. We'll step outside. Sip your coffee and try to relax."

John followed him out with ill grace.

Moments later they returned to the office. John dropped back behind his desk, and Alex returned to the chair next to Miss Sheridan. *Good,* he thought. *The freckles sprinkled across her nose look like freckles now, instead of dark splatters of grapeshot on parchment.* "All right, Miss Sheridan . . . let me tell you what we do know. The man who passed that note to you, down in North Carolina, goes by the name of Horace Topper. He's what Avery Paxton calls an 'associate,' which is a euphemism in this case for fellow criminal."

She flinched, and Alex paused, sweeping her in a brief but thorough look. Shaken to the soles of her sturdy pegged shoes she might be—but her backbone remained unyielding as a railroad spike. Relieved, Alex pressed on. "Horace Topper is a shy, amiable man with a rare talent.

Unfortunately, he's chosen to use his artistic ability to create some of the best forgeries and counterfeit bills we've seen in years. He free-lanced for a while, until Avery Paxton took him up as one of his associates."

Miss Sheridan carefully placed her mug on the tray. "And why would an expert forger be involving himself in helping to arrange my . . . untimely demise?"

"I believe he's being used both as a sort of middleman—a catalyst, perhaps—and a decoy. It was Topper who passed you the note in North Carolina. I witnessed that, you may recall? Ah—I see that you do. Don't scowl, Miss Sheridan. You'll wrinkle your lovely brow."

"*Mr.* MacKay," John growled.

Alex sat back, folding his arms across his chest. "Topper is a busy man," he continued blandly. "He has spent the past several days driving back and forth by your residence. Looking, I think, for some sign of a missing fellow associate, one Joe Leoni, the man who attacked you at the Lexington last week. The man—if you're correct in your observations—who has been shadowing your house this past week, waiting for an opportunity to finish the job. I would say, Miss Sheridan, that there are some powerful guardian angels watching over you."

He sat forward. "We learned recently of a brutal slaying in New York of a . . . ah . . . a 'lady of the night.' Nobody paid too much attention until a red wig was discovered, caught on the edge of a sewer drain a block from the sight of the murder."

Across the room John stirred. Alex exchanged another stringent look, then finished, his voice a rough growl: "Our operative in New York claims the victim was the new courier Avery Paxton hired a month or two ago."

"I . . . see."

She spoke so calmly that Alex was almost fooled. Then he peered more closely into her face. "Miss Sheridan . . . perhaps you should sit back in your chair for a moment."

"I'm perfectly all right."

"Miss Sheridan," Alex tried again, even more gently.

She ignored him. "I need to go home. It's late. My mother will worry, even though she's used to my ways." She stood, looking lost and uncertain. "I need to think. I . . . would appreciate an escort, if one is available."

John came around the desk and stood next to Alex. "Of course," he concurred instantly. "I'll have Mr. Peabody arrange for a hack, and he—"

"I'll see Miss Sheridan home," Alex said.

John scowled, his complexion purpling, but it was Eve Sheridan who spoke first, in a polite, pedantic voice. "Thank you, but I'm sure you've other things to do, Mr. MacKay. Mr. Peabody—"

"I said, I'll see you home," Alex repeated, even more softly. He watched her eyes widen, the dazed look of a trapped animal. He escorted her out the door of Hostler's office and reached for his cap and coat.

"I'll have a minute of your time first, Mr. MacKay." John enunciated each word deliberately, warning Alex of a pending eruption.

"Wait here," he said to Miss Sheridan. Her nostrils flared, but she merely nodded. Alex returned with John to his office and shut the door. "I realize you'd like to transfer me to Santa Fe," he began, "but—"

"I want to know why you didn't ask her about Giles Dawson. If the man's above board, no harm is done. But if he's a Paxton associate—or even an innocent dupe, we need to know."

He glared at Alex and reminded him heavily, "Especially considering the possible significance attached to those particular initials. You had her exactly where you wanted her, Mr. MacKay, and don't think you can cow *me* with that look. Earlier, I wanted to wait and confront her father, but no—" He jabbed a finger at Alex. "You insisted that we first alert the girl so she could better protect herself." He stomped over to his desk and snatched up his pipe. "So . . . I repeat: Why didn't you interrogate her about Giles Dawson?"

"She'd had enough."

91

John snorted. "The 'Bluebeard Case' is one you have personally been pursuing for almost five years now, Mr. MacKay. It's been your Holy Grail. But I will remind you that our first loyalty is owed to American Eagle Insurance Company, who—"

"Our first loyalty is to find out the truth!" Alex shot back. "For the love of God, John—Eve Sheridan's *sister* is married to the man! I'll no' be party to trampling, any further than I already have, the spirit of a very brave young woman. She's had enough for now, I say."

Muscles corded, Alex waited in tense silence, knowing that if John lost his temper, this time Alex might lose his own as well.

For a full two minutes John puffed on his pipe, chewing the stem and breathing like a bellows. Abruptly he slammed the pipe down and threw up his hands. "Have it your way. For now." He jerked open the door. "I'll be waiting to hear from you. Immediately."

"You may depend upon it," Alex bit out. They exchanged a last look. Then Alex shut the door behind him, took a deep breath, and pondered how to convince a frightened, hostile Eve Sheridan that her life might depend on her willingness to trust him.

17

Cambridge, England

A SHROUD OF MISTING RAIN BLURRED the majestic cluster of buildings that comprised King's College. It was a little past two in the afternoon, and Dante Gambrielli had been standing beneath the stone arch entrance to the college for close to an hour. He caught sight of a young woman on the other side of the narrow cobblestone street; today she was carrying a cumbersome bundle while trying to hold her umbrella aloft.

Dante dodged bicycles, passing carriages, and the hordes of pedestrians, and crossed the street to intercept the young woman. "May I be of assistance?" he inquired.

She looked up, a pair of large gray eyes framed by thick lashes revealing both gratitude and doubt . . . with a touch of coyness. "I'm not sure—I've only another two blocks," she answered.

He was pleased by the cultured, well-modulated tone of her voice. "And I *am* a stranger." He smiled, bowing. "Permit me to introduce myself. Denham Granville, at your service. I'm on holiday, from Norfolk, to peruse the Trinity and King's College libraries."

"I am Beatrice Linwood." She slanted him a look that told him she was not unaccustomed to gentlemen introducing themselves on the slightest pretext. Then her umbrella tilted, and the bundle toppled through her slipping fingers.

Dante plucked the bundle from her hands and tucked it beneath his arm. "Oh dear." The girl dimpled, and her cheeks, already rosy from the wind and rain, deepened to the color of sun-ripened plums. "Thank you kindly, Mr. Granville. It would seem that, under the circumstances, I should clearly allow you to escort me home."

"It would be my pleasure," Dante responded with a formal cordiality that earned him another giggle.

"I'm staying with my aunt. She lives right across the river, there. I love to watch the young men rowing in the summertime."

Dante did not respond. This one, he realized, would offer a tantalizing—but painful—challenge. Tantalizing because he enjoyed the chase more when his victim wasn't a simpering, simpleminded miss. Painful . . . because her manner reminded him of Rebecca's.

"I've noticed your aunt's residence," he commented. "Sixteenth-century, half-beam construction with jettied walls, isn't it? And overlooking the river. I walk by most every afternoon—except, of course, when the weather is frightful, as it is today."

"You must come in for tea and meet my aunt. She's very scholarly, and thoroughly enjoys a good chat." The gray eyes crinkled at the corners, frankly baiting him, Dante decided.

Miss Linwood would have to learn who controlled the circumstances. "I'm afraid that won't be possible today." He smiled politely. "I have another appointment."

"Oh." She looked momentarily disconcerted. Dante walked beside her, not saying a word, waiting. "Perhaps . . . if you are going to be here awhile longer . . . you could come to tea another day?"

He waited until they were on the arched stone bridge, a block from her aunt's house. "Very well, Miss Linwood. I will look forward to meeting your aunt," he said formally. "I do enjoy a lively discussion. What, do you know, are some of the authors she favors? Perhaps I could bring along some choice volumes."

Miss Linwood's nose wrinkled in dismay. She had a long, narrow one, Dante saw, totally unsuitable for wrinkling. Rebecca's, on the other hand . . .

Abruptly he became aware that Miss Linwood was talking. "Um . . . I do beg your pardon, Miss Linwood. I'm afraid I was admiring your aunt's house. Such a fine example of medieval timber framing. I attended a lecture once . . ." He let his voice trail away and affected an air of sheepish confusion. "Oh dear. What must you think of me? How terribly rude, and so boorish."

"Not at all, Mr. Granville. Well . . . shall we say Tuesday, then? Half past four?" She held out her hands and Dante handed over the bundle, which was—judging from the shape and fragrance—several loaves of bread.

"I shall look forward to it very much." He bowed, doffed his hat, and returned the way he had come. Across the bridge, out of earshot, he laughed and began whistling. Miss Linwood's father was an extremely wealthy farmer, and Dante happened to know that upon the occasion of his daughter's eighteenth birthday the previous month, Thaddeus Linwood had settled on her a considerable dowry. She had also come into a thousand acres of her deceased mother's estate in Suffolk.

If Dante was very careful, he might be able to settle comfortably in England for the rest of his life, safe from the pernicious Pinkerton bloodhounds. The dilemma of Avery Paxton, unfortunately, was another matter entirely.

Dante daily regretted the impulse that had chained him to an unwelcome association with a man whose ruthlessness rivaled Dante's own. He regretted even more his present situation.

Avery might have initiated Dante's introduction to Rebecca, but as far as Dante was concerned, the five thousand he had paid Paxton for that favor acquitted Dante of further obligations.

He refused to be blackmailed.

And yet . . . the refusal could prove to be even more costly.

Dante's jaunty walk slowed. Thoughts of Avery inevitably led to thoughts of Rebecca. Thoughts of Rebecca created pain, loneliness—and fear. Resolutely Dante erased his mind of her image, superimposing instead the delectable form of Beatrice Linwood.

He'd give it five months, this time.

18

New York

AVERY PAXTON STROKED THE CARRARA marble
statue of Aphrodite which now graced the landing at the
foot of the stairs. His fingers caressed the cool, satiny surface with the touch of a lover. This was his newest purchase, special ordered all the way from Italy; the shippers
had placed her here in the entrance foyer just the previous day. He thought she complemented perfectly the
cherubs flanking the newel posts.

"Isn't she beautiful, Amos?" He turned to the butler,
eager and excited. "Have you ever seen anything like this?
I saw a statue by Michelangelo in Rome once, and ever
since then I promised myself that one day I'd have something like that in my home. . . . Isn't she beautiful?" he repeated almost dreamily.

"Yessir, Mr. Paxton." White teeth gleamed in Amos's
normally impassive black face. "That's one mighty fine
statue."

"And wasn't it a stroke of genius to have it placed right
here, at the bottom of the staircase? Just like she's greeting me . . ." His voice trailed away as he looked around
the immense Italian-style foyer of his Fifth Avenue mansion. Right down the street from the Vanderbilts and the

Goulds, he liked to point out to his friends.

He beamed at Amos. "How long have you been with me now, Amos?"

"Goin' on a year, come December, Mr. Paxton."

"I hired you right after Mr. Gould died, remember? You like it here much better, don't you?"

"Yessir." The butler stood straight and tall. "Much better, Mr. Paxton."

Pleased, Avery reached into his pocket and tugged out a silver dollar. "Here. On your next day off, go buy something for yourself, or your missus."

"Thank you, sir." The butler carefully tucked the coin away, bowed, and withdrew.

Avery rubbed his hands together. He enjoyed pleasing his servants, enjoyed knowing they talked and whispered among themselves about his generosity, about the magnificence of his home. Avery Paxton was destined to be a legend—he already *was* a legend.

"Cablegram, Mr. Paxton."

Avery turned to one of the housemaids, grinning as he accepted the cablegram. "Thanks, Della. How's that boy of yours?"

The homely girl's face lit up. "A lot better now, thanks to you, sir." She blushed. "I thank you for asking, sir." Avery headed toward the library, tapping the cablegram against his palm. It was from England—probably Gambrielli. Avery chuckled. One of these years, perhaps he'd buy himself an English castle. . . .

Avery sat back in the chair, his hands clenched on its overstuffed arms. On the small table beside him steam spiraled upward from the coffee a servant had brought. The delicate bone china cup tilted precariously in the saucer. Dark splotches stained the cutwork doily covering the inlaid table, but Avery barely noticed.

He rubbed his finger over and over the tiger's-eye ring, breathing deeply until he was calm. Then he picked up the cablegram in his lap, lips pinched in a thin, straight line as he reread the message. "You will be sorry," he whispered, then repeated the threat aloud. "You *will* be sorry."

Shiver. He needed Shiver. *Blast* the man, where was he? Avery knew of his favorite associate's propensities. But Shiver should recognize Avery's absolute authority by now, especially after that regrettable episode the previous year. Avery had had to bribe half a dozen bluecoats—as well as P.C. Commissioner Byrnes himself—to keep Shiver out of Dannemora State Prison. If it happened again, Avery had promised, Shiver could rot in jail.

Regrettably, Shiver was the only associate who could recognize Dante Gambrielli—and carry out Avery's orders. In spite of his lapse concerning the Sheridan female, only Shiver could finish the job. Frustrated, furious, he twisted the tiger's-eye ring around, his mind sorting out alternatives.

There were none. He had no choice. Eve Sheridan was still alive, and might even write him again, since he had not replied to her original inquiry. *Blast* the both of them, her and her vain little sister who had started this whole coil in the first place. Who would have thought that a coy, blushing bride would have attached any significance to his single meeting with her new husband, at Shang Draper's? The danger to Avery now constituted a serious threat. He would have to formulate his escape carefully.

Yesterday, following instructions, Topper had placed a call to Avery's Fifth Avenue mansion, utilizing Avery's brand-new telephone. Over the wire his associate's whining voice practically blubbered with fear, apologizing because he hadn't located Shiver.

Avery had known all along that Topper would fail—the man could barely find his way out of a one-horse hack. On the other hand, Horace Topper *was* a forger of brilliant proportions, whose craft had almost doubled Avery's profits the past year. It was a shame, really, that the man was such a Philistine. The only reason Avery had ordered him to Richmond was because the Pinks were sure to spot him immediately and, if Avery's hunch was accurate, they would flush Shiver out of hiding in the process. With the Pinks hot on the trail, Shiver would finally escape to England.

Momentarily cheered, Avery picked up his coffee cup, then caught sight of the stain. He hurled the cup across the room. It slammed into the wall, shattering. Avery walked over to the bellpull and rang for Amos. "I seem to have dropped my coffee," he told the expressionless butler. "Clean it up. I'm going to my club."

As he changed clothes, he decided to stop by a certain billiards parlor and drop a few hints in the right ears. "It's a poor man—and a half-wit," his father always said, "who keeps all his money in one bank." The lesson could be applied many other ways, Avery had found.

An hour later, after verifying that William Sheridan was still in town, Avery strolled into Shang Draper's. "Bring my drink along to my private table," he instructed the bartender. "And make sure I'm not disturbed."

19

Richmond

THE STREETLAMPS CAST WAVERING puddles of
light among the deepening shadows as Eve rode home in
a horse cab with Alexander MacKay. Numb with fatigue
and apprehension, Eve watched the silent Pinkerton operative, wondering why he continued to study the street
so intently.

Part of her was still terrified of this man who moved
with the silent grace and economy of a peregrine falcon.
Yet there was also a warmth, a gentleness in him she
could sense even through her fear. He was unlike any man
she had ever known, and she wondered why—though he
terrified her—she still felt compelled to challenge him.

"What are you looking for?" she finally asked. "Surely
he can't know where I am right now."

Mr. MacKay replied without turning his head. "I'd like
to think so, knowing how resourceful you are. But the
fact remains that, clever and bright though you may be,
you're still no match for Joe Leoni. He's known as 'Shiver'
on the street—for good reason, not the least of which is
due to his favorite weapon."

Eve fiddled with the frog of her cloak. She hated to
admit that he was right. She hated even more the fear

crowding her as relentlessly as the onset of night. She only hoped Mr. MacKay wouldn't sense her fear. Eve forced herself to stop fidgeting; even in the concealing shadows of this carriage, her restlessness could give her away to an observant man like Alexander MacKay.

Three blocks from home he spoke, his vigilant gaze still out the window. "I need for you to promise me something."

Alarmed by the deep somber tone, Eve braced herself. "That depends."

"Now, why," he returned with disconcerting humor, "does that not surprise me?" Then he became very sober again. "Miss Sheridan, Joe Leoni is as vicious and cold-blooded as they come. The man is devoid of any humanity."

"I'm painfully aware of all that, Mr. MacKay."

"Ach, but you don't seem to comprehend that the man is a hired assassin—and in his mind, you're a botched job. I fear he won't leave stalking you until you're dead." He paused. "Unless the law can nab him first. So, Miss Sheridan, this is why you must trust me, or at least trust that I can better protect you."

"A week ago you wanted to arrest me," Eve pointed out.

His head swiveled around. "That was a week ago, and you comprehend very well the reasons why." To emphasize the point, he turned back to the window as if even in the past few seconds he might have missed something important. "This is not a battle you can win, Miss Sheridan. At any rate, don't you see that we need to join forces, so to speak, and fight on the same side?"

"Mr. MacKay, I don't want to . . . do battle . . . with *any-one*. But when people are treated with suspicion, the natural human response is defensive. Tell me," she charged bitterly, "that you're convinced I *am* an innocent bystander in a scheme about which I know nothing. Are you willing to trust *me*, Mr. MacKay?"

The hack pulled to a halt in front of her house. Eve

put her hand out to open the door, but Mr. MacKay fore-stalled her. "I'm convinced you're not a criminal, Miss Sheridan," he murmured. "But as to trusting, that's looking to be a little more difficult. We'll see after the next few minutes, perhaps."

Flustered, Eve stammered, "In the next few minutes? What does that mean?"

"It means I'm going to walk you to the door and see you safely inside. But I must have your promise, here and now, to *stay* inside until I personally inform you otherwise . . . or you won't be leaving this carriage." His voice had softened to a rumbling burr, the threat spoken so gently Eve almost didn't recognize it.

When she did, curiosity outweighed indignation. "How would you stop me?" she asked. "Somehow, Mr. MacKay, I can't see you physically restraining an unwilling woman who, I assure you, would scream loudly enough to arouse the entire neighborhood."

A deadly quiet descended, prickling the fine hairs on the back of Eve's neck. She held her breath, darting surreptitious glances between the door handle and Mr. MacKay's ominous bulk.

"Can't you, now?" his voice purred. "Shall I give a demonstration, then? I once promised you would regret defying me. I don't lie, Miss Sheridan."

"I think," Eve retorted, her mouth dry as rice powder, "that I'm as frightened of you as I am of Joe Leoni."

The tingling aura of danger vanished instantly. Mr. MacKay shifted back, relaxing against the opposite side of the buggy, arms folded across his chest. Light-headed, Eve gripped a trembling hand over the handle of her umbrella. Mr. MacKay chuckled.

"Miss Sheridan . . . I think you've a streak of recklessness as bold and vivid as your hair." He did not respond to her smothered gasp. "Bedevil and torment me if you must, for there's no way I could ever deliberately harm a woman," he promised. "I've four sisters and a gentle mother, and my father would flay me to the bone for showing even a glimmer of disrespect, no matter what the provocation."

Dazed, Eve blinked. Was he *smiling* at her? But with his next pronouncement, she decided the smile must have been a trick of the streetlamp.

"That doesn't mean I won't carry out my promise," he finished. "It just means I'd be taking you down to the city jail, and request that you be made comfortable there for a while. Now—do we have an understanding?"

Eve entertained no further delusions concerning the Pinkerton operative's persuasive powers. "I can see why Mr. Hostler threatens to send you to Santa Fe," she murmured. Then she sighed. "Yes. We have an understanding."

"Good." He leaped down, paid the driver, then came around to Eve's side, holding out his hand.

Slowly Eve placed hers in it, startled not so much by the warmth and hardness as by the bewildering sense of security she felt when his fingers closed about hers. Wordlessly she allowed him to escort her up the walk. He continued to stay close by her side all the way up the front porch steps, his gaze constantly monitoring the surroundings.

Maggie opened the door.

"Maggie, this is Mr. MacKay," Eve introduced him, wondering what else to say, if anything. "He escorted me home."

"Doubtless you've gone and landed yourself in a spot of trouble again," Maggie snorted. She raked Alexander MacKay with a suspicious eye. "What would you be doing with Miss Eve, if I might ask?"

"She'll explain as much as she feels comfortable with," was the unperturbed response. "I've things to do at the moment." He touched the brim of his flat cap, then turned and ran down the steps, blending into the evening shadows so silently that Eve shivered afresh. She stared at the darkness and suddenly realized he'd left up to her the ticklish task of relating any or all of the week's incredible events.

"So then, what is it this time?" Maggie grumbled, wiping her hands on her apron. "Your mother's been home this hour past, let me tell you, and after reading your note, 'twas all I could do to convince her to wait a bit before telegraphing the mister up in New York, then marching down to the police station herself."

"Well, I'm home, but Mother still might end up marching down to the police station," Eve warned. She crossed the hall and hurried into the kitchen. Mr. MacKay, she decided, had gone far enough. He couldn't order a self-sufficient woman like Eve Sheridan around. . . .

Her hand was reaching for the back porch door when common sense belatedly arrived. Her hand fell from the latch.

Alexander MacKay was *not* the sort of man to cross heedlessly. He had ordered Eve to stay inside, and though she resented his manner and feared the consequences of disregarding his orders, she knew he was right.

"Maggie," she announced as the housekeeper huffed into the kitchen behind her, "perhaps you'd better have Mother and Sophie gather in here immediately. There are a few things I need to tell you all."

Alex scouted the Sheridans' front yard, his movements soundless. He'd had to wait for several minutes until his vision adapted to the night, but now every sense was alert, heightened, his skin itching. When the search of the front yard failed to flush his quarry, he struck out for the back, hugging the wall of the house, silent as a shadow.

A carriage rolled by in the street behind, the horse's hooves ringing on the pavement. Somewhere off to the left a dog barked. Crouched and motionless, Alex waited to see what the barking signaled. A screen door slammed—then silence.

Alex crept from behind a rose trellis at the corner to the base of a pine tree, its trunk just thick enough for concealment. Inch by inch, he moved his head until he could scan almost a quarter of the Sheridans' backyard. Covered with trees, bushes, and several dark, boxy shapes at the back, which he decided must be storage sheds, the scene loomed as a logistical nightmare. Light shone through a single window, probably the kitchen.

There. At the corner of his vision—movement. Alex froze. A breeze sifted through the trees, and in the distance a river barge's mournful horn wailed. The clump of bushes where he had sensed movement was about fifteen feet away, near a footpath; Alex was just able to discern the flagstones.

Stealthily he crouched down, then drifted closer to the clump of bushes. His right hand closed tighter over a stone he'd picked up earlier. When he was about ten feet away, he threw the stone in a shallow, vicious arc.

Nothing happened.

For five solid minutes he waited in absolute stillness, watching and listening. Finally, when his racing pulse slowed almost to normal, he risked straightening enough to scan the other side of the yard. Soon a golden harvest moon would be rising, but at this moment the Sheridans' backyard might have been the blackest bog in Scotland, save for the faint strip of light from the kitchen window.

Alex crouched back down, preparing to slip across to the trunk of a huge elm, when he sensed another movement. The primitive tingle shot down his spine, screaming an alarm. His only warning was a whispering current of air; Alex dropped, throwing himself backward, and the quick action saved his life.

He heard the sound of ripping cloth, felt a brief, white-hot pain slash his shoulder, then his body slammed into Leoni, hurling them both to the ground. Leoni hissed a savage curse, and Alex rammed his forearm toward the sound at the same time his other hand shot out. Somehow he connected with Leoni's wrist. He twisted it viciously.

Leoni countered with a bruising jab to Alex's midriff.

Alex gasped for air, his hold slipping enough for Leoni to jump up. Alex lunged, catching one ankle and yanking the fleeing man off his feet again.

They fought in deadly silence. Alex was larger, stronger, and skilled—but Leoni fought with the viciousness of a trapped weasel. And Alex was weakening rapidly from the searing pain in his left shoulder.

Without warning, a stream of bright light spilled onto their thrashing bodies, momentarily blinding both men—but also illuminating the knife, dropped in the fracas. With a chilling, obscene grunt Leoni rolled, scrambling for the knife. Alex surged to his feet, his gaze fastened on the other man, whose mouth was stretched in a feral, gloating smile.

From out of nowhere a torrent of hard grit engulfed Leoni. He yelled, sputtering and coughing, blindly stabbing with the knife hand while trying to shield his eyes. Alex didn't hesitate; he crashed into Leoni's knees, grabbed the knife-wielding wrist, and slammed it against a tree trunk.

Both men thudded to the earth in a choking shower of birdseed. Another brief struggle ended when Leoni managed to twist free. His fist caught Alex a head-ringing blow to the jaw; by the time Alex's vision cleared, Leoni had vanished into the darkness. Seconds later, Alex heard the sound of cloth scraping against brick. Then there was silence, except for his tearing breaths and the faint hissing sound of the lantern.

He straightened carefully, each movement an agony of screaming pain. His gaze moved from the formidable figure of the woman holding the lantern to the housekeeper beside her. Next to the housekeeper a young, large-boned servant girl wrung her hands, gawking. Slowly Alex turned, searching until his gaze at last found and focused on the determined, dead white face of Eve Sheridan, her arms holding an empty bucket.

She lifted her chin. "I disobeyed you, I know," she admitted. "But I was afraid of what could happen to you, out here in the dark, in an unfamiliar location. There are so many places to hide. . . ." Her arms began to tremble, and she dropped the bucket.

Alex attempted a smile. "As to that, lassie, it's no' a new thing for me to go hunting in unfamiliar territory." Another lightning bolt of pain hit then, almost bringing him to his knees. Eve Sheridan's face blurred to a pale oval surrounded by a tumbling red-gold halo. "But I'll be forgiving you, since there's a fair possibility you might have just saved my life."

"The man's bleeding like a fresh-gutted pullet," Maggie snorted. "Best come into the house, Mr. MacKay." She sounded more irritated than alarmed.

Ach, but that was the Irish for you. Always contrary . . .

"I'll send Sophie for Dr. Towser," the older woman said. She stepped forward, holding the light higher to peer at Alex's back. "You've a nasty wound, Mr. MacKay, so I'll save the lectures and recriminations for now."

"Be grateful," Eve murmured at his elbow. "When Mother lectures, you'll think a knife wound pleasant in comparison."

Dazed, bemused, Alex allowed himself to be led into the house. It was a wonder, he thought, light-headed and dangerously near to passing out, how these gentle ladies were treating the whole affair as if they'd merely happened upon a couple of schoolboys tumbling about the yard.

20

Bramble Cottage
Norfolk, England
November

THE TRAIN WAS LATE. GILES DAWSON sat at the window, one foot tapping impatiently. He glared out at the passing countryside: barren fields of turned-over earth and dry, stubbly meadows, checkered by the interminable hedges, which now were nothing but bare, twisted branches. The sullen sky glowered a sickly grayish yellow, as if it were jaundiced.

Giles had written Rebecca that he would be home in time for supper, but his wife probably hadn't appreciated the gesture. He stroked his chin, frowning, dreading the pending reunion. Suspicion and petulance had replaced Rebecca's adoration, and for the past month she had been hinting that she might return to America for a visit with her family.

"And I might stay there until you're able to join me," she had flung out. She was testing him, Giles knew.

On that occasion he had still been able to kiss and caress her into tearful compliance. Giles shifted, crossing and recrossing his legs. Beneath the starched white shirt, his armpits dampened. Avery's last cablegram was burning a hole in his pocket.

Paxton! It may have been a mistake to provoke the little man, with his megalomaniac delusions. It had *definitely* been an error to reveal his Cambridge address. An error, he reminded himself—but one from which he could recover. The association with Avery was proving to be more trouble than it was worth—except that if it hadn't been for Avery Paxton, Giles would not have met Rebecca. The situation was proving to be more difficult than he had realized, but in the end, Dante Gambrielli would prevail, regardless of what happened to Giles Dawson.

He tugged out his watch, then with a muttered oath shoved it back. *Rebecca.* What *was* he going to do?

The whistle shrilled as they pulled into another small village, the steam and cinders clouding Giles' view. Travelers hurried to board the train, and he watched the scene without seeing it. All he could see was Rebecca's face if she ever found out who Giles Dawson really was.

In the end, he would do whatever was necessary. Giles leaned back against the seat and closed his eyes. Oh yes, there would be fear, at the last . . . and there would be nothing he could do about it. The harsh lines bracketing his mouth deepened, and his hands clenched into fists. He would do what he had to do.

He always had, and this time he could not afford to deviate, not with Avery's threatened blackmail dangling over him like a hangman's noose. The train jerked and pulled slowly out of the station. Giles opened his eyes, forcing himself to envision the expression of joy and satisfaction that would certainly light Beatrice Linwood's face when, some four days hence, he formerly requested permission to court her.

Twilight had fallen when he hurried up the path toward the brick and slate cottage where he and Rebecca had lived these past months. The acrid tang of coal peat and musty ashes stung his nostrils, and he coughed. Inside, a fire would be burning, the lamps trimmed low, a kettle on the range. Perhaps some scones, covered by a cloth, would be waiting on the sideboard.

And Rebecca would be waiting as well, her eyes filled with bitterness and suspicion instead of welcome and love.

He would do what he must do.

He opened the ornamental iron gate and strode up the uneven path to the front door. Inside, as always, he carefully hung his cape and hat on the hallstand. This time, he did not remove his gloves. "Rebecca? I'm home, love. . . ."

Giles stumbled out the back door, sides heaving, his vision a sickening mist that swam in a thick crimson tide. Lifting his hands, he stared at the red, sodden gloves. There had been so much blood. . . .

He turned then and was sick, retching until he collapsed weakly onto the cold, damp ground. Much later, he rose with the unsteady gait of an old man and reentered the house. There was a lot to be done, and very little time left in which to do it.

21

Richmond

A GUST OF WIND FLATTENED THE LAST of the
chrysanthemums and blew most of the remaining leaves
off the trees that lined the street in front of the Sheridan
home. Eve watched the approach of the wind-buffeted
mail carrier. The sky had no right to be such a deep, jewel-
toned blue on such a cold and windy day.

It had been over three weeks since Joe Leoni attacked
Alexander MacKay in their backyard. Not since four
years ago, when Eve yielded to impulse and hired a trap
to drive alone down to the river to watch shorebirds, had
her parents exhibited such a fever of emotion. Her father,
she knew, still had difficulty accepting the attack. But he
had—along with her mother—employed every tactic of
emotional blackmail to convince Eve to leave for an extended visit with Great-aunt Effie, out in Denver. Mother
insisted that Sophie accompany her. Maggie crossed her
arms and flatly denounced that idea, maintaining that
Eve would manipulate Sophie far too easily.

The postman mounted the steps, and Eve rose from
her musings on the front porch swing. "Good day to you,
miss," he greeted Eve, his grizzled face reddened from the

wind. "Have another letter for you to
Your sister again, eh?"

Eve thanked him. For some reason, he
ing. She hurried upstairs to the privacy of
and sank down onto the window seat, opening
thin envelope with mounting dread. It was su
crumpled, the address barely legible. Inside, the
was streaked in several places, as if from drops of
. . . or tears. A month had passed since Becca's last l
Throat aching, Eve began to read.

> *Dearest Eve,*
> *It's very late here, almost midnight, but I can't sleep. Giles was supposed to have returned home three nights ago, but hasn't. This time, he's been gone over two weeks. Eve, I wish you were here. I'm very sorry to worry you, but even writing all my feelings in the journal has not been able to ease the heaviness of my heart. Dear sister, how I despise myself for burdening you, but I've nowhere else to turn, no one I can trust.*
> *I'm afraid of my husband.*

The letter fell into Eve's lap. She stared at it blindly, while her lips formed a wordless prayer. Eventually, with hands that felt like blocks of ice, she picked the sheet of paper back up and read through it twice more, then paced the floor, her thoughts churning.

When she returned the letter to the envelope an hour later, her mind was set. She went searching for Maggie to inform the housekeeper that she would be going on a journey after all. Only she wouldn't be going to visit Great-aunt Effie in Colorado; she was going to England on the first ocean liner available.

Horace Topper sat in the office of John Hostler, his knees shaking. He had placed his top hat in his lap and pressed his palms down flat on the crown as hard as he

...uld, hoping Hostler and the Pinkerton operative with ...m hadn't noticed his knees.

"Mr. Topper, I've explained that we're not interested in disturbing your vacation," Hostler repeated for the third time. The deep, booming voice was beginning to lose its patience. "All we need from you is any information you can provide on Joe Leoni."

Topper exchanged a wordless, pointed glare with the other operative—Mr. MacKay, he had introduced himself.

"We know you both work for Avery Paxton," MacKay put in. He walked over to stand behind Topper. One hand tossed what looked like a small piece of wood up and down. "Make it easy for us . . . and it will go better for you."

Topper slid an uneasy glance upward. On first inspection, MacKay wasn't all that remarkable in appearance, and Mr. Paxton would have sneered at the casual sack coat he wore. Why, the man wasn't even wearing a tie! Except . . . Horace chewed the inside of his cheek, trying to analyze what it was about this particular operative that set him so on edge.

Mr. Paxton might boast of his ability to outwit the Pinks, and Topper himself had witnessed the ease with which the New York coppers were either bribed or bamboozled. *"Just stick with me, Tops,"* Mr. Paxton always promised. *"Stick with me and watch the fools chase their own tails."*

Topper took a deep, quavering breath. Mr. Paxton had never met the operatives here, or he would have had to change his mind. But though the Pinkerton operatives were a fearsome lot, Topper would never betray Mr. Paxton. He owed his employer too much. Besides, if Mr. Paxton ever found out Topper had been squealing— Shiver would be stalking *him* instead of that stupid Sheridan girl.

MacKay strolled over to stand in front of him, so close his scuffed boots touched the tips of Topper's patent leather shoes. Horace shrank back against the seat, his throat muscles working. "There's no need to be so nervous, Mr. Topper." MacKay spoke the words as smooth as clover honey, but the mesmerizing blue eyes sizzled Topper's nerves. "If you truly don't know where Joe Leoni is, why, we'll all shake hands and you can be about your business. But you see . . . Leoni *is* our business. And we thought, since of course you know Leoni is a low-down, murderous snake—"

"Mr. MacKay," Hostler growled, his voice warning.

Topper didn't understand why the two men would be angry at each other, but he didn't care as long as it released *him* from the bite of MacKay's soft but stinging voice and those searing eyes. This fellow unnerved him far more than Hostler's grizzly-bear size and thunderous scowl. And yet MacKay, Topper realized, hadn't so much as raised an eyebrow.

In fact, right now he was looking down at Topper almost with . . . with compassion. Horace gulped, suddenly wanting this man to understand the awkwardness of his position. Maybe if he *did* explain, Operative MacKay would help. "I was to locate Sh—I mean Mr. Leoni," he blurted, wiping his sweating palms on his trousers. MacKay plopped down in the chair opposite, his silence encouraging. Horace leaned forward, eager now to unburden himself. "This is the *second* trip I've made down here since the beginning of October; I've looked everywhere, but I haven't seen or heard from him." Hostler snorted and Topper shot him an aggrieved look. "I haven't! I've looked and looked, every day, just like Mr.—" He stopped abruptly, great droplets of perspiration popping out on his brow. "What I mean, is—"

"That's quite all right, Mr. Topper." MacKay stood and rested his hand momentarily on Topper's shoulder. "We know Paxton would not look kindly on an associate turned stool pigeon for the authorities." The hand squeezed, then lifted. "He might even feel compelled to teach you a lesson, might he not? Even someone as . . . useful . . . as you."

Topper squirmed. "He wouldn't. . . ."

"Well, we can hope so." MacKay smiled. "But were I you, Mr. Topper—I'd watch my step until I returned to New York and could hear Mr. Paxton's reassurances for myself. I'm sure he'll understand, you being such a valuable associate and all."

Topper bolted upright, his voice beseeching. "Can I leave now? I don't know any more. I don't!"

Hostler leaned back in the chair, smoking his pipe and pondering the ceiling. Finally he waved the stem. "Scram."

Topper rushed to the door, stumbling in his haste. Mr. MacKay held it open, his expression impassive.

"Mr. Topper?"

Topper froze, hunched shoulders stiffening with dread.

"When you do return to New York, you'd be doing me a favor if you'd pass along a message to your employer." The smooth voice softened into almost a whisper and froze the perspiration on Topper's brow. "Tell him, if you will, that down here we don't take kindly to low-life gooneys skulking about the bushes of peoples' homes, waiting to murder innocent young ladies." He leaned down, and now the blue eyes were fiery as the hottest fire in a steel mill. "And that the next time I encounter Joe Leoni— and there *will* be a next time—I'll be doing some marking of my own."

Topper's eyes bugged, and he lifted a shaking hand to pass over his mouth. "I don't know what you mean," he denied hoarsely. He scuttled down the steps as if the building were on fire, and didn't pause until he was safe back in his room at the hotel, with the door firmly bolted.

"Permanent desk duty," John told the ceiling. Then he glared across at Alex. "In Santa Fe."

Alex grinned, a savage bearing of teeth. "There was nothing to be gained by pretending ignorance of Paxton's motivation for sending Topper to Richmond. And you

116

knew it, else you would have stopped me."

"I'd sooner step in front of a runaway train."

Both men stood in frustrated, furious silence, having debated for a quarter of an hour, with neither man giving an inch.

Finally John stalked across the room, snatched his cape and top hat off the hatstand, and marched toward the door. "I'm having lunch with the commissioner. Thanks to you, Mr. MacKay, I've a monstrous case of dyspepsia, and doubt I'll be able to eat."

"My apologies, sir—but to my way of thinking the cause of your dyspepsia is that you hate to admit I'm right." He stuffed his thumbs inside his suspenders, rocking back and forth on his heels.

"Blast you, MacKay, that's beside the point!" John exploded. But Alex saw the betraying glint in the superintendent's eye. He shook his head and stomped toward the door, his voluminous cape billowing. Then he paused and, without turning, tossed back, "How's your shoulder?"

"It's healing well. Dr. MacPhail vows I've either the luck of the devil or the blessing of the Almighty."

"There's no doubt in my mind as to which it would be," John growled. He slammed the door behind him.

22

THE SHERIDAN TRUST AND Securities office was located on East Main, in the Mutual Assurance Society building. Because the day was clear and blustery, Alex walked, enjoying the freedom. He swung his injured arm and smiled. The pain was diminishing; in no time he would be good as new.

After three weeks, his feelings of weakness and fury had faded, along with the physical discomfort, although he would carry the mark on the back of his shoulder to his grave. "You're a fortunate lad, Alex, me boy," Dr. MacPhail had observed the previous day after examining the six-inch scar. "No poisoning of the blood, no excessive redness or tenderness. Stiffness seems to be lessening, probably because"—he glanced over the tops of his spectacles—"you're such a braw lad. Although you do insist on moving about more than's wise, ignoring your auld family doctor's advice."

"I've been careful," Alex promised. "And the stiffening is easing because I *am* exercising it."

He rotated the shoulder now, wincing a little. But overall, he was satisfied that in another week, like Jacob, he would be able to wrestle an angel and win the match.

At that moment a blurred figure burst through the door of a jewelry pawnshop two doors down and pelted toward the street. "Stop! Thief!" The angry shopkeeper ran out onto the sidewalk behind him. "Stop that man!"

There were shouts of consternation, and a woman screamed. A horse half reared, whinnying in alarm. Alex sprinted down the walk, his eye fastened on the fleeing thief. Down the street an open-air trolley approached from the other direction, bell clanging, electric wires humming. In a desperate burst of speed the thief hurled himself toward the car, hoping to escape, Alex realized, by hopping aboard and eluding any pursuers.

Alex swerved and cut across the street behind the trolley. Using the car and passengers as a screen, he jumped on board, keeping his gaze glued to the thief. "Don't be alarmed," he reassured the angry conductor at the turnstile. "I'm after that man there. He just robbed Robinson's Pawnshop."

Even as he spoke, the panting thief leaped aboard the opposite end, shoved aside two indignant passengers, and plowed a desperate path toward the other side of the car. Alex had anticipated this move, however; as the thief prepared to jump, Alex slipped up behind, then clamped a commanding hand on his shoulder. "I'm afraid not, lad."

The miscreant jerked around, gaping at Alex in astonishment. He lowered his head like a bull preparing to charge, though he more resembled a squat, red-faced bullfrog. The trolley lurched to a halt, and with a foul oath the man swung his bag of pilfered loot at Alex's head. Alex ducked, then in a series of swift moves that wrenched his shoulder considerably, wrestled the man to the floor of the trolley.

Two policemen dashed up and jumped aboard, ordering curious onlookers and the trolley passengers out of the way. The younger one glanced from Alex to the subdued man sprawled on the floor, Alex's knee firmly planted in his back. "Thank you, sir. That was right fast thinking." His face was full of admiration.

His older companion snorted. "And no blasted wonder, ya young pup. That there's 'the real MacKay' himself." He dropped down beside Alex and hooked a beefy hand around the cowed and trembling thief. "You're lucky he didn't break your neck—which is still a distinct possibility if you don't come along nice and quiet-like for me."

The young copper's eyes widened, and he looked at Alex as if he were the chief attraction at the county fair. "Alexander MacKay? The Pinkerton operative who wrestles on Friday nights down at Mahoney's? I heard about you! There's not a man between here and Boston who's been able to best you on the mat."

"Well . . . I haven't been lately," he muttered, rubbing his aching shoulder. He shot a rancorous glare at Sergeant Porter, who winked at him as he manhandled the thief off the trolley. Alex glanced down at his grimy clothing, then back at the young policeman. "Hadn't you best be aiding your sergeant there?" He was beginning to feel not only uncomfortable but surly from the aggravation to the healing wound.

The young officer obediently turned and left, still shaking his head. Alex apologized to the conductor and the passengers, then thanked the boy who had retrieved his cap. All the way across the street he endured the gawking stares, inwardly groaning at the wildfire gossip that inevitably fanned higher the farther down the street it traveled.

The shopkeeper stuttered and gushed his gratitude, collaring passersby to regale them with Alexander's skill and cunning. It took a full fifteen minutes to escape, so by the time he arrived at William Sheridan's office, he was late.

"Mr. Sheridan," the prissy bookkeeper testily informed him, "has been waiting. He does have another appointment at two." He pointed at the door and returned to his work.

"Alfred's always a little irritable toward the end of the year," William Sheridan apologized, shaking hands and gesturing toward a pair of chairs. "What happened? You look like you've been rolling about in the street."

"Close." Alex explained briefly.

William listened, his head cocked, his eyes sympathetic. "Shoulder bothering you some, I see," he remarked when Alex finished. "Nothing irreparable, I hope?"

Alex shrugged, heartily tired of the whole episode. He gratefully accepted the glass of water William Sheridan offered, complete with chips of ice. William, Alex had discovered, might have a reputation as a shrewd investment broker, but he had also turned out to be one of the kindest men Alex had ever met.

Alex had tried to convince John to arrange a meeting with William upon his return to Richmond. Hostler refused. He had received a letter from the New York office detailing Avery Paxton's movements over the previous month. On two known occasions he had entered the hotel where Sheridan had booked a room, and remained there for several hours.

When Alex protested that meetings between the two men could in fact be legitimate business concerns, Hostler fixed a jaded eye upon him and inquired, "Are you willing to risk Eve Sheridan's life on that?" He leaned across the desk. "For the past two weeks you've escorted the girl all over town. When you're not available, Captain Hall details a patrolman, as a personal favor to me. We'll see to Miss Sheridan's safety. You persuade her to keep her own counsel another week or two."

"I don't like it."

"Your liking has little to do with it, MacKay. What if the old man *is* involved? We can't keep watch over the girl in her own home, now, can we? So . . . you introduce yourself to Mr. Sheridan, ingratiate yourself as his daughter's knight in shining armor—and keep Paxton's name out of it until I tell you otherwise."

"I've some things to discuss with you," Alex told Sheridan now, his voice dragging. He might have originally urged Hostler to confront William Sheridan—but now that the moment had finally arrived, Alex dreaded the confrontation. "The first issue remains your daughter's persistent refusal to go to Denver."

Sheridan groaned. A tall, stately man, William Sheridan possessed a deep, unruffled calm Alex greatly admired. Confident, paternalistic, but surprisingly indulgent in some areas, he and Alex had developed a comfortable rapport within hours of their first meeting. Alex—to his dismay—could also see why Eve continued to shield her father. The older man maintained a hopelessly idealistic concept of mankind's inherent decency. *God, You knew this would happen. Why do I have to like him?*

Unaware of Alexander's black mood, William was adopting a jocular tone about his older daughter. "Most girls in her position would have taken to their beds. I'm afraid the only way Eve would stay there would be if I had her chained to the headboard."

In the past few weeks Alex had discovered many new things about Eve Sheridan, but nothing had changed his initial opinion of her: an impulsive bluestocking whose unconscious vulnerability appalled Alex. "I don't think that would be a workable solution," he agreed, smiling briefly. "At any rate, I don't think it's necessary. We have reason to believe that Joe Leoni has left the city."

"Based on—?" Like his daughter, William was not a man to be placated by vague reassurances and generalities.

"We've had a couple of operatives working the local depots, as well as a man down at the docks. That particular fellow glimpsed a man who fit Leoni's description, boarding a sloop bound for New York late last night."

"That's not definitive, Alexander. At night, most figures are indistinguishable."

Not to Simon, Alex wanted to promise, though he merely inclined his head. "Perhaps not, though I give you my word this operative is one of the best. There's also

Horace Topper, still floundering about, totally ignorant. He hasn't been approached, or had any messages delivered locally. Of course, the man who we believe ordered the attack is not one to allow that much laxity on the part of his associates. Since it's been well over a month since the attack on Miss Sheridan, I'm afraid we also have to consider the possibility that Leoni is now acting independently. He's a bit uncontrollable."

William grunted. "You keep referring to some conspiracy, Alexander. I appreciate your skills and your powers of deduction, but frankly, the whole idea is preposterous. Who would set out to deliberately harm an innocent young woman?"

Alex steeled himself, tension gathering at the back of his neck and in his jaw. "My superintendent has given me permission to be more specific, if necessary. We're pretty sure Horace Topper was sent to flush Leoni out—sort of like a bird dog. But Topper hasn't a clue as to whether he has succeeded, else he would have left days ago."

A heavy silver eyebrow arched. "That's still weak, and you're still being evasive, Alexander. I've allowed it the past few weeks out of respect for your professional integrity." He leaned forward. "This whole situation is bizarre—we're talking about my daughter, not some enterprising female spy. Now, you keep maintaining there's 'a man' orchestrating all of this, ostensibly out of New York. I want to know the name of this man. I have some pretty powerful connections of my own there, and if there *is* such an individual, perhaps I can help." He looked straight at Alex. "I need to tell you something. I've read everything I could on Pinkerton's, and asked around on my own—very discreetly, I assure you. My conclusion is that . . ." He paused and studied Alex for another protracted moment. Then he lifted his hands in a pacifying gesture. "My conclusion is that I'd not want to be an enemy of Pinkerton's National Detective Agency."

Alex wondered what he had started to say. "You don't know how glad I am to hear that."

William's expression relaxed. "No offense intended. I'm aware of the slanted, generally negative tone adapted by much of the press, and I try to formulate my own assessments from a more positive approach." He chuckled a bit. "All the same—I wonder how the two of us would have fared had I been a member of the Amalgamated Association."

Alex winced. "We've no friends among the Union crowd, I'm afraid—particularly after this past summer at Homestead. I'm relieved you don't believe everything you see in the papers."

"I'm not that big a fool, Alexander."

No, you're no fool, Alex realized with increasing disquiet. *But I'm beginning to fear your reaction to the dark powers and principalities you refuse to see.*

William lifted his hands in a dismissive gesture, then dropped back to stroke the smooth oak chair arms. "All of this is beside the point. I just want you to understand that I'm willing to help you in any way I can." Abruptly his hands clenched and unclenched on the chair arms, and a tic jumped beneath his left eye. "It's unconscionable!" he burst out. "All of this! I just can't . . . that something like this should be happening to Eve . . . it makes no *sense!*"

The passionate cry echoed through the room. Alex stood and walked to the window, staring out over Main Street. *Do You know, sometimes I dislike it when I'm right?*

Outside, there was no sign of the earlier disturbance. Two more streetcars rattled past, followed by a lumbering mule-drawn wagon. On the corner a shiny green cabriolet pulled up to a hitching post and a dark-suited man jumped out. Over his head the wind whipped store awnings, along with the flags flying over Berry & Company, Outfitters, and the American National Bank farther down the street. Nothing out of the ordinary. Just another weekday afternoon in downtown Richmond. *You'd better take over here, Lord. I'm having a bit of a struggle, as You see.*

124

He could almost hear the unruffled, compassionate reply: *I know.*

"Alexander?"

Alex took a deep breath and turned around. "William, I must ask you some questions . . . this is difficult for me." He faced the older man without flinching; he owed William that much, if not more. "Would you mind telling me about your dealings with Avery Paxton?"

There was a long silence.

"I perceive your difficulty." William stood as well, clasping his hands behind his back. "You think Paxton is involved in this somehow, perhaps even knows a few . . . ah . . . unsavory characters, since he does live in New York?"

God . . . help me to do the right thing. "Not exactly," Alex replied. "Um . . . Miss Sheridan tells me Paxton introduced Giles Dawson to her and her sister."

William's face lit up, a soft smile playing about the corners of his mouth. "He made a good matchmaker. You wouldn't have met Dawson, of course. They're in England until spring, combining the bridal tour with business. Dawson's a solid fellow, positively besotted with Rebecca. I opened a bank account and deposited some shares in it when they married. Giles tried to refuse—said the concept of a dowry in the 1890s was an insult to him as well as my daughter."

"He said that, did he?"

William shrugged, waving aside the matter of Giles Dawson and his younger daughter. "You're not here about them. Blast it, man—come back over here and sit down. You look like you're facing a firing squad." When Alex made no response, William added more somberly, "What *is* it, Alexander? Asking me to involve Paxton? He's a little bit too much the dandy for me, and of course I don't know him as well as some of my other—"

Angry disbelief swept over William Sheridan's face. "Wait a minute. You're not—are you accusing Avery Paxton of *planning* this—this atrocity against my oldest daughter?"

Alex plunged both hands deep in his trouser pockets. "Yes, I'm afraid I am."

"Rubbish!" William exploded. "The man's fastidious to a fault, I tell you, and he is not at all violent. He prides himself in his cultural élan, even brags about his membership in various clubs and organizations. He's as rich as Croesus—he bought a mansion last year on Fifth Avenue, and he's so proud of it he's like a little boy with a new Christmas toy." He shook his head. "Besides, we do business together. You're mistaken about this. You and your Agency must look elsewhere on this one, Alexander."

"William—"

"Let me contact some of my friends in New York. I'll let—"

Two long strides and Alex was standing directly in front of the irate, incredulous man. "William. I'm telling you the truth. We have the note luring Miss Sheridan to the Lexington, as well as a verified piece of Avery Paxton's correspondence. They match, William. Pinkerton's would never make accusations of this nature without due cause." He waited, watching William struggle to regain control. After a moment, he touched the older man's shoulder. "Let's sit down, and I'll tell you what we know, and how. We've been . . . watching him, for several years now, you see. And, William—there's one other thing I must share with you. It's not just your daughter whom Paxton intends to eliminate. For some reason, he's trying to destroy you as well."

23

Richmond

BY THE TIME HER FATHER ARRIVED home that evening, Eve had secured passage on a ship leaving New York in four days. With surprisingly little dissension, her mother had acceded to Eve's hurried but methodical arrangements and was helping her pack.

At least, Eve thought as her mother folded and wrapped, *this is one area where we're compatible.* Packing a steamer trunk efficiently might seem a frivolous bond to most, but Eve had learned to accept whatever she could. "What about this muff?" she asked, holding it up.

Her mother paused from wrapping a pair of shoes in tissue paper. "Definitely not. You've had that since you were nineteen. We'll go to Thalhimer's first thing in the morning. You could use some new gloves as well." Her hands stilled, and her mouth began working as a sudden sheen glistened in her eyes. "Eve . . . you must take care."

This unexpected show of emotion shook Eve, threatening the fear-induced calm in which she had functioned since Rebecca's letter arrived. "I will, Mother. Please try not to worry. I can take care of myself quite adequately—as well you know." She managed a smile.

"In some ways, yes." Her mother gratefully smiled

back, dabbing the corners of her eyes with a lace-edged handkerchief. "You're really very like me when I was your age, as much as it pains me to admit it. But in other ways, Eve . . ." She shook her head. "You're very like your father. Besides—you'll be in another *country,* you and Rebecca. I can't . . ." Her throat muscles quivered. "While Trude will be a proper chaperone, I just don't—she hasn't been in *our* service—oh bother!" She resumed folding a chemise, the momentary softness ruthlessly banished.

Eve reached for a stack of collars, her mouth wry. Mother had proposed Trude and made arrangements earlier in the afternoon for her to accompany Eve. The daughter of Pastor Sidney Jamison's housekeeper, Trude was a phlegmatic woman of some thirty years whose husband had died the previous year. She had been wanting to visit relatives in Germany, and was more than agreeable to serve as Eve's chaperone, in return for the cost of her passage. Eve hadn't cared a jot and would have gone alone if necessary, though she knew better than to voice *that* intention aloud.

The front door slammed, followed by the sound of her father's voice—and Alexander MacKay's. Eve exchanged a swift, frowning glance with her mother. She had wondered why Mr. MacKay hadn't appeared to accompany her to the steamship company ticket office.

Downstairs, Eve's mother immediately took charge. "Mr. MacKay, what a . . . surprise. Sophie, show him into the parlor and have Maggie prepare some cocoa." She smiled. "I know how much you love a hot cup with a good froth at the top." She helped her husband shrug free of his muffler and coat. "You look tired this evening, Mr. Sheridan."

Eve smiled shyly over their heads at Alexander MacKay. He nodded, and she realized he was amused by her mother's bustling domination. The deep blue eyes were twinkling, and beneath the thick moustache his mouth curved in a smile. But as Eve continued to study him, she noted deeper lines furrowing his brow and the ill-concealed aura of tension.

She tilted her head, and his gaze instantly returned to her, searching her face. Eve still found his discernment a shock. Alexander MacKay possessed an unnerving ability to not only interpret—but share—her thoughts and feelings. *Eve,* she warned herself, *be very careful.*

"*I'll* show Mr. MacKay into the parlor," Eve told Sophie, her manner crisp. "As it happens, I've something to discuss."

"Yes, I think we should all adjourn to the parlor," her mother chimed in. "William, I suggest you add more coal to the fire. There's going to be frost tonight. Mr. MacKay, give me your cap and cape and quit dawdling."

"Yes, ma'am." He obediently handed them over, but Eve saw the understanding look he exchanged with her father. Few gentlemen could withstand Mother's forcefulness, but there had been only one occasion when Alexander MacKay had meekly succumbed.

"Miss Sheridan?"

Eve abruptly realized he was waiting for her to precede him. She blushed, averting her face as she slipped by. In the parlor she deliberately chose the barrel chair facing the sofa. Father walked over to the fireplace heater and turned up the flame, while Mother engaged Alexander MacKay in the kind of mindless social repartee Eve had never been able to perfect.

Something must have happened. Eve braced herself, glancing from her father to the Pinkerton operative. Father's manner was grim, abstracted—almost as if he were in shock. He hadn't even spoken to Eve. Nameless dread gripped her heart as a horrifying possibility pricked her consciousness. Had Mr. MacKay disclosed Avery Paxton's contemptible nature, told him Paxton had hired someone to kill her? Even worse—what if Mr. Paxton himself had corresponded with her father regarding the letter Eve had written in Rebecca's behalf?

When Maggie appeared with the pot of steaming cocoa and matching demitasse cups, Eve jumped up to pour, unable to sit still. She avoided any further eye contact with Mr. MacKay.

"What's going on?" Mother finally demanded, her voice loud in the strained silence.

24

Henrico County

ALEXANDER WAS EXTREMELY BUSY the next few days. Nonetheless, he spared an afternoon to rent a horse and ride out to visit his parents, soaking up the warmth of the rambling clapboard house ten miles out of the city, in Henrico County. As always, his first concern was his grandfather, who now spent his days by the huge open fireplace in the parlor, ensconced in the rocking chair he had designed some sixty years earlier.

Dom immediately asked if Alex had solved the latest puzzle, cackling with glee when Alex confessed he was still stumped. He was looking more frail these days, Alex saw with a pang; the long scholar's fingers were skeletal, as fragile as bird bones.

His father wasted few words after the initial greetings. "You're off again, aren't you, lad? How long this time?" Duncan MacKay had been a surveyor for the county for over thirty years, but now spent most of his time tending his flower garden and arguing politics. A weathered, wiry man with fixed notions, Duncan's intractable personality alternately challenged and vexed Alexander.

But he had never lied to either of his parents, and today would be no different. He took a deep breath. "I can't

131

say. But you need to know that it might cost me my job."

Duncan MacKay grunted. "You've said that often enough. Why should this time be any different?"

"Because this time, for the first time since I joined Pinkerton's, I'll be disobeying a direct order from my superintendent." He paused. Telling his father was far more difficult than defying John Hostler. "I wanted you to know. I've had to examine my conscience, and I've—" Abruptly his control broke, and he slammed his fist against the wall. "Father, I *have* to do this!"

The impassioned words gushed forth in a torrent as Alex faced his father, a man to whom God was more a Being of Judgment than a loving Father. A man who would never comprehend that doing one's duty and following one's conscience were not always the same. "It may be contrary to orders," he admitted, each word spoken as a vow, "but I'm doing what I know in my heart is the *right* thing to do." From the other side of the room he heard the sound of footsteps ascending the cellar stairs. "If I don't do this," he finished more quietly, looking his father in the eye, "God would forgive me—but I would never forgive myself."

His father slumped a little, the rigidity leaving his shoulders. "You've always had the conscience of a minister, Alexander, but the independent spirit of a Highlander. 'Tis an uneasy mix, and I daresay you'll be paying dear for it. But I've always told you to do what is right. Just don't get yourself killed, son. Your mother's roaring an' grating would send us all to the grave."

"I promise to do my best," Alex returned, flexing his shoulders in relief. In truth, he had expected much worse.

"Ach, what would the pair of you be doing over in the corner, sober as the Grim Reaper?" Mary MacKay's round face, wreathed in wrinkles, bathed Alex in warmth and bottomless love. Her apron laden with apples from the cellar, she smiled at him and gestured toward the table. "Plant yourself over here by the bucket with me, laddie, and help peel these apples. I'll tell you all about your sisters, and you can tell me your plans." The faded blue eyes were gentle as they rested on Alex's face.

So he peeled apples, listened to the soothing burr of his mother's voice—and tried not to think of what the following weeks would bring.

PART TWO

———

TRIAL

November 1893

25

TRUDE HUNG UP CLOTHES, ARRANGED toiletries, and set about straightening their cubbyhole of a room. Hat and gloves cast aside, Eve pressed her nose against the porthole and vowed not to become ill. Her stomach was playing leapfrog with her heart—though it wasn't from seasickness.

As New York's jumbled skyline diminished, Mother's and Maggie's stalwart figures blended with the waving crowd left behind on the quay. With a last resounding blast of the horn, the *S.S. Etruria* plowed from the harbor, past the Statue of Liberty. The mournful wail lingered in her ears as Eve finally accepted that she was irrevocably on her way across the Atlantic Ocean.

She wanted to feel anticipation and excitement. Instead, her gaze fell to the white-capped waves undulating in the ship's wake; deep, treacherous, cold as death, they beckoned with endlessly seductive splashes. The fear dogging her steps and her sleep would no longer be denied.

Rebecca.

And it was there, in the tiny cubbyhole cabin of the

S.S. *Etruria,* where Eve first admitted that she might never see her sister again.

After a while Eve turned away from the porthole. Trude, dressed in severe black bombazine, was busily dusting spotless fixtures with a hand towel. "What time is our seating for dinner?" Eve asked, as much to divert Trude from the relentless straightening as to control her own upsurge of emotion.

Trude barely paused from her labor. "Eight o'clock. You'll be wanting to change, miss." The calm voice and pale blue eyes betrayed no emotion.

"Yes . . . well, I think perhaps I'll go up on the deck for a few minutes." Eve hastened to add, "You needn't join me. I'll be perfectly fine, and will be back down in plenty of time to change for dinner."

That earned her a stolid, unblinking stare. "Very good, miss."

It promised to be a long voyage.

Laughing couples strolled about the deck, oblivious to the choppy seas and stinging salt-encrusted gusts of wind. Seabirds dived and swooped about the ship's wake, cawing and calling to one another.

Eve leaned on the railing and watched. This particular crowd consisted of herring gulls—*larus argentatus.* Saucy and brave they were, indifferent to the perils of both sea and land. Wrapped in her new gray traveling cloak, her new hat pinned so firmly a gale wouldn't dislodge it, Eve felt as weighted and earthbound as an African elephant.

She dug out the piece of roll left over from the meal Maggie had packed, and held it up. Immediately an enterprising gull swooped down, his elegantly curved beak opening to snatch the morsel right from her gloved fingers. "Oh, you're such a beautiful creature." Eve blinked back tears, overwhelmed by the bird's fearlessness and amused by its audacity.

She wished God would miraculously endow *her* with that kind of spirit. And, because her new book was meticulously researched, she also knew that even a mundane house sparrow was promised the kind of divine watch-care for which Eve had searched—and never found—all her life. It would be so much easier to be a bird. The thought was perhaps vaguely blasphemous, and she found herself glancing around almost sheepishly.

Alexander Mackay stood some four feet away, his ankles crossed, his hands deep in his pockets. The top cape of his brilliant plaid ulster flapped wildly in the wind. Framed by the lowering sleet gray sky and churning gray-green ocean depths, his rugged profile and solid presence offered strength, safety . . . and irresistible allure.

"Mr. MacKay?" Eve's voice cracked.

He turned, and the blue eyes—vivid as a blue jay's wing—trapped her as surely as a snare. "I have matters of my own to attend to," he said as if they had already been conversing for hours. "Since there's no longer the need to protect you from murderous miscreants, this seemed as good a time as any to make the trip."

Tears sprang to Eve's eyes, and she swiftly averted her head.

"You're not about to weep, are you?" He sounded so dismayed that Eve was able to swallow the choking lump in her throat, and even managed a watery smile. Plainly relieved, he gestured to several hopeful gulls, all hovering above them, black eyes trained on Eve. "You'll scare your new friends away, just when they've discovered your soft heart." He smiled. "Which, you'll discover, I also possess over weeping ladies."

"I'm not crying. It's just the wind." Eve shivered as an obliging blast of salt spray tugged at her cloak and wilted the stiff rows of ribbons on her new hat.

"Well, then." The broad shoulders relaxed. "I was afraid my presence had upset you, and I would have to spend the next eight days ducking into strange cabins and diving down smokestacks to stay out of your way. Of course this *is* a large ship, and if it would make you feel more comfortable—" He cocked an inquiring brow.

The feeling of coldness and isolation eased, and Eve relaxed for the first time in four days. "It's no use. I can tell when you're teasing me now," she warned. She shook her head, the tears and turmoil fading as well. From under the flat peaked cap his eyes danced, and beneath the heavy moustache the left corner of his mouth curled upward in a crooked half-smile. When he looked at Eve like that, it always caused the strangest sensation in her middle, as if she had fallen off her bicycle and couldn't catch her breath. "Tell me, Mr. MacKay, do you *really* have business to attend to?"

"Eventually." His gaze returned to the horizon. "I talked with your father. He agrees that you haven't revealed the true reason behind your decision to visit your sister, particularly when your original argument for staying in Richmond was due to a pressing commitment." He didn't elaborate on the nature of her "pressing commitment"; Eve was grateful for her father's discretion—and for Mr. MacKay's. Instead of probing further, he continued speaking. The deep voice was calm, nonthreatening. "I believe your father is concerned that you haven't accepted your sister's marriage. He told me the two of you were very close."

Months of denied grief clambered for release. Eve could see Rebecca as clearly as the man by her side, waving an exultant farewell from the ship, radiant in her blue gown, one arm clinging to Giles. The afternoon June sun had caught on her face—and on the brooch pinned at her throat. *Dear God, why won't You help me with this pain?*

Eve's hands clenched on the railing. Standing next to Alexander, she felt as if she were holding her palms over the kitchen stove, reveling in its welcoming warmth. But in eight days, she and Alexander would go their separate ways. She might yearn for the warmth, but Eve was too mindful of the consequences of thrusting one's hands into the hot coals. *But oh, how I want it. I must be brave, and very strong. The Lord has more important concerns than easing my pain—and so does Alexander.*

140

"It's not your concern, Mr. MacKay."

For a long time Mr. MacKay did not respond. A damp, numbing chill began to seep through Eve's cloak and into her bones. She watched the disappointed seabirds turn back to the safety of land and thought about the indifferent Presence of an unfathomable Almighty.

Mr. MacKay finally stirred. "That remains to be seen," he said, so low Eve had to strain to hear. "And God help the two of us if it *does* turn out to concern me." He turned, and his gloved hand wrapped about her elbow. "Come. You're shivering. I spied some deck chairs on the level below. We can talk there."

Alarmed and defensive, Eve tugged it free. "Who says I want to talk?"

He looked at her. "I have four sisters," he mused. "Whenever they're frightened and unsure, they bristle and spit, when what they really want is for me to give them a hug and listen to all their troubles."

"I didn't—"

"Now . . . you're a wee bit different, probably because you've no older brothers, and all the men you've known are either intimidated or appalled by your striking appearance and independent behavior." The knowing gaze touched on her hair, her mouth.

"Obviously you're neither, Mr. MacKay, but if you think propinquity gives you license to—to—" She stopped, unable to continue, because she couldn't lie to herself. If Mr. MacKay offered *any* form of physical comfort, including a hug, she would welcome it, and her face flamed with the acknowledgment. But instead of departing in righteous indignation, she stared wordlessly up into the narrowed blue eyes.

His face gentled, and he spoke as if her outburst had never happened. "My family and friends call me Alex." He lifted his hand, and without releasing her from the intensity of his gaze, he brushed back a wildly blowing strand of red hair. "And since we've saved each other's lives, perhaps—in spite of Mrs. Sherwood's *Manners and Social Us-*

age—you could find the use of Christian names between us acceptable."

Eve couldn't breathe. Her heart hammered wildly as he continued. "I'll confess I've been thinking of you as Eve for weeks now." *There it was again, that teasing glimmer and the rakish half-smile.* "When I'm not calling you a red-bird, that is. . . ."

"Mr. MacKay—" Was that breathless squeak really her voice?

"Alex."

"Mr. Ma—" He put his finger against her lips, a fleeting pressure gone almost instantly. Eve froze. Nobody except Rebecca—not even her parents—had ever treated her with such *intimate* familiarity. Grief and longing swept through her in an overpowering flood; she closed her eyes, then whispered, "Alexander. . . ."

"Well . . . 'Alex' would be better, but I won't quibble." He stepped back, gesturing toward the passageway. "After you . . . Eve."

Her lips tingling from the touch of his fingers, Eve obeyed. She *had* saved his life, as he so rightly pointed out, and surely an adult woman with a college degree and one published book to her credit could make the decision to call someone by his first name.

But she would call him Alexander—not Alex. And she would *command* her unruly heart to remember that in eight days they would go their separate ways.

26

Nettlesby
Lincolnshire, England
November

SHIVER SAUNTERED INTO THE DIM, smoke-filled pub. Except for the unlikely moniker of The Lamb, this place was indistinguishable from countless other country pubs he had visited in the past weeks. A couple of blokes were playing darts, egged on by several old geezers nursing their tankards. One gent wearing a three-piecer sat at a table by the fire, eating. At the opposite side, beneath a couple of stuffed animal heads, a table of rough-looking characters were playing dominoes.

Shiver made his way up to the bar and ordered a pint. He had quickly learned that no order meant no answers. "I'm lookin' for a man," he told the barkeep. "Fancy swell, name of Gambrielli. I was told he used to come here a lot." He chugged back several swallows of the foul-tasting ale. "Good beer."

The barkeep, a red-faced man with a walrus moustache, wiped a meaty hand across his brow. He began swabbing the high countertop, lips pursed in thought. "Chap live 'ere abouts, y'say?"

Shiver shrugged. "I was told he had a new wife, married her sometime last fall. Name's Priscilla? They were living somewhere near or in this village." He pulled another long swallow. "Nettlesby. That's what I was told."

The barkeep eyed him with a closed expression. *Limeys,* Shiver grumped in disgust. It was like sweating a clam to worm information out of them. He snagged a nearby barstool and settled on the worn, smooth seat. "I've come all the way from America," he tried, thinking what pleasure it would be to plunge his sticker in this jowled porker's ribs.

"Well . . ." The barkeep kept mopping the counter with long, irritating sweeps. Finally his head swiveled and he yelled to someone in the back, "Alf! Got some Yankee bloke looking for a friend."

A tall, pimply-faced young man appeared, his pale eyes watering and a little vacant. "Whole village be crawling with 'em, seems like," he grumbled.

Shiver stood, then casually spat on the wooden floor. "Tell me where I can find Gambrielli, and there'll be one less."

The dolt named Alf twitched, giggling a high-pitched laugh that earned an elbow to the ribs from the barkeep. "You sound like a blooming idiot, Alf. Do you know this Gamberilly gent or not?" To Shiver he added gruffly, "Alf here makes deliveries in the village. If your chum's about, he'd know."

Alf sobered, blinking his eyes rapidly. He looked too stupid to know day from night. Shiver sat, drank the ale, and waited. "I knew Prissy. That's what we called her, growing up like." Alf swallowed, his prominent Adam's apple bobbing up and down. Shiver thought in growing irritation how easy it would be to pop it out with his knife. "She was always nice to me, but she's gone now. So's Ga— gum—" He ducked his head. "Both gone. There was some talk—"

Beady eyes wary, the publican shoved Alf toward the back. "The gent ain't interested in your stories, Alf." He turned to Shiver. "'Twould appear you're out for a duck, mate. Sorry."

Shiver tossed some coins down. He didn't thank the barkeep or waste any more time. There were too many villages between here and Cambridge, and obviously Gambrielli was going to make Shiver sniff through every last one of them. From the sound of it, the clever coxcomb was up to his old tricks. In spite of Avery's orders to eliminate the man, Shiver was perversely pleased.

On his way out the door he passed by a poster advertising Cadbury's chocolates. A dimpled, smiling young girl posed, fat white hands holding out a tin of cocoa. Shiver whipped out his blade and with lightning-quick precision slashed the poster girl's smiling throat.

The stunned silence that followed him out provided Joe Leoni his only relief in the past crummy fortnight. *When I finally find you, Gambrielli, you're gonna beg before I'm through. . . .*

27

S.S. Etruria

A VIOLENT ATLANTIC STORM confined passengers to their cabins the third day out. Alex, queasy and claustrophobic, spent a lot of the time wondering if this was his punishment for defying the Agency. He occupied miserable hours discussing the matter with the Lord.

"Maybe I should go topside and be swept overboard," he groused to the shifting ceiling at one point. "I'm beginning to wonder if Jonah was relieved to end up in the belly of a fish." On the other hand, Jonah had been defying the will of God—not the will of Pinkerton's National Detective Agency. "Does this mean I should have left Eve on her own, then? You know better than I what she will find—that's why I had to come. Isn't it?" *Ach, Alex. Is it?*

The question was unanswerable, as were the feelings with which Alex wrestled during those interminable hours confined in the dark belly of the *S.S. Etruria*.

"I wonder how Mr. MacKay is faring." Eve grabbed the wardrobe to keep from losing her balance as the liner dipped into another swell.

Trude, repairing the lace ruching on one of Eve's shirtwaists, was unperturbed by the rolling ship, the raging storm, or the fate of other passengers. Eve had decided Trude was a Jules Verne character come to life—an alien machine in human form, right here in the cabin of the *S.S. Etruria.*

Unaware of Eve's uncharitable analysis, Trude didn't even lift her head. "His welfare is not your concern, miss." She sewed two stitches, then finally glanced across at Eve. "You've spent a good deal of time with him, until this storm. I'm not sure Mr. and Mrs. Sheridan would approve."

"They would probably announce the news in the *Dispatch,* with Roman candles and Mr. Sousa's brass band. Mr. MacKay is the first man, other than Pastor Sidney, with whom I've developed a rapport." *Alexander,* she thought to herself. *I can call him Alexander.* She retrieved her ivory comb and brush, then lurched back toward the bunk. "It's not as though I'm a gushing, blushing ingenue."

Trude sniffed. After a few moments of comfortable silence, she snipped the thread with a minuscule pair of manicure scissors, then lay the waist aside. "The pastor showed me your book. He's very proud of you."

Hot color, followed by cold prickles of insecurity, stung Eve's skin. She felt stripped, exposed. "I'm glad," she mumbled.

"You love birds." Trude picked up a pair of lisle stockings with a hole in the heel. "Though painting, or feather pictures, would be more appropriate than cavorting about Richmond on that bicycle of yours."

"Trude, how would you feel if your hands were chained to your side, and you couldn't mend, or clean, or restore order to a room?"

The chaperone's fingers stilled, and for a brief second Eve detected the first glimpse of genuine emotion in Trude she had ever seen. "I wouldn't care for it," was all she would say, though the pale blue eyes were troubled.

Eve collapsed in her bunk, braced her feet on the floor, and began removing pins from her hair. "If I had to sit around the house all day, painting pretty pictures and sticking feathers on paper—feathers from birds no longer alive and soaring about the sky—my soul would shrivel up, and something inside me would die." She dropped all the hairpins on the bed and began combing out her hair. It was thick, long, and unruly, and brushing it out made her arms ache.

After a while, Trude cleared her throat. "My mother used to talk about you and your sister a lot as the two of you grew up. Whenever your mother brought you along to visit the reverend, you'd do naught but pester him with theological questions, while Miss Rebecca would show off her new dress. I can see why you're wanting to see her, miss."

Rebecca.

The ship rolled again, plunging down, then up as it battled the high seas. For the first time since the storm hit, nausea lay like a stone in Eve's stomach, and she closed her eyes. *Becca. Becca.*

"Miss? Are you all right?"

She opened her eyes and began plaiting her hair. "I'm fine. Just a trifle queasy. I wish this storm would hurry up and blow itself out." *Please, God, don't let anything happen to my sister. I'll do anything, be anything . . . just let Becca be all right.*

"You look pale. Did the storm make you ill, too?" Alexander came to stand at the railing beside her.

Eve shook her head. For over an hour she had been engrossed in the splendid panorama of a cardinal red sun staining the sky in brilliant sunset hues. The contrast from the preceding days held her enthralled, oblivious to the frigid wind and invasive dampness. "I've missed this, even without birds. It's so open, so vast . . . I can breathe out here." She shrugged, feeling self-conscious.

"You hate being cooped up, too, don't you?" Alexander

lifted his face to the wind. Like Eve, he was obviously enjoying the fresh air and freedom after two days of riding out a storm.

She examined the rugged profile, surprised by how pale Alexander was beneath the shadow of his afternoon beard and the bushy moustache. "Unless I'm working, yes," she finally said. "When I'm confined, I'm afraid I tend to become irritable. It makes my skin . . . itch, almost as if I need to shed free of it, like a butterfly from the cocoon."

"What? No avian analogies? These two days *must* have addled your brain more than mine." Eve gave a fleeting smile. After a moment Alexander propped his elbows on the railing beside hers. "What is it?" he asked quietly.

Well, she had known this moment would arrive, and in fact had been preparing for it the last hour. "I'm worried about Rebecca," she admitted, simply and without elaboration.

"Why?"

Eve turned her head, irritably shoving her hat brim back so she could see. Her hand froze, suspended in the air. Alexander had gone still, an absolute stillness fraught with repudiation.

Eve's hand dropped. His reaction told her everything she had needed to know. "It's nothing. Nothing. I'm just being overly maudlin. I haven't seen Rebecca in so long and there wasn't time to write her before I leaped aboard the ship. My father is probably right; I'll be intruding and—"

"You're babbling, Eve." His hand closed warmly over her shoulder. "We've become good friends, you and I— there's no need for you to be shy, nor is there any use to prevaricate." The hand squeezed. "You're no good at it. Tell me what's troubling you."

If he had sounded patronizing or preoccupied she could have stood her ground. Her face colored, but she ignored the warm hand and compelling voice as best she could. "I'm worried that something is wrong. Rebecca's last few letters haven't sounded like her. That's why—" Abruptly she moved away. "It's just that I didn't want my personal misgivings about Giles to exaggerate my interpretation of what she wrote."

"Eve . . ." He hesitated, obviously uncomfortable. "Perhaps I should—"

There it was again, the dragging reluctance. Stiff and ashamed, Eve retreated. "You're right. I shouldn't have said anything. Like you said, I'm no longer your responsibility, and you've matters of your own to attend to."

"That's nae the problem at all," Alexander snapped, the burr licking through the words in a growl. He shoved away from the railing, his ulster flaring wide in the wind.

"It's that I've nae been entirely straightforward about—"

"Excuse me, sir. Are you Alexander MacKay?" a uniformed steward inquired. In his white-gloved hand he held a cablegram.

Alexander turned, a quick, lithe movement that raised the steward's eyebrows and caused him to step hurriedly back. Alexander didn't even notice. He rummaged for a tip, then stood staring at the paper as if it were a coiled rattlesnake.

"Aren't you going to open it?" Eve asked. Concerned, she tried to inject a note of levity. "Maybe it's from Mr. Hostler, and he's finally banishing you to Santa Fe. On the other hand, perhaps he's forgiven your incorrigible behavior."

"Not in this century, girl." He continued staring at the cablegram, deep blue eyes frowning, shadowed.

Eve waited. She wanted to pry—and yet she longed to vanish discreetly. He was really concerned, she saw, her own apprehension rising.

With a quick, impatient movement he ripped the paper opened and scanned the contents. The strong muscles in his throat tightened. Anger, tightly controlled, settled over him like a storm cloud.

"Alexander?"

"It's from John, right enough. Fortunately, I haven't been fired." His head dropped, and in mounting fear Eve heard him utter a brief, heartfelt prayer: "God Almighty, I need Your help in a mighty way." Then he turned to Eve, his mouth twisted. "No . . . I haven't been fired, and in fact he's glad I'm such a pigheaded Scot." He was looking at her, though she had the uneasy sensation that he wasn't really seeing her. "That's one of his favorite appellations for me, don't you know."

"Alexander, give me the cablegram." She didn't wait but lifted it from his unresisting fingers. The message was short. *Sorry to admit you were right after all. Joe Leoni left for England at least two weeks ago. Contact Inspector Rudge, Scotland Yard, immediately upon arrival.*

28

Upper Dereford
Norfolk, England

HARRIET CRABTREE HURRIED down the lane, wanting to reach the house before any prying eyes were up and about. It was a little past seven, a cold, dreary morning with the sun only now rising above the thatched roofs and brick chimneys of the still-quiet village. Harriet clutched her shawl tightly, her chilblained fingertips white in their fingerless gloves.

He had told her that, after she tidied the place so it looked as though they had left, permanent-like, she could keep whatever trinkets she wished.

"Just make sure you don't keep anything that will make people suspicious," he warned, the handsome face pale, gaunt as a corpse. *Poor man*, Harriet thought as she unlatched the iron gate and scuttled down the path. *Grievin' right proper, he was, over the missus.*

She had been a pretty little thing, though a trifle self-ish, to Harriet's way of thinking. A little too possessive of her husband, always wanting his exclusive attention. Harriet unlocked the door, using the key he had given her. Inside, she hung her shawl on the hallstand, pausing to study her reflection in its oval mirror.

Not too many years ago she had been the village

beauty, chased and pestered by all the lads. Curse it, she never had been able to resist a smooth tongue, and when a curly-headed lad selling horse harnesses filled her head with the enticing vision of his snug cottage on a grand estate in Lincolnshire, Harriet hadn't been able to resist.

They had only been married a year when the drinking started, then the wenching. Harriet stared in the mirror. Little was left of the comely black-haired girl of seventeen. Now the reflection that stared back at her revealed a slump-shouldered woman with thickened waist. The once peachy complexion now had the consistency of day-old Yorkshire pudding.

"Men!" She spat the word as an epithet, remembering how Mistress Dawson's face gradually changed from bright and expectant to secretive and bitter. "They're scoundrels, the lot o' them. . . ."

But didn't that Giles Dawson have an irresistible smile, and those dimples! Harriet smiled a secretive smile at her reflection. When he looked down at her that special way, talking in that rich chocolate voice, why, there weren't nothing she wouldn't do for him. And really, she'd only let him kiss her once . . . well, all right. Twice, it was.

But she had to give him credit—he hadn't philandered near as bad as some. She turned away from the mirror with a sigh and set to work. It was a shame, it was, to be sure. Such a nice-looking man, and for all his flirting ways he had been in love with his wife.

The way he had looked that night, Harriet would never forget it—nor the sight of poor Mrs. Dawson's body, sprawled there in a puddle of her blood. To take your own life like that, just because your husband has to travel a bit. Harriet clucked, remembering Mr. Dawson's hoarse, almost incoherent voice as he begged Harriet's help in keeping the matter quiet.

"I loved her. I don't want her memory shamed." He had choked up a bit then, and Harriet had offered her bosom for comfort, to let the poor dear sob all his grief out.

As she cleaned the four rooms of Bramble Cottage, her eye greedily examined all the potential treasures. Bless a bodkin, but she had never understood why two such well-heeled Americans wanted to hide out here in the country!

Harriet spent a long time in the bedroom, eagerly pawing through Mrs. Dawson's jewelry. It wouldn't be like she was stealing or nothing, and she would be careful not to help herself to too much.

By noon the cottage gleamed with spit and polish. Harriet folded the missus' clothes and packed everything in the steamer trunk Mrs. Dawson had brought from America. It was a shame she had been such a slender girl; Harriet would have particularly enjoyed that fancy blue gown with all the lace and ribbons. But wearing that would create wagging tongues for sure.

In the end, she only took a few trifling things, items she could easily explain away if ever she were asked. As she tied on her shawl and pinned her old felt hat in place, her eyes returned to the rug in the parlor. It was a shame about the stains. Whoever rented the house next would have to replace that rug for sure.

29

S.S. Etruria

ALEX HAD ARRANGED TO MEET Eve in the ship's chapel, empty at this time of the day. The room offered privacy, shelter from the frigid North Atlantic winds— and the promise of a sustaining Presence. Alex thought of the Eve he had left earlier: pale, composed, her brown eyes scared but defiant.

"England's a big country, and he must have fled here trying to escape from *you*," she had insisted. "It's ironic, in a way, but he can't have any idea of *my* plans, so I shall be quite safe on my own." She slanted him a shrewd sideways look. "I do hope chasing down Mr. Leoni won't prevent you from seeing to the other matters that require your attention."

Tired, bedeviled, Alex hadn't minced words. "You know as well as I that the only reason I'm here is because you are, Eve."

In another place, another time, those words would have implied something entirely different. Alex withdrew the chamois pouch and began fitting the puzzle pieces together. *That particular implication is lost on her, isn't it? She simply has no awareness of herself as a woman, whereas I . . .* His hands closed into fists, the small

155

wooden pieces digging into his palms. He could not afford to consider Eve Sheridan as anything but the endangered daughter of the Agency's newest client.

"I gave him—them, I thought—twenty thousand dollars when they married," William Sheridan had confided to Alex. "*Gave* it—it was their wedding gift! And it was so obvious Giles loved her. There was simply no reason to suspect that he and Avery Paxton . . ." The tic next to his eye jumped. "I'll arrange matters with Hostler, pay your expenses if you—you, personally—escort Eve to England. . . ." His voice had exploded in a tortured cry. "God . . . dear God, why—*both* my daughters! Alex, please! Help me." And the cultured, proud man had broken down, covering his face with a shaking hand.

"Your scowl is fierce enough to melt the smokestacks on this ship." Eve removed her cloak before Alex could help her, draping it over the wooden pew. She sat down in the pew in front of him, twisting to face Alex, her chin propped on folded hands on the back of the pew. "I've been thinking."

"Aye. I was afraid of that." His gaze wandered over her, admiring the gleaming red hair and slender neck, an enchanting contrast to the reserved elegance of her neat gray dress.

"You needn't trot out your famous Scottish charm on me—that's one of the things I've been thinking about." She cleared her throat. "I'm not going to let you manipulate me any longer, Alexander. I know it will be difficult—with you, it seems, I'm easy enough to manipulate. I hope that's only because you're a master of the art."

"You make me sound like some kind of sinister mesmerist." Ach, but the girl knew how to goad a man with that earnest, forthright manner of hers! How the devil was he supposed to respond? Rankled, even hurt, Alex struggled to curb his temper.

Eve sat up straight, looking contrite, the gloved hands fluttering in the air. "I didn't mean for you to interpret it *that* way. You have an extraordinary gift, Alexander. You must be aware of it, because everyone talks about it. I wish *I* could . . . could intuitively understand people like you do. Sergeant Harris told me he's seen you talk a raving madman with a loaded pistol into a—"

"I think you can shake down Sergeant Harris's tales and find they're mostly chaff, not wheat."

"Into a docile child," she finished firmly. "But not like a mesmerist, or some evil sorcerer." She twisted her face as if searching for a word. " 'Manipulate' was a poor choice of terms. Perhaps . . . 'persuade' would be more accurate. That's what I should have said. You're very persuasive, Alexander, and I'm no more immune than the next person." The corners of her mouth twitched. "Felon or innocent, male or female."

Alex leaned over until their noses almost touched. "You can be a saucy little baggage, don't you know. Can you feel my 'persuasive powers' now, then?—urging you to . . ." He sat back, folding his arms across his chest. "To yield to my lacerated ego, drop this ridiculous discussion of my 'powers,' and address the matter at hand?"

After a moment of silence, she ducked her head. "I don't want to address it," she whispered. "I'm afraid of the answers."

"Eve—"

"It's Giles, isn't it? Your other 'affairs to attend to' concern Giles. I've been piecing it together ever since this morning, and that's what it leads to. Avery Paxton introduced Giles to us, and you think if you talk to Giles, you'll . . . *persuade* him to provide enough evidence to arrest Avery."

God, what do I do here? What, then?

Eve was too intent on voicing her feared conclusions to notice Alex's strained indecisiveness. "And if you're willing to spend the time and risk the censure of Mr. Hostler, just to track down Giles for whatever information he might reveal—then the only logical conclusion I could draw is that Giles is not the person *he* claimed to be, either. That's it, isn't it?"

Alex closed his eyes briefly. Then, letting his breath out on a long sigh, he faced her directly. "You've the essence of it, yes."

Her fist lifted to her mouth. "Dear Lord." She swallowed convulsively and her eyes shone with pending tears. Once again she brought herself under control, focusing on the chapel's altar. Her gaze was agonized, but no tears fell.

You're a game, plucky . . . bonny lass.

"All right." Her chin lifted. "Please—tell me what you know. I promise not to confound you with tears . . . or denials."

She would likely do both, Alex knew. He also knew, after the past several weeks, that this was an individual like himself, who would accept nothing less than the truth. And unlike her father, Eve would refuse to allow it to defeat her. "I can't tell you very much yet," he replied, stilling her protest with a look. "The evidence is flimsy, speculative, and mostly based on what I can only call 'instinct.' All good detectives rely on instinct—Allan Pinkerton, founder of the Agency, was matchless. What I feel comfortable sharing with you right now is that I don't think his name is really 'Giles Dawson.' "

Eve's face paled, but her jaw clenched with determination. "And just what *do* you think his name is?"

Alex closed his eyes and prayed for wisdom. He had no choice but to tell her the truth, even though he hated the very idea of causing her more pain. He drew a deep breath. "We *think,*" he said with as much calmness as he could muster, "that his real name is Dante Gambrielli. We're not certain, but your sister's husband may be a character we have been chasing for a long time."

Eve's eyes bored into his. "And what is this . . . this Dante Gambrielli . . . accused of?"

Alex shook his head.

"Tell me!"

"He . . . marries wealthy women, takes their money, and then—"

Eve shuddered, bowing her head. "I . . . see." Throat muscles working, she had to try twice before continuing. "That means . . . my sister is in grave danger, isn't she?"

Alex reached out and took her clenched hand. "Yes."

For a few moments they sat in silence.

Finally Eve spoke, her voice halting, thick with suppressed emotion. "I've known . . . I don't know why . . . maybe her letters. . . ." She stopped, fighting for control. Alex shifted closer, refusing to release her hand even though she tried to pull free. "I think—I think there is a chance she's—"

Alex blinked back the dampness in his own eyes. "I'll be going with you, lass," he promised, his own voice husky. "Whatever we find—I'll be there with you."

She shook her head, slowly at first, then with increasing violence. "No. No. You have to go to London. To Scotland Yard. Not Norfolk . . . that's where he took Becca. She said it was the most beautiful stone cottage, with climbing roses and ivy, and—and how much I would love the English birds."

In a flurry of motion she yanked her hand free and surged to her feet. "I'm sorry, Alexander. I know you hate tears, but I can't—" She snatched up her cloak, her gaze ricocheting wildly. "I prayed. I begged God . . . why is He punishing my sister when it's *me*?" In a swirl of petticoats and rustling skirts, she flew from the room.

More slowly Alex rose, his gaze on Eve's departing form. He would be a long time forgetting that look of soul-scorching agony and the utter despair of her words.

If ever he could.

30

Cambridge, England

BEATRICE LINWOOD TURNED FROM side to side, admiring her new day gown. The blue poult-de-soie silk was a flattering color, setting off the chestnut highlights in her hair. Its fashionably wide puffed sleeves and gored skirt were sure to bring out those marvelous dimples in Mr. Granville's cheeks.

"Meg, fetch my new lace fan. It will perfectly complement the lace in the gown."

"Yes, mum." The girl's head bobbed. Beneath her starched white mobcap, wiry curls and merry green eyes danced in unspoken conspiracy. "The gentleman won't be able to take his eyes off you, miss."

Beatrice giggled. "I hope not." She picked up a spray of silk pansies and twirled it around in her fingers. "I'll tell you a secret, Meg. I think this afternoon he's going to ask permission to court me!"

The girl's eyes rounded. "Ooh, mum. He's ever so dashing. The mistress favors him as well. I heard her telling Mrs. Ambrose over tea yesterday that Mr. Granville's a gentleman with brains as well as breeding."

"Even if he *is* American," Beatrice added, her voice mimicking the snootish Mrs. Ambrose perfectly. "Well, I'd rather marry an American like Mr. Granville than some of the callow boys and crotchety old men approaching dotage that Father and Aunt Imogene keep pressing upon me."

"Beatrice, dear. Mr. Granville is here," Aunt Imogene announced, her rather plain face animated, a blush staining the sallow cheeks. "He looks as if a matter of grave concern is preying on his mind." She eyed her niece with satisfaction. "Hopefully you'll soon put his mind to rest."

"That," Beatrice returned archly as she sailed from the bedroom and descended the stairs, "will depend."

She paused between the fringed portieres framing the doorway to the drawing room. The salmon pink drapes with the gold fringe ought to provide a becoming frame for her gown. "Good afternoon, Mr. Granville."

He turned from his examination of a volume of poetry, and an expression she had never seen flashed through his handsome countenance. "Miss Linwood. You look . . ." He stopped, and incredibly, turned his back to Beatrice.

Nonplussed, she glanced down to make sure her corset cover or something equally indelicate wasn't showing. "Mr. Granville?"

His back was as stiff as the spine on a new-bound book. When he did turn around again, Beatrice gasped. The man looked positively haggard, the skin stretched tight across his face, its complexion colorless. "Mr. Granville, what's the matter?" She hurried to his side, coyness and dreams of courtship set aside. "You look dreadful."

He removed a silk handkerchief from his pocket and wiped his face, trying to smile. His eyes were black, tormented. "I most humbly beg your pardon, Miss Linwood." His gaze flickered over her beautiful new gown, then slid away as if he couldn't bear the sight. "You . . . that gown . . ." He took a deep breath.

Mesmerized, Beatrice watched the vein at his temple throb. Then he seemed to bring himself under control, lifting her hand to his lips and brushing it with a smooth courtliness that always weakened Beatrice's knees. "You

161

look ravishing, if I may be so bold as to comment on your appearance."

"Thank you." Beatrice was in no mood for parlor games. "Mr. Granville, if you are ill—"

"I'm perfectly all right," he assured her. "And I most humbly apologize. I hadn't wanted to distress you, especially today."

Well, that at least was a hopeful sign. "You could only distress me by pretending cordiality when something is obviously weighing upon your mind." Beatrice sat down on the divan and patted the striped brocade. "Sit here, beside me, and tell me what is troubling you. I'm not just a featherheaded nit, Mr. Granville."

There it was again, the flicker of an almost . . . sinister . . . look. Abruptly a tiny warning thrill shot down Beatrice's backbone. "No," he agreed, and smiled the devastatingly attractive smile. "No, you're most certainly not."

He sat down. Beatrice subtly shifted closer, enjoying the fresh fragrance wafting from his starched shirt and the impeccably cut morning coat. Mr. Granville's smile deepened, and Beatrice decided the earlier expression had merely been the glare from the table lamp. "My sister has died," he said. "Quite suddenly." He glanced at Beatrice. "She had a gown very like the one you're wearing, which is why . . ." He lifted a patrician hand in a brief apology.

"Oh." Crestfallen, Beatrice fiddled with her fan, and wondered what Aunt Imogene would have to say about this dilemma. A young lady of good breeding certainly could not offer to remove her gown to avoid offending a gentleman caller.

"Forgive me. You must think me the most callous of boors. This is a new gown, isn't it? For me?"

Beatrice searched his face, wondering at the ease with which he changed his emotions. She would have pursued the matter if she hadn't heard Aunt Imogene descending the stairs, signaling that their few moments alone were over. "Now, Mr. Granville, no young lady with any sense would ever admit that her dress was selected merely for the gratification of a gentleman's pleasure."

Mr. Granville's gaze narrowed. The creases on either side of his face deepened, and he laughed. "Miss Linwood, I believe you have just issued me a challenge. And I'll tell you right now that I never refuse a challenge. Never."

31

Liverpool, England

TRUDE, HER FACE STIFF IN ITS disapproval,
agreed to proceed to Germany as planned, leaving Eve behind in England to find Rebecca on her own. Alexander,
dour and ubiquitous, watched without interfering as Eve
won the battle of wills.

"I'll be fine." Eve repeated the meaningless phrase as
if she were a talking parrot. "Mr. MacKay will escort me
to London as arranged. From there I won't have a bit of
trouble making connections to Norfolk. It's no different
from my riding the train alone in America."

In the end, Trude had to give in. "As you wish, miss.
But I must say I find your behavior improper."

She finally boarded the train, and Eve's last view of her
erstwhile chaperone was the sight of Trude industriously
wiping the dirty window clean as the train chugged out
of the Liverpool station.

While Alexander saw to their luggage, Eve purchased
tickets to London, then sat on the end of a crowded bench
and watched Alexander. His taciturn manner and irrita-
bility might be understandable—Joe Leoni on the loose
would unnerve even the stoutest of souls. Still, Eve had

164

grown accustomed to his big-brotherly attitude, and she missed it.

A pigeon strutted up to the bench, pecking at the ground. With a grateful sigh, Eve crumbled the remainder of a doughnut and fed it to the bird. For a few moments at least, she could divert her thoughts from a future devoid of Alexander's presence altogether.

The train's compartment was crowded, the ride from Liverpool to London slow, interrupted by stops in quaint villages Eve was too exhausted to appreciate. They arrived at Pancras Station at half past four in the afternoon, dirty and bedraggled.

At the hotel, Eve didn't know whether regret or relief prevailed over Alexander's immediate departure for New Scotland Yard. After they choked down a high tea in the hotel restaurant, Alexander reluctantly took his leave.

"Promise me," he entreated one last time, "to stay here until I can return. Eve . . . promise me."

"I'll be here until tomorrow morning. Alexander—"

"I know. Forget I asked." His hands clenched. "Take care of yourself. Like it or not, you're my responsibility."

Eve flushed. "You may have made some kind of arrangements with my father, but I thought you had learned that I've a mind of my own, Alexander."

"And don't I know that," he muttered.

She bridled at his comment but refused to back down. Not when it concerned Rebecca—and not when Rebecca's peril was Eve's fault. "I'll wait until morning. Beyond that . . ." She let the implied conclusion fall into a thickening silence.

"Have it your way, then." Alexander leveled one last frustrated look toward her, his blue eyes sizzling. Eve felt a little sick; she hadn't wanted him to look at her *that* way ever again. His mouth twitched, then he swept out the door.

Oppressed and exhausted, Eve climbed the stairs to her room. But instead of collapsing, she merely removed her outerwear and shoes, then sat down next to the window with her stockinged feet propped on the radiator. A pretty table lamp with crystal prisms sat on a piecrust table beside her. Eve turned up the lamp, then toyed with the prisms, admiring the colored facets in the lamp's yellow glow.

Finally she picked up Becca's last letter. Her mind was tortured by doubt and crippling fear, largely because of her *own* letter written to Mr. Paxton months ago, asking for his advice. She had thought she could help ease her sister's anxieties; instead, she feared she had sown a wind that now was reaping its deadly whirlwind.

I should never have taken it upon myself to write that letter. Cringing inside, her mind recalled the words, the innocent, innocuous . . . *imbecilic* words: *From my sister's correspondence with me, it is obvious you and Mr. Dawson know each other well, and I thought perhaps you might be able to set her mind—as well as mine—at rest. Let me explain. . . .*

What would Alexander MacKay think of her when she marshalled the fortitude to confess what she had done?

What if she were wrong?

What if . . . ?

A bellboy delivered the note early the following morning. It was, as she suspected, from Alexander.

Miss Sheridan:
Circumstances force me to accompany Inspector Rudge today, though I should be back this time tomorrow. Since this regrettable development will tax your character beyond restraint . . . please, at least, send me your sister's address, care of Inspector Thomas Rudge, New Scotland Yard, C.I.D. That way, I'll be able to catch up with you faster. Be careful, though. "Auld sparrows (as they say) are ill to tame."

> *Your humble servant,*
> *Alexander MacKay.*

Somehow she had known this would happen. Even so, her conscience smarted from the unsubtle censure. Alexander's disapproval, however, would not override Eve's determination: she had made a gross error of judgment, and it was fitting that she face the consequences alone.

She resolutely finished dressing, her mind sifting through tasks, organizing everything that needed to be done. As she pinned on her brooch, her fingers fumbled, and the pin pierced her thumb. A tiny drop of blood welled up.

Eve stared at the innocuous smear, her heart aching.

If she begged with tears like drops of blood, could she finally pierce the impenetrable heart of the Almighty so that He would heed her agonized pleas?

Eve pressed her handkerchief over her thumb to stop the bleeding. Then she sat down at a small table and spent the next few minutes composing several notes, her handwriting rapid but neat.

Rebecca used to tease her unmercifully about her penmanship, which had won awards throughout school. Becca also used to try to wheedle Eve into completing Rebecca's lessons. "You could disguise the writing a little—just enough so that it wouldn't look too much like yours. Please, Evie. You know how I *hate* making my letters."

Oh, Becca. . . .

Eve ruthlessly suppressed the painful memories. At ten o'clock, avoiding the recently opened underground trains that traversed the city, Eve hired one of the shiny black English hansoms to convey her across town. At two minutes past noon, the train pulled out of the station. Eve settled back against the worn cloth seat, her face and her heart resolutely set toward Norfolk. *And please, God, Rebecca.*

"Mr. Farley, this is Operative Alexander MacKay, from Pinkerton's National Detective Agency, America." Inspector Rudge introduced the comptroller of the small private London bank.

The comptroller was a pale, weedy man whose face was deeply pitted from smallpox. He wore a monocle, an affectation that made Alex's skin crawl with irritation. "This is highly irregular," Mr. Farley announced in a nasal Oxford accent—probably also affected, Alex decided. "I must reiterate again to both of you that all of the business transacted at this bank is of unblemished character."

"No one has implied otherwise," Inspector Rudge returned. A tall, cadaverous man who fairly burst with nervous energy and restless intelligence, Rudge strode back and forth across the floor. While he talked, he cracked his knuckles without pause. "Our desire here, Mr. Farley, is to ensure that the reputation of this establishment *remains* unblemished."

The comptroller's chest swelled. Resignation flitted across his brow. "Very well. Since Mr. Tewkesbury has spoken with me, I will assist you in any way I can."

Alex clasped his hands behind his back. "As Inspector Rudge explained, Pinkerton's—in cooperation with Scotland Yard—is investigating the activities of an individual whose real name is Dante Gambrielli. He has, unfortunately, established several aliases."

"Based upon certain pieces of evidence gathered by Pinkerton's Detective Agency, we believe Gambrielli might have opened an account with your bank using the name of Giles Dawson," Rudge inserted. In the last twenty-four hours, he had not allowed Alex to complete but a handful of sentences. "Date should be this past June, a bank-to-bank draft from The State Bank of Virginia, in Richmond."

"Those records will have to be brought from the vault. That will take several hours, as I couldn't possibly—"

Alex stepped closer. "I think you can," he enunciated,

very softly. "Why don't you see to it, and the inspector and I will wait here."

Above the stiff, upright collar and striped cravat, the florid face deepened to an ugly plum color, and the superior expression underwent a rapid transformation. The monocle dropped unnoticed from Farley's rapidly blinking eye. "Ah . . . perhaps I could . . . yes. I'm sure I can arrange something. If you'll just excuse me. . . ." He scurried from the room.

"Any chance you'll leave the Colonies and come work for us?" Rudge chuckled deep in his throat, nodding his head up and down. "You have a way about you, Mr. MacKay. Puts the fear of God in a man."

Alex sat down in a delicate-looking chair with legs as curved and spindly as a newborn foal's. "The fear of the Lord is the beginning of wisdom, so Proverbs tells us, Inspector. I wouldn't be wanting to do more than help Mr. Farley gain a little more. Assisting Scotland Yard's Criminal Investigation Department in its pursuit of justice strikes me as a prudent manner in which to acquire a bit of wisdom."

The inspector laughed out loud.

They waited fifteen minutes in a tense but compatible silence. Rudge wore a path in the carpet and cracked his knuckles, while Alex sat unmoving and gnashed his teeth over Eve Sheridan.

The woman was going to land herself in a boiling kettle of trouble and would likely end up with her throat cut—or worse. And because Alex had felt honor-bound to search out Inspector Rudge—partly as compensation for defying John over his initial decision to come to England—Alex was helpless to protect Eve. He knew as surely as he knew his name that the headstrong girl wouldn't be waiting for him at the hotel.

Why, Lord? Could You tell me that, now? Why arrange matters for me to escort her over here, knowing she needs protecting—then fasten me to a rack that is ripping me—

"Ah . . . here we are, gentlemen." Farley bustled back

into the room, carrying a large ledger, his manner officious. "I trust you'll duly note our cooperation with your . . . ah . . . superiors."

"Duly noted." Inspector Rudge and Alex jostled each other in their eagerness to peruse the ledger. Farley refused to be hurried; he turned each page with pursed lips, the monocle firmly back in place.

"Ah . . . yes. I believe this would be the entry . . . the sixth of July, 1893. A banker's check from The State Bank of Virginia. Authorized both by a director and the cashier. The sum of twenty thousand dollars, which at current exchange rates of the day, minus transfer fees, amounted to . . ." He read the figure, then lifted his head, peering at the two men. "Is that satisfactory, then?"

"And subsequent transactions?" Alex prompted. He casually shifted positions.

Farley hastily scanned the rest of the ledger. "Dear. Dear me. How . . . odd."

Both men leaned forward.

"Highly irregular, in fact." The comptroller splayed pasty white hands on top of the pages he had been reading. "But not—let me hasten to add—against the law of the land." He cleared his throat and adjusted the monocle. "Ah . . . just this past month, Mr. Dawson transferred his account to another bank and closed his account here. Most unusual. We are one of the most prestigious banks in London outside of the Bank of England. I don't understand." He shook his head. "As I recall, I was on holiday at the time, so—"

"To what bank was the account transferred?" Rudge interrupted impatiently.

"I'm afraid that would not be—" He stopped, his affronted gaze taking in the rapidly diminishing tolerance of the two men hovering over his desk. Another bout of throat-clearing ensued. "Ah . . . let me see . . . yes. Well, perhaps since your visit *is* an official one, and we *do* pride ourselves in our cooperation with the Yard . . . yes. Ahem." He cleared his throat a final time, then mumbled

170

the bank's name. "In Peterborough, Cambridgeshire." He slammed the book shut.

"Thank you. You've been most helpful." With a terse nod Inspector Rudge stalked out. Alex followed more slowly, trying to recall the exact location of Peterborough.

By the time they stepped out into the deafening noise of the London traffic, he knew.

32

New York

HORACE TOPPER RETURNED to New York in fear and trembling. His only hope for salvation was contained in the false bottom of his Gladstone bag, and he presented the contents to Mr. Paxton on a snowy evening, two days after his return from Richmond.

Immaculate in formal evening wear, Avery was on his way to a party at the Waldorf-Astoria. He inspected Topper from head to toe. "Welcome home, Tops. But I'd appreciate it if you'd not drip on my Persian rug."

"I . . . I beg your pardon, Mr. Paxton." Topper shifted uncomfortably, then scuttled after Avery to a massive marble fireplace that dominated the wall of the room. "I've brought what you requested." He held out a file folder wrapped in string.

"I never doubted you for a moment, Tops." Avery poured a drink from a Waterford crystal decanter. He picked up the matching goblet, glanced across at the acutely uncomfortable Horace, and smiled. "I'm not even overly angry by your failure to locate Shiver. He did proceed to England, as he was ordered, and I'm expecting a cable any day now."

Topper eyed the decanter longingly. "That's . . . a relief,

172

Mr. Paxton. Has he—" He clamped his mouth shut when Paxton's expression chilled. "I . . . I beg your pardon, sir," he stammered. "I forgot."

"Don't forget again." Paxton swallowed the brandy and set the delicate goblet down nearly hard enough to snap the stem. "All that matters to me concerning *certain* activities—which *shall* remain unremarked upon—is that they are accomplished." He picked up the folder and unwrapped the string. "This, I trust, will please me very much?" The fierce gaze swept over Topper, causing him to perspire heavily.

In this, at least, Horace could project confidence. "I was able to requisition five different selections, Mr. Paxton. The bookkeeper had gone to lunch, and the janitor who let me in thought it was because I'd forgotten my umbrella. Nobody in the office ever knew I was there." He finished almost confidently, "I can have identical copies to you before Christmas."

"Excellent. Excellent." His smile glowed. After examining the contents, he stuffed them back in the folder and poured another drink. After a brief pause, he also poured one for Topper. "You've done well, Tops. Very well, in fact. I forgive you for your bungling efforts to locate Shiver." He handed Horace the drink, gesturing to the folder. "I predict that, thanks to your exceptional talent and my incomparable—shall we call it *business acumen?*—this promises to be a windfall year."

Topper relaxed and took a careful, noiseless swallow of brandy. Paxton's smile broadened further. "It's good, Tops. It's good. And promises to be even better." He pulled out his watch. "Well, I must be off, my friend. You dry out here, by the fire, and enjoy the brandy. Tomorrow, you work. And then we'll send William Sheridan a Christmas present he'll remember for a very long time."

33

Upper Dereford
Norfolk, England

EVE ARRIVED IN BRANDON DURING the middle of a rainstorm. Covered with soot from the long journey north, soggy and shivering, she secured from the station agent the name of a respectable boardinghouse that catered to lone ladies.

Her room there was small but clean. She choked down an unappetizing meal of boiled beef and vegetables, then arranged for a pot of tea to be sent to the room.

Rivulets of rain splattered the filmy window with its yellowing lace curtain. A steady stream of chilly air seeped beneath the warped sash. Wrapped in a scratchy wool blanket, which smelled of dried lavender, and sipping the blessedly hot tea, Eve spent the remainder of the evening in a lonely vigil.

Frost coated the earth the next morning, and rain puddles gleamed through gossamer sheets of ice in the frigid daylight. Steam escaped in puffs from people's mouths and horses' nostrils, while all the chimneys billowed thick gray smoke. Eve rented a hooded buggy from a nearby livery and paid for three days' use. After receiving friendly but barely intelligible directions, she headed down the muddy road to Upper Dereford, some eight miles to the south.

The sullen gray sky promised snow; Eve wrapped the lap robe tightly about her knees to stave off a relentless wet wind. Small farms surrounded by fields and woods dotted the almost flat countryside. Ditches on either side of the tree-lined road were full of brackish water; Eve hoped nothing spooked the horse.

She hadn't handled the reins much in the last several years, but thankfully the livery horse was a placid beast, and they arrived safely in the village of Upper Dereford at eleven in the morning. She directed the horse down High Street—the British equivalent of Main—until she came to the bakery shop.

A cheerful red and white striped awning flapped in the wind, and trays piled high with mouth-watering sweet breads were displayed in the window. According to Rebecca's letters, she came here at least once a week.

Inside, a plump, red-cheeked lady was stocking the wooden shelves and bins behind her with loaves of fresh bread. She stared at Eve. "Yes, miss?"

"I'm from America." Eve forced a smile. "I've come to visit my sister, but I need directions. She wrote me that she loves to come to your bakery."

The woman's face changed, closing up. "Your sister?" she repeated carefully, dumping the last loaf of bread into a bin and wiping her hands on her apron. "And what might her name be, miss?"

Eve's mouth was dry, her hands damp. "Rebecca," she spoke, almost in a whisper. "Rebecca . . . Mrs. Giles Dawson."

"Blessed Lord, have mercy!" the woman breathed. She glanced around as if to see if Eve were alone.

Eve stepped forward, her heart beating so fast she was slightly dizzy. The ringing in her ears intensified, overlaid by a loud buzzing. She was unable to tear her eyes away from the plump woman whose compassion was rapidly eroding to alarm. "My sister?"

"You might be wanting to sit, miss." She called back over her shoulder. "Bobby! Fetch me a stool, and be quick about it. Mistress Dawson's sister is out here!"

From the dark confines toward the back of the shop, a stocky man with wisping white hair and a clean-shaven face appeared, carrying a high three-legged stool. He plunked the stool next to Eve. "You best sit down, then, miss," he repeated. The gruff voice was kind.

Eve sank down onto the hard stool. She pressed her knees tightly together and clasped her hands. "Tell me," she ordered through numb lips. "I must know."

" 'Twould be better coming from the vicar, Agnes."

"Then fetch him. I'll stay with her." Agnes came round the counter and stood in front of Eve, chin tucked, eyes troubled. "You know it's not good?"

Eve nodded. She was numb everywhere, and each breath rasped in her throat. "Is she—" She couldn't finish the question, couldn't do anything but stare at the neatly arranged loaves of bread. Her lips began moving soundlessly as she counted them, and she was up to eighteen when the baker's wife answered.

"Aye, dearie. A little over a week ago, it was. I'm so dreadfully sorry. . . ."

Eve shook her head. "No." Tremors took hold, and she surged to her feet. "No. It's not true. It can't be true!" Teeth chattering, chest heaving, she swung around to face the other woman. "I *begged* God to keep her safe! I *promised* I'd do anything, be anything. . . ." She gasped, jamming her fists over her eyes. "No. Not Becca. Not—" The pain was unbearable. She stood, shaking, finding no comfort in the arm that circled her shoulders, hugging her briefly.

"I'll make you a cup of tea. Here—sit back down, now."

Rebecca. "No. God—please no." She repeated the words over and over, until they ran together in a burning litany that scorched her heart, her soul. Dead. *Dead.* Rebecca was really dead. Eve sat on the stool, rigid, her eyes and throat burning like the fires of hell and her blood frozen colder than arctic ice floes.

When the vicar arrived with Bobby, moments later, Eve was still sitting, her only sound of life the deep, uncontrolled breaths torn from her lungs.

Shiver hated trains. He always felt trapped, because there was no escape from a moving train. The English trains, with their individual compartments and doors opening directly onto the outside, were preferable, except that guards kept the doors locked.

He slid farther down in the hard seat, tugging his cap over his eyes, trying to doze. The trip to Upper Dereford took two days, and the closer he got the more he dreaded his return. What if some nosy villager recognized him and remembered enough for a description? It was a risk he didn't want to take.

Shiver almost hadn't bothered, but Paxton's letter, which had reached him the previous day, gave him little choice.

> _There is a journal somewhere in a house called Bramble Cottage, which I'm given to understand might contain certain unfortunate references. Since you've failed to carry out your original assignment, you must return to Upper Dereford immediately, before Gambrielli finds this journal himself. His last letter to me indicates that his intentions were to remain in England, which might prove difficult for my future arrangements. Find that journal before you see to Gambrielli. We have no way of knowing either who, or how many, his contacts are there. Cable me upon completion of this task. Do not fail. It would be very simple for me to draft a letter to New Scotland Yard, providing dates, names, and other pertinent information._

Shiver huddled inside his coat. He would do as the boss asked this time, but if Paxton thought Joe Leoni was a pug dog to be brought to heel every time Paxton jerked a leash, it might be about time to teach the master a trick or two.

"Good morning, Mr. Dawson. How may we be of service to you today?"

"I am closing my account here, I'm afraid." Dante paused, allowing the shocked bank manager time to observe his black mourning garb. "My wife passed away, and I plan to return to America shortly." Of course, he had no such plans, but no one at the bank needed to know that.

"I . . . see." The manager, a formal but courteous man, did not wallow in emotion or vulgar curiosity. Lifting his hand to summon the clerk, he informed Dante: "We'll take care of the necessary arrangements, Mr. Dawson. This will require several minutes. You may wait in my office, if you are so inclined, and I will arrange for some refreshments."

Dante nodded, grim but equally courteous. Thirty minutes later he left, a bank draft for slightly over forty thousand pounds securely tucked away in a hidden pocket.

It was a damp, bitingly cold day. Dante lifted his cane, and a hansom approached. "Take me to the train station," he ordered. If British Rail cooperated, he could be back in Cambridge in time to share high tea with Rebec—

His hand closed around the handle of his walking cane. Drawing deep, even breaths, he forced himself to summon the image of Beatrice Linwood, with her pouting lips and dove gray eyes. "Beatrice," he whispered to himself, his gaze following the magnificent lines of the Peterborough Cathedral, visible through the cab's window. *Beatrice.*

If British Rail cooperated, he would be back in Cambridge in time to share high tea with *Beatrice.*

In his youth, Alex had hunted many a deer, riding with reckless abandon through the gentle rolling hills of Virginia, as well as the wilder and rougher lowlands surrounding Edinburgh. Then, he had ridden for excitement and pleasure. Now, flying down a muddy road flanked by towering trees, his heart galloping in rhythm with the horse's hooves, he rode with grim urgency.

Upper Dereford was a small, largely agricultural village, a picturesque collection of thatched cottages, stone and flint houses, with the requisite pub and collection of shops to supply the villagers' needs. From inclination as much as instinct, Alex first stopped at the village church, a medieval stone structure with a square tower, flanked by uneven rows of tumbling gravestones. A square brick house behind the church displayed a plaque that read, "Rectory." Alex tied the horse and ran up the path.

A plain, middle-aged woman in a neat black dress answered the door.

"I'm looking for a young American woman," Alex began.

34

Upper Dereford

"WE SIMPLY COULDN'T KEEP HER from going to the cottage. The rector had another engagement and was unable to accompany her, and she resisted my offer so stringently I felt I had to respect her wishes." Mrs. Mitford dabbed a handkerchief to the corner of her eyes. "It's a terrible business, Mr. MacKay. Terrible, indeed."

"You say Mr. Dawson found his wife?"

The vicar's wife tilted her head, mouth pursed. She was a petite, silver-haired woman whose bright eyes read human nature very clearly, Alex suspected. "Yes, he did, and a more distraught, grief-stricken soul I've never encountered in forty-three years of serving by my husband's side . . . until today, that is."

Distraught and grief-stricken? Giles Dawson? Perhaps . . . though he could *still* be Dante Gambrielli. The man was a consummate actor. Evil incarnate.

"The poor girl just sat here, staring. We couldn't coax her to speak a word other than Mrs. Dawson's name, and that it was her fault. Most distressing. My husband tried everything. Talking, reading some Scripture. He would have prayed, but the poor dear—" Mrs. Mitford clucked

180

her tongue, shaking her head. "That's when she insisted on leaving."

Torn momentarily from his desperation to find Eve, Alex arched an inquiring brow. "Why do you think she didn't want the vicar to pray?"

"Ah. The rector and I discussed it, very briefly. Miss Sheridan seems to feel she's to blame for her sister's death, and that puts her beyond the reach of God's grace. A very confused, misguided girl." She stood, smoothing her dress down, appraising Alex.

He stood as well, picking up his cap and moving with Mrs. Mitford toward the door. "I've come to know Miss Sheridan fairly well. Her attitude doesn't surprise me at all . . . which is why I should be off now. She doesn't need to be alone."

"God go with you," the kindly woman said. "Please feel free, both of you, to make use of the rectory. We've a guest room upstairs, and the divan in—"

"Thank you." He opened the door and stepped outside. "I'll remember." He touched his forehead. "Thank you." Anxiety, fear, grief—and cold anger—poured unchecked through his body in a deadly flood tide. *Dawson, if my suspicions prove to be true—you've killed your last innocent girl.*

Bramble Cottage was situated about a hundred yards beyond the village, down a narrow lane choked with overgrown trees and shrubbery. The cottage was almost hidden beneath the spreading branches of two gigantic oaks. Alex tied the horse to the gate and sprinted up the path. Withered ivy vines and decaying roses framed the portal; he had to clench his teeth to keep from yelling out his pain and anger.

He pushed open the door and stepped into a dark, narrow hall. To the left was a parlor, where a dim flickering light illuminated Eve's tragic figure in a heart-wrenching tableau.

"Eve."

She didn't respond in any way. Alex walked across the

room to where she sat unmoving in a straight-back chair, her hands lying limply in her lap. Her gaze remained fixed on the floor; the smoky kerosene lamp illuminated a dark, irregular stain, which had ruined the sheepskin rug.

Dear God, Alex prayed, swallowing hard. "Eve." He moved in front of her, knelt down. Her face was cold and still, dead white with her dark eyes staring unblinkingly at the stain. Alex stripped off his gloves and tossed them aside, then cupped her face in his bare hands. "Eve. Look at me."

Her lips moved. Slowly, stiffly, her gaze lifted, vaguely focusing on Alex. She tried to take a breath, and failed; her eyes dimmed, then started to slide away.

Alex slid his hands to her shoulders and administered a firm shake. "Let it out, Eve. Please! Look at me. Talk to me."

"She's dead. And it's my fault."

"Aye. She's dead, Eve, but it is *not* your fault. Come along, now. You don't need to stay—"

"NO! No—no—nooo!" Without warning she erupted, arms flailing out wildly. She struck him—hard—with her fists, her head shaking violently from side to side. Hat and pins flew, releasing a wild cascade of hair, which tumbled about her face and shoulders. Alex caught her fists in his two hands, then hauled her to her feet and dragged her away from the bloodstained rug. Eve struggled every inch of the way.

"Shh—shh. Go on, then, lass—weep. It's all right to grieve, girl. . . ." He kept talking, holding her clenched hands against his chest until, with a great racking sob from the depth of her soul, she collapsed against him, crying as if her heart would break.

As if her heart were already broken.

The train came to a grinding halt at the Brandon Station. Shiver jumped out the moment the guard unlocked the door, shoving past two uppity Englishwomen.

It was too far to walk. He'd have to risk going to the livery, which made his innards cramp. Liveries were always crawling with bored locals, all too ready to poke their dripping noses into a stranger's business.

On this occasion he was lucky. A one-seater road cart had just been returned, and because it was a little before four, the hostler was the only person left at the stable. Within five minutes Shiver was headed down the lane. He whipped the tired horse to a bone-jarring trot, ignoring the hostler's admonishment to go easy with the animal.

35

Upper Dereford

HER THROAT BURNED, HER EYES felt as if she had
rubbed cayenne pepper in them . . . yet she was enfolded
in a snug cocoon of warmth. A voice crooned in her ear,
flowing in low, soothing syllables.

Gradually Eve realized someone's arm was wrapped
around her shoulders. She stirred.

"That's it. Quiet now. The worst is over." The voice was
masculine, deep and warm. But it wasn't her father. Who
could it be, then?

"Poor dear. She looks quite spent. Shall we try the tea
again?"

"Yes. I think that's a good idea."

Someone patted her hand. "Gracious Father, in Your
infinite mercy, soothe the grieving spirit of Your hurting
child."

Eve forced her eyes open. She wasn't at the cottage.
The instant her brain formed the word, her mind re-
coiled, still unwilling to reconstruct the immediate past.
She struggled to free her shoulders of the restricting embrace.

"Easy, now. I'll let you go as soon as you can look at
me. I need to see your eyes, Eve."

That was definitely *not* her father. Her eyes opened, and she stared up into a deeply lined face, with a bushy moustache and vivid eyes, as blue as a blue jay's—

"Alexander." She winced from the croaking syllables.

"Aye." He turned his head. "I think she could take the tea—ah, yes. That looks wonderful, Mrs. Mitford."

The hot tea, laced heavily with milk and sugar, soothed Eve's throat. After the first sip she was able to hold the cup, and Alexander moved away. Without his arm she felt freezing cold and utterly alone.

"There's a little color coming back now."

"Thank You, blessed Lord."

Eve's gaze lifted to the English vicar and his wife. "Thank you." She grimaced. Her voice still sounded hoarse and creaky. "I'm . . . sorry."

"Dear, dear child. Whatever for?" The vicar's wife blinked back tears. Astonished and ashamed, Eve reached out a trembling hand. The older woman clasped it between her own. "You've suffered a grievous shock. I'm just thankful Mr. MacKay arrived in time to help you." She patted Eve's hand. "He carried you here, you know, because we told him to. Poor child, let us help."

Eve turned to regard Alexander. She opened her mouth, but to her horror more tears welled up in her swollen eyes. Incredibly, he didn't retreat in disgust or embarrassment, but instead tenderly wiped the tears away with the pad of his thumb. "I didn't mean to cry," she whispered.

"Hush, now," Alexander said, his voice low, anguished. "I wanted you to. You needed to."

Eve drank some more tea, relieved when a modicum of strength flowed back into her limbs. Mrs. Mitford led her to a bedroom and poured cool water into a basin. Eve washed her face, then tied her hair at the nape of her neck with the velvet ribbon the vicar's wife gave her.

She returned to the parlor a few moments later. "I'm better," she assured the three concerned people hovering over her. She tried to smile, but the pain was still too fresh, too raw. "Or at least, I will be." She drank some more tea, but the moment couldn't be postponed. She set the cup on the little nesting table the rector's wife had placed by her knee. "I'd like to see her grave."

Both Alexander and the older woman protested, but the vicar held up an admonishing hand. "She needs to say goodbye. This will help." He leaned forward, the elderly face above his clerical collar full of understanding. "I prayed for your sister's soul, dear," he promised. "And over her husband's objections, I performed the Order for the Burial of the Dead, even though she wasn't Church of England." He smiled a serene, beatific smile. "I have a suspicion our dear Lord cares naught for earthly labels. At any rate, I thought her family would be comforted. We would have notified you, of course, if Mr. Dawson, in his extreme grief, had not forgotten to provide your address before he left."

"Thank you." Eve glanced at Alexander, wary of his expression. "Will you—"

"I will. Don't look at me like that. I hate for you to endure more pain and grief, that's all."

Relief shook her, but she had recovered enough now to function. "Is it very far?" She stood, both ashamed and grateful for Alexander's help. After a moment her knees supported her without trembling.

The vicar's face, incredibly, suffused with color. "I . . . um . . . since the church does not permit . . . I felt perhaps it was better . . ."

His wife laid a gentle hand on her husband's arm. "She's buried in a corner of the garden, behind Bramble Cottage, dear. She seemed happy there, for a while."

Eve was staring at the vicar. "Exactly how," she asked carefully, the trembling catching hold again, "did my sister die?"

The vicar and his wife exchanged uneasy glances. Alexander stepped over to Eve and reached for her hand. Eve thrust them behind her back and sidestepped, inching backward across the small room. "How?" she repeated.

"Eve, we'll discuss it later. It's going to be dark in a little while, and if you feel the need to see her grave we need to leave now."

"Miss Sheridan—"

The coldness was coming back again, rolling over her like wet, suffocating fog—except this time, a bright beam of rage shone through the gathering mist. "She *was* murdered, wasn't she? Why avoid telling me? I've known for weeks. Don't try and cushion me. I'm not some silly little girl. Just because—"

"Oh dear, oh dear." Mrs. Mitford started for her, the thin face alive with pity and consternation.

Alex stalked her with grim determination.

Eve whirled and ran for the door. The last thing she heard, as her fingers scrambled for the latch, were the vicar's incredible words: "Oh, my poor, dear child. She took her own life, Miss Sheridan. That's why we couldn't bury—"

But Eve didn't hear the rest. She ran down the path and, in spite of her heavy skirt and petticoats, was halfway to the cottage before Alexander managed to catch up.

A mile from the village Shiver's flagging horse stumbled, almost falling. Shiver raised the whip, then with a vicious curse threw it aside. The animal was spent. Sides heaving, head hanging, it stopped still in the road, steam huffing from reddened nostrils. Shiver jumped down, eyeing the lathered, trembling body with disgust. He cursed again, looking up and down the deserted road. Then, with clumsy movements he unfastened the shafts and grabbed the horse's bridle.

Sweating and cursing in the cold, wet wind, he tugged the unwilling animal across the shallowest part of the water-filled ditch and into the woods. After about a hundred yards he reached a dense thicket of undergrowth in the trees, where he tied the horse to a sapling. Then he hurried back to retrieve the cart. The delay was infuriating, but he could still make it to the village by dusk, which would suit his purposes just fine. He carved a notch in the bark of a nearby tree, then set off down the road.

"She didn't take her own life, Alexander." Eve stared down at Rebecca's grave, marked with a fresh white tombstone and a spray of withered dahlias across the settling mound.

Beside her, cap in hand, Alexander laid a comforting hand on her shoulder. "I don't know if we can prove that now." His voice was very gentle.

For a brief moment she weakened enough to lean, savoring the strength, the warmth emanating from him. Then she straightened, knelt down on the cold, damp earth, and rested her hand on the grave. "I'll prove it," she vowed. "One way or another, I'll prove it, if it takes the rest of my life. Giles Dawson—or whoever he is—murdered her. You know it, and I know it." She stood, and in the settling dusk she confronted the Pinkerton operative. "I have her letters—and somewhere in that house is her journal. She told me that she wrote everything down in that journal. All her suspicions, all her fears, all her feelings. I'm going to find that journal, Alexander."

He expelled his breath in a long sigh. "Why didn't you tell me?"

She didn't pretend to misunderstand. "It was private. As long as she was . . . alive—" Her voice caught, but she finished levelly. "I had to honor her privacy. Beyond that . . ." She braced herself, then admitted without wavering, "I wrote a letter to Avery Paxton, betraying what Rebecca had written me. I . . . I was trying to help, but now . . . now it doesn't matter. My arrogance and stupidity killed her." The bitter little announcement fell between them.

"Eve, you did what you thought best," Alexander said after a long period of heavy silence.

"I killed her. Even without the letter I wrote, by my silence I killed her." A cold wind swept through the garden, rustling the dying vegetation, and the smell of decaying earth filled her nostrils. A jackdaw flitted across the yard, scolding. Eve didn't even turn her head.

"There's no use arguing the matter now," Alexander muttered tiredly. "Come. We'll have some supper—then I'll bring you back to the cottage and we'll search for the journal. Together, if you can bring yourself to trust me that much."

"I'm not hungry." She brushed the dirt from her skirt and gloves, avoiding what she knew would be a very censorious look. He had every right to condemn her, but she still couldn't face him. "I know I need to eat. I can't remember . . ." She stopped.

"You'll feel better if you try." He took her arm, and this time Eve didn't protest. "In an hour we'll be back. While we eat, you can let me see the letters, if you're so inclined."

"I'm sorry, Alexander."

He pulled her arm through his, covering her hand with his own. "At least you left me the address here. As for the rest—" He paused and squeezed her hand. "You've suffered enough. Don't punish yourself any more."

The wind had blown all the clouds away by the time Alexander drove Eve's hired buggy down the lane to the cottage. A waning moon in a sky the color of India ink lit the way. Eve shivered at the soft moaning hoot of an owl, and Alexander turned his head.

"It's just an owl."

"I know. I'm . . . uneasy and numb and agitated, all at the same time." *And I'm suffocating with the choking guilt.*

189

At least Alexander wasn't acting angry or distant with her anymore.

"You have cause. Eve, are you sure you don't want to wait until morning, or stay at the rectory while I search? This isn't going to be pleasant."

"I won't break down again, or try to hide anything I find."

"I wasn't concerned about that." He sounded aggravated. Eve thought she heard him mutter something about stubborn women, but she decided against querying him on the matter.

They rounded a curve in the lane. Eve strained her eyes ahead, toward the cottage, when suddenly Alexander pulled back on the reins, stopping dead in the center of the road. One hand closed over Eve's arm in a viselike grip, tugging her close as he leaned down. Eve felt his lips brush her ear. "Don't move or make a sound," he murmured, so softly she barely heard. "There's someone in the cottage."

36

THE LANE WAS TOO NARROW TO turn the buggy, and Alex couldn't risk sending Eve back to the village on foot alone. He eased the horse as close to the ditch as he could safely risk, until the overhanging branches of an ancient oak safely concealed them in shadows. "I want you to stay here," he whispered against her ear. Soft tendrils of hair tickled his face, and a faint fragrance of violets teased his nose. *Poor lass. She didn't need this now. She was doubtless terrified, and he—*

Then Eve spoke. *"I WILL NOT!"* she hissed in a vehement whisper, shoving her face right up next to his. "Don't you *dare* even think—"

Alex clamped a hand over her mouth, his eyes following the wavering yellow glow in the parlor. Seconds later it disappeared. He gripped Eve's shoulder so tightly she squirmed in mute protest. Alex loosened his hold. He knew *exactly* what would happen if he left her here unattended. "All right," he muttered. "All right, you little wildcat. At least if you stay with me, I'll not be attacking the wrong person." He breathed deeply, evenly. He had to think fast.

"I have an idea," Eve whispered. He groaned, and Eve

kicked his shin. "Listen—I'll go to the front entrance, making enough noise to alert whoever's in there. You can sneak—"

"Absolutely not."

"Why? Have you a better plan? If we both go to the front entrance, or even the back—whoever is there can escape out the other door. Besides, it's probably just a vagrant, or one of the villagers, instead—"

"Instead of your sister's vicious, amoral murderer," Alex finished. "Who might also be after that journal." He clenched his fists. "I'll no' be havin' you risk your life!" His control broke, and his hands reached, cupping her face. "I don't want you hurt—or worse!"

Eve was stiff as a pike. "And I won't have you risk your life, either," she shot back. "Alexander . . . while we sit here arguing, Giles—if that's who it is—might *find* the journal, or some other clue. Besides . . ." She wrenched free, and her words spewed out as heatedly as his, "You can't let him escape! Not this time, Alexander. . . ."

"Ach . . ." He wanted to pull out his hair, or tie Eve to the buggy. Yet he couldn't deny the sheer admiration he felt—albeit reluctantly—as he watched her metamorphosis from weeping, vanquished girl to feisty, avenging angel. *You have to protect her. You can't allow this spirit to be dimmed. You can't . . .* "All right." His hands swept down her shoulders in a caress he couldn't control, then closed over her hands. He lifted them to his chest. "Eve—"

"I promise I'll be careful, Alexander." Incredibly, he heard the ghost of a laugh, which almost became a sob. "I'm trusting you to do *your* job. All you have to do is trust me in return. I know that might be asking too much, but I promise: I'll be careful."

He dropped his head, and his lips brushed the back of her gloved hands. "If he tries to run at you, or attack—scream as loudly as you can and—" He chuckled. "Throw something in his face. If you can't find birdseed, maybe dirt would do the trick."

Her breath hitched, and he heard her swallow. "You

be careful too. Your shoulder—"

"Is healed." He jumped down and handed her the reins. "Let's go."

Alex stayed behind the buggy until Eve pulled the horse to a stop in front of the gate. Then he ducked behind the low, crumbling brick wall surrounding the cottage and slipped free of his ulster and cap. The biting wind ruffled his hair and nipped his skin, but Alex barely noticed. Slowly feeling his way, he came upon another huge oak, this one split in half, its dead branches crumbling the low stone wall into a jumbled pile.

Somewhere behind him he heard Eve open the gate, rattling it loudly, and then scuff her boots on the path. Alex ground his teeth together and pushed through the thick undergrowth on the other side of the wall.

Clouds banked across the moon, blocking much of its light. Breathing a prayer of thanks for the darkness, Alex inched carefully through the remains of a rose garden. Vicious thorns from the unattended, overgrown bushes gouged his clothing and tore at his skin. Maybe the moonlight would be preferable, after all.

A loud knock echoed in the night.

Muttering gaelic threats, Alex hurled himself through the garden, tripped over a compost heap, and went sprawling. Spitting earth and dead leaves, he scrambled up and pelted across the yard. The clouds blew past, and bright moonlight flooded the yard again.

"Who's there?" Eve's voice demanded from the front of the cottage, loudly enough to be heard in London.

Alex made it to the wall of the house. He pressed against the dank, clammy stone, inching his way to the back door. It was bolted on the outside—no escape here. The walls were too thick to detect inside noise. He couldn't hear anything at all except the rising moan of the wind rustling the trees. Moving as rapidly as possible, heedless of noise, he edged along the wall. Wet, prickling shrubbery blocked the corner. Alex forced his way past.

Without warning, bats exploded from beneath the eaves.

He slammed back against the wall, automatically shielding his head. Sweat, cold as the dripping bushes, gathered in the small of his back and on his forehead. His pulse thundered.

At the corner he dropped to all fours, then inch by inch stuck his head around until he could see. Eve was nowhere in sight. Alex took a long, deep breath, emptying his mind of all emotion. Deadly quiet spilled through his veins, calming the racing heart, relaxing tensed muscles. Silent as the clouds, he drifted closer, his vision acute, his ears alert to the slightest noise.

Eve's cape lay on the front porch, in a dark heap.

The front door gaped wide open.

Inside, light from the intruder's lantern shed a single sliver of yellow across the hall. Alex eased up the steps and into the cottage, his eyes searching corners, his body supple, ready for attack.

"Alexander? Is that you?"

At the first hint of sound and movement Alex had gone into action, catapulting forward with the reflexive speed honed from years of practice. He checked himself at the last second, twisting his body so that as the two of them hurled to the floor, Alex took the brunt of the fall.

Eve screamed. Her face was buried against his shoulder, and the sound emerged like a muffled roar. Alex would have reassured her, but he found himself attacked by a clawing, panting tigress. "Eve!" he barked, fending off fists and elbows and almost suffocating in billowy sleeves and a waterfall of hair. "Be still. It's Alexander . . . ouch!"

He managed to grab her wrists, then turned, and with surprising difficulty pinned her to the floor.

"Eve!" he repeated. "Open your eyes. You're safe."

The squirming body stilled, her eyes snapped open, and in the thin beam of light Alex watched recognition—then rage—spark like kindling. "You *attacked* me!" she spat. Her head twisted from side to side as she struggled to move her wrists. "You're *sitting* on me!"

Light-headed from relief and the dizzying aftermath of fear and anger, Eve's display of indignant outrage—so ludicrous under the circumstances—tipped Alex over the edge. He started laughing. "Aye. And considering what I almost did, count yourself blessed, girl." He shifted, then easily hauled her to her feet.

Eve jerked free. "I called your name so you would know it was me," she fumed, rubbing her wrists. Her blouse had pulled free of her skirt, which was twisted sideways, and two buttons had popped off her jacket. With her hair streaming down her face and back and her eyes shooting daggers at him, Alex thought her the most magnificent sight he had ever seen.

Hands on his hips, he raked an unrepentant, admiring look over her that swept from the tip of her head to her boots. "You were the one who insisted on swimming in water over your head, Miss Sheridan. Next time, listen to me."

"Instead of lecturing, you might inquire as to the whereabouts of Joe Leoni," she fired back, killing his laughter in a single breath. "That's who it was, in case you're interested. Not Giles. I caught a glimpse of his face before he dived out the bedroom window, at the back of the house. Which is where"—she poked his chest with her finger—"you were supposed to be." Chest heaving, she lifted her hands and furiously began to gather up her heavy hair. "Now he's probably halfway to the next village, no thanks to you."

"You're absolutely sure it was Leoni?"

Eve froze in the act of separating her hair into three sections. She opened her mouth, looked up into Alex's face, and nodded. Wisely, she remained silent.

Alex stalked down the hall, retrieved Leoni's lantern, and used it to rummage for matches. Then he prowled throughout all the rooms, lighting every lamp and candle he found, until the cottage blazed with light. By the time he finished, he had gotten himself back under control.

Eve was sitting on a kitchen stool, her hair fixed in a single braid, her clothing restored to order. She looked up as Alex entered the room. "I'm sorry. You frightened me."

He nodded. "I know. I meant to." He grinned crookedly. "You frightened *me*. You're a braw lass, Eve Sheridan—but you've led a sheltered life. I never should have listened to you out there in the lane." He took a deep breath, his hands digging into his pockets and closing over his grandfather's wooden puzzle. Incredibly, it was still there. "Paxton must have sent him." He paused. "He could have killed you!"

"I know." She bit her lip. "I wonder why he didn't. He heard me, I know. But he just ran."

Alex walked over to where she sat, her back and shoulders straight, her head averted. She looked subdued now, and very vulnerable. "Eve."

She turned.

"Have you realized the significance of Joe Leoni here, pawing about Giles and Rebecca's house?"

He saw her throat muscles tighten, and a quiver rippled the slender form. "Giles . . . and Avery Paxton . . . must be . . . they must have planned . . ." Her voice dried up, and her shoulders slumped abruptly. "And my letter made me a blind, gullible *Judas* goat."

It was all Alex could do not to pull her into a comforting embrace. "We'll know," he promised, his hand lifting to touch one dirt and tear smudged cheek, "as soon as we find Joe Leoni. Eve—if it helps, this would have taken months to plan. Your letter may have inadvertently helped, but it did *not* cause Rebecca's death." He could tell she still didn't believe him. "We'll know when we catch Leoni," he repeated.

"And find Rebecca's journal."

"Aye. That, too." He hesitated, hating to cause more pain. But a suspicion that could not be ignored raised the hackles at the back of his neck. "Eve . . . do you think you can search for it now?"

196

"Of course. That's why we came, after all." She rose. "I'll start in the bedroom. I doubt if she hid it there—much too obvious. Still, I've learned that it's best to be methodical."

"I'll join you as soon as I snoop about the yard a bit."

Fear flooded back into Eve's face, turning her expressive eyes black. "Alexander, no."

"I'll be careful, Eve." He kept his voice calm, reasonable. "We can't both of us be in here, our heads buried in bric-a-brac. If he returns . . ."

"All right. You don't have to convince me." She closed her eyes, and when she opened them again, the expression took Alex's breath. For an endless moment they stared at each other without speaking. Then her lips moved soundlessly, shaping his name.

Alex smiled. "I'll be careful—and I'll be back. Say a prayer for me. It will help us both."

"Alexander—" Her voice broke.

"Say a prayer, Eve. The Lord will hear. Trust me." He touched his forehead, then strode out of the room.

37

Bramble Cottage

SHIVER WATCHED THE COTTAGE blaze to life. He cursed, rubbing his hands to try to stay warm. The three-sided hay shed at the corner of the field might offer the perfect hiding place, but it was colder than Satan's laughter.

He had wanted to kill the woman, who was probably an interfering villager, but it was too much of a risk. And she hadn't been alone. As Shiver had lit out across the yard, he had glimpsed someone else sneaking around the corner. He kicked a bale of hay. The woman could also be one of Gambrielli's limmers. The rake had them stashed everywhere. Stupid, stupid females. Show 'em a pretty face like Gambrielli's, fill their ears with pretty words, and they were dumb as cows.

Shiver blew on his fingers. This cursed country made his bones ache, with its damp cold and endless wind. *Avery Paxton, this is the last time I do your dirty work.*

He huddled in the shadows of the open doorway, his gaze fastened on the cottage. He would have to wait and hope their poking about wouldn't take a long time. As soon as the lights went out, he would go back.

"Hurry up," he growled at the female whose voice had

alerted him to danger in the nick of time. *Hurry up.*

The cottage was full of Rebecca's touch. Heartsore, Eve noted the scrapbook albums, and the many beaded pillows—one of Becca's favorite pastimes. Her sister had been quintessentially feminine, and as a consequence Eve had always felt like a horsefaced old maid in comparison.

She stood in the middle of the bedroom and tried to force her brain to work in a logical pattern instead of wallowing in guilt and grief. If she were Rebecca, growing suspicious of her husband, trusting no one but her older sister—where would she hide the journal?

Her clothes? Becca delighted in every aspect of dress, from her lace-edged undergarments to the ridiculously elaborate hats she preferred. Perhaps she had created a secret pocket in one of her cloaks or gowns. Eve opened a large wardrobe, but it was empty. Giles obviously had packed away her sister's clothes—or more likely, had someone else do it. But where were they? Frustrated, she glanced about the room, seeing signs of Joe Leoni's hurried pawing in the tumbled bedcovers and opened drawers.

Had the journal been packed away as well?

Sighing, Eve gritted her teeth and searched every nook and cranny of the room; there was no other way to know *anything* for sure until a thorough search was completed.

Alexander appeared in the doorway. "Any luck?"

"No." She had heard his return; he had been careful to announce his presence. Eve had been crawling along the floor, searching for loose boards. Now she sat back on her heels and blew a strand of hair out of her eyes. "I've searched in here. All her clothes have already been packed and sent off somewhere. You can search after me, if you'd like, or start in the kitchen."

"Why can't I take the parlor, and *you* the kitchen?"

Eve's mouth dropped open. He was smiling, trying to

tease—but Eve could tell immediately that he was distracted. "What is it?" she asked, tiny pinpricks of fear prickling her spine.

A corner of his mouth twitched. "Sometimes," he murmured beneath his breath, "I wish you weren't so astute." He stuffed his hand in his pocket and tugged out a small pouch. "I found tracks. He headed into the field—but I have no way of knowing how far he went."

Eve lifted her gaze from the pouch to his face. "So he could still be out there, waiting," she finished. This wasn't real. None of this was actually happening. Her sister wasn't really dead . . . and she wasn't really standing in a strange cottage in a foreign country, three thousand miles from home, with a Pinkerton operative who had just informed her that her attempted killer might be lurking outside, waiting to pounce. That wasn't real, either.

"Eve—I *will* take care of you. Don't be frightened."

"What *is* that?" Eve pointed to the pouch. "I've seen you fiddling with it lots of times and wanted to ask . . ." Her voice trailed away as Alexander lifted her hand in one of his, then tipped the contents of the pouch into her palm. "Pieces of wood?"

"My grandfather loves to carve. I've always been a lively, curious sort who had to be about something, so Dom—that's what I call him—started carving wooden puzzles for me. At first they were figures—animals, identifiable objects. When I pieced them together too fast, he started creating mazes. That's what this one is, but I've only figured out the fitting for about half a dozen pieces." He deftly worked them together. "See? I have a suspicion this one will be octagonal."

Fascinated, her fear subsiding for the moment, Eve fingered the smooth, fragrant wood, warm from his pocket. "It's cedar."

"Aye. Dom loves the fragrance."

"Do you always carry one in your pocket?"

He smiled sheepishly. "They help me think, calm me

when I'm troubled . . . relieve boredom when I'm having to sit still."

"I don't mind sitting still. I had to learn so the birds would come to trust me."

He studied her, the enigmatic blue of his eyes glittering darkly in the small bedroom. All of a sudden Eve realized where they were, and in spite of herself a blush crept up into her cheeks. "I—here." She thrust the pieces back into his hands. "We shouldn't . . . I'll take the kitchen!" she blurted. "I don't mind."

"All right," he returned equably. He started to say something else but stopped. Eve stood, twisting her hands, embarrassed but reluctant to abandon the warm oasis of his presence. Alexander watched her in silence, then lifted his hand and softly cupped her cheek in a tender caress, over before it began. "Go on, then, lass," he whispered, the deep voice as caressing as his hand. "We've plenty of time."

She obeyed, and it wasn't until she had emptied the cupboard of all the crockery that the import of his words registered. Scattering dishes and bowls, she leaped to her feet and hurried into the parlor. "We have to stay here all night, don't we?"

Alexander was down on the floor, rummaging behind the fire screen. His shoulders stiffened; he stood but didn't turn around. "The darkness provides Leoni with as much protection as it would us. In the cottage, at least, there's a little more protection than out in the open. I think you should try and sleep a little, though."

"I . . . don't think I can."

"Then keep searching." His voice was gruff, and he still didn't turn around. Puzzled, Eve started across the parlor, which looked as if a herd of small boys had been allowed to run loose. "Go back to the kitchen, Eve."

His tone was so sharp that she froze, hurt to the point of tears. He had no cause to speak to her that way, especially now. He had to realize that she was torn with emotion, hanging on to her control through sheer dogged de-

201

termination. He wouldn't even face her. "I might be more inclined to do so if you'd at least do me the courtesy of turning around when you ask." She winced; even to her own ears she sounded like a priggish old maid.

Alexander grumbled something unintelligible beneath his breath. Then, looking as if he were facing a firing squad, he turned. He kept his hands behind his back.

Eve went cold. "What . . ." she asked, the words slow, reluctant, ". . . what are you hiding behind your back?" She walked across the room to his side. "Alexander? What have you found?" she repeated.

He grimaced, then with a fierce shudder thrust out his hand. In it he held a Russian nesting doll. *Matryoshkas* they were called.

The smiling face was covered with dried blood.

38

Upper Dereford

MRS. DAWSON'S SISTER WAS IN the village. Harriet Crabtree heard it from Edith Pulham, who had found out from Agnes Thirkettle at the bakery.

Harriet didn't reveal her nervousness by so much as a twitch. Calmly she finished making her purchases at the village shop, then just as calmly laid them on the counter. "Where is the lady staying?" she asked Edith, whose love of gossip equalled her fondness for sweet breads.

"Nobody's sure." Full of gloom, Edith Pulham shook her head. "Last I heard, she was under the care of the vicar. 'Tis a terrible thing to have happened in our village."

Everyone nodded in solemn agreement, including Harriet.

"Would anybody know the gent who galloped into the village earlier this afternoon?" The blacksmith clumped up behind Harriet, an aggrieved scowl on his sweating face. "The vicar asked would I bed his horse down for the night. What I want to know is, who'll be paying?"

"He had the look of a highwayman, I hear."

"Poppycock, Edith! Highwaymen don't come calling on the vicarage."

"Mr. Neaves, over to the pub, said he's with Mrs. Dawson's sister. And he's a *Scotsman*."

Fresh speculations swept the crowded shop. Harriet paid for her purchases, slipped through the jawing crowd, and scurried home, heart pounding.

The cottage. Of course they would go to the cottage, to pilfer about, make arrangements for the trunk, even. Harriet would have to tell them about the trunk.

Well, what of it? Harriet put away the groceries, arguing furiously with herself. She had nothing to hide, nothing of which to be ashamed. The few objects she had helped herself to were payment for services rendered. Harriet had only been doing her Christian duty, like—cleaning up the place at the request of Mr. Dawson. She did wonder why he hadn't returned to meet with his sister-in-law. Poor cove. Likely he was still off somewhere, grieving alone.

That evening, sitting in front of the fire, she decided that, come morning, she would call on the vicar and see what he had to say about Mistress Dawson's sister. Likely the lady would be as distraught as Master Giles . . . perhaps she wouldn't even notice a few missing trinkets at the cottage.

Harriet's eye lifted to the mantelpiece, covered with her treasures. The strange little wooden doll's face smiled at her, so cheerful-like. It wasn't a doll, precisely; it reminded Harriet more of a large, flat-bottomed eggcup, with a doll's features painted on it in some sort of gypsy-looking dress.

The object fascinated Harriet, because she had discovered that by twisting a seam in its middle she could pull it completely apart. Inside she had found a smaller painted doll, a replica of the larger one. The smaller one could be opened too—just like cracking an egg on the side of a crock.

Delighted, Harriet had no idea how many other dolls were hidden inside, for—try as she might—she had been unable to twist open the smaller doll. She had carefully reassembled the pieces and placed the doll on the mantel, next to her prized figurine of a handsome soldier, where everyone could see and admire them both. She had no intention of giving up the doll.

Even if the vicar himself asked.

39

"MY PARENTS BROUGHT THEM BACK for us years ago, mementos from a European tour. I have a similar one." Eve stroked the dainty blue flowers at the doll's waist. "Only mine has birds along with the flowers." Her voice wobbled. "I loved birds, even then."

Alex lifted the toy from her fingers. Despite his objections, Eve had insisted upon washing the blood away, and he had given in. A blood-spattered toy, after all, hardly constituted evidence strong enough to prove that Rebecca's death was murder instead of suicide.

"The wood-carver did a nice job," he observed. "Dom would enjoy studying this."

"I'll lend it to you, if you like." Eve glanced around. "I wonder where the rest of it is. Mine has a total of six smaller dolls inside the largest one." She glanced at Alex. "Did you find the others?"

"No." The dainty piece he had found opened to reveal the smallest doll, a quarter of the size of a thimble. "Actually, I had just stumbled upon this when you came into the room. It had rolled under the coal scuttle." He paused, and Eve smiled at him, a bittersweet expression that made Alex want to gather her back into his arms.

"I'm all right, Alexander. You don't have to tiptoe around my emotions. The Matryoshka doll rattled me because of—well, it rattled me. But I'm all right now. Let's go look for the rest of them, along with the journal." She stood, her expression resolute, and marched over to an oak barley twist table in the far corner. Its surface was almost hidden beneath a scattering of various objects.

Alex ran a hand over the back of his neck, massaging the twitching muscle at the top of his spine. After a while he quietly rose and prowled through the rest of the cottage again. All the windows and doors were securely latched; they should be safe for the night. He hoped.

"Alexander?"

He returned to the parlor. "What is it?" Eve stood in the middle of the room, a frown on her face.

"Two things." She twisted her hands together. "The first is that I can't find the other pieces of the doll anywhere." She hesitated, looking suddenly so uncertain that Alex walked over and gently took her hands, holding them in a comforting grip between his own.

"Go on, then. Tell me."

"I . . ." She looked down at their clasped hands, then over his shoulder, and swallowed several times. "I can't, when you're—holding my hands. I'm sorry, but it makes my thoughts all jumbled."

Even in the smoky kerosene lamplight, Alex could discern her rising color. He laughed low and released her hands, lifting one of his to brush her cheek. "Lass, you never cease to surprise me."

Eve retreated behind stilted dignity. "I'd appreciate it if you didn't make fun of me right now. This is difficult as it is."

"I'm not making fun of you." *But if you don't stop gazing at me with those great, dark eyes, I might end up kissing you.* He stared down at his boots and clasped his hands behind his back. "What is it you want to tell me, Eve?"

"Rebecca . . . could be sneaky. She used to hide things a lot, to tease me. It was just a game, of course. But I'm wondering—there's enough room inside the larger dolls to hide things. A note, perhaps. It would have been like Becca to leave a clue to the location of her journal inside one of the nesting dolls."

"All of which seem to have disappeared."

They looked at each other.

"Leoni, or Giles, could have the doll by now—or the journal," Alex said finally, his voice flat, bleak. "But we'll continue searching. We've got all night."

Eve's answering glance was wry. "Don't worry about my sensibilities, Alexander. Right now, what's 'proper' seems a bit absurd, with my sister murdered, her murderer doubtless weaving another web somewhere for another victim—and Joe Leoni skulking about the bushes."

"Sounds like a dime novel, does it not?" Alex rubbed his palms together and strode across the room. "I'll have a go at this secretary, while you finish in that corner. At least we have a way to pass the time."

For more than an hour they searched, without result. When a wall clock chimed ten, Eve collapsed onto the settee. Alex was in the hall, searching through the seat of the hall tree. He glanced into the parlor. "Why don't you take a nap?" he suggested again, keeping his voice matter-of-fact. "I'm used to all-night vigils."

"I don't think I can sleep."

He stood up, dusting off his trousers. "I've told you I won't let anyone hurt you. I wish you could trust me."

"It's not that."

Slowly he walked back into the parlor. "Would you like me to sit in here with you? I don't mind." He dropped down into a comfortable parlor chair and pulled out Dom's puzzle, acting as if the circumstances were as ordinary and natural as a trip to the market. "How about a bedtime story?"

Eve's stiff posture and averted face didn't budge. After a minute she spoke in a stifled voice. "I'd like to ask you a question instead."

Alex was hard-pressed not to blurt out his growing admiration of her dauntless character, if only to generate a smile. Not once had she whined or complained, not once had she succumbed to hysteria. The wild grief had been brought under control, and all her energies focused on accomplishing her goal.

He fiddled with the puzzle, wondering how much longer he would be able to hide his feelings from her.

"Ask away."

"Why haven't you yelled at me for not telling you about the letter I wrote Mr. Paxton?"

"Why *didn't* you tell me about it, Eve?" he countered.

Her shoulders lifted, then dropped. "I . . . was ashamed, because in retrospect I came to realize how ridiculous I must have sounded. And he never replied anyway. I used to pray the letter never arrived. Then . . ." she swallowed hard, "I became petrified by what my letter might have precipitated. If I hadn't, in my arrogance, told Rebecca I would find out more about Giles for her by writing Mr. Paxton—maybe Giles wouldn't have killed her."

Alex continued to stroke the puzzle pieces, forcing a bland expression to mask his inner turmoil. Eve was convinced Dawson had murdered her sister—but evidence remained circumstantial. Alex had had to convince *himself* to maintain an open mind, in spite of his growing conviction that, not only had Dawson killed his wife—he was in fact the infamous "Bluebeard": Dante Gambrielli.

A court of law doesn't care about your hunches, Alex MacKay.

He studied Eve. Would it help—or hurt—if he warned her that Rebecca might have been doomed from the moment Dawson slid a ring on her finger?

What if Giles Dawson was innocent, and Rebecca *had* killed herself? *Ach, let it go, man, and concentrate on comforting the poor lass.*

"Eve, past actions might be regretted, whether they're right or wrong. But *nothing* can change what has already happened. Regardless of the consequences, God has forgiven you—and so have I. The motive of your heart was pure." He smiled sadly. "Misguided, perhaps, but driven by the genuine desire to help your sister." His fingers slipped a puzzle piece in place.

"Why didn't God punish *me* personally, instead of allowing my sister to die?" she cried, as if she couldn't hold the words back any longer. "*I* deserve the punishment, even though I was trying to help. But I was *wrong*. So why didn't God punish *me*?"

Puzzle pieces scattered all over his lap. "Is that how you perceive God? A vengeful Deity who doles out punishment, but never grace?" Alex retrieved the pieces while his thoughts spun madly. *I wasn't expecting this, God, d'You hear?*

Silence. Alex glanced up, catching an expression of such agonized shame that he almost dropped the pieces again. He forced his own expression and voice to remain carefully neutral. "You blame yourself for your sister's death and have steeled yourself for retribution. You're a Christian. Tell me, are you not entitled to God's grace? His forgiveness? His love?"

More silence. Finally, Eve gave a brief shake of her head, then a savage chewing of her lip. *Hmm,* Alex thought. *This promises to be a bit of a challenge.* "Lass, you don't have to crucify yourself any longer. That's taken care of, forever."

Eve looked at him. In the dim light her dark eyes filled a face still pale from shock. At some point she had pinned her hair back into a severe twist and removed her jacket. Her striped lawn blouse was rumpled, with several dark smudges streaking the balloon sleeves. Above the starched collar, in the slender column of her throat, a pulse beat as frantically as that of a frightened hare.

"Eve?"

"I've tried to—to be a good Christian all my life," she began, the words strained, hesitant. "But it's never enough. I can't . . . I don't . . ." She stopped, her hands clenching into fists.

Alex waited without speaking, giving her the time she needed. He prayed the dam would burst without his having to force it. Suddenly he realized that—far more than the mystery of Rebecca Sheridan's death, or even the true identity of Giles Dawson—he was determined to solve the mystery of Eve Sheridan's complex, confused personality.

"I don't *feel* God," Eve blurted out abruptly. Alex made an encouraging noise in his throat, but quick as a blink her head jerked away. "I can't pray. It's as if I'm inside a box, or—or one of the Matryoshka dolls. I've tried for years, but no matter how hard, no matter what I try—it's the same. I know it's not God's fault, so it has to be mine."

Alex's own communion with the Almighty was as natural to him as breathing. He could scarcely imagine what a spiritual desert his life would be without it. Or until now, he corrected himself, when a struggling young woman bared her tortured soul.

He knew instinctively that Eve would be offended, even angered, by trite platitudes and scriptural quotes. Sometimes, Alex thought, she was too intelligent for her own good. *Miss Sheridan,* he asked her silently, *how do I help you to comprehend that it isn't necessary to understand* how *something works, as long as you accept that it does?*

This time, he had waited too long to respond.

"I'm sorry. I shouldn't have said anything. I . . . I think I'll search for the journal, or the doll, some more." She started to rise, but Alex moved faster, pressing her back down onto the settee with firm but gentle hands.

"I'm glad you told me," he said. "Very glad . . . and grateful for your trusting me with your feelings. I'm trying to think through my words, so I won't patronize, hurt, or insult you." He lifted a brow at her. "You see, your very nimble brain intimidates me, Miss Sheridan."

She was in no mood for levity. "My brain intimidates most men. Does that mean God cursed me—or are all men mentally deficient?"

He stifled a laugh. "You sound like a suffragette. No—

don't bristle. I'm teasing you, doubtless inappropriately, but there it is." He grinned. "I must be mentally deficient."

She didn't want to smile, he could see, and she whipped her head away to hide it. But her shoulders finally relaxed, and after a moment Alex spoke, this time with heartfelt sincerity. "I can't answer for others, Eve, but I *can* promise you that God has no stringent list of qualifications that an individual must satisfy before He grants them an audience, so to speak. Or forgiveness. Or His love. You're a Christian—or at least," he amended at her pained expression, "you earnestly live as if you're a Christian. From what I've seen and heard, you've a willing heart and the desire. That's all you need."

"Then why haven't I felt Him? Why doesn't God answer my prayers? Why do I always feel this . . . this suffocating fear and guilt that I'm doing something wrong, or never doing enough?"

She jumped to her feet, and the cry burst forth, "Why did my sister have to die?"

40

Bramble Cottage

IT WAS MIDNIGHT. SHIVER KICKED A bale of hay, then whipped out his blade and hacked the bale to pieces. The couple hadn't budged from the cottage, and it was unlikely they'd be leaving before morning. Shiver had passed several hours imagining what *they* might be doing to pass the time. Meanwhile his fingers and toes were rapidly losing all feeling, and his belly gnawed from hunger pains.

Smashing his hat down over his head until he could barely see, he left the cursed shed and dashed back across the moonlit field to the cover of the trees behind the cottage. When no alarm sounded after ten minutes, he approached the cottage itself with growing confidence. He planned to slip back in the same window from which he'd escaped.

They would probably be asleep by now. He would take care of the bloke first, then the limmer. He briefly considered enjoying some of what the bloke had obviously been sampling these past hours; he figured he deserved something for the long, cold hours he'd suffered in that blasted lean-to.

The window was firmly locked, from the inside.

Growling beneath his breath, Shiver crept around to the two other windows in the house. Through the diamond panes of the parlor window, he glimpsed the blurred silhouette of a man sitting in a chair. The woman was nowhere in sight.

Shiver retreated to the back of the house. Crouched behind thick bushes, he spent several moments casting about for a plan, anger and uneasiness rising with each passing minute.

The quiet out here in the country unnerved him. Back in New York, there was always noise, from the El, or passing streetcars, or rattling carriages . . . clanging and banging and shouting, and the unending shuffle of footsteps, no matter the lateness of the hour. Here, the only sound he had heard in hours was the rasp of his own breathing, and the wind whistling a mournful wail that near drove him to a murderous frenzy.

Doggedly, he settled on his course. Once committed, he knew his only chance to avoid capture would be surprise, speed—and ruthlessness. But if necessary, he would sacrifice the journal before risking his own skin. If Paxton tried to follow through on his threats, well, Shiver had a plan for his employer too.

41

Upper Dereford
Norfolk, England

EVE WOKE TO COMPLETE DARKNESS and a man's hand covering her mouth. She tried to turn her head, groggily swiping at the arm with both hands. The hand tightened.

She roused in a terrifying rush.

Her arms flailed upward, and she bit down on the encroaching hand as hard as she could.

"Ach, are you part vampire, then? Eve, wake up, girl!" Alexander's voice hissed in her ear, sounding both irate and urgent. "My hand is covering your mouth to keep you quiet, all right? You must stay absolutely quiet."

Eve's eyes popped open, straining in the darkness to see his face. As soon as she saw his face, she quit struggling. When had he extinguished all the light?

Alexander slowly removed his hand from her mouth but wouldn't allow her to rise. "Someone is trying to break into the house," he whispered, a soft trickle of sound that shot through Eve like a jolt of Mr. Edison's electricity.

Her mouth shaped the word *Leoni?* but she had to moisten her lips and swallow before her parched throat

215

managed to whisper the name aloud. Would this nightmare never end?

Alexander, kneeling by the settee, squeezed her shoulders reassuringly. His breath was warm in her ear, the only warmth Eve felt. "He's at the front door, probably trying to pick the lock. I'm going to sneak out to the hall—"

"No!" Eve grabbed his wrist. "That's what he *wants* you to do."

"Shh, now, lass. I know that." In the darkness his teeth flashed white. "I've learned a bit about Mr. Leoni since our last encounter."

A scratching, rasping noise floated into the room.

Eve shuddered. Instantly Alexander's hand covered hers. "I mustn't keep our guest waiting."

"Alexander—" Her voice broke, and she turned her head into the cushion.

His hands gently forced her head back around. "Eve . . ." He crooned something incredibly musical but totally incomprehensible. "I'll be back." His lips brushed her forehead, then lifted. Seconds later, she was alone.

This time, Eve was determined to obey his wishes to the letter. She huddled on the settee, clutching a pillow, eyes and ears strained wide. And with every heartbeat she remembered the touch of Alexander's hands enfolding her face, the feel of his lips against her skin.

The scratching noise returned. It sounded, Eve decided, as if Leoni were scratching the door with a twig. He was teasing, taunting them. She knew—and prayed Alexander did as well—that the noise was designed to provoke one of them into opening the door.

The scratching stopped.

Silence.

Where was Alexander? Curiosity pricked at Eve. Slowly, holding her breath, she slipped her feet to the floor and sat up.

"Eve?" Alexander called, the deep voice barely above a hushed growl of sound. "He's making his way around the corner of the house. I just heard him at the glass in the kitchen." He paused. Eve's heartbeat doubled. "I want you to tiptoe as quietly as you can to the hall. Do you hear?"

"Yes." She didn't waste time with further words. Seconds later she met him by the hall tree.

"What are you holding?" he asked.

"A bronze statue of an elephant."

A soft chuckle tickled the hairs on her forehead. "I could almost feel sorry for Joe Leoni."

Something heavy thudded against the kitchen window, followed by the ominous sound of tinkling glass.

"Watch—and listen," Alex ordered, taking off down the hall.

He must have eyes like an owl, Eve decided.

Behind her, the parlor window rattled, then exploded into thousands of fragments.

Eve jumped, biting her lip hard enough to draw blood. Alexander materialized at her side, his hand finding her shoulder and giving it a squeeze. "He'll wear himself out, the way he's circling the cottage like a demented harpie."

He sounded completely unruffled, almost amused, but Eve knew him now. "He can crawl through any of the windows."

"Aye. 'Twould be simpler to use the door, but there's no accounting for some individuals." He took two steps and flung open the door. The heavy oak panel crashed against the wall. "There. Now he has another option."

Eve stood, straight and still, locking her knees and clutching the elephant in slippery fingers. Alexander urged her into the tiny space between the hall tree and the corner by the front door. His breath ruffled her hair, warmed her cold cheek.

"We'll just wait here a bit. I'll be in front of you, just like this," he whispered. "Keep your back to the wall, and you'll be safe . . . from me as well as Leoni."

Indignant, Eve opened her mouth to deliver a sharp retort, then clamped it shut. Her body still smarted from being hurled to the floor earlier. Besides, Alexander didn't need his attention divided, which it would be if he weren't certain of her whereabouts. That was a lesson she wouldn't forget again.

She concentrated on listening and staying as unmoving as the statue she held. "I'd rather be watching for birds," she murmured to herself—but Alexander heard.

"I'd rather you were, too."

He also had the *ears* of an owl.

When Leoni made his move, it was almost a relief.

Another large object crashed through the kitchen window, landing with a solid thunk on the stone floor. Eve jerked, but Alexander didn't move except for his head, which swiveled to face the passage leading to the kitchen.

Leoni appeared without warning, his swooping shadow spilling through the doorway. Moonlight glinted on an upheld knife. In a soundless rush he plunged it down toward Alexander's unprotected back.

Eve didn't think—she reacted. Her body rammed into Alexander, propelling him forward, while at the same time she slammed the heavy elephant down across Leoni's knife arm. Leoni howled, and the knife clattered across the floor. Eve hit him again, this time against the side of his head.

Leoni stumbled back against the doorpost—and Alexander catapulted past Eve in a blur of motion. Seconds later, Leoni lay in an unconscious heap, half inside, half outside. Alexander rose, retrieved the knife, then lit a wall sconce. In its wavering light he surveyed Eve, who stood trembling, one hand shielding her eyes from the sudden flame.

"Well, lass." He grinned down at her, a reckless, exultant grin. "You may be sheltered, but you've the courage of a warring Highlander." He gestured to the elephant. "Your choice of weapons was certainly more effective than birdseed." He reached and gently unfastened her cramped fingers from the object. "I don't think you'll be needing this anymore."

Eve stared down at Leoni. "Is he—"

"Nay, more's the pity." He nudged the limp body with the toe of his boot. "But I daresay he'll be sleeping the rest of the night, at least."

She took a light, uneven breath. "I . . . didn't think. He was just there, with the knife pointing toward—" Her voice broke, and then she was in Alexander's arms, clinging to his broad shoulders and burying her face against his chest.

42

Richmond

THE SUNNY NOVEMBER AFTERNOON was unseasonably warm. Avery Paxton briskly walked into Mutual Bank, his cane tapping on the marble floor. It was just before closing time. The lobby was crowded, and all of the tellers were busy with customers. A small line had formed.

Excellent. He enjoyed timing maneuvers in his head, then executing them with flawless perfection. He consulted his watch several times. At precisely the moment he stepped up to the next available teller, a man rushed through the bank doors and dashed up to the first teller's window.

A thin, old codger was slowly counting out some bills onto the high counter. He glared at the rude intruder.

"Please," the man gasped. "I must withdraw my money *now*. I have to catch a train in twenty minutes."

"Sir," the flustered teller protested, "I'm afraid you'll have to wait your turn. This gentleman came first."

The desperate man proceeded to the next window, this time confronted by a militant woman who firmly turned her back on his pleas. "What kind of bank is this?" he shouted. "What kind of people who have no Christian charity—"

The customers shifted uncomfortably, while the tellers glanced at each other, uncertain what to do.

"Sir—" Avery lifted his cane and gestured to the emotional man. "Please. You may conduct your business here. I don't mind waiting."

The man hurried over, wiping his face, his relief palpable. "Bless you, sir. Bless you. . . ."

The relieved clerk barely glanced at the payroll slip the man thrust through the window. His movements crisp, manner censorious, he counted out the appropriate bills.

The man grabbed them and dashed out, his babblings of gratitude ringing in the lobby.

Avery discreetly cleared his throat. "If you don't mind," he explained, "I, too, have an important engagement, and would appreciate an expeditious handling of my business as well."

The teller's face flushed. "Certainly, sir." He glanced down at the check Avery slid through the window. "Um . . . you wish to cash or deposit this, sir?"

"I need a bank draft, my good man, which I will deposit into my bank when I return to New York, where I live. Mr. Sheridan and I are business associates," he added, as if an afterthought.

Relieved, the teller glanced from the check to Avery. "William Sheridan presented you with this personally, then?"

Avery stiffened. "Of course." His voice dropped and he began tapping his cane on the marble floor. "I trust you won't further delay my engagement by questioning either my integrity or the authenticity of this check."

The teller's flush deepened. "Certainly not, sir. It's clear you're a most considerate gentleman." He coughed. "Normally . . . ah . . . the amount here would require verification from the manager, and—" He gulped, then immediately began the necessary paper work, goaded by the frigid blast of displeasure Avery sent him in a wordless glare.

Moments later, Avery strode from the bank, a certified draft for a little under forty thousand dollars tucked in his wallet. Two blocks down the street, he glanced casually about to ensure nobody was paying attention to his movements. Then he climbed into a burgundy cabriolet waiting at the curb.

"Any trouble?" he asked the man handling the reins.

"Not a bit." The man chuckled, looking as smug as a cardsharp holding the winning hand. "Easiest wad I've made all year. You were right. That teller barely glanced at the receipt after the fuss I raised."

"If you continue to follow instructions, there will be more in the future." Avery settled back in the seat with a satisfied smirk. "A very profitable day's work." He nodded, then pulled out his watch. "And now, I *do* have a train to catch." He glanced at the other man. "I'll be returning in ten days, remember."

"I remember, Mr. Paxton. Don't worry about my end of it." He urged the horse to a fast trot. "It's a pleasure working with you, sir."

Avery beamed. "Thank you, Mr. Hanks. I've always found that an organization works best when the employer knows how to treat those who work for him."

At the depot, he jumped from the buggy, then turned back. "Mr. Hanks?"

"Yeah?"

"If for some reason you are approached, or questioned—you won't mention our association, of course."

The man's exultant demeanor vanished. He sat up straight. "Questioned, Mr. Paxton? Why would the bluecoats be questioning me?"

Avery lifted his cane, so that the point hovered inches from Hank's abruptly uneasy face. "It's not the police, Mr. Hanks. It's the *Pinks*." He spat the word like an epithet, viciously. The cane dropped. "Good-day, Mr. Hanks."

He headed for the platform, whistling, his diamond stickpin glinting in the afternoon sunshine.

43

Upper Dereford
Norfolk, England

THE NEXT MORNING THOMAS RUDGE rode into Upper Dereford, windblown and mud-splattered in an equally mud-splattered chaise. Alex had been watching for him since dawn, and hailed him from the rectory gate.

"Did you find your two recalcitrant damsels?" Rudge leaped down, his bloodshot eyes snapping.

Alex nodded. "Miss Sheridan's okay, but her sister is dead. The villagers think it was suicide."

Rudge swore, slapping a frustrated hand against his thigh. "Gambrielli, you think?"

"It would seem so. Miss Sheridan is, of course, convinced, and—"

"Dash it—the bounder has escaped again!" Rudge interrupted. "They telegraphed Cambridge, and the station guard passed the message along to me. Got here as soon as I could. Dawson has closed his account in the Peterborough bank. Claimed his sister died and he was returning to America. Of course the sister would actually be Miss Sheridan's."

"It's possible." Alex sensed movement behind them. Mrs. Mitford had opened the door, her face questioning. At Alex's reassuring nod she withdrew, shutting the door.

"There are complications. Miss Sheridan claims there is a—"

"How did the sister die, then? This development certainly lends a woeful credibility to our hypothesis that Dawson is actually Dante Gambrielli. How did she ring off, did you say? Gambrielli usually strangles his victims, though your report claims there have also been a drowning, two arranged falls—"

Alex straightened and fixed an unblinking gaze upon the inspector. After a moment, Rudge stopped midsentence, then began cracking his knuckles. "Beg pardon, MacKay." He shrugged. "It's just that my mind . . ." He hunched his lanky shoulders and jammed his hands into the pockets of his shapeless mackintosh. "Ah . . . what was it you were saying?"

"Miss Sheridan," Alex repeated patiently, "claims her sister hid a journal somewhere that contains enough evidence, if not to convict her husband, at least to lead us to evidence that *will* convict him. Until we find it, though, proving Dawson and Gambrielli are the same will still take a bit of digging."

Rudge's face lit up. "Ah yes. Forgot to tell you. We received word just before I left London, from the chairman of the Parish Council in a village in Lincolnshire, concerning the disappearance of a local villager there." The hands popped out and Rudge rubbed them together, then enthusiastically cracked every knuckle. "It appears she married a gent this past summer whose moniker happened to be 'Gambrielli.' I'll be headed there after you apprise me of the developments here."

"Any chance of locating a sample of handwriting? Something we could compare to Dawson's signature at the London and Peterborough banks?" Alex queried. "And do you have the Rogue's Gallery file cards I gave you on Gambrielli, with his other aliases?"

Rudge nodded. "I'll have a go at the handwriting. I'm off to Peterborough after my investigation in Nettlesby." He stared at Alex, then scanned the vicarage. "I . . . ah . . .

rather expected you would accompany me."

Alex glanced over his shoulder. Mrs. Mitford hadn't returned, so Eve must still be sleeping. "I have more pressing commitments here," he revealed, smiling a little at Rudge's surprise. Then he added, his voice so calm as to sound prosaic, "Leoni is here."

Rudge gawked, and for five solid seconds he remained speechless. Alex's smile deepened. The exhausting night and subsequent pacing while he waited for the long arm of Scotland Yard's Criminal Investigation Department melted away at the spectacle of a momentarily flabbergasted Inspector Rudge. "I believe Avery Paxton ordered Leoni here, not to escape from us, but to hunt down Giles Dawson, and probably kill him. Motivation at this point still unknown."

"Where is he?" Rudge sputtered, shaking his head. "Don't tell me you've allowed his escape. And what about Miss Sheridan? Taken to her bed, has she, from the shock? I trust the villagers here have provided sufficient succor. Poor lady, this is a nasty business for—"

"Last night the *poor lady*," Alex informed him dryly, "saved my skin—for the second time." The memory alarmed, amazed, and amused him still. "She walloped Leoni with a bronze statue of an elephant."

The front door reopened and Mrs. Mitford waved to Alex, then approached, her manner contrite. "I do beg your pardon, but you asked that I inform you immediately upon Miss Sheridan's awakening."

"It's quite all right. Thank you, Mrs. Mitford." Alex introduced her to Inspector Rudge, and after a gracious greeting the vicar's wife excused herself. Alex turned to Rudge. "Leoni's locked in a stall at the blacksmith's. Go down High Street, take the first right—he's at the end of the lane. I'll join you shortly."

Rudge snorted. "I would have thought you'd sweated him already and secured whatever information you could."

"He was still unconscious when I left him last night,"

Alex said, striding up the path. "Thanks for arriving as soon as you could." He was speaking to the gatepost; Rudge had already leaped into the chaise and was turning the horse.

Shaking his head, Alex loped up the path and ducked inside the rectory. Mrs. Mitford smiled. "She's quite all right this morning, Mr. MacKay. A most unusual young lady."

"You have the way of it, Mrs. Mitford, but then . . ." He swept a courtly bow, grinning. "So are you."

The woman's cheeks pinkened, and she laughed. "Oh my, but you're a rogue, aren't you, Mr. MacKay?" She led the way into the sitting room, shaking her head. "Sit yourself down, and I'll bring you a cuppa. Miss Sheridan should be along shortly."

Alex was gazing through a stereopticon, enjoying three-dimensional views of the Holy Land, when Eve entered the room. "Good morning," she greeted him, looking amazingly fresh, as if last night's encounter had never happened. Alex straightened, his gaze moving over her. He reconsidered his first impression. She *did* look composed in her fresh shirtwaist and gored skirt, hair again bound in the severe figure eight at the base of her neck. But the dark eyes and somber face still reflected the strain of the past twenty-four hours.

"You look lovely," he announced gallantly. "No nightmares, lingering aches, or residual terrors?"

That prompted a shy smile. "No. *You* certainly act like a barn cat who's tipped over the butter churn." She walked over to his side. "I looked through this last night. Mrs. Mitford says it was a gift from an American minister they met in the Holy Land."

"A somewhat extravagant gift," Alex observed.

"Perhaps, but not when you learn that Mrs. Mitford nursed the gentleman through a bout of dysentery, and the rector prayed by his bedside for four solid days."

"They are good people," Alex agreed, stacking the stereographs back in a neat pile. "This village is fortunate to have such godly spiritual shepherds." He slanted Eve a sideways glance. "Tell me how you are," he commanded, his voice soft, but determined.

She made a dismissive gesture with her hand. "I slept. It still doesn't seem real, somehow. Giles Dawson and Avery Paxton . . . Joe Leoni. Rebecca. Probably not having seen her for so long is helping to cushion the reality. I . . . I'm still trying to avoid thinking about it, I suppose."

"But you've accepted that what happened was not a manifestation of God's wrath inflicted upon the innocent to punish your indiscretions."

Eve wrinkled her nose at him. "You *are* feeling your oats this morning, aren't you, Mr. MacKay?" She sighed. "I'm trying. When I woke up, I spent a long time mulling what you told me last night. I . . . *want* to believe you, if that matters. I want to believe your interpretation of God's more loving eye." Her mouth curved. "A bit like the Agency's motto, but with spiritual overtones. *The Eye That Never Sleeps.* Actually . . ." A look of dawning wonder lightened the shadows in her face, "I believe I *do* feel more . . . peaceful."

Alex wanted to sweep her into his arms. "Ah—here's Mrs. Mitford, with what looks to be some delicious tea cakes. You're spoiling us sinfully, madam."

"Piffle," Mrs. Mitford scoffed good-naturedly, rolling a tea trolley into the room. "Such a golden tongue you have, Mr. MacKay. Are you sure you're not Irish?"

Alex effected horrified dismay, causing both ladies to laugh. In the midst of their merriment, the front bell jangled, followed by frantic pounding on the door.

"Heaven above!" exclaimed Mrs. Mitford.

Alex strode for the door, glancing at Eve as he passed. Her skin had bleached to the color of salt, but she met his concerned look with a brave smile and followed him out of the room.

"The inspector sent me along here," puffed a gangling young man wearing a rumpled butcher's apron. "Be you Mr. MacKay?"

"I am."

The agitated fellow waved behind him, words tumbling forth in a torrent. "The rum blighter's escaped! He whopped the smith somethin' proper, he did, and the inspector sent me to summon the Pinkerton man at the rectory." He paused, gasping, and Alex plunged into the lull.

"Joe Leoni has escaped? When was this discovered? No—never mind. I'll come immediately."

"I'm coming too," Eve piped in at his shoulder.

Alex looked down at the messenger. "Tell the inspector I'm on my way." He dug into his pocket and flipped the surprised and pleased youth a coin. "You're a good lad. Thanks."

"I suppose," Eve ventured after a moment of stunned silence, "we need to consider how best to proceed next?"

Alex stuffed his hands deep in his pockets. "Aye. I'll go fetch Inspector Rudge." He looked down at Eve, his expression fierce. "Wait here, inside—and stay alert. Will you do that?"

Slowly, she nodded. Alex relaxed a bit, then looked beyond Eve to the vicar's wife. "With your permission?"

"She'll be safe here, Mr. MacKay," the astute Mrs. Mitford promised. "But it might be best if you refrain from dawdling at the smithy."

Alex nodded shortly, looked once more at Eve, then stepped outside, quietly shutting the door.

44

THIRTY MINUTES LATER ALEXANDER returned with a fuming Inspector Rudge. Mrs. Mitford ushered them into the parlor, then excused herself. "I promised to meet the organist at the church. Please, my dears—stay as long as is necessary."

"A tactful woman," the C.I.D. inspector observed after her departure. He strode over to Eve. "Inspector Thomas Rudge, at your service, Miss Sheridan. I am deeply sorry for the circumstances, but am pleased to make your acquaintance."

Eve started to reply, but Inspector Rudge had already turned back to Alexander. "The blacksmith told me Leoni struck him some time around dawn, to the best of his knowledge."

Alexander crossed over to Eve. "The inspector," he told her dryly, "shares your distaste for frivolous social chitchat. I suggest, however, that we at least enjoy the rest of Mrs. Mitford's tea cakes, while we discuss the best way to proceed."

Inspector Rudge clapped his hands together. "Capital idea. Ah . . . Miss Sheridan? Would you care to pour?"

Eve chewed the inside of her cheek to keep from smiling, and obediently poured tea for them all. The realization that she even *wanted* to smile was a relief. "I've been wondering," she ventured at last, "about a couple of things."

"Only a couple?" Alexander inserted.

Eve glanced down, a saucy retort springing to her lips, until she caught the strain in his face. *Why, he's as upset and angry as the inspector!* she realized, touched by his efforts to nurture her flicker of humor in spite of the circumstances.

She sat down on a low stool across from the two men and mustered a reciprocal grin. "Only a couple of questions *right now*," she amended. "Joe Leoni—and the journal. Is that why he was at the cottage?"

"Very good question, of course. I would say—"

"Ah yes," Inspector Rudge inserted, almost as if he hadn't noticed that Alexander was speaking. "I suggested to Mr. MacKay here that Joe Leoni would not have remained in the area, deliberately attacking you in the cottage, risking detection and the gaol, if he did not have a rather strong motivation to do so. Unfortunately, until we track him down, his knowledge, or the lack thereof, of Mrs. Dawson's journal cannot be definitively ascertained."

"That's why I suggested—"

"To that end," the inspector plunged on, cracking his knuckles and ignoring Alexander, "I feel it would be prudent to interrogate the villagers. Perhaps in their interaction with Mrs. Dawson, before her—" He paused, stroking his nose, then changed direction. "Perhaps we can discover additional information."

Inspector Rudge finally paused to sip his tea, and Eve jumped in at the lull. "I noticed when I was searching the bedroom that all of Rebecca's clothes are missing. Mr. Dawson might have already shipped them to America, but I did wonder." It was difficult to say his name without shuddering.

Alexander smiled down at her, almost as if he understood. "A very good question indeed," he murmured. "Inspector, perhaps while you continue your interrogation of the village from this end, Miss Sheridan and I will proceed to the other, and we can meet at the village shop."

The inspector leaped to his feet, scattering crumbs and almost overtipping the cup he placed on the edge of the table. "Excellent. I'll be off, then. Miss Sheridan, New Scotland Yard will do its utmost to bring your sister's murderer, as well as Joe Leoni, to justice." He grabbed a dusty black bowler. "Mr. MacKay, I will meet you at the tea shop presently."

After he left, a ringing silence descended. Eve began gathering the dishes. "Alexander?"

"Hmm?" He was watching her with a steady regard Eve found unsettling, though she tried to ignore it.

"About Rebecca's clothes—shouldn't we also look for the person who packed them? I can't imagine Giles would have done that, after he . . ." She swallowed hard and busied herself stacking plates on the tea trolley. "I just wondered," she finished feebly.

"We'll start with those row houses closest to the cottage." Alexander rose and reached Eve's side in one long step. "I'll take this to the kitchen for you, then we'll leave." He nudged her aside and pushed the trolley toward the doorway, then paused to glance over his shoulder. Your questions show a canny sense of detecting, Miss Sheridan. If ever you tire of studying your birds, I think you'd make a bonny Pinkerton operative."

45

Brandon
Norfolk, England

THE RED LION HOTEL CATERED to a constant flow of railway travelers. Dante Gambrielli, clean-shaven but for a false pencil-thin moustache, calculated that no one would recognize him in his present guise.

Few people paid attention to other individuals around them unless they were remarkably different, or drew undue attention toward themselves. Dante had learned how to make use of both those human predilections. He swept back the folds of a new fur-lined cape, doffed the matching beaver top hat, and donned a pair of Franklin spectacles. Then he stepped up to the desk, peered down at the clerk, and pompously demanded the best room available.

"I shall be here at least a week," he announced. "I expect a working radiator in the room, a window—with a view, of course—and tea service promptly at my door by seven each morning." He produced a ten-pound note and slapped it down in front of the bug-eyed clerk. "If those demands are met sufficiently, I will in turn sufficiently reward an obliging staff."

The clerk, a young man whose high-necked collar forced his chin to tilt at an uncomfortable angle, eyed the money, then Dante. "I'm sure we can handle all your needs to your satisfaction," he promised. The bank note disappeared, and with a flourish Dante signed the guest register. The clerk turned it around, his eye scanning the signature. "Thank you, Mr. . . . Dorset."

An hour later, dressed in casual clothes and wearing a false beard, Dante strolled through the lobby and out the front door. He looked completely ordinary, like any middle-class Britisher on holiday. The clerk didn't acknowledge his presence by so much as a lifted brow. Dante struck a match on the bottom of his scuffed work boot, then lit a cigar. A small courtyard off the hotel restaurant was filled with wrought-iron benches and tables, now deserted. Dante consulted his watch, then wandered over to one of the benches to smoke his cigar and plan.

Beatrice would be expecting him for Boxing Day, the day after Christmas. That gave Dante almost a month. Smoking and thinking, he assessed his activities of the past few weeks, making sure he had covered his tracks sufficiently.

His first warning letter to Avery had reached New York weeks earlier, threatening the same exposure with which Avery had threatened Dante. The arrogance of the bloated toad, who didn't even possess the strength of character to take charge of his own destiny!

He wished he could have been present to watch Avery squirm over the revelation of Rebecca's journal. His dear wife, he had told Avery, used to talk about "Mr. Paxton's skillful matchmaking," all of which had been recorded— with every detail—in the journal.

Dante leaned forward, his elbows on his knees, his cigar dangling from limp fingers. Memories engulfed him, images still so painful that he winced at their recollection. When he found the journal, he still didn't know whether he would keep or destroy it.

A noisy crowd of men and women streamed into the hotel, their laughter jarring him back to the present. He ran his hand gingerly over the full beard and sideburns to make sure everything was still in place, and suppressed all memory of Rebecca.

The courtship with Beatrice Linwood was progressing nicely, and he planned to seal their betrothal on Boxing Day, with her father and aunt as eager witnesses. By the following summer, as Denham Granville, he would be living on a comfortable estate in Suffolk, safe from Avery Paxton and those blasted Pinkerton detectives.

Only one small task remained unresolved.

Dante ground out the cigar. He would enjoy a leisurely meal as the demanding Mr. Dorset, then reapply the full beard and hairpiece and don the casual middle-class clothes that assured his anonymity. Upper Dereford was less than an hour's jaunt, and it would be a simple matter to slip into the cottage unnoticed, around midnight. All the villagers would be asleep then.

He discovered a livery some six blocks from the hotel, one with which he had had no past dealings. He waited while a couple returned a wagon, and two young men argued over the condition of their mounts. Finally the phlegmatic little hostler cocked a long-suffering look at Dante. "I require a lighted conveyance, enclosed, for one night, with a horse that doesn't spook on dark country lanes," he said.

"That's what they all want," the hostler observed, casually spitting into a filthy brass spittoon. "Which road will you be taking?"

Dante thought about ignoring the question, then shrugged. "Upper Dereford. Why?"

"Been a lot o' rain hereabouts. Some roads are impassable in a gig. That one'll do, though." He scratched a bristly chin, looking thoughtful. "Lot o' folk taking that road lately."

"Oh?"

The hostler shuffled down the dimly lit aisle of the barn, talking over his shoulder. "Aye, lot o' folk. You be the second gent in as many days—he was American, too, he was."

Joe Leoni pushed through the pub's door, his mood vicious. He ordered whiskey, then made his way to the darkest corner where he sat nursing the drink, a bruised arm, and a throbbing headache.

He still couldn't believe what had happened. The Sheridan skirt. Again, here in England. He was sure of it. Even in the moonlight, her red hair had been impossible to miss—and the crafty mug who'd floored him had to be a Pink. Shiver could smell 'em a mile away, and he figured this was probably the gent he had slashed back in Richmond. If so, he had suffered a long voyage for nothing, because very soon now Dante Gambrielli would be joining all his unfortunate wives. Shiver, of course, was too smart for *any* flatfoot—as he had proven many a time.

A sly grin inched across Shiver's face, and his hand slid down to pat his knife before he remembered that it was gone. Fresh rage consumed him. His fingers *itched* for that knife. It had been one of his favorites, with an elaborately carved ivory handle . . . and now the Pink had it. *You'll get yours,* Shiver promised silently. *Both you and that interfering canary will get what's coming to you.*

46

Upper Dereford
Norfolk, England

AT THE ROW OF CONNECTED HOUSES down the lane from Bramble Cottage, responses to Alex's polite inquiries ranged from avid curiosity to suspicion, with one blistering harangue from an elderly man who accused them of being Irish anarchists.

"Perhaps I should do the talking," Eve suggested after the door was slammed in their faces. "Your brogue is showing."

Alex ducked his head sheepishly. "It will do that," he acknowledged with a slight smile. Then he sobered. "I'm not liking the feel of this," he muttered, half to himself. How many of the sidelong glances and inhospitable attitudes stemmed from the local perception that Rebecca's death had been a suicide? Grimly he took Eve's arm as they started up the path to the last house.

She gave a tremulous smile. "You don't have to coddle me, Alexander. I didn't expect anything different."

God, Alex fumed heavenward, *do something, won't You?* After a reflective pause, he tacked on a more conciliatory prayer: *But if not yet, I'll try to keep my frustration from throwing a spanner in Your workings. . . .*

He knocked on the door, then stepped aside with a

mocking bow. It opened to reveal a woman wearing a voluminous striped apron. Her thick black hair was covered by an old-fashioned muslin mobcap. She glanced at Eve only briefly, then transferred her gaze to Alex. A hint of coy speculation flitted across her face. She would have been pretty some ten years earlier, Alex observed. He returned her smile, though he didn't speak.

"My name is Eve Sheridan," Eve began. "I'm Rebecca Dawson's sister, and—"

"I know," the woman interrupted. "The whole village is nattering about you and the Scotsman here." The coy gaze warmed to frank flirtation. "Are you really a highwayman?" she asked him, ignoring Eve.

"Don't be ridiculous," Eve snapped, earning startled looks from Alex as well as the woman. "He's a detective, and he's helping me find out about my sister's death. It was *not* suicide."

The woman's face closed up as completely as if Eve had just called her an uncomplimentary name. "I only met her a time or two, in the village. I can't help you." Now her tone was guarded, even grudging.

Alex heaved an inner sigh. Eve had little understanding of rural English villages, and unfortunately, when she decided on a course, her manner reminded him of a team of runaway horses. "Well, we're sorry to hear that, of course," he said. His smile banished some of the woman's hostility. He touched the brim of his cap. "Do hope we didn't disturb you unduly." He clasped Eve's elbow in a firm grip.

"Well . . . I can't say as I minded overmuch." Placated, the woman opened the door wider, stepping completely outside. Her manner might be more conciliatory, Alex noted with rising interest, but she was hiding something. He sensed it, *felt* the undercurrent of fear even though he had been able to charm her into lowering her guard a bit.

"I think I would have preferred a highwayman to a detective, but I still can't help you." She wiped her hands on her apron, the movement tugging its bib down so that the top gaped open at the woman's neck.

Eve gasped. She elbowed past Alex to grab the older woman's arm. "Where did you get that?" she demanded. "The brooch—*where did you get it?*"

The woman pulled free, her hand protectively covering the brooch pinned to her collar—pearl and turquoise, shaped like two intertwined hearts. She stepped back. "Get away from me! What manner of person are you, attacking a—"

Eve cut her off. "That brooch was my sister's." Her voice raised the hairs on Alex's neck. "And it was a gift. From me. And as for what manner of person I am, I'm the person who will personally rip every strip of clothing from your skin if you don't—" Her voice wavered. "If you don't remove that brooch and give it to me immediately!"

Consternation, alarm, and guilt chased across the black-haired woman's countenance. She would have fled back inside, but Alex inserted one of his big feet across the stoop to prevent the door from closing. He glanced down at Eve, whose expression stabbed into him like Leoni's knife. "There's a C.I.D. inspector at the other end of the village," he rumbled, his voice uncharacteristically hard. "You've no hope of escape, and lying will only make the ordeal worse for us all. Tell Miss Sheridan now, and quickly, how you came by the brooch." He held out his hand. "What's your name?"

She pressed her lips together, but she was no match for Alex. "Harriet Crabtree. Mrs. Crabtree to you. And I didn't steal it!"

"Perhaps you should hand it over," Alex murmured.

Harriet Crabtree glared at Eve. "Maybe *she's* lying. . . ."

Alex stepped closer. "Hand it over."

Mrs. Crabtree paled. Her fingers felt for the brooch and fumbled with the clasp. "Here, then. But I didn't pinch it!"

"She wouldn't have given it to you," Eve said, her voice hoarse. "I gave it to her on her wedding day, and she promised me she'd always . . ." Her fist pressed against her mouth, and she averted her head.

Mrs. Crabtree's defiance and hostility withered. "I'm sorry," she repeated, and this time Alex could see she meant it. "I didn't know."

"How did you come by it?" he asked.

"Mr. Dawson asked me if I'd clean the place up, like." She gestured to her mobcap and apron. "I've a thing for being orderly. Me mum . . ." She sighed, tucking a strand of hair behind her ear, her gaze resting on Eve. "He was in a sorry state over your sister. Mr. Dawson's a fine gentleman. He . . . he came to me first. After he found her, lying there on the floor with her throat split wide open, all covered with—"

With a little gasp, Eve fainted into Alex's arms.

47

CONSCIOUSNESS RETURNED in uncomfortable stages, as if she were viewing blurred scenes through a faulty stereopticon. Eve groaned, a sound of frustration more than pain. "What a stupid, useless thing to do," she mumbled.

A strong arm moved around her shoulders, steadying her. "Easy, Miss Sheridan."

Eve's vision focused, sharpening first on Alexander, then on Harriet Crabtree, who was just coming into the room with a tray and three glasses. "Where's my sister's brooch?"

"I have it in my pocket," Alexander promised. "It's quite safe."

Eve pressed a hand to her throbbing temples and glared at Alexander. "I do *not* faint," she insisted. "I experienced a . . . a momentary dizziness is all." Her fumbling fingers moved to her throat, where she discovered that several of the buttons had been unfastened. "What. . . ?"

"You needed to breathe freely, to . . . ah . . . alleviate your dizziness," Alexander replied. He took a glass from

240

the tray and pressed it to her lips. "Here. Mrs. Crabtree fetched some lemonade."

Eve snatched the glass and waved Alexander away. "I'm fine." She drank, embarrassment warring with stubbornness . . . and pain. "That was certainly a useless thing to do. I . . . beg your pardon. It won't happen again."

"I shouldn't have said what I did about your sister," Mrs. Crabtree offered. She had removed her mobcap and apron, and Eve realized the woman was actually very attractive.

Eve's discomfort deepened. To hide it, she began refastening buttons, her gaze wandering about the tiny room. It was plain but tidy, with none of the clutter that filled Rebecca's cottage.

Alexander intervened, his voice kind. "Mrs. Crabtree, would you mind terribly if Miss Sheridan stayed here with you a few more moments, until she's recovered completely? I need to fetch Inspector Rudge, who will want to talk with you as well."

Mrs. Crabtree flushed. "Why should I talk to *him*?" she retorted. "I gave you the brooch, didn't I?"

Eve sneaked a quick glimpse, first at Harriet Crabtree, then at Alexander. She was not surprised when the older woman stepped back.

"I haven't done anything wrong!" She whirled, appealing to Eve. "Tell him!"

"That's not for me to determine," Eve returned slowly, a modicum of self-respect restored when a look of approval warmed Alexander's eyes. "Perhaps, while he's gone, you can talk with me. You say Mr. Dawson asked you to . . . to clean their cottage? Was it you who packed my sister's clothes?"

Mrs. Crabtree drew herself up. "I did. Mr. Dawson promised he would have them shipped back to America but asked if I'd keep them until he made the arrangements. I haven't seen him since the funeral. The trunk is in my bedroom." She jerked her chin at Alexander. "I told him there already, while you were—"

241

"Thank you. That was very kind." Eve dropped her gaze to her hands, inwardly squirming. A loosened hairpin slipped free, falling into her lap. She covered it with her hand and tried not to think about her frazzled appearance.

"Mrs. Crabtree," Alexander said, "I'm sure Miss Sheridan would appreciate some kind words of comfort. Something, for instance, that will provide . . . gentler? . . . memories of her only sister."

Iron over down feathers, Eve mused. That's what Alexander was—a strong, dangerous man who tempered his extraordinary power with phenomenal control. For some reason, he was angry with Harriet Crabtree, far more than Eve felt the circumstances warranted. *But why?*

"Alexander—" she began. She realized she had called him by his first name only when Mrs. Crabtree shot her a swift look of astonishment.

He put on his cap. "I'll be back soon, Miss Sheridan," he promised. At the door, he turned. "Mrs. Crabtree?"

Beside Eve the older woman stiffened. "Yes?"

"Consider, if you will, the benefits of returning any other objects with which you might have . . . rewarded yourself before I return with the inspector. Your conscience will rest much easier." The door shut gently behind him.

Eve sat back on Harriet Crabtree's faded, old-fashioned settee. *Something* was afoot here, but her fuzzy brain couldn't fit any of the pieces together.

"You don't look anything like your sister."

Flushing, Eve inclined her head. "I know. Rebecca was very beautiful, full of gaiety." Her throat closed.

Mrs. Crabtree was looking at her with a peculiar expression. "She may have been . . . before. But she changed. You're not exactly an ugly duck yourself."

Eve shook her head. "Rebecca was beautiful," she insisted. She halfheartedly lifted a hand to rearrange her hair, then dropped it, too dispirited to bother. Besides, she would *never* be beautiful. Not like Rebecca, or even this Harriet Crabtree, who in spite of her work clothes and jaded air had captured Alexander's immediate interest.

She should be digging for answers instead of fretting over physical appearances. Her sister had been murdered. Eve sat up, irritated with herself, refusing to wallow further in self-pity. "What did Mr. MacKay mean by his last remark?" she asked.

Mrs. Crabtree shrugged. "Would you like some more lemonade, or perhaps tea?" she inquired.

"Thank you, but no. What I would like is an answer to my question." She stood, steadying herself on the back of the settee, her gaze searching the room. "Mrs. Crabtree, Mr. MacKay is not the sort of gentlemen with whom a person ought to trifle." She smiled a little. "He doesn't react very well to deception—trust me on that."

"Who does he think he is?" the woman sniffed. "Big, ruddy bully, that's what. Treating me like a common thief, he was."

"I witnessed nothing but courtesy," Eve refuted. "And he never so much as raised his voice."

"He didn't need to." Harriet Crabtree's countenance turned speculative, almost dreamy. "I've always had a soft spot for a man like that . . . Mr. Dawson, you know, has that certain way of looking at a woman, too."

"Comparing Giles Dawson to Alexander MacKay is like comparing a vulture to a golden eagle," Eve snapped. "They are nothing alike. *Nothing!*"

Mrs. Crabtree tilted her head to the side, a knowing grin spreading across her face. "So that's the way the wind blows, ducky. Well, I did wonder a mite, when you called him by his Christian name, so familiar-like. And the way he looked at you when he carried you in here after you swooned, as if you were—" She stopped. "Ah, well. Never mind, then."

With a deprecating grimace she left the room, returning a moment later with a dilapidated bandbox, which she dumped on the settee beside Eve. "After what he said, and the way he looked at me . . . I'll never have a moment's peace if I don't at least let you take a gander. Mind you," she finished a shade defensively, "Mr. Dawson *did* tell me I could help myself, so I *wasn't* filching none of it."

Eve stared at the box, then up at the blowsy, defiant woman. With unsteady fingers she untied the string and lifted off the lid.

She barely noticed the jumbled tangle of Becca's lace-edged hankies, two pairs of gloves, a glass paperweight, and several other trinkets; her gaze fell transfixed on the smiling face of the Matryoshka doll, tossed carelessly on top of the pile.

48

"*YOU* HAD IT." ALMOST IN A TRANCE, Eve lifted the wooden doll out. "Did you open this?"

Mrs. Crabtree nodded, her gaze anxious. "I was careful—it's not been damaged. I had never seen anything like it. They're so clever, what with the smaller dolls inside, each one exactly like the others."

"Was anything inside one of the smaller dolls?"

"No—but then I couldn't open but two of them." She hesitated, then blurted, "Can I have it back?"

Eve was twisting them open, dropping each piece in the box, but at the plaintive question she paused. "I'm not sure," she began, her hands struggling with the next two pieces. As Mrs. Crabtree had warned, they were stuck fast. "My parents gave one to each of us when we were children. This one was Rebecca's."

"Oh." Her face fell.

Eve barely noticed. "Do you have any sort of lard, or cream? No . . . perhaps a sharp knife would be better. Something we can pry between the crack."

"I'd hate for it to break. It's the most wondrous trinket I've ever owned. Nobody in the village has anything like it." She left the room and returned shortly with a butter knife. Reluctantly she thrust it out. "Here. Try this."

"Thank you." Eve took the proffered knife and, after several attempts, managed to slip it under the top half of the doll. She worked it back and forth, and though she tried to be careful, in her desperation she still chipped off some of the paint. Hovering at her shoulder, Mrs. Crabtree groaned in despair.

Eve twisted the halves again—and the doll broke open. A smaller doll tumbled out. In spite of Eve's hurried fumbling, those two halves easily twisted apart . . . and a small brass key fell into her lap.

Alexander found Inspector Rudge at the village shop, where he was chatting with the proprietor, a phlegmatic chap who also served as the village postmaster.

"Mrs. Dawson posted a parcel two days before she died," Rudge greeted Alex, cracking his knuckles in elation. "It was addressed to Miss Sheridan!"

Alex greeted the proprietor and asked a few questions of his own. After thanking the relieved man, he and Rudge left.

"Cable your superior," Rudge ordered. "He can fetch the parcel from Miss Sheridan's residence and determine the contents. If it is in fact the journal, your Agency can cable back any pertinent findings. In the interim—"

"You and I will return to the home of Mrs. Harriet Crabtree," Alex finished smoothly. He related the events of the past hour to the inspector as the horse headed down High Street at a teeth-rattling trot.

Mrs. Crabtree opened the door, her expression resigned. Behind her, Eve leaped up from the settee. "I found a key!" she proclaimed, waving it. "Mrs. Crabtree had the rest of Rebecca's nesting dolls, and the key was inside. Just like I predicted!"

Alex removed his cap, then casually smoothed his rumpled hair. "I'm relieved you chose to do the right thing," he murmured to Mrs. Crabtree.

The woman ducked her head, then lifted it to meet

Eve's bewildered look. "I was hoping he wouldn't notice. When you fainted, and he was looking after you, I slipped it out like, while his back was turned. But he had already seen it on the mantel." She tilted her head, then observed archly, "You've a fine pair of eyes, Mr. MacKay. I'd not mind them looking upon me like you did your lady friend, even if you *are* a blooming detective."

Eve began sputtering, her complexion turning a deep rose. Alex grinned without replying and walked over to Rudge. He was examining the key, oblivious to Mrs. Crabtree's impertinent observations. "Could be to a diary, or a small box," he muttered. "We'll have to search the cottage."

"Harriet and I have already searched through Rebecca's trunk," Eve announced. "There was nothing there that the key fit."

"Better have another go at the cottage, then." Rudge rubbed his hands together. "I will be able to assist you for a while, then I'm off to Brandon to catch the evening mail express. Mr. MacKay?"

"Miss Sheridan and I will follow a little bit later."

"What about Joe Leoni?" Eve asked.

"He might have recognized you last night. You won't be safe until you're out of the country," Alex warned.

Eve, naturally, embarked on a spirited debate. "It was too dark, and I was behind him."

"I am not willing to risk your life on it," Alex shot back. He picked up the jumbled halves of the nesting dolls and began putting them back together. "We'll go back to the cottage with Inspector Rudge. But we need to leave for Brandon before dark. The road between here and there is a desolate, lonely stretch."

"Ah. You will be joining me, then?" Rudge concluded, sounding pleased.

Alex shook his head. "Not until I've escorted Miss Sheridan back to Liverpool and seen her onto the first available New York packet." Before Eve could launch any more objections, he turned back to her. "Rebecca mailed you a parcel over a week ago. It would be helpful, don't you agree, for you to return immediately to Richmond? There's a very good possibility she has mailed you the journal."

"And if this key goes to something entirely different?"

"We won't know that until we find the journal." He glanced at Rudge. "We'll ride over together in the buggy. But once we're there, it might be best to let you precede us into the cottage. I'll keep an eye on you while I stay with Miss Sheridan in the buggy. When you verify that the cottage is still empty, we'll join you."

"You'd send him in alone?" Eve shook her head. "What if Leoni *is* hiding in there, like a rattlesnake waiting to strike?"

An unnerving expression of bloodthirsty anticipation filled Inspector Rudge's face. "Madam," he promised Eve, bowing and clicking his heels, "that is a prospect devoutly to be wished."

Alex grinned. "Save a piece for me, if your wish is granted. I owe him."

Moments later they took their leave. Dumfounded, Alex watched Eve's parting from Harriet Crabtree. Eve held the bandbox, her fingers lovingly caressing all the contents. Suddenly she thrust it back into the other woman's hands.

"I want you to have it," she explained haltingly to the stunned Englishwoman. "It's not my place to judge your actions, and I *am* grateful that you chose to give it back. Besides, I think perhaps Rebecca would have wanted you to have everything, especially the Matryoshka doll. You're as fascinated by it as she once was." Her voice thickened. "My sister did *not* commit suicide, Mrs. Crabtree. She was murdered. When I find the lock that belongs to this key, I know I'll be able to not only prove that—but also prove who did it."

Alex's last memory of Harriet Crabtree was of her standing in the doorway, hugging the nesting doll to her bosom.

It was a little past one. Shiver's luck at last seemed to be changing for the better; the lane from Weeting to Upper Dereford had been deserted, and he reached the hay shed undetected. There was just enough room inside for the horse and cart.

Shiver slipped out and made his way down the rutted path that followed the edge of the field. The sun blazed in a clear blue sky, warming his back. It also made his head ache. He felt the side of his head, probing the swollen, still-tender bruise that ran from temple to cheek. He had a matching one on his arm.

Eve Sheridan would not escape a third time, because he wasn't—

Abruptly he dropped to all fours. Curse it! He couldn't believe his eyes! His hand closed over the long knife he had pinched from the fishmonger's an hour earlier.

A buggy was headed down the lane toward the cottage, filled with three people. Two gents and a girl . . . with *red* hair. Shiver lay unmoving, his eyes following the buggy until the trees hid it from view.

They were going to the cottage.

Joe Leoni pounded the dirt in rage. It didn't take a genius to figure out who they were.

Paxton could retrieve the journal himself if it was in that cottage. Squirming on his belly in the moist, stinking earth, Shiver inched his way back to the hay shed. As for Gambrielli, the limeys were welcome to him as well. Truth be known, Shiver had never been too wild about hunting him down.

His association with Avery Paxton had been wearing thin, anyway. Shiver backed the horse and cart out of the shed and headed back down the road toward Brandon. Tomorrow he'd cable Paxton, but the message wouldn't be the news the boss hoped for.

If the big man wanted Gambrielli out of the way, he'd have to find himself another "associate." Joe Leoni had decided to go into business on his own.

And his first priority was a return trip to Richmond. That meddling piece of petticoat wouldn't hang about England very long.

49

Richmond

WILLIAM SHERIDAN STARED AT HIS bookkeeper in disbelief. "What did you say?"

"That was *my* reaction, sir." In the thin, bony face two spots of color burned bright on his cheekbones. "The bank insists the check *was* one of ours, Mr. Sheridan. I've personally investigated the matter with both their head teller and the individual bookkeeper."

William surged to his feet. "I'll have him strung from a flagpole in the middle of Wall Street!" he roared. His eye skewered the nervous clerk. "Where did he lay hold of our check, Alfred? You know my orders."

"I . . . don't know, Mr. Sheridan." The bookkeeper's Adam's apple bobbed convulsively. "If I'm not at my desk, I lock the checkbook in the drawer. The key is always on my person." He dug out a chain and dangled it from his waist. "See? It's just that . . . the checks used were from the end of the register, which is why I didn't discover the theft earlier."

Planting his palms on the desk, William bowed his head. He was boiling with such violent emotion that he was afraid to speak, for fear of saying words he might later regret. After a few moments of crackling silence he straightened. "Draft a letter immediately to every financial institution in the city. Tell them to hold all checks from Sheridan Investments and Securities until I personally vouch for them."

The harrowed bookkeeper wrung his hands. "Mr. Sheridan . . . sir . . . what if he writes a check in another city?" A sheen of sweat filmed his pallid face. "We could be ruined, Mr. Sheridan! Wiped out! Sir—what are we going to do?"

"We won't be ruined," William stated, his voice dead. *Damaged, hurt, and betrayed—but not ruined.* "We're going to notify Pinkerton's, Alfred." He walked over to the window and gazed out over Main Street. "If anyone can catch the filthy blackguards, *they* can."

"This is an outrage, Mr. Sheridan, particularly with the city just now recovering from financial panic earlier this year. Why would he *do* this to you, Mr. Sheridan?"

William didn't answer for a long time. Eventually, his voice hoarse, he said without turning around, "Go back to your desk, Alfred. We still have business to attend to, and many *honest* people who are depending on the financial well-being of this company."

"If we can't stop Mr. Paxton from writing checks on Sheridan Investment and Security funds, we'll have to close, like those other businesses, Mr. Sheridan! We'll go bankrupt!" He left, his fearful, whining voice echoing in William's plush office.

Unmoving, William stayed by the window, his gaze fixed down the street, on the waving American flag.

New York

Avery Paxton studied the report spread out on the massive rosewood desk, then glanced at the malodorous stool pigeon shifting from foot to foot in front of him. "You wouldn't be trying to deceive me, now, would you,

Sootie? You're prepared to swear what you just told me is the absolute truth."

Sootie twisted his cloth cap in his hands. "I swear it, Mr. Paxton!" His beady eyes darted about, looking, Avery realized, like a fearful rat searching for a hole. "I heared it straight from a—a friend of mine who just busted out o' the big house. He heard some big cheeses talking to a couple of gents, and one of them it was that said that name, plain as St. Patrick's church bell. It was 'Topper.' I swear it on my mother's grave. They were going to discuss it with the commissioner, he says." He wiped his runny nose on his sleeve. Avery shuddered. "I wouldn't lie to you, Mr. Paxton."

"Of course not, Sootie." He flipped open the lid of a cloisonne box and took out a quarter. "Here. I'll expect you next week, unless of course you hear mention of more names in which I would be interested."

After the grateful stooge scurried out, Avery rang for Amos, ordered brandy, and told the butler to bring it to the library. Over the next hour or so, sipping the brandy and thinking, Avery reached several inescapable conclusions.

If the Pinks had gotten to Topper, it was only a matter of time until the trail led back to Avery himself. Perhaps it was time to leave New York, to take his operation elsewhere.

"Amos," he inquired as the butler cleared away the tray, "have you been back down south since the war?"

"No, suh, Mr. Avery."

"I've always had a yearning to try a mint julep, Amos. And it's beginning to look as if this just might be the right time. . . ."

50

Upper Dereford
Norfolk, England

A THOROUGH SEARCH OF BRAMBLE Cottage
yielded no lock that fit the small brass key, no journal, and
no further clues. Inspector Rudge left for Brandon after
promising Eve that he would not rest until he tracked
down Giles Dawson's whereabouts. If her sister's widower
still roamed about England, the long arm of New Scotland Yard would eventually collar him.

"But without proof," Mr. Rudge reminded her, "I can't
arrest the man."

"I will find proof," Eve promised. The words bore the
weight of a sacred vow.

After the inspector disappeared around the bend, Eve
and Alexander returned to the rectory long enough to
thank the Mitfords and retrieve Eve's traveling bag.
Choked with emotion, Eve hugged the petite woman and
tried to thank the rector for Becca's funeral service.

"I only wish we could have helped her more while she
was still with us," the vicar confessed.

"My sister was a wonderful person," Eve told him,
"but she could be very shallow, and spiritual matters were
of little importance to her, I'm afraid. I used to try to talk
with her, but with little success. She avoided our minister

253

as well." Her voice frayed. "I can't help but wonder if I—"

Alexander interrupted. "Eve, you were not responsible for your sister's soul, any more than you were responsible for her death. You must accept that whatever decisions Rebecca made, she made herself."

"But I could have forced her to listen!"

"Miss Sheridan, God Himself doesn't *force* anyone to listen," Rev. Mitford reminded her. "The journey toward faith is one that must be taken alone."

"But God uses people for signposts," Eve argued. "We're supposed to point the way. I should have tried harder." She clutched her umbrella and the box of sandwiches Mrs. Mitford had prepared, then turned toward the buggy. "And I should have told my father about my misgivings over Mr. Dawson. Regardless of what you or anyone else tells me," she insisted, jerking her chin toward Alexander, "I didn't do what I should have done. And my sister is dead because of it."

"Your sister is dead because a vicious, evil man killed her," Alexander stated flatly, his face set. He turned to the vicar and his wife. "We *will* stay in touch. I thank God for you both." Before Eve could say anything else, his hands clamped about her waist and he lifted her into the buggy. The Mitfords waved, and with a touch of the whip Alex and Eve left Upper Dereford behind.

"Have you always been a bully?" Eve asked a little while later, mostly in a desperate attempt to keep from weeping. "Throwing me in the buggy, handling me as if I were a sack of flour—and in front of two godly people who probably won't respect me any longer."

True to form, Alexander chuckled. "Since when have you concerned yourself with being respectable?" He began whistling through his teeth. "As to handling you like a sack of flour, I'd have to disagree, though I suppose I *could* compare your waist to a stalk of wheat. Slender but firm it felt beneath my hands. I'm glad you don't wear a corset, by the way . . . not that you need one of those contraptions in the first place." He turned his head briefly, his eyes very blue in the chilly afternoon sunlight. "I enjoy holding you, Eve Sheridan. You're a bonny lass, with a spirit that flames as bright as your hair. Which," he tacked on in the same breath, as if he were remarking on the weather, "is about to slip free from the pins again."

"Wh—at?" Her hands fumbled beneath her hat. "Why are you talking to me this way?" she finally stuttered, looking everywhere but at Alexander. "You never have before."

"You're not feeling weepy any longer, are you?" he observed with a cheeky grin. "Wasn't that what you were after with your inflammatory observations?"

Eve's indignation—and that peculiar breathlessness—disintegrated. "I . . . yes." She lifted her chin and produced a smile. "Of course. How well you know me, Alexander. And I don't feel the least like weeping anymore." She jammed the last hairpin back in place, smiled another bright smile, and turned to contemplate the passing scenery. "November is a dreary month everywhere, isn't it? Everything is draped in grays and browns."

Alexander drew the buggy to a halt. A moment later Eve felt his hand, warm and strong, on her arm. "Eve . . . I didn't mean to hurt you just now."

"Don't be silly. I'm not hurt."

"Then why won't you turn around and face me?"

His gentle voice and warm hand disconcerted her, making her feel as if she were on the deck of a ship in the middle of a raging storm. "I'm looking for . . . pheasants. They're beautiful birds. Did you know that I abhor the obsession with using bird plumage in ladies' hats? You may have noticed my hats never have feathers because I feel so strongly about the matter."

"Eve . . ." Alexander whispered something low and musical sounding, the brogue caressing her as surely as the touch of his hand.

Eve glanced over her shoulder. "I will *not* be soft-soaped with your Scottish brogue, Alexander MacKay.

Besides, I thought only Irishmen could speak Gaelic." She shifted uneasily. "Hadn't we better be going? You said you wanted to be back in Brandon before dark."

"We've plenty of time." All of a sudden his hand clutched her shoulder. "Look! Over yonder!" His arm whipped out, inches from her nose, pointing beyond the fringe of woods to an open field. "A pheasant—a big rooster pheasant."

"Where?" Instantly diverted, Eve searched the field, following the direction of his finger. "Oh . . ." She held her breath, suspended in joy at the sight of the magnificent bird, calmly scratching through the stubble some thirty yards away. Sunlight danced and shimmered through the rich mahogany feathers. "Oh . . . isn't he beautiful?"

All of a sudden Alexander's hands were turning her around, drawing her closer. "Alexander?" she squeaked.

"The pheasant is beautiful—but not nearly as lovely as you, Eve." His finger stroked her cheek. "I do know you, you see, and because I do—I think it's time you and I admitted the truth."

"The truth?" Eve echoed. She felt hot, breathless, yet goose bumps rose on her skin, and she couldn't seem to still the trembling that had seized her. "The truth is, you're making me feel very uncomfortable," she admitted weakly.

His arms gathered her closer, so close his warmth seared her. With every breath, she inhaled the unique blend of wool, leather, and cedar that emanated from Alexander MacKay. Her hands lifted to push him away—but she might as well have shoved the trunk of a towering oak.

"Look at me," he ordered in a deep, lazy voice she had never heard before.

Eve shook her head. "No. You're—I'm—"

"You're what, Eve?"

"I'm afraid of you!" she blurted out. Her hands bunched into fists, and then, irrationally, she clung to the wool ulster. "I'm afraid of what I feel when you behave like this." She tried to take a deep breath but failed. "You make me feel safe, and warm, and . . . and *cherished*, almost as if I could be more of a woman, like Rebecca. But I know that's just a fanciful longing brought on by everything that has happened, and when I'm home again it will all be over. I'll be alone again." She stared hard at the triangular patch that secured the throat fastening of his cloak. Hot prickles chased the cold goose bumps up and down her spine, and she felt slightly nauseated. "Don't . . . do this, Alexander. Please. It will hurt too much, and I've had all the hurt I can bear."

His hands came up to cover hers. "Are you finished?" he asked.

Eve nodded, tensing.

"I'm glad you told me. At least I better understand what kind of demons I still have to battle." His fingers began removing the long hatpins, and before Eve found breath to object, her hat was tossed to the floor behind the buggy seat. "There," Alexander announced. "It's difficult, you see, to kiss a lass wearing a hat with a broad brim and rows of ribbons and bows."

Kiss? The last of Eve's breath exhaled in a whoosh. She tried to draw another, but Alexander's hand was cupping her chin, lifting it so that her eyes met the narrowed blue flames in his. Slowly his head lowered. Eve's eyes closed, and her body jerked as she felt the warm pressure of his lips against hers, the prickly brush of his moustache.

"Easy, lass," he murmured. "It's all right. Eve, you *are* an incredibly beautiful woman. . . ."

Eve's eyes opened. "I've never been kissed before," she whispered, color heating her cheeks.

"What a surprise," he teased, and his head ducked so that he could kiss her again. "You told me once that perhaps men were mentally deficient. It must be true." His finger stroked her cheekbone, then her jaw. "Because you're lovely."

She shook her head, but she couldn't bring herself to

257

push him away. "I'm not. Alexander . . . it's late."

The horse snorted and shook its head, rattling the harness. Across the field the pheasant screeched, then clumsily ran for cover. Eve jumped as if struck with the buggy whip, and laughing, Alexander drew her into a close embrace. "Aye . . . it's late." He hugged her, then set her back on her side. One long arm retrieved the hat and expertly placed it on her head. "There. Not a hair out of place, which for you is extraordinary. Of course, I must be extraordinary too—but then having four sisters helped. Would I make an efficient lady's maid, do you think?"

He was being kind, Eve thought. She had behaved like an empty-headed schoolgirl, and very doubtless her wretchedly expressive face had revealed the depth of her longing. Now, not only would Alexander know that she was an old maid who had never been kissed—he would also be burdened with the awful weight of her schoolgirl crush.

"Eve? You're gazing at me with such sad, solemn eyes. Was stealing a kiss so bad, then? Do you need to slap me, to remind me that you're a respectable young woman who would never dream of behaving with such *un*ladylike abandon? Whose life is the very picture of staid decorum, of careful, restrained—"

"All right, enough!" Eve blurted. For a minute they looked at each other, then Eve shyly laid her hand on Alexander's arm. "You made your point. Subtle, deft, as always—but you made your point." A reluctant smiled inched across her face. "Actually, until I met you, I always wondered why girls and their gentleman escorts seemed to disappear at all the picnics and riverboat excursions and fairs." Her color deepened. "Now I understand."

"Ah. So you *did* enjoy our kisses?" He lifted her hand on his forearm and brushed a kiss across her knuckles. "I'm glad, little redbird. Because I very much enjoyed kissing you." He released the brake and picked up the reins, clucking to the horse. "As for the future—that's in God's hands. But I promise you this, Eve Sheridan: no matter where you are, you're not going to be alone any longer."

For almost a mile they rode in silence, except for the steady clip-clopping of the horse's hooves and the rattle of the wheels. Eve couldn't tear her gaze away from the man beside her, nor could she curb the rise of hot air crowding her lungs, pressing against her heart.

When Alexander slowed the horse to a walk in order to maneuver a particularly deep rut, his head turned toward her. "Do you understand what I'm telling you, Eve?" he rumbled. His voice was deep, all traces of humor vanished.

Slowly, Eve nodded. She clasped her wrists in her lap very tightly. "I understand, Alexander," she whispered. But the rest of the way to Brandon she couldn't help but wonder if she had told Alexander a lie.

A large crowd from Norwich had arrived in town, and the boardinghouse where Eve had spent the previous night was full. The clerk sent them along to a large hotel farther down the street. "The Red Lion is quite nice," he promised.

There were two rooms available, to Eve's relief. While Alexander made the arrangements, she wandered about the lobby. A number of people were sitting on the chairs and sofas scattered around an indoor arboretum. Since it was a little past five, many of them were enjoying high tea. Too tired to pay much attention, Eve's gaze swept over a man sitting alone at a small table next to a large potted palm. His elegant hands, holding a copy of the London *Times*, tightened into fists, crushing the pages.

Alexander beckoned, and Eve hurried over. As they climbed the stairs after the porter, she glanced back around the lobby, wondering at the sudden unnerving sensation of being watched. Then she shook her head, gathered her skirts, and told herself to stop imagining the spectre of Giles Dawson lurking about, waiting to pounce.

51

Brandon
Norfolk, England

DID THEY KNOW ABOUT REBECCA?

Dante waited until Eve Sheridan and her escort disappeared up the stairs. Then he folded the paper, rose, and returned to his room. He locked the door and stared at his hands. They were shaking.

Eve Sheridan had come to visit her sister. That was all. She hadn't known . . . it was too soon for anyone in America to have found out. *Blast* the girl! It was too soon.

If she had been alone, her immediate elimination would have proven inconvenient, but not difficult. Unfortunately—incredibly, for Eve Sheridan—she had brought along a male escort.

He was probably the man the hostler had mentioned, which meant they had arrived at least twenty-four hours earlier—and would have already been to Upper Dereford.

Eve must have decided to surprise Rebecca with a visit. That was the only explanation. Even if someone in the village *had* found the Sheridans' address after Rebecca's death, then journeyed all the way to Brandon to cable Richmond . . . no. The simpleminded villagers almost never ventured farther than the next town.

It had to be incredible timing, mere coincidence.

Dante cursed Rebecca's independent, enigmatic older sister. She had never liked Giles Dawson, though at the time Dante had attributed her reserve to shyness as much as hostility. The hostility he had discounted; Eve, apparently, was a social misfit more at home pedaling about Richmond on her bicycle, studying and reading about birds.

"I'm the only real friend she has," Rebecca had sighed once, batting her lashes at Dante over her fan. "My poor sister. I do wonder what will become of her after you and I are wed. I'll try to write her a lot, I suppose." And she had looked at him with that intoxicating blend of siren and coquette, adding, "If I can find the time. . . ."

Dante dampened a cloth and mopped his face. Perspiration had loosened the thin moustache, and he yanked it off. His throat ached with tension.

Obviously Rebecca *had* found plenty of time to write her older sister, because Dante's plans forced him to be gone for weeks at a time. He slammed his fist on the marble-top sink.

What had she written in her letters? He might never know. He did know that he must find the journal before they did, or he would lose his only leverage with which to control Avery Paxton. An even worse complication than Eve's untimely appearance would be if Avery—in a fit of jealous spite—ordered that despicable little worm Leoni to come after Dante.

He paced the floor, fighting an unsettling sensation of panic he'd never experienced, not even after he had killed his first wife, all those years before, for a paltry five-thousand-dollar insurance policy.

He was smart. He could wriggle out of this unexpected complication. He forced himself to think of Rebecca, remembering how in those last weeks she had grown suspicious and secretive. She liked hiding things, and he cursed himself for not confiscating that journal months earlier, when he had had the opportunity.

He must think, plan. He would *not* be deflected from

his chosen course. All he had to do was use his head. He had been fooling people for years, effortlessly, because of his superior wit and intelligence. After all, hadn't he just now been downstairs in the lobby, in the same room with Eve Sheridan, and she hadn't recognized him?

Women, Dante reminded himself forcefully, were empty-headed, malleable fools. Delightful companions, physically satisfying—but easily discarded. In fifteen years he had not met one who hadn't deserved her fate.

Until Rebecca.

Pressing his mouth into a flat, grim line, he withdrew from his bag the photograph that Beatrice had given him. He stared at the stiffly formal likeness of Beatrice Linwood until he no longer saw Rebecca's face.

Then he set about revising his schedule. He would do what he must do, and it would work. Regardless of Eve Sheridan's unwelcome appearance here in England, Dante's carefully laid-out future would come to pass.

Like a restless ghost, he prowled the empty cottage, shrouded in midnight darkness. Memories dogged every step. The journal, disturbingly, was nowhere to be found.

He checked all of Rebecca's favorite hiding places, chilled when he realized that someone else had found them as well. It had to be Eve Sheridan again. The sisters had been close and would know each other's habits and idiosyncracies. Rebecca *had* written many letters, Dante recalled.

Bitterly he recalled an occasion when he had come upon her by surprise; she had stuffed the letter out of sight, as if she hadn't wanted him to see what she had written.

Dante stood in front of the fire screen in the parlor, his gaze riveted on the stained sheepskin rug. That blasted journal—and Eve Sheridan—changed everything. For the last hour, every time he swallowed, Dante could feel the choking sensation of a hangman's noose around his neck.

He had to find the journal.

If it wasn't here, perhaps Harriet Crabtree had it among the things of Rebecca's she had packed. No, surely Rebecca had hidden it, and the only logical conclusion to draw was that Eve now had it. Everything came back to Eve Sheridan. Dante glanced around the deserted cottage one last time. Gloomy and dank in the cold November night, the silence was oppressive, almost menacing. "I won't let you do this to me," he vowed, his voice loud in the darkness.

As he drove back to Brandon, the buggy's single lantern cast a dim pool of light, barely enough to see the road. He should have demanded a second one. Annoyed by the unfamiliar jitters, Dante forced himself to resolve his immediate future.

Unlike Rebecca, Beatrice was a very sympathetic girl, who understood and accepted that Denham Granville's business obligations required constant travel. If an unexpected trip to America arose, she would accept his absence with the same resolve she manifested at their last parting a week earlier. "Don't look so forlorn, Mr. Granville," she had remarked. "I'll be here when you return."

Then she smiled Rebecca's smile and added, "But don't let it turn your head. I've plenty of activities to keep me occupied—and my choice of fine young gentlemen as escorts, should the need arise in your absence."

Dante had learned to curb the possessiveness of his response. "Certainly you will. And I trust, each time you smile so coyly up at them, it will be my face you see."

Her wry response filled him with satisfaction. "Mr. Granville, you know your face is quite unforgettable."

Dante had laughed, humor and confidence restored. "It depends on who is gazing upon it," he had returned.

Now, driving down the dark, deserted road, he laughed again, remembering Eve Sheridan strolling past him, oblivious to his presence. "It depends," he amended, "upon which of my faces they are gazing."

He promised himself that, when the time came, Eve Sheridan would carry the face of Dante Gambrielli with her into eternity.

PART THREE

TRUTH

December 1893–January 1894

52

Richmond

THE WEEKS PRECEDING CHRISTMAS passed in a blur for Eve. Carolers sang beneath the streetlamps, and the delicious smells of fruitcake and spiced cider and evergreen boughs filled the house. But an oppressive atmosphere dampened the joy of the season, though Eve's mother had insisted that the house be decorated and all traditions observed. Rebecca, she pointed out with uplifted chin and over-bright eyes, would have wished it. Christmas had been one of her favorite holidays.

Eve's father had changed the most. Where once he brimmed with vigor and moved with confidence, now Eve noted painfully the signs of aging that accompanied his grief. He crept from house to office, his face gray and lifeless; he spent hours in the library, staring into space. Sheridan Investments had been dissolved, then reorganized under a new name, its depleted funds transferred to a different account. But he was still tortured by the calculated perfidy of the two men he had trusted and admired.

Nobody spoke aloud the name of Giles Dawson, much less that of Dante Gambrielli. Eve had reluctantly told her parents the whole story—but only after hours of her mother's pointed badgering. Now they knew everything, but by mutual consent did not discuss the issue further. Reminders of the grim truth were too difficult to bear, especially for her father.

John Hostler paid a visit two days after Eve's return, his matter-of-fact acceptance of Rebecca's death strangely acting as a balm. He gripped Father's hand, nodded to Mother, then turned to Eve, studying her for a moment. "Mr. MacKay's letter is full of praise for your courage and fortitude in the face of tragedy," he finally boomed in his gravelly voice. Eve had hand-carried the letter from England. "You acquitted yourself well, Miss Sheridan."

Eve's father cleared his throat. "She always has, in some things. Have . . ." Above the full beard his sunken cheeks flushed, and Eve's mother tucked her hand around his arm. "Have you . . . is there any word on Paxton? Or . . . anyone else?"

"Nothing on Dawson. Paxton, the wily little ferret, boarded the Lake Shore Limited for Chicago yesterday— but never arrived," Mr. Hostler admitted with a growl. He thanked Maggie for the steaming mug of hot cider, then planted his feet in front of the fireplace. "I received a letter from our New York office, where I had forwarded the note used to entice your daughter to the Lexington this past September. One of our operatives had finally secured a piece of correspondence in Avery Paxton's handwriting, enabling us to compare the two." He sipped the hot drink, one hand patting his pocket—looking, Eve suspected, for his pipe.

"What did he find?" Father bit out, his voice hoarse. Mother, manifesting a new tenderness, urged her husband to a chair and forced him to sit, then pressed a mug of cider he'd refused earlier into his hands. Eve's father drank automatically, but his anguished gaze never left Hostler's. "What did he find?"

"The handwriting of the note, though disguised somewhat, matched Paxton's correspondence definitively enough that the police were notified." Hostler's voice was grim. "Regrettably, Paxton had been alerted somehow, and he escaped. We have operatives working around the clock, however. When he surfaces again—and he will—we'll catch him. I promise you." He heaved a sigh. "Mr. Sheridan, I regret very much that you and your family have been the victims of a craftily planned conspiracy designed to extort a goodly amount of funds from your company. As for the death of Mrs. Dawson—"

Her father slammed the cider down, shattering the mug. The hot liquid splashed over his hand and onto the table.

"William!" Her mother leaped into action, whipped out her handkerchief, and began mopping her husband's hand while she ordered Eve to fetch Maggie, and some rags.

"Mr. Hostler, perhaps you'll join me in the library?" Eve suggested as she hurried past the superintendent.

In the big downstairs library a few moments later, she offered a wan smile. "My father has taken this hard. Please forgive him."

"Don't be idiotic!" came the irritable response. "Your father has suffered misfortunes that have killed stronger men than he." He glared at Eve. "You, on the other hand, stand with the light of battle shining in your eyes, yet you look as if a puff of wind could knock you flat." A growling, half-baffled laugh escaped. "Mr. MacKay was right about that as well."

Eve did not want to talk about Alexander MacKay. "If you'll tell me the rest of what you know," she insisted, "I'll share it with my father later, when he is in better condition to receive it."

Mr. Hostler shook his head. "I'll wait for your father, miss. Intrepid though you may be, your father remains the proper authority in this matter."

"I . . . see." Eve's hand lifted to stroke Rebecca's brooch, which Alexander had given to her just before she sailed. "In that case, whenever the parcel from my sister finally arrives, I'll enjoy the same discretion with whom I choose to share the contents."

Mr. Hostler's face froze in disbelief, then gradually turned the color of boiled tomatoes. His mouth worked furiously, and the look he bent upon Eve could have melted the kitchen sink. Eve clasped her hands behind her back and faced him down. She hadn't survived the past month by having her sensibilities shielded from life's bitter realities.

"Miss Sheridan," he growled at last, "I have reached the conclusion that one of my best operatives has at last met his match. Tell me," he inquired testily, "has your character always been this obdurate?"

"I don't know," Eve shot back. "Has yours?"

Mr. Hostler emitted a crack of laughter, shaking his head. "Very well. I yield, Miss Sheridan." All amusement vanished. "But . . . I'll have no displays of feminine vapors when you don't like what you hear, is that clear?"

Eve swallowed her indignation. His comment rankled her; though Alexander had promised that he would never reveal to another soul her lamentable fainting spell in Mrs. Crabtree's cottage, the memory still stung. She walked over to her father's floor globe and spun it around. "What have you uncovered about Giles Dawson?"

"Miss Sheridan, it is my regrettable duty to warn you that we are in the process of gathering the necessary evidence to establish his identity as Dante Gambrielli." The superintendent's voice was harsh with anger . . . and regret. "His introduction to your sister was probably deliberately arranged by Avery Paxton, with the intention of him wooing either of you into a marriage. We believe they calculated that such an alliance would be accompanied by a significant amount of funds." He clasped his hands behind his back. "Unfortunately, I doubt we'll be able to recover the money."

The superintendent—still looking uncomfortable and irritated—pulled out his pipe, then with a muttered imprecation stuffed it back in his pocket. "Mr. MacKay's letter informed me that Dawson had transferred his funds to a private London bank, using the moniker 'Giles Dawson.' He then transferred those funds to a third bank in Peterborough, probably under yet a different name. Scotland Yard also uncovered a marriage between a Dante Gambrielli and a girl named Priscilla in a village in Lincolnshire, only thirty miles from Peterborough. Mr. MacKay and Inspector Rudge hope to secure more information soon, even if the monies are beyond reach."

"Anything else?" Eve asked.

Mr. Hostler's head tilted, and he tugged at his beard. "Not yet," he answered, but Eve had the uneasy sensation he was withholding something. Then he announced without warning: "Joe Leoni is back."

Eve's hand crept up to cup Rebecca's brooch. "Here?" she asked, her voice faint.

Hostler shook his head. "We're still not sure. He was spotted in New York but disappeared. Miss Sheridan, it will be my strong recommendation to your father—and you— that you be removed from the city until this killer can be apprehended and jailed. Dawson is likely to remain in England, but Leoni is the type who won't rest until he avenges the blow to his . . . ah . . . professional pride."

"He's been apprehended and jailed at least twice. He escaped both times." Eve took a deep, careful breath. "I won't run again. You've seen my father. My family needs me here; they've never needed me before."

"And what will it do to your family when Leoni succeeds in accomplishing what he's tried to do twice before? When your parents lose *both* their daughters to vile murderers?"

Eve paled. "I can't leave," she whispered, almost to herself. "If I do—I'll never be able to look in a mirror again." An endless ocean voyage consumed with loneliness and hours of soul-searching had taught her that much. She looked up. "Besides, where could I go that we would have absolute assurance Joe Leoni wouldn't find out, and follow? Look what happened when I went to England."

"MacKay told me that would be your response," Hostler grumbled. He stomped down the hall to the front door and opened it, with Eve trailing behind, bewildered. Mr. Hostler stepped onto the front porch; when he returned seconds later, another man followed him, quietly shutting the door.

Eve blinked. She had seen no sign of the second man's approach, heard not a whisper of sound.

"Miss Sheridan," Mr. Hostler announced, his tone resigned, "this is Operative Simon Kincaid. At the . . . ah . . . *urging* of Mr. MacKay, he's volunteered to be your shadow until Joe Leoni is apprehended. Though highly irregular, and against company policy, I've agreed." A fleeting grimace of humor crossed his face. "I've enough troubles without Alexander MacKay browbeating me for not arranging for your proper protection."

Simon Kincaid was whipcord lean, his clean-shaven face framed by thick hair several shades darker than Alexander's. He inspected Eve's heightened color with a pair of hard green eyes. "Don't worry, Miss Sheridan," he promised, "I'll be your shadow—not your constant companion. Wherever you go, I'll be along, silent but close. Just ignore me." His voice was hard, like his eyes.

"A shadow." Eve suppressed an involuntary shudder at the prospect of being constantly watched again, even by benevolent, protective eyes. After another swift, sideways review of Mr. Kincaid, she deleted the description of benevolent. "Mr. Kincaid, I can *try* to ignore you, or rather my awareness of your presence nearby. But I'm not much of an actress."

"You've something far more important than acting ability, Miss Sheridan," the Pinkerton operative responded. "You have . . . character."

The quiet pronouncement stayed with Eve over the following weeks, stiffening her spine and goading her faltering courage when she walked the Richmond streets shopping for Christmas presents or slipped outside to feed the birds. But though she knew a dark-haired man with cat green eyes monitored her every step, it was Alexander MacKay's teasing smile and eyes the color of a jay's wing that comforted her uneasy sleep.

53

New York

SHIVER SLIPPED PAST THE PORT authorities with contemptuous ease. By noon the following day he was stowed away on a freighter headed down the coast, bound eventually for Richmond.

The bosun's mate stumbled over his hiding place behind a pile of cargo net. Awakened from a sound sleep, Shiver was unable to reach his knife in time, and after a brief scuffle, the two-hundred-pound man knocked him senseless.

The next time Shiver awoke, he was in the ship's hold, trussed like a turkey. The freighter docked at its next scheduled stop, and Shiver was trundled down the plank and tossed in a foul-smelling, overcrowded jail in some nameless Maryland burg. It was two weeks before he finally escaped.

Twyndham House
Norfolk, England

Denham Granville stood and lifted his wine goblet, its

cut glass sparkling with the same glow as the elaborate crystal chandelier blazing above the twenty-foot mahogany dining table. He smiled at Beatrice. "I would like to propose a toast to my beautiful bride-to-be."

"Hear, hear!" Beaming, Thaddeus Linwood raised his goblet as well. "To the man who managed to put a bridle on my fickle filly of a daughter." A plump, congenial gentleman when sober, Linwood's tipsy condition had loosened his tongue as well as his manners.

"I must disagree," Denham demurred. "This is a toast to the lovely young woman who accorded *me* the honor by consenting to become my wife."

Beatrice smiled gratefully. Her aunt Imogene sniffed, "Much more appropriate. Thank you, Mr. Granville." She glared at her brother. "You would do well, Brother, to emulate the civility of your son-in-law-to-be."

Linwood waved an expansive hand. "I'm doing better than that." He thrust out his goblet, and a servant hastily refilled the glass. "I've already signed the papers giving him the deeds to the estate in Suffolk. And—" He toasted Granville. "As a reward for his devotion, persistence— and success in the face of overwhelming odds—"

"Father, really!"

"I've arranged for the sum of twenty-five thousand pounds to be deposited in the account Mr. Granville opened at our bank in Cambridge, the day after your vows."

In the uncomfortable lull following the announcement, Denham sat down and covered Beatrice's hand, clenched in a white fist on the table. "My dear," he murmured, "the land and funds are irrelevant. I would marry you even if you were a poor milkmaid from a small country village." He squeezed her hand. "Be gracious. This is merely your father's way of thanking me—extravagant and unnecessary, but he insisted."

"I detest being made to feel as if I'm a commodity." Beatrice glared at her father, whose broad face, reddened from wine and weather, continued to beam at his daughter with the gregarious smile of an infant. Beatrice rolled her eyes and turned back to her fiancé, her gaze challenging. "My father needs to find an opportunity to learn moderation of drink, and decent table manners."

"Indeed," her aunt chimed in.

"I trust," Beatrice concluded, "that after we're married, you'll carry me somewhere far away, for an *extended* length of time."

"My dear Miss Linwood—Beatrice." Denham smiled an intimate smile, the twin creases in his cheeks deepening. "I have plans to do exactly that." His voice lowered. "We'll go someplace only the two of us will know about."

Denham straightened and turned back to his host. "Now, regrettably, I must impart some frustrating news, on an occasion that would normally number among the happiest in my life." He paused, studying the three people at the table. "I have to return to the States to take care of some unfinished business which, sadly, has been neglected these past months. I sincerely pray it will only be for a short time."

"That's all right, Mr. Granville." Beatrice rose to the occasion, a brave smile belying her disappointment. "I expect I'll be extremely busy planning the wedding. Why, I'll probably not even notice you're gone . . . just like all those other times."

"When do you have to leave?" Linwood asked.

"I'm booked on the *Campania*, leaving the day after New Year's. I hope to return within a month, at the latest."

"Just make sure you finish your unfinished business," Beatrice ordered, flashing him a saucy grin.

"Don't worry, I'll finish it." Denham downed the rest of his drink, hiding the savagery of his expression.

54

London, England
January 1894

"YOU SAY SHE WAS STRANGLED?" Alex turned the half-finished maze puzzle in his fingers, trying to fit a stubborn piece. He glanced up at Thomas Rudge.

The C.I.D. inspector nodded. "But we've found no photographs in the cottage where they lived, no samples of Gambrielli's handwriting. He's a careful bloke, isn't he? Not even a wedding portrait. The mother, as well as the villagers, all wondered what had happened to him and Priscilla—but nobody knew what to do about it. None of them wanted to involve outsiders, much less the authorities." His voice was bitter. "So . . . with their unknowing help, Gambrielli was able to cover his tracks well. As I said, a careful bloke."

"Not careful enough." Alex continued fiddling with the puzzle. "We're closing in on him, Thomas—I feel it."

"I trust you're right, old chap. This Gambrielli is as despicable as Jack the Ripper—even more so, perhaps." He shrugged his shoulders restlessly. "I've never understood the gullibility of females to that sort of swell. Did you know Priscilla's mother told me the girl married Gambrielli after only a two-month courtship? It was the village scandal."

Alex's voice was deadly quiet. "I don't plan on allowing Gambrielli to slip into the world of romanticized legend. This time, justice *will* be served."

The inspector's cheeks reddened. "My sentiments exactly."

Alex lifted his head. "Sorry, Thomas." His mouth twisted in a grim smile. "I know the Ripper case is a sore point with Scotland Yard." He rubbed a tired hand against his throbbing temple. "Pinkerton's has raw spots as well—and the newspapers delight in making them bleed. But—" His hand closed into a fist and pounded on his knee. "I *will not let Gambrielli murder another girl!*" He wanted to shake his fist at heaven. "Where *is* the swine?"

"Alexander, you look exhausted. Why don't you catch a snooze?" The detective shook his head. "You've barely closed your eyes these past weeks. At least we *do* finally have the evidence to link Gambrielli with Giles Dawson." He rubbed his hands together. "And if the independent corroboration of two bank managers in different cities isn't sufficient for the court, we also have the handwriting analysis, remember. It's only a matter of time until—"

"Not for me!" Alex surged to his feet, sending the chair in Rudge's cluttered pigeonhole of an office slamming against a wooden file cabinet. "I'm trapped over here, waiting for word, wasting time following clues that turn out to be dead ends . . . while across an ocean a vicious little worm of a cutthroat crawls about. And I'm not there to squash him!"

"Ah." Rudge cracked his knuckles and sorted through papers. "Joe Leoni and the redoubtable Miss Sheridan. She is still unharmed, isn't she?"

Alex nodded wearily. "But it can't last forever. A local sheriff in Maryland identified Leoni. He had been jailed, but with Leoni's devilish luck he escaped again. He's after Eve Sheridan. I know it." He stared across the room at Rudge, battling a grinding despair—and fear—that he had never confronted in his life.

"Why not return to the States, then?" Rudge persisted,

the clipped British voice reasonable. "Gambrielli will ultimately be caught, tried—and hanged—here, since he made the error of practicing his despicable wiles in Her Majesty's realm."

"My job—my *duty*—is to track Gambrielli down and see that justice is served, regardless of our respective countries' muddled extradition policies." Alex dropped back down in the chair. "Eve's—Miss Sheridan's—father hired me to follow her over here, so that I could protect her. Now he wants me back, in the same capacity, in America—which is not Pinkerton's normal policy, I'm afraid. But Southern States Insurance Company hired Pinkerton's three years ago to track down Dante Gambrielli—alias Dexter Greaves, alias Giles Dawson . . . and as long as they continue to pay expenses, they command my first loyalty." He heaved a long, defeated sigh. "God help me," he mumbled, mostly to himself, "but every day that loyalty is tested . . . and I find it weakening." He lifted his head to meet Rudge's understanding expression. "I know as surely as you and I sit here in this office that you don't need me any longer. It's a waiting game now, gathering all the facts with sheer dogged persistence, which Scotland Yard does as well as Pinkerton's." He mustered a feeble joke. "Well . . . *almost* as well as Pinkerton's."

He and Thomas exchanged brief smiles. Alex shook his head, then ran agitated fingers through his hair. "I also know that I *am* needed back home. The longer I'm away . . ." He couldn't finish.

The longer he was away from Eve, the more he feared for her life. He needed to be there, not only to protect her, but to nurture her, to bring to flower the stirring of her faith in herself as a woman—and her faith in God's affirmation of her *worth* . . . not her works.

He couldn't do either from across the Atlantic Ocean . . . and he *certainly* couldn't if she were dead.

55

Richmond

"YOU'RE LOOKING BETTER TODAY, Eve. I'm glad."
Pastor Sidney fumbled at the cloth cover and inhaled the
spicy fragrance of his favorite hot cross buns. "These
smell heavenly. Maggie spoils me."

"Maggie's a manipulator. She baked them to get me to
come see you; she knew I would bring them to you when
she refused to do so." Eve's gaze darted to the window, an
automatic habit she had given up trying to control. She
still hadn't caught so much as a glimpse of Simon Kincaid
in the past month.

Of course, she hadn't glimpsed Joe Leoni, either.

"I wondered if you might help me with a problem?" Eve
jerked her thoughts back to the elderly man. He was watching her with a luminous compassion that never failed to
surprise her, because she knew he lived in constant pain.
"You still look for your shadowy bodyguard, I take it?"

"I can't seem to help it." Eve grasped the handles of his
high-backed wheelchair and pushed him back to the library, where a fire blazed, its crackling flames as welcoming as the pastor's smile. "I suppose it's comical, in a way.
Part of me is afraid I will see him—which would mean he's
not as good as he needs to be. And part of me is afraid I

279

won't see him—which might mean he isn't really there."

"Ah." The twisted, gnarled hands slowly stroked the afghan draped across his lap. "At the risk of sounding like a preacher, there's a spiritual application here, if you choose to see with a spiritual eye."

"I suppose," Eve mumbled after a minute.

"Perhaps," Pastor Sidney returned, his words gently nudging, "you should explain it to me."

Eve stepped around the chair and sat in front of him. The Reverend Sidney Jamison was not a man to push a sensitive issue without cause—nor was his motivation ever to wound. Eve swallowed a rising lump in her throat. In that, he reminded her of Alexander MacKay. "I've known for years my feelings toward God are confused," she confessed, her troubled voice low. "Part of me is afraid that, because I can't see Him, perhaps He really isn't there."

Pastor Sidney inclined his head. "And?"

"And . . . if He *did* reveal himself to me in a miraculous moment, I'm afraid I would either discount it, or not trust enough in spite of the reassurance of His presence."

The pastor made no effort to hide his satisfaction.

"Acknowledging the problem," she reminded him as she stood, "is only half the battle." She walked over to a small writing desk and sat down, opening at random one of the books piled there.

The pastor also knew when to change the subject. "So," he nodded to the table at his elbow, neatly stacked with more books and papers, "would you like to work today, while you're here? We've yet to search out references in the book of Revelation, and you told me your publisher was hoping to have the completed manuscript by spring."

Spring . . . the season of rebirth, of new life. Of hope renewed and joy fulfilled. Eve closed her eyes, fighting for breath. A year ago this week, Giles Dawson had come calling on Rebecca for the first time, with his handsome face and rotten soul. *And I suspected something, almost from the beginning. Why couldn't I have seen it in Avery Paxton as well?*

The front door's buzzer startled Eve so badly that she leaped to her feet, her heart hammering.

"Someone's at the door," Sidney observed with a twinkle. "Would you like me to see, since Berta's still at the market?"

"No, I know it hurts your hands to push your wheelchair," Eve responded. "You stay here, by the fire."

Simon Kincaid waited on the stoop, his striking green eyes the only hint of color in the cold January day. "I'm here to escort you to the Pinkerton offices," he informed her, his expression unrevealing. "It's time for a council of war."

Eve gaped at the tall, dark operative. She hadn't seen him since Mr. Hostler introduced them a month ago, yet he acted as though they had spoken the previous day.

Mr. Kincaid continued to wait calmly, allowing Eve to recover from the shock. "We need to leave immediately," he finally prompted.

"Why? What's wrong?"

"I'll wait on the porch. Explain to your friend." He turned away, ignoring her questions.

Pastor Sidney held her hand, gently stroking the cold fingers. "Go with your dark guardian angel, child," he murmured. "Try to remember that the Lord *is* watching—over *both* of you."

"I know." She pulled free and turned away to fasten her cloak. "But if I know, why am I still afraid?"

"Why must we endure winter before spring?" the pastor countered. "Eve . . . you're human. You cannot deny your humanity, nor is there the need to be ashamed of it, since you are as God made you. Besides, it's not the presence of fear that's a sin—it's your response."

"My response," Eve retorted, near tears, "is the overpowering urge to run and hide under the bed."

Pastor Sidney's calm, confident words followed her out. "But you're not hiding there, are you? You never have—and you never will, Eve. God *is* with you, and one day you'll realize His presence is as real as your Pinkerton shadow outside—and the one in England to whom you've given your heart."

Eve was not surprised by the private hansom waiting out front. Nor was Mr. Kincaid's silence during the entire drive into the city unexpected. She was not surprised when he held her arm as they climbed the stairs, his body poised and alert, ready to defend her with his life.

She *was* unprepared when the door opened, however—and Alexander MacKay pulled her inside. He held her at arm's length, a look of pure relief . . . and something else . . . blazing from his blue eyes.

The postman eyed the gray sky as he climbed the steps to his next delivery. A storm was coming, he saw, and he sniffed the air. Wet, it was . . . cold enough to bite. He adjusted his heavy pack, then rang the buzzer instead of depositing the mail in the letter box. While he waited for the door to open, he studied the soiled, sadly tattered parcel in his hands, wondering what it could be.

"Mr. Akins," the Sheridans' housekeeper glared sourly at him. "What would you be doing—" Her gaze fell to the crushed, smudged box, and all the color drained from her thin face as she clapped her hands over her mouth.

"It's in pretty sad shape," Mr. Akins admitted. He shuffled uncomfortably. "But maybe there weren't nothing breakable . . ."

The housekeeper snatched it from his hands, not even thanking him. The door slammed in his face, but not before his astonished gaze caught a glimpse of the dignified servant scampering down the foyer, screeching for Mrs. Sheridan like an Irish banshee.

Shaking his head, the postman continued his rounds. But the rest of the afternoon, he wondered about the contents of that tattered parcel from England.

56

Richmond

EVE WAS EMBARRASSED, ALEX knew, yet he couldn't stop hovering. His hands lingered on her shoulders as he took her cloak, and brushed her arms as he seated her in a chair. His gaze followed her every move.

"Leave her be," Simon finally drawled. "I told you she was all right."

Alex ignored his friend. "You look . . ." *Beautiful, fragile, poised—and haunted.* ". . . well, Miss Sheridan." He wondered how long it would be before his tongue tripped him and he addressed her by her Christian name.

"As do you, Mr. MacKay," Eve returned, her voice breathless. She made a production of smoothing her skirts. At her throat, fastened to her collar, the brooch Harriet Crabtree had pilfered glinted in the lamplight.

Alex smiled down at her, wanting to brush the hair from her forehead and press a kiss against the delicate veins tracing her temple. "I trust Mr. Kincaid took proper care of you?"

Eve's gaze surveyed Simon Kincaid, lounging with folded arms against Mr. Peabody's desk; the secretary had been dismissed for the evening. "I would assume so," Eve muttered. "I've seen nothing of him—or Joe Leoni—for over a month." Her eyes began to twinkle. "It's been a dull life, hereabouts, without you, Mr. MacKay."

John's office door flung open, and the superintendent blew into the reception area with hurricane force. "I've just received a telephone call from William Sheridan's office," be bellowed. Then he caught sight of Eve, and relief lightened his thundering scowl. "Ah. Kincaid brought you in already. Good. We can leave immediately."

"What's wrong with my father?" Eve demanded, surging to her feet.

"What? Nothing is wrong with your father," John tossed over his shoulder as he grabbed his bowler and cane. "Your sister's package from England—it's arrived! One of your family servants brought the news to your father. Hurry up—we've been waiting for weeks." He paused at the office doors. "Why are you standing around like lizards in the sun?" He barreled down the stairs.

Alex refused to hurry, not when Eve stood there with tragic eyes and her gloved hands twisted together like snarled ropes. He looked over her head to Simon, whose mouth twitched into the semblance of a smile.

"I'll be off as well," he announced. "Take care, Alex. I can watch your back—but I'll leave it to you to guard the rest." He nodded once to Eve, then left.

Alex waited until she looked up. "Are you able to leave now?" he asked, his voice light, unhurried.

"Why wouldn't I be?" She made a fuss of fastening her cape, tugging at her gloves.

Alex glanced around. They were alone. He stepped close and took her hands. "Eve . . ."

She froze, the expression on her face so tortured Alex almost dropped her hands. "I didn't know," she whispered, "that it would hurt this bad. . . ."

"I know." He squeezed her hands, then lifted them to his chest. "But I'll be with you. Hovering, if you like, as I was just now. Whatever is coming, Eve, you won't have to bear the pain alone." He stopped. Eve was shaking her head, tugging her hands, every movement of her body proclaiming her desire to distance herself from him. "Eve?"

"It's not the journal!" She broke free, stumbled against the chair, then scurried behind it, facing Alex as if he were about to attack. "It's not the journal that's troubling me." Her hands gripped the back of the chair, and her eyes closed. "I can't bear it. I don't know how to handle this." She opened her eyes. "It's you, Alexander. I didn't know—" She clamped her mouth shut.

"Lass . . ." Alex protested. "What have I done, then? I came back as soon as I was able. The *last* thing I would do is hurt you, but—"

"It's not *you!*" Eve burst out, incoherent words tumbling forth. "I mean—it's you, but it's because of what you are, not how long you were gone. I saw you—and it was as if my heart would burst from joy. Then I had to accept that the feelings wouldn't be going away—but *you* will, one day. Especially now that Becca's journal has arrived. But I didn't realize it would hurt so bad, and . . . and— Alexander! What are you doing?" Her voice rose to a squeak.

Alex shoved the chair aside, hauled her into his arms, and crushed her against his chest. Her hat slipped sideways, and he yanked out the two hatpins and tossed them and the hat aside. "Don't ever do that to me again!" His hands slid to her shoulders and held her at arm's length. "I won't be going away, Eve Sheridan. Ever. Do you ken what I'm saying?"

Her great brown eyes searched every feature of his face. Slowly, she nodded. More slowly, the corners of her mouth lifted. "Alexander," she whispered, "can you loosen your hands a bit? You're leaving bruises."

He instantly gentled his hold. "Sorry," he apologized, his voice husky in its relief. He knew he shouldn't, but he brushed his lips to her forehead, her eyelids, and finally her mouth. "Later, we'll talk," he promised, and released her. "For right now—unless you're prepared for a scalding blush the color of your hair, we'd best hasten over to your house before Mr. Hostler comes looking for us."

He rummaged for the hatpins and Eve pinned her hat in place while they hurried down to catch a streetcar. Thirty minutes later they alighted, two blocks from Eve's house.

"Alexander?"

"Hmm?"

"This is the first time in a month I haven't been afraid when I walk down the sidewalk."

"Simon Kincaid's the best, girl. You should have trusted him, or at least trusted that I would provide the best protection I could for you." His hand reached to clasp hers in a warm, brief squeeze. "All the same, 'tis a joy to hear you trust me *more*."

They reached the house, but when Alex would have ushered her up the porch steps she stopped.

"Alexander?"

"Aye?"

"I want to read Rebecca's journal alone, the first time. I might *want* you hovering at my shoulder, but I . . . I need even more to be alone." She looked up at him anxiously. "Do you understand?"

"Aye, lass. I understand." One last time he touched the wisping red curls peeking beneath her old homburg. "More than you realize."

57

EVE SEQUESTERED HERSELF ALONE in her bedroom while the others waited below in the parlor. Her fingers shook as she first removed the ripped and soiled outer paper, then the crumpled layers of tissue in which Rebecca had wrapped the journal.

A note, hastily scribbled, was attached to the top.

Eve, I've little time. He's due back any moment. If something happens, perhaps what I've written here will help. I've locked away the evidence you'll need, and will try to send the key in my next letter. For now I've hidden it away so he won't find it. Don't forget to talk to God for me, Evie. I know I used to scoff, but, now ... especially now, dear sister, I've realized how much I depended on your faith. Talk to God for me. I know He listens to you.

Eve sank into her favorite chair, her eyes brimming. *I know He listens.* . . . She had talked to God all of her life, but until recently, she had never believed He ever bothered to listen.

No longer. Now, even through her doubt and guilt and fear, she made the conscious decision to *believe* what

Alexander had told her back in the cottage in England; what—reaching beyond the grave—Rebecca affirmed. *I'll keep talking, Becca. Because . . . I choose to believe that at last God has given me the answer I've sought.*

She swiped at the tears, lifted her head, and smiled toward the ceiling. Besides, it was better to live a life of "foolish" hope than sink in the endless despair of intellectual pragmatism.

Outside, the lowering sky thickened, casting an ominous gray light through the window. As Eve opened the clothbound journal with trembling fingers, pellets of freezing rain splattered onto the roof and into the street below.

Less than thirty minutes later she returned downstairs. Alexander crossed to her side, and Mr. Hostler's prowling figure froze in midstep. Her father, sitting next to her mother, watched Eve approach with lifeless eyes, and Mother's chest swelled as if preparing to receive a blow.

Eve's step faltered. Since she had told them of the mounting evidence against Giles, she had been forced to watch her parents' daily struggle with grief and hopeless despair. Eve had lost a sister—but they had lost a *daughter*. They had given Rebecca's hand in marriage to Giles Dawson, and he had taken her away forever.

"I've read all I can," Eve confessed, her voice as colorless as the sleet. "I couldn't find anything in the first twenty pages, other than the note on top. The key . . ." She stopped.

Alexander took the journal, then led Eve to a small chair with a matching footstool and pressed her down.

"I'm sure you'll find something," she finally managed. "The only . . . reference to the key is . . . the note, and I was unable to find anything at all in the journal. But I couldn't . . . I'm terribly sorry I—"

"Don't worry, Miss Sheridan," Alexander promised. "We'll find it."

He followed the girl into the confectionery, elated by his stroke of luck. The domestic was a new one, and would not recognize him. Inside the store, he stood behind her while she ordered a selection of pastries. Outside, driving sleet had turned the street and sidewalks to dirty slush. He brushed frigid droplets from his shoulders and the brim of his top hat, then stepped closer to the counter. When the girl turned around, she bumped into him, and the brimming sack spilled its contents onto the mud-covered floor.

"I am so sorry." He caught the distressed girl's arm when she would have stooped down. "No—they're ruined now." He looked over the glass display case to the clerk. "Please, refill the young lady's order and have it delivered to—" He glanced at the girl, "—where?"

"Um . . . Sh-Sheridan. Mr. Sheridan's, on East Franklin." Her lips trembled as she wrung her hands. "I need them right away. Mrs. Sheridan ordered me to hurry as fast as I could."

"I've a carriage outside. I can have you—and your pastries—there in ten minutes." He paid the clerk and ushered the befuddled girl outside. "What's the hurry?" he asked while they waited for a couple of trolleys and several pedestrians to pass. He smiled at her as he guided the horse into the busy street.

The smile unleashed a torrent of tumbling words. "Oh . . . there's ever such a fuss right now! I've never seen the like! I've only been helping out these past weeks, for the holidays, and I don't usually stay past six o'clock, but the missus asked and I said yes . . . I like it there ever so much better than the orphanage." She fairly bounced on the cracked leather seat. "At any rate, several gentlemen arrived, all without warning, and Miss Eve looked very upset. Maggie was sore put out, she was, because she hadn't enough refreshments."

"Why all the fuss? Tell me about it." He looked into the vapid eyes.

The girl flushed but eagerly responded, "I'm not rightly sure. The postman delivered a parcel earlier, and I had to fetch Mr. Sheridan. Then the other gentlemen and Miss Eve arrived, and Mrs. Sheridan said for me to hurry. . . ."

"I'm sure everything will work out," he soothed. "That parcel must have been something very important."

"I suppose, though I don't understand why everyone is making such a bother over a book. Maybe it's because it was from England. The Sheridans had another daughter, you know. She married and went to England, but she passed away, sudden-like. It's been very sad lately, at the house."

"I'm sure things will change soon." The sleet had subsided, and even the whistling wind was still. Icy droplets from the tree branches dripped to the ground. He pulled the buggy up a block from the house. "I need to turn down this street. Will you mind if I let you off here?"

"Oh, no sir. You're most kind. I appreciate it. . . ." She wrestled open a huge umbrella, took the sack of pastries, then hurried down the walk. He drove off with a satisfied smile, stroking the two matching creases on either side of his clean-shaven cheeks.

58

ALEX AND JOHN CLOSETED THEMSELVES in the superintendent's office. Every time the wind howled and the sleet rattled the windows, the new electric lamps flickered. While Alex read the journal, John studied all the notes and information Alex had compiled in England.

Time passed slowly. The journal, for the most part, revealed Rebecca Dawson as a self-centered, probably over-indulged girl who had depended on her sister for guidance and counsel far more than Eve realized. A wave of tenderness engulfed Alex. Eve might be incapable of perceiving her own spiritual strengths—but her sister had known. *When this is over, Lord, I'm going to claim her.*

I hear you, Alexander. Why else did I bring you together? Outside, the storm raged; inside, on the desk in front of Alex, turbulent human emotions spilled forth. Yet in the silence of his mind, he plainly heard the soft affirmation.

"What?" John growled, looking up. "Did you say something, MacKay?"

"No, sir. I'm still reading." Alex smiled to himself and resumed scanning the pages of abysmal handwriting.

The longer he read, the more his feeling of foreboding intensified. Rebecca Dawson had begun to suspect her husband within weeks of their wedding.

"Mr. Hostler, perhaps you should hear this."

"What is it *this* time?"

"There's a paragraph or two that refer to a meeting Dawson had with Avery Paxton at his club in New York, before the Dawsons sailed to England."

John lifted his head, his eyes gleaming. "Continue, Mr. MacKay."

"She talks about how vulgar the club is, and wonders why Giles and 'that sweet Mr. Paxton' would want to be seen in such a place. Her wording here indicates that she plans to write Eve another letter about it—*another* letter." He and John traded glances. "Another letter," Alex mused again. "Eve received at least one, possibly more, letters from her sister soon after the wedding. They could even have been posted before the Dawsons sailed."

John grabbed his pipe. "The courier!" he said. "We thought the false trail of a red-haired courier had been designed primarily as harassment. Now it would seem that Paxton may have discovered Mrs. Dawson's growing suspicions—and the fact that she shared them with her sister. Probably heard it from Dawson himself."

Alex could feel the pulse throbbing in his temple. "It wasn't Dawson," he said quietly.

At five o'clock a delivery boy brought sandwiches and a pot of coffee. The sleet had turned to driving rain, Alex noted absently while he ate and read.

At a little past six a telegram arrived. John ripped it open, read the contents, and his face darkened with fury. Alex sat back and stretched his cramped muscles. "Bad news?"

John didn't answer immediately. He tucked the telegram into his pocket, fetched more tobacco for his pipe, and made a production of lighting it. He wouldn't look at Alex.

Alex rose from the small corner table and walked over to John's desk. "What is it?"

"The Atlanta office needs help." John puffed for a moment, then removed the pipe and looked straight at Alex. "It's the Crump family again. They've bought off another railroad near the western Florida border by 'persuading' the president to sell. The last two operatives the Atlanta superintendent sent were discovered and barely escaped with their lives. They need someone to go undercover."

"I won't go, John."

"I wasn't going to ask!" John roared, slamming down the pipe. Then he took a deep breath, glaring at Alex. "But I *am* going to send Kincaid."

Alex stalked over to the windows, his hands clasped behind his back. "You're risking her life," he stated flatly after a moment of tense silence. He couldn't say her name; if he did, he'd go after the superintendent with bare hands.

"I'll try to arrange for some sort of protection—I only allowed Kincaid to keep an eye on her as a personal favor, MacKay," he reminded Alex. "You knew that at the time. Well . . . now Kincaid's needed elsewhere, and that's the end of it."

"How do you know he'll go?"

Hostler swore, his temper rekindling. "Unlike *you*, Kincaid keeps his mind on the job—*and* obeys orders!"

Stunned into silence, Alex jammed his fists into his pockets. John was right, and Alex needed to apologize. "You're right, of course." *This time, at any rate—much as I hate it.* His fingers closed over the chamois pouch, squeezing so hard that a pain shot up his wrist. "Sorry." His back teeth clenched. The truth was, he was terrified out of his skull for Eve.

Staying behind in England had been difficult, bearable only because Simon had been here for her. Now Eve would be alone, vulnerable. Plucky—but helpless as a lamb with a hungry wolf. *I'm doing my duty, Lord, and it's the same as before: doing one's duty might cost the life of an innocent bystander. Don't You understand that?*

This time, the silence in his mind produced not affirmation, but steadfast illumination—another time, another deliberately vulnerable Innocent. In furious shame Alex stared out the window. Dusk had settled over the city in an opaque gray shroud, and rain slashed down on hunched pedestrians scurrying to safety beneath the flimsy protection of their umbrellas. The wind moaned, mimicking the despair of Alex's heart.

He went back to the small table and sat down. "I'm going to finish reading this," he snarled. He looked across the room at John. "But if anything happens to Eve Sheridan, you'll be having my resignation on your desk."

At seven o'clock, in a thick silence broken only by the sound of rain and wind, Alex stumbled upon the solution to the riddle of the key. "The key!" he exclaimed. "I've discovered the lock for the key!"

This time John ignored him. Alex surged to his feet, strode out the door, and returned with the small brass key Eve had found inside the Matryoshka doll. He tossed it down on the papers John had been analyzing. "There's a box in Rebecca Dawson's old room at the Sheridans', with something inside so detrimental to Dawson that she felt compelled to hide this key."

Even as John reached for the key, Alex's hand scooped it up, and he headed for the door.

"Mr. MacKay."

Alex paused, slowly turned. He and John Hostler exchanged a long, wordless stare. At last John said, his voice grave, almost subdued, "Watch yourself, Mr. MacKay. It's nasty out there."

Alex jammed on his cap. "I know." Without another word, he shut the door behind him.

59

THE SHERIDANS, MAGGIE INFORMED Alex, had just finished supper, a dismal affair where everyone picked at the soup and fried croutons she had prepared. "So I'll thank you to take yourself off and return in daylight, like decent folk."

"Then tonight I'll have to be *in*decent." His voice crackled with warning. He shouldered past the outraged housekeeper. "Either announce me, or I'll do it myself."

"Maggie, I thought I heard—Mr. MacKay!" Letitia Sheridan's hand lifted to her throat. She dropped it immediately, darting an alarmed backward glance down the hall. "What has happened? Maggie, do stop glaring at the man and take his cape."

"I'm sorry to disturb you at this time of night, but I've been studying the journal, and it appears Mrs. Dawson may have hidden something in her bedroom here, sometime before she left for England." While he talked, Alex's gaze had been busy scanning the house. "Where is Miss Sheridan?"

"Working in the library, on her book." Mrs. Sheridan's voice was exasperated.

Alex relaxed. "Her book?"

The older woman waved her hand. "She writes. About birds. For some reason, she doesn't like to talk about it. Mr. MacKay, what did Rebecca hide? I've had her room cleaned, of course—but I confess I've as yet been unable to pack up her things. . . ." Her voice faltered, and she impatiently tugged at her lace jabot.

"She seems to have had a special box of some kind . . . Mrs. Sheridan, under the circumstances, would you permit me—?"

"Don't be ridiculous, Mr. MacKay. Of course you may search the room. I . . . can't accompany you, but I will explain to Mr. Sheridan."

"Is he any better?"

For the first time the indomitable woman looked uncertain. "Somewhat. My husband is a strong, *decent* man, Mr. MacKay. He has never been able to see any evil in other people. This has been a . . . dreadful blow." She turned away and tugged a handkerchief from her sleeve.

"He'll recover, Mrs. Sheridan. Give him time." Alex glanced toward the stairs.

She turned, gesturing down the hall, and Maggie approached. "I'll join you as soon as I—I'll be there shortly." The struggling woman nodded to Alex, then spoke to the housekeeper. "Maggie, please show Mr. MacKay to Miss Rebecca's room. Perhaps you'll alert Miss Eve as well?"

The housekeeper muttered beneath her breath all the way up the stairs. Feeling very much the interloper, Alex perused the Sheridans' inner sanctum. Family portraits and a pair of fine English prints lined the stairwell. At the top, several samplers graced the walls leading down the hall.

Alex stopped. Three of the works bore the initials "RS" and displayed a fine skill with the needle. The last one, of gaily colored birds, bore the initials "ES"; the needlework was atrocious. Stifling a grin, Alex lengthened his stride to where Maggie waited with baleful eye by a closed door.

"It's disgraceful," she announced, her thin nose quivering as she flung open the portal. "An outrage." Then her eyes filled with tears. Alex followed her into the dark room, waiting while she turned on the lamps. "But since you're here, Mr. MacKay, you'd better make good use of your time. That blackhearted scoundrel . . ." She turned away, and in a muffled voice told Alex she would warn Miss Eve of his intrusive presence in the upstairs chambers.

Rebecca's bedroom was tomblike in its quietness. Alex took swift inventory: good-quality walnut furniture, and the same profusion of bric-a-brac that cluttered Bramble Cottage. Two solemn-eyed dolls watched him from their perch among the lace and beaded pillows at the head of a canopied bed. With a brief twinge of pity, Alex began a methodical search.

He had just opened a satin glove box on the dresser when Eve flew into the room, Maggie on her heels.

"Al—Mr. MacKay!" She covered the slip, but the color rose in her cheeks. "Maggie says Rebecca might have hidden something in here. I don't understand. *Here?* Did you find something in the journal?"

Alex tried to tear his eyes away from the picture she made, all rosy and disarrayed, her shirtwaist crumpled and two pencils haphazardly sticking from an unraveling chignon. "Yes. Some sort of box? She called it—"

"Her treasure box!" Eve smacked her palm to her head. "Oh, why didn't I think of it weeks ago? Rebecca tucked everything she wanted as a keepsake in that box, from dance cards to pressed flowers to notes she received from Giles—oh!"

She flew across the room, dropped to her knees, and yanked open a pair of doors in a massive chiffonnier. "She hid it in here, I believe . . . why I don't know, since she made me promise never to peek—but then she was always doing things like that."

"I remember." Alex and Maggie crowded behind Eve, and only the maid's presence prevented Alex from snatching Eve into his arms.

"Here!" Flushed and triumphant, Eve held up a flat

leather box. She jumped up, almost losing her balance in the process.

Alex steadied her, holding on a lot longer than was necessary. "Here's the key." He released Eve and dug it out.

Eve backed away, hugging herself. "You open it," she whispered. Then she bit her lip. "I should have recognized the key in England. I'm so sorry."

"Don't be. Even if you had, the box was over here." Alex laid it on top of the dresser. Rebecca's "treasure box" *was* a handsome object, decorated with an elaborate bronze applique and elegant hinges. He inserted the key and flipped open the lid. The gardenia-scented interior overflowed with notes, snippets of ribbon, cards, pressed flowers, and a multitude of other fripperies. Unearthing the evidence to which Rebecca had referred loomed as a monumental task.

Dismayed, Alex glanced at Eve, who was staring at the box in agonized silence. Less restrained, Maggie was quietly weeping in her apron.

"Miss Sheridan—" Alex began, his voice soft, caressing.

"I'm all right." She smiled the most heartbreaking smile he had ever seen. "Don't worry. I'll do it. You might want to sit down, though. It could take a while."

"Why don't we take it downstairs, then?"

She shook her head. "I don't want my father to see. It would hurt him too much."

As if it's not hurting you, love. . . . The word slipped past his subconscious, unbidden, but Alex didn't try to stop the emotion flooding his veins. It was too late to deny his feelings . . . it had been too late for a long time.

The tiny door of a cuckoo clock hanging on the wall popped open and a little bird announced the hour of eight o'clock. Instantly Alex grabbed Eve, thrust her behind him, and whirled to face the unexpected noise before the bird chirped the second time.

Maggie gaped as if she'd never seen him before.

"Faith, and would you look at the man!" she whispered after the doors shut and silence filled the room. "I've never seen a body move so fast. When you and that muck-souled scoundrel squared off last fall, I thought to myself, 'Hmph, too bad he hasn't the fists of Gentleman Jim.'" She eyed Alex with new respect. "Perhaps I'll be changing my mind about you now. . . ."

"You should have seen him in England, Maggie." Eve grinned at Alex, a hint of mischief stirring as she retrieved a number of scattered papers that had blown to the floor.

Sheepish, Alex bent to help her. "I'm sorry. I've been a little—Eve? What is it?"

She was reading what looked like a receipt, her expression bewildered.

"I don't know why she would have kept this—I don't even know where it came from." She held up the slip of paper. "It's the receipt from a hotel in Georgia I've never heard of. Rebecca never even *visited* Georgia. Who . . ." She squinted at the signature. "This is signed by a Mr. Greaves. The first name is smudged. D-E-S? No, 'X'. Oh . . . Dexter. Dexter Greaves." She held it out to Alex. "I wonder why she would keep a stranger's—" The significance registered, and she stared wordlessly back at an equally dumbstruck Alex.

Everything depended on timing, Dante knew. Timing, and his trademark careful planning. This risk presented the ultimate challenge of his career, but the reward was more than worth the risk. If he were successful, he would have unencumbered freedom to pursue the idyllic life of an English country gentleman. Acquisition of the journal would free him from Avery Paxton; Eve Sheridan's death would free him from the last of Rebecca's lingering influence.

As for the Pinkerton's National Detective Agency operatives . . . *they* would learn the utter futility of trifling with Dante Gambrielli. He contemplated the sheet of paper lying on the table in front of him, and pictured the irritating, elusive flathead's expression when he read the words Dante had written.

The timing *must* be absolutely perfect. Dante rose, pacing the rough, creaking floorboards of the shabby room in the boardinghouse. Located a block away from the railroad tracks, the endless coming and going of the trains shook the entire frame structure every time they rumbled past.

Dante froze in the middle of the room, and an expression of fiendish delight filled his face. The solution to one of his most ticklish problems lay practically on his doorstep.

He laughed aloud, then hurriedly dragged down the Gladstone bag with its secret compartments and false bottom. First, an appropriate disguise. . . .

For the next several days he worked from dawn until late at night, making careful, detailed preparations. He pored over all the notes he had made, double-checked arrangements, dates, and the growing collection of equipment. He concealed everything in a locked strongbox on top of the wardrobe, where the slattern of a landlady couldn't reach—evidenced by a repulsive layer of dust coating its surface.

Several times while he was out, Dante felt a tingling sensation at the base of his spine, warning him of watching eyes. He could never pinpoint the culprit, however, and concluded that his heightened perception was merely overdramatizing the innocent interest of casual passersby. Doubtless they would all be feminine.

On an unseasonably mild Thursday afternoon, he packed his bags, paid for his lodgings, and walked toward the Richmond, Fredericksburg, and Potomac passenger depot. His step was brisk, confident. With the set of keys he had procured, he stowed his bags in the predetermined location, then spent the next hours painstakingly tracing his route one last time.

The time had arrived.

60

ON A DISMAL SUNDAY AFTERNOON, two days after the discovery of the hotel receipt, Eve responded to a knock on the door. It was Alexander.

"What's wrong?" she asked without preamble.

Alexander pondered her in resigned silence, then the corners of his mouth quirked. "You know me too well, I'm thinking. How did you know my mood's as dour as the day?"

Eve shrugged, her gaze bouncing away from Alexander. She was grateful for the task of hanging up his ulster and cap, though she was unable to prevent her fingers from caressing the soft Scottish wool, or brushing it next to her face. When she turned back to Alexander, her response faltered at the look in his eyes. "I . . . we've spent a lot of time together." She couldn't seem to catch her breath, or swallow. "What's wrong?"

"Where are your parents?" Alexander asked. "No— don't panic. Just tell me if they can hear or see us right now."

"N-no." The intensity of his expression should have warned her, but Eve was still unprepared when Alexander lifted her hand and carried it to his lips.

"Eve, you're the brightest spot in my day, lass." His moustache brushed her knuckles as his mouth pressed a lingering kiss first on the back, then in the center of her palm. "A cardinal," he continued, the words as caressing as his actions, "in a dank, cold world of endless mist." He enfolded her hand in his, and straightened.

"I wish my parents were out visiting, instead of waiting for you," Eve blurted out, then felt her cheeks flush.

Alexander laughed. "Ach, but I needed that," he admitted, the light in his eyes dimming. "Eve . . . we must talk, but first, I've some information from England. I think your parents will want to hear it."

"Not bad news? I don't want Father to hear any more bad news."

She thought he hesitated, then he tucked her hand into the crook of his elbow. "Just good," he promised, his fingers stroking hers. "I'll share only the good."

As Eve led him down the hall toward the kitchen, she wondered at the way he had phrased his answer.

During the last month, her mother had fallen into the habit of baking hard gingerbread—Eve's father's favorite—every Sunday afternoon. While Mother worked in the kitchen, Father would sit by the boiler in the big old rocker. Sometimes they talked, sometimes Father idly leafed through the Richmond *Times*. Less often now, he would stare into space, his stern features a mask, unresponsive even to Mother's bullying concern.

Today, thankfully, Father responded to Alexander's deliberately cheerful greeting with something of his old warmth. "What brings you out on such a bleak afternoon?" He glanced fearfully at Eve.

Alexander smiled. "How did you guess?" he confessed easily. "I'm here to steal your daughter away for an afternoon drive, if I may. First, though, I thought I'd share a bit of news we received from Scotland Yard."

"News?" Eve's mother chimed in, turning away from the huge worktable.

Alexander waited until she hung up her apron and

wiped her hands free of flour. "A local bookseller in a Cambridge bookshop recognized one of the likenesses of Dante Gambrielli the C.I.D. has been circulating all over England. Apparently he's clean-shaven now, going by the moniker Denham Granville. Local gossip yielded the information that he's been courting the niece of a wealthy, well-respected widow whose brother owns a fair-sized farm in Norfolk."

Eve saw her father's hand clench, pounding on the chair arm. Her mother moved closer and directed Alexander a warning look.

"The girl?" Eve asked for them all, dreading the answer.

"She is still alive, as far as we know. Banns were posted for a May wedding, so she should be safe for now. The C.I.D. has detailed a number of detectives up to Cambridge, as well as King's Lynn, the town nearest the father's farm. They're closing in like hounds who've caught the scent," he finished with grim relish.

"Has anyone warned his unfortunate bride-to-be?" Eve's mother asked, her voice tart.

Alexander shook his head. "That I can't answer. I'm telling you everything that was in the cable Mr. Hostler received last night. I thought it would encourage you, help you to know that we *are* closing in on the blighter. He won't get away this time." He smiled and clapped his hand on Eve's father's shoulder. "Now, with your permission, I thought I'd take Miss Sheridan for a drive. It's a raw day, to be sure, but I thought the fresh air might offer an invigorating respite."

Eve watched, disbelieving, as her parents exchanged secretive, satisfied looks. "Make sure your gloves match, dear," Mother admonished. "And for heaven's sake, do *not* impinge on Mr. MacKay's generosity by asking him to take you to some muddy, windblown field so you can watch the birds!"

They were halfway down the hall when Eve heard her father calling Alexander's name. Alex turned around.

"Take care of my daughter, Mr. MacKay," Father implored. "For the love of God, Alexander—take care of my daughter."

"What is it you need to share that you couldn't, back at the house?" Eve asked some thirty minutes later. Alex had driven them out Monument Avenue, where the statue of Mr. Lee had been unveiled several years earlier. On either side of the wide lane, cows huddled together in open fields, their backs to the wind.

"How about if we enjoy the drive a little longer first?"

"That," Eve retorted in some exasperation, "quite effectively kills any hope of my enjoying this outing, Mr. MacKay."

"We're alone. You can call me Alexander now." He transferred the reins to one hand, then picked up Eve's hand with his free one. The horse continued a steady walk, its mane blowing in the stiff January breeze. "Do you know, I think your parents are matchmaking?"

"It's because Maggie gleefully reported your slip. You called me by my Christian name in front of her the other evening—Alexander, stop that!" His fingers were stroking the tendons of her wrists, and he could feel—even through her gloves—the rioting of her pulse.

"Do you really want me to stop, lass?"

Eve swallowed hard. "No," she admitted, the blunt admission touching Alex. "When you're close, I'm no longer cold, or lonely. Or afraid."

Overwhelmed—and burdened with knowledge—Alex didn't immediately reply. Eve shifted in the seat, and his heart banged into his ribs when her hand lifted to caress his wind-stung cheek. "When I'm not with you," she continued, the words low and shaky, "just the thought of your voice warms my blood and makes my heart beat faster."

Ach, don't I know that as well. Alex closed his eyes, savoring the burning shy honesty of her touch.

"And in spite of everything that has happened, I'm beginning to understand . . ." Eve's voice wavered, ". . . truly understand for the first time, why my sister followed the man she loved across the ocean, away from everything familiar—without a qualm."

Alex jerked the buggy to a halt, dropped the reins, and drew her into a tight embrace, his throat choked with emotion. He stripped off his gloves, then buried his face in her hair, inhaling the poignant fragrance of spring violets. "You make me feel humble," he whispered. His hand cupped her chin and lifted it, reveling in the exquisite softness of her skin. "But I will confess that being compared to the likes of Dante Gambrielli tends to dampen my ardor somewhat."

Eve's face flamed. "I didn't mean . . . I was trying to . . . all I meant—"

His mouth stopped her words. After a moment, he murmured against her lips, "I understand what you're telling me, love. It's all right." Tenderly his fingers traced a caressing path over her heated cheeks. "Besides, you're such a joy when you're flustered, it's almost irresistible to tease."

"I do *not* appreciate being teased about some things," Eve mumbled, burrowing her face into the folds of his ulster. "I've never felt like this before, and you must know I never expected to. So when you tease . . . I'm not quite sure whether you're teasing or . . . or just making fun of me."

He cupped her cheeks again, and his eyes burned into hers until her lids lowered, veiling both uncertainty and dawning awareness. "I won't have you belittle yourself any longer," he ordered softly, in a tone vibrant with restrained passion. "Nor do I want you casting any more base interpretations on my actions or words." He shook his head, then dropped a quick kiss on her reddened nose. "For such an intelligent woman, with a heart stout enough to face down a cold-blooded killer, you have the least amount of self-confidence of any female I've ever known."

Eve sputtered, pummeling his chest with her fists.

"And I've known quite a few," Alex persisted, enjoying her rising temper, "not including my four sisters. Females, don't you know, have this predilection for focusing a great deal too much on themselves. I've often wondered if that's what the good Lord intended when—ouch!" Eve's elbow dug into his ribs.

Then, incredibly, she threw her arms around his neck and squeezed so tightly Alex could barely breathe. When he felt hot moisture dampening his skin and shirt collar, his breathing suspended altogether.

"Eve? Lass, what is it?" He tried to pry her loose, but she shook her head and tightened her hold. Uncertain, terrified that somehow he had hurt her again, Alex gave up and held her, rubbing his hands in soothing circles down her back until at last he felt her relax.

She tried to dig inside her cloak, her hand casting about; Alex shifted, allowing her to retrieve a handkerchief. After a minute she lifted her head. "I don't know why I did that," she admitted, "but for some reason, now I feel better." The smile began in her eyes, then her mouth twitched. "I'm willing to argue the issue of who's more self-centered—ladies or gentlemen—but in light of *my* behavior, I will concede that ladies often do behave more irrationally."

The choking sensation in his chest evaporated. A smile spread across his face as Alex leaned down. This time, her response to his deepening kiss affirmed the feelings of his heart—with perfect communication.

61

"SIMON HAS BEEN ORDERED to another case," Alex revealed much later. "He left as I was arriving at your house."

Eve stirred, lifting her head from his shoulder. "Since I never saw the man, I can't promise to miss him much. Will you take his place?"

"No." His voice was strangled. "No, lass. I cannot."

"Who . . . or have you caught Joe Leoni, and nobody needs to . . . guard me anymore?"

Alex searched for her hand, clenched in her lap inside the folds of her cloak. "Mr. Hostler is discussing the matter with the Chief of Police. We're hoping to at least have a patrolman always in the vicinity."

"I . . . see." He felt her heave a sigh, then she lifted her head. "Alexander, please don't look like that. I'll be fine. I've learned, you see, how to be observant of my surroundings even when I'm *not* bird-watching. Besides—" Her voice was hopeful. "Maybe Joe Leoni has given up. Mr. Kincaid never saw him, did he?"

"No. And that, I grant you, is a good sign. Simon's stalking abilities are unequaled."

"There you have it. I'll be careful, the police are

alerted, and Joe Leoni hasn't been sighted in over a month." She smiled brightly. "I'll just finish my—" she stopped abruptly.

"Your book on birds of the New Testament?" Alex finished, his voice tender. He stroked the bright strands of hair at the base of her neck.

"How did you—never mind. 'The real MacKay' knows everything." She sounded more resigned than outraged.

"I'd like to see your first one."

Her head lifted. "I thought you would." She took a deep breath. "I don't mind . . . if you'll promise to be honest with your response." She searched his eyes. "I can bear any criticism, Alexander, as long as you're honest. What I can't bear is pity or condescension."

"I've warned you about your faulty interpretations of my motivations."

"So you did." She swatted his arm. "Just as I've warned *you* not to try and bully me . . . which is what you're doing now. I'll accept your admonition if you'll accept mine."

Life with Eve Sheridan, Alex was beginning to realize, promised to be lively. "I concede," he surrendered. "Now . . . shall we seal the pact with a kiss?"

Eve blushed. "I thought you'd never ask!"

They returned home as evening shadows settled over the street in soft layers of purple and gray. Alex secured the reins, his gaze drifting to a delivery wagon trundling past. The hunched driver didn't even glance their way. With a grin, Alex stole one last kiss as he helped Eve down.

At the corner, the wagon driver lifted his head.

Only the horse's ears flickered at the sound of a deep, malevolent chuckle.

62

"SNOW'S COMING," MAGGIE ANNOUNCED. The back porch door banged shut as she hung the broom on a nail.

"Your bones aching again?" Eve asked.

Maggie sniffed. "There's nothing wrong with my bones, miss. I read it in the Farmer's Almanac, if you must know. Besides, there's a feel to the air."

Eve finished filling the bucket. "Perhaps I'll double my portion of seed."

Maggie shook her head, muttering. Her hand paused in the process of reaching for her long woolen coat. "I need to be taking this basket of clothes over to Sheltering Arms Hospital. Your mother's expecting me. How long will it take you to scatter that about?"

Eve wanted to stomp her foot in exasperation. "As little as ten minutes or as long as two hours, depending on my mood. For heaven's sake, Maggie—take the basket and go! I'll be perfectly safe. If it would help, I'll carry Father's old Army pistol with me." She sucked in her breath and mumbled the names of twelve bird species before she faced Maggie again. "I'm sorry."

"We'd all of us be less grim were that black-souled

Leoni found drowned like a sewer rat."

"Mr. MacKay told me yesterday that another operative received an unconfirmed report of a fight down in Petersburg involving a couple of men, one of whom fit Leoni's description. Mr. Hostler sent Mr. MacKay to investigate." She tugged on her old work gloves. "At least it should be safe for me to putter in the backyard a bit, Maggie. Take the basket to Mother, and grant me one small hour of freedom."

Shaking her head, Maggie tied on her bonnet. "All right, but 'tis against my better judgment. . . ." The housekeeper finally departed, grumbling dire warnings and a litany of disclaimers.

Elated by the rare freedom of being *alone*, Eve barely waited for the gate to swing shut behind Maggie before she grabbed the bucket. If it hadn't been so heavy with its load of seed, she would have skipped down the garden path. Nobody to fret if she stayed outside longer than three minutes . . . nobody watching her with anxious eyes . . . nobody lecturing her about keeping her eyes open and her senses alert to her surroundings.

She decided to clean the bird feeders before replenishing them, for the hushed stillness in the air warned her as clearly as Maggie's voice of a pending storm. "It's a troublesome chore," she grumbled aloud to a pair of snowbirds watching her from the bare-branched dogwood next to the shed. "I hope you appreciate my efforts."

The door to the shed pushed open easily. Whoever had been out here last—probably Sophie—must have forgotten to latch it. Heady with her momentary freedom, Eve completely forgot Alexander's repeated warnings to be alert.

As she reached for a scrub brush hanging on a nail, unseen hands jerked her backward. A cloth slapped down over her mouth and nose, and the last thing Eve remembered was a sickly sweet smell . . . and the sensation of falling.

Bone-deep tired, furious at the trip to Petersburg, which had proven to be a complete waste, Alex stomped up the stairs to the Pinkerton offices. He snarled at Raymond, who with a guarded glance handed him the afternoon mail.

He tried to ignore the persistent prickling at the back of his neck. In the past, he would have heeded the instinctive alarm, which had saved his life on numerous occasions. Now, calculating how long it would take to reach the Sheridans' house, he strode irritably across to his office, a sectioned-off corner in a room shared with three other operatives. None of them were in. Alex glanced at the untidy desks, his grim mood lifting a bit. *We're all of us a trial to John, to be sure.*

He tossed the day's collection of letters and advertising leaflets onto his own month-old pile of unfinished paper work. Indifferent to the backlog, his mind, as always, returned to Eve. What was she doing right now? He curbed the growing obsession to swoop down and carry her away, far away, from the likes of Dante Gambrielli, Joe Leoni, and Avery Paxton—whose escape still rankled.

It's not over, Paxton, Alex vowed to himself. *After we put Gambrielli and Leoni behind bars, I'm coming after you.* No matter how long it took, Alex planned to ensure that the little snake paid for his poisonous attack on the Sheridan family.

Stifling a groan, Alex sat down and rubbed at his neck, massaging the shoulder Leoni had stabbed. It was aching—a sure sign of bad weather.

His glance caught on a plain white envelope about to slide off the desk. He picked it up, idly wondering at the lack of a postmark.

Perhaps Eve had left a note for him. Eagerly he tore open the envelope and scanned the contents. As he read, rage welled up in him. Rage . . . and fear. *"No!"* he roared. *"Not Eve! No!"*

Raymond burst into the room, his face white with alarm. "Mr. MacKay! Are you all right?"

Alex didn't answer. Raw terror pulsed through his mind. "God in heaven . . ." he groaned. "Not her!" His hands shook as he lifted them to the ceiling. "Not Eve . . . not Eve!"

The secretary hovered in the doorway. "Shall I fetch someone?" he faltered, then scuttled backward as Alex surged to his feet.

"No! I won't let him do this! It *isn't* Your will, God! I *refuse* to believe You'll allow this to happen." He stood gripping the desk, his mind reeling, scrabbling to reestablish the formidable calm for which he was famous. *You will NOT allow this! Eve! My God . . . please!*

Raymond backed out of the room and slammed the door behind him.

Shaking, Alex dropped into his desk chair again. He couldn't think, couldn't move. Could barely pray. "God, help me," he whispered hoarsely.

His fingers fumbled for the note, smoothing the crumpled paper he had crushed in the first onslaught of emotion. Silence engulfed him. He tried to focus on the words written there—the pitiless, sadistic clarity of the words.

Giving in to fear isn't going to help Eve, Alexander.

Had someone spoken? He lifted his head. "Raymond?" There was no response. Alex swiveled about, his movements wooden.

Quit wasting time. You've precious little of it left.

Alex stared down at the note, then resolutely lifted his head again, listening. He cleared his throat, surprised at the pain, surprised when he couldn't control the fine trembling in his hands. For a moment the corroding despair swelled up in him again, then was swept aside in a rising flood of gritty determination. The woman he loved—dear, feisty, uncontrollable Eve—was in danger. He could not let his fear for her freeze him into uselessness.

Alex breathed more deeply, ignoring the pain. Then he

bowed his head. When he raised it again, he knew he was not alone.

A moment later he shoved back the chair and stood, folded the note, and tucked it inside his shirt. Then he retrieved his ulster and cap and dashed out of the office.

Thirty minutes later Alexander MacKay extinguished his bedroom lamp and headed for the door. Dressed like the night in shades of black, he moved with the soundless stealth of smoke.

On his way out he paused at a small cabinet. With steady hands he unlocked the door, retrieved his Smith and Wesson New Departure revolver, and tucked it away.

It was time to go hunting.

63

NAUSEA. PAIN. SEEPING COLD. Eve didn't want to open her eyes, but the cowardly alternative to facing reality prodded her back to consciousness. She forced her eyes open.

Fresh panic assailed her. She couldn't see, even with her eyes open. She tried to lift her hands to rub her eyes, and vicious pain streaked up her arms. Her hands were tied behind her back.

Her breathing shallow, Eve sat very still and took stock. The nausea was abating, but her head still ached, and all her muscles felt as if they were stretched over an open fire. Cautiously she turned her head. A thin strip of light, about a yard from her bound feet, revealed the location of a door. She must be locked inside a small room.

The piercing blast of a train whistle shattered the silence, and as a growing rumble of sound crescendoed, the tiny dark room began to shake. Eve bit back a scream, every muscle rigid, braced for the fatal impact. With a heavy, grinding clatter the train rolled by, so close that the sound buffeted her eardrums in a terrifying cacophony of metal and iron and steam.

Finally the noise faded, and the vibrating room stilled.

Farther down the track the train whistle sounded again. At the same instant the door flew open, and Giles Dawson's silhouette filled the entrance like a looming, ravenous vulture.

Lantern light flared. Eve winced, blinking. When her vision adjusted to the light, she immediately recognized her surroundings. She was chained to the wooden pedestal of a train seat, in a private compartment with the shades drawn. They weren't moving . . . Giles must have broken into a stationary car on a sidetrack. Did that mean she was still in Richmond?

"So . . . you're finally awake," he said. The smooth voice, with its macabre timbre of culture and class, ignited a fury in Eve she hadn't known she possessed.

"You filthy, murdering *swine!*" she yelled. "You killed my sister!"

He appeared unmoved by her rage. "More to the point is whether or not I plan to kill *you*, Miss Sheridan." He held the lantern higher, his mouth spreading in a loathsome smile. "You look sufficiently pathetic. I daresay when Mr. MacKay arrives he'll find the sight . . . ah . . . *stimulating* enough, shall we say, for him to meet my demands."

He wanted to toy with her, amuse himself with the spectacle of her helplessness. Eve lifted her chin, then mimicked his indifferent voice. "I find you even more pathetic, Mr. Dawson. Or should I call you Dante Gambrielli . . . or Denham Granville. Or—" She stared straight into the dead pits of his eyes. "Dexter Greaves?"

The slashing crease in his right cheek jumped. *Interesting*, Eve thought. The matching one in his left cheek didn't move at all. Neither, regrettably, did his indolent pose. "Miss Sheridan, since you seem so fond of namecalling, perhaps *you* should choose."

"Certainly," she retorted, cudgeling her brain to think . . . *think* of a solution instead of panicking over the problem. "I'll call you Giles, like my sister did," she flung out, though the words betrayed an unfortunate hoarseness.

"Was she crying your name when you killed her . . . *Giles*? Was the last sound she made before you plunged the—"

"SILENCE!" The lantern swung crazily as he hooked the handle onto an overhead pipe. Then he knelt, and his hands closed like steel manacles around her upper arms. Eve flinched, but her gaze never wavered. Giles thrust his face inches away from hers. "Don't taunt me with Rebecca," he whispered. "Do you understand me, you ugly redheaded bluenose? Do not even speak her name in my presence again."

"I . . . won't." She licked her lips and tried to take a careful breath. "Could you please release my arms? You're hurting me."

With a contemptuous thrust he shoved her back and stood, his breathing harsh. "Don't provoke me again." He paused, then added, "Since you've just let slip your knowledge of my past lives—perhaps you'll also comprehend the ease with which I could . . . and would . . . dispatch you." He snapped his fingers. "Just like that."

Eve shook her head without speaking. She had just learned a very important lesson about Giles: talk of Rebecca's death triggered a dangerous display of violence. She wanted to ask what he was going to do, but he grabbed the lantern and stalked out, slamming and locking the door.

This time the darkness did not terrify her. She began tugging on the bonds, ignoring the pain and lingering effects of the chloroform. Giles, of course, *would* have to kill her now, thanks to her unforgivable stupidity.

She twisted and tugged until the pain in her wrists brought tears streaming down her cheeks, but Giles had bound her too well. Her frantic struggle only depleted her strength and sapped her resolve. With a strangulated moan she collapsed against the cold wood siding, her breath ragged.

Gradually, as the cold seeped into her aching bones and her muscles screamed from their unnatural confinement, Eve was forced to confront the frightening reality of her complete helplessness. Even her intellect—the pride and sometimes despair of her life—offered not a single solution.

There was nothing she could do to help herself. Nothing. What lesson must she need to learn for God to bring her this low?

Perhaps if she remembered some of the Scripture verses she had studied while writing her books. All good Christians were expected to memorize verses that they could spout forth on the appropriate occasion—and Eve had spent much of her childhood fervently winning all the prizes for her excellent memory.

She was supposed to mount up with eagles' wings . . . and the Lord was supposed to swirl down with heavenly horses more swift than eagles. *Why can't I remember any verses dealing with other birds?* Eagles were strong, magnificent, invincible. *Eagle verses are NOT appropriate under these circumstances, Lord. I'm helpless. Is that what You want me to learn? That I'm never going to soar on eagles' wings because my faith is not worthy enough? I'm just one of Your sparrows, so small and insignificant, nobody notices.*

For some reason, Eve remembered a conversation she had shared with Alexander.

"Remember the sparrows, then," Alexander had told her after she'd confessed her difficulty in accepting her importance in the eye of the almighty God. "And think of how you feed all those birds in your backyard. You do feed a lot of birds, don't you?"

Eve had grinned. "Lots, but never enough," she had told him. "There's always room for more."

"A noble sentiment. And you don't mind feeding the sparrows, along with the brighter cardinals and blue jays and goldfinches? You don't ignore them because they aren't as cute or playful as your chickadees?"

"Of course not!" Eve had retorted, instantly indignant. "They're still birds, and they can't help the way God made—"

Eve straightened so fast that the ropes jerked her arms, but she barely noticed the white-hot bolt of pain. *It didn't matter!* "It doesn't matter," she exclaimed aloud. "You don't *care* whether I have the faith of an eagle, or a sparrow—because You've promised to watch over me . . . to *care* for me regardless."

The revelation stole into her spirit, loosening bonds far more restrictive and painful than those shackling her now. She didn't have to *prove* her devotion to anyone—herself or the Lord! As the spiritual chains loosened, she began to relax, and as she relaxed, a gentle peace stole into her heart.

Along with the peace, a faint glimmer of resolution returned: if *she* couldn't arrange for her own rescue, then she would simply have to wait for someone else.

Alexander.

A shaft of hope leaped up in her. Giles had mentioned Alexander, hadn't he? Had *taunted* her about the probability that he would try to rescue her! He would have sent a ransom note, of course. If he hadn't planned to use Eve as some kind of leverage, he would have killed her already.

When Alexander knew where she was, he would find a way to free her. Eve knew it as surely as she knew the birds in her backyard.

That's truth, Eve. Now, let it set you free—then trust Me with your life, exactly as you're trusting Alexander.

Fresh resolve poured into her battered body, stimulated by the flood of illumination to her mind.

"Alexander will need some help, though," she muttered. "I might be an ugly redheaded bluenose to you, Giles—but not to those who matter." She drew her bound feet up, relieving a little of the pressure on her arms, and settled back to wait . . . and think.

Another train passed, and once she heard the distant sound of men's voices. Farther away a horse whinnied, and a dog barked, the sound strangely remote, muffled. She tilted her head, absently staring at the window shade above her—and a shadow drifted across the panel. It disappeared so swiftly she might have imagined it.

Alexander!

It had to be. Galvanized by hope, Eve decided now was the appropriate moment to employ the one other recourse Giles had left to her. She screamed Alexander's name as loudly as she could.

64

ALEX SLIPPED INTO THE DOORWAY of a shoe repair store, brushing wet snow from his back and shoulders. His gaze scanned an almost deserted 17th Street, methodically cross-sectioning until he was satisfied that nobody was shadowing *his* movements.

He left the doorway and continued down the street. A block later, he ducked down an alley. At the back, a rusting ladder led to the roof of the building. Alex vaulted up the rungs with catlike speed. He negotiated the roof, slippery and treacherous with an inch of snow, with the same single-minded skill. Down the other side, then several running dashes between more dark, snow-shrouded monolithic buildings.

Moments after he had left the journal by the fireplug, he was approaching the drop-off site again—but from the opposite side. He checked his watch. Four minutes . . . and the parcel was still there. *Thank You.*

Now, if only Gambrielli had enough arrogance to put in an appearance. . . .

Ten minutes passed, then twenty. Shivering cold in spite of his thick wool jacket and stocking cap, Alex waited patiently beneath the concealing shadows of a water tower. With Eve's life hanging on the erratic delusions of a murderer, he could wait all night without twitching a muscle. He blanked his mind to the possibility that Gambrielli wasn't going to come at all.

A freight train approached, rumbling through the stormy night, the shriek of its whistle borne on the gusting wind. The rhythmic creak and sway of the cars grew louder, and another blast of the whistle signaled its passage by the Chesapeake and Ohio depot.

Under cover of the rattling cars, a shadowy figure crept from the direction of the coal yard, headed straight for the drop-off site. Muscles tensed, breathing suspended, Alex watched.

Movements fast but furtive—like a rat scuttling toward a garbage heap—the figure approached the parcel, almost hidden now beneath drifting snow. He stopped, scanning the surroundings, and Alex expelled a triumphant breath. It was Dante Gambrielli. After a pause, which for Alex stretched toward infinity, he grabbed the parcel, shook it free of snow, then thrust it beneath his coat.

He hadn't taken time to look inside.

Thanks for the storm, Lord. It's annoying—but I do believe it tipped the scales in my *favor this time.* From his position beneath the water tower, Alex watched until Gambrielli disappeared. He was headed toward the freight yard . . . where a multitude of railroad cars sat idle on sidetracks.

Alex ran like a hunted stag; the storm, as well as the moving train, would conceal him as well as it had Gambrielli. The last of the swaying cars rumbled by, a bright red light winking from the caboose.

A lone Wagner palace car stood on a sidetrack adjacent to the passing freight. As the caboose disappeared into a vortex of swirling snow, its red light momentarily reflected on a man's figure climbing the vestibule steps of the palace car. He disappeared inside, and seconds later the freight's whistle screamed one last time.

Got you, you murdering blackguard.

Alex quickly scanned his surroundings. Several box-cars sat on the siding beyond the palace car, then a stretch of open space before the freight shed to the northeast. Behind and in front, railroad tracks. A dark, jumbled collection of buildings to the southeast offered the most viable bolt-hole. Alex briefly spared a fleeting wish that Simon was about.

Suddenly his ear pricked at the sound of crunching gravel. Heedless of the snow and sharp stones, Alex dropped, belly to the ground, behind a stationary boxcar. Had Gambrielli already discovered that Rebecca's journal was missing several carefully selected passages? If so—where was he going now?

More critically—where was Eve?

From the direction of the freight depot a shadow darted across the tracks and disappeared behind the passenger car. Alex frowned. Either Gambrielli had slipped out without Alex seeing him, or the figure Alex had just spotted was a third man.

A third man?

Gambrielli had always worked alone. His arrogance, his perception of his "superior mentality," precluded the encumbrance of underlings. And Alex would have staked his professional reputation that nobody had been shadowing his own movements. Who could it be?

Joe Leoni. It had to be Leoni.

Out in the corridor, running footsteps thudded. A man's shout, hoarse and indistinguishable, silenced Eve's screams. She held her breath, straining to hear.

The door wrenched open. It was Giles—his face a rictus of hatred, evil . . . and fear. In spite of herself, Eve shrank back. Then he attacked, and her terrified eyes glimpsed the point of a knife. With a single slash Giles cut the cord that bound her to the bench.

"Hurry . . . have to hurry!" he muttered, the whisper almost incoherent. He sawed furiously at the cords binding her feet, then jerked her upright. Her hands still tied behind her, Eve would have fallen, but Giles caught her waist in a merciless grip. He cursed beneath his breath. "Run!" he hissed in her ear, and shoved her into the narrow corridor. "Run, or you're dead!"

Overhead the lantern swayed, light and shadow shifting in broken, distorted patterns. From the other end of the car footsteps scraped down the aisle, out of sight behind a pair of heavy curtains.

"Alexander!" Eve managed to choke out, but Giles was at her back, one hand shoving her shoulder blades, between her still-bound arms. The other wrapped around the cord he was holding, keeping her bound to his side. "It's not the Pink!" he grated, scattering the words like bullets.

Eve turned so suddenly he slammed into her, knocking her against the side of the train. She stumbled back against Giles. "You're a liar!" she yelled, and her boot connected with his shin.

"There's nowhere to run, Gambrielli. I jiggered the door at that end. It's you . . . me—and the skirt."

The guttural voice spun Eve toward a spiraling black void; for a moment her vision wavered. The man stalking them was *not* Alexander MacKay: it was Joe Leoni.

The low, faintly nasal voice flowed toward them like a poisonous cloud, drifting closer, closer. "I would have left you alone, Gambrielli. I really would have. You and I— we're a lot alike." With a hushed rustle the drapery parted. "But you wouldn't stay in England, with your plump English chippies. Even worse, Gambrielli—you're interfering in *my* business." His malignant shadow leaped down the aisle.

"I told you I'd take care of it," Giles snarled, turning to face the oncoming man. "And I also warned you that the Pinkerton flatfoot is on the way. I sent him a note. Don't be stupid, Shiver. Get out while you can."

Eve risked a slow, cautionary step away from Giles, praying he wouldn't notice. She tried to wriggle her arms to restore some circulation, tried to lift her numb feet without shuffling. *Keep talking,* she begged them silently.

Leoni maintained his slow, stalking pace, the fitful light touching the pallid moon of his face. Without turning his head, Giles' foot ground down on the hem of Eve's skirt at the same time his hand closed over her raw and throbbing wrists.

"What's the matter, Dante? Or should I call you 'Giles'?" Leoni jibed in a macabre echo of Eve's attempt to goad her captor. "You want to save the interfering red-haired limmer for yourself, is that it?" His laugh rustled like dead leaves against a tombstone. "Best leave her to me, Gambrielli. You kill your unsuspecting wives all the time—but this skirt's nothing but trouble. Not like her pretty little sister at all."

"Shut up!" Giles burst out hoarsely, his hand grinding Eve's wrist so tightly the bones shifted. She clamped her teeth against a moan.

Joe Leoni sauntered forward a few more steps, drawing level with the first compartment past the car's kitchen. Only one more compartment—a bare two yards—separated them. "You can watch, if you want to. How's that for professional courtesy? You can watch, *Giles Dawson*—while I slit her throat as neatly as I did your wife's. I've been waiting a long time. . . ."

The words exploded in Eve's ears. Then Giles shouted, a sound borne of fury, anger—and raw pain. *"I'll kill YOU, you stinking little tinhorn!* You killed her! You killed Rebecca!"

Suddenly he thrust Eve aside, leaping with an enraged snarl at Joe Leoni. Dazed, Eve staggered upright, her back pressed against the corridor wall.

Leoni, she accepted with terror-induced calm, would kill Giles, who seemed to have gone mad. And then . . . and then he would kill her like he had—Eve closed her eyes and bowed her head. A strange sort of acceptance washed over her; pain and fear swept away in the gentle river of peace flowing through her. *I can die with dignity, after all. Thank You.*

There was the sickening sound of a falling body, followed by an obscene grunt. Then a gurgling rattle of sound, and a heartbeat of thick, unbroken silence. Eve shuddered, an eddy of fear swirling in her mind. She flinched when dragging footsteps moved toward her, accompanied by wheezing sobs of exertion.

I will not fear, for Thou art with me. The words, so familiar that the meaning often blurred into trite insignificance, cascaded over Eve and filled her with a resurgence of power and warmth. She opened her eyes and lifted her head. But it was not Joe Leoni creeping toward her with lust in his eye and blood on his hands. It was Giles. In one hand he held a knife, the blade shining dark and wet. His eyes looked straight through Eve.

Reeling with shock, Eve opened her mouth to speak, to try to reason with him. She wanted to understand before she died. Only a wisp of sound emerged.

Giles—he would always be Giles to her—walked straight up to her. Now the black gaze mirrored the torture of the condemned. "He killed my wife." He stared down into Eve's disbelieving face, his mouth working. "He killed my wife . . . but he won't be killing anyone else."

Eve searched the stark face, then glanced toward the dark heap sprawled in the corridor. "You . . . didn't kill Rebecca?" She couldn't grasp it, couldn't believe it. After all these months of fear and despair and festering hatred, the man responsible for her sister's death now lay dead in the corridor behind her.

And the man standing in front of her, the man who had just cold-bloodedly extracted vengeance for his wife's murder—this man manifested soul-rending grief, much like the pain Eve daily confronted in her father's face. Joe Leoni had killed Rebecca—not Giles Dawson.

Then Eve remembered Giles Dawson's *real* identity.

She stared down at the knife, clutched loosely in his trembling fingers. "If Leoni hadn't killed her, were you planning to? Like you have all your other . . . wives?"

His shoulders hunched with tension. He lifted the knife, stared at it, then tugged out a snowy white handkerchief and wiped it clean. "I loved her." The words were low, choked—so soft Eve barely heard.

Her heart lurched, and she watched Giles carefully tuck the knife inside his boot. When he straightened, some of the old aloof condescension had returned. "I can tell you don't believe me. Well, I did, Miss Sheridan—and it's for *that* she died."

"I . . . don't understand."

He gave a dry, mirthless laugh. "The journal. The cursed journal."

65

JOE LEONI. THE VERY NAME CAUSED every nerve in Alex's body to leap in warning. Tucked in a low crouch, he inched along the base of the boxcar, peered out behind the coupling, then dashed to the far end of the Wagner palace car.

Foot and hand prints smeared the steps and rail. A gust of wind whistled around the corner, blinding him in a blast of whirling snow. He vaulted up the steps and found a crowbar jamming the inner door, preventing anyone inside from escaping.

Alex was debating whether to remove the crowbar or to slip down to the other end when he heard Eve's voice, screaming his name. The sound was faint, barely audible, but Alex heard it. His hands, clumsy and stiff from cold, tugged at the crowbar. It was jammed so tightly he couldn't pry it loose.

Moving on blind instinct, he leaped down and ran to the other end of the car. If that door was blocked, he would break a window, and devil take the hindmost. *Never fear, lass! I'm coming. God . . . don't let him kill her.*

With a faint sucking noise the door swung open. Alex slipped inside the dark car, where instant quiet enveloped him. He heard the sound of bodies thudding against the walls, the floor. A weak stream of light haloed the pantry and kitchen area at the center of the car, beyond the drawn-back curtain.

The sounds of the fight abruptly ceased. A thick silence filled the air.

Alex dropped back into a crouch, then crept along the narrow aisle, his pulse throbbing the deadly cadence of his warring ancestors. He was cold and very calm, his mind clear as a Highland loch, every sense focused.

Then he heard Eve's voice: "You . . . didn't kill Rebecca?" And incredibly, unbelievably, Dante Gambrielli replying, in the tone of a man stretched on a rack, "I loved her."

She was still alive! Eve was *alive.*

Each movement slow, cautious, Alex straightened. Standing just behind the concealing folds of the heavy drapery panels, he listened to the incredible conversation taking place, and waited. His timing had to be perfect, or Eve could get hurt.

"So Avery Paxton threatened to tell her who I was if I didn't pay," Gambrielli was telling Eve. "I . . . knew she would never stay with me—"

"You mean you knew you'd have to kill her," Eve interjected, her tone accusing.

Don't, love. Alex altered his stance and peered briefly through the curtain panels, his hand thrusting inside his jacket. Then he ducked back. He couldn't risk exposure yet. Dante had drawn a knife out of his boot, and Eve was standing too close to him. *Move back,* he urged her with his mind. *Eve, step away.*

"Yes, I would have killed her. Just as I will you, Miss Sheridan." Gambrielli's voice changed. "Now, come with me. I have something to show you—and we'll both find out if your Mr. MacKay is as clumsy and inept as all the others."

Alex ground his teeth, and pulled back behind the curtain, then relaxed when Eve snapped tartly, "*I* already know the answer. The fact that you don't know tells more about *your* lack of intelligence than Mr. MacKay's." Then Alex heard her exclamation of dismay. "The journal!"

"That's right, Miss Sheridan. The journal. And now . . ."

There was the sound of rustling pages, and Alex held his breath, his hand slowly . . . slowly withdrawing the revolver. Ach, if only he could see what was going on! He could hear the restless swirl of Eve's skirt, and Gambrielli's excited rasps as he turned pages.

It shouldn't be long now.

"The conniving cheat!" Gambrielli roared abruptly, and Alex grinned a savage, satisfied grin. "Some pages have been cut out! I should have known he'd pull a stunt like this."

"Now who is the *inept* one, *Giles*?" Eve's voice sounded triumphant.

Ah, love, you need to learn to curb that tongue. . . .

"Did you think he'd be fool enough to allow you to keep both the journal and me?" Eve continued.

Gambrielli's answering retort could not conceal his growing agitation. "Of course not, you silly twit. Though I did think he valued your life more than this. Obviously he needs to be taught a lesson."

"No matter what you do to me, Alexander will see justice done—and he won't let you escape—oh!"

At her cry of pain, Alex flinched. Sweat gathered on his temple and forehead, but he forced himself not to move. Not yet. Dante couldn't afford to kill her, not when she remained his only bargaining tool. Still, he didn't think he could stand much more of her pain.

"That was only a tiny cut," Gambrielli murmured, his voice oozing with threat. "He won't wait much longer to put in an appearance—I made sure my movements were easy for him to follow." He chuckled. "Of course, with this storm, one never knows. And let's not forget Shiver, there. Perhaps Mr. MacKay is lying outside, on the tracks, with *his* throat slit."

Eve sobbed aloud, and Alexander heard her extraordinary courage faltering for the first time. "No." But the word lacked conviction.

"You don't sound so sure. Perhaps another tiny slice? Where shall I—?"

Alex stepped from behind the curtain. "I don't think that will be necessary, Gambrielli." He raked a rapid glance over Eve, noting with curdling rage the paper white face and lines of pain, her bound arms—and a small, widening stain smearing the sleeve of her shirtwaist, right below the shoulder. "Let her go," he said. Alex wanted to smile at Eve, to reassure her, but he couldn't take his eyes off his prey.

Dante laughed again, a high, crazed sound. A muscle twitched in his jaw. "First, hand over the journal pages you tore out." Alex watched his hands, especially the one holding the knife to Eve.

"They're not here. I'm really not a fool, Gambrielli."

The stone-dead eyes darkened with anger. "Neither am I. Quit stalling—or I'll kill her in front of your eyes, you blasted Pinkerton!" He spat the word like an epithet.

"Kill her," Alex murmured, very softly, "and you won't leave this car alive."

Gambrielli was finally losing control, Alex saw, but Eve stood still, her gaze never leaving Alex. "It seems we're at an impasse," Gambrielli ground harshly. His arm moved. Eve jerked, her skin turning the color of putty. Gambrielli held up the knife, showing Alex the reddened point. "I wonder," he continued, his gaze vicious, ". . . how many times I can slice into Miss Sheridan before you learn that I *will* have things my way."

"I think," Eve interjected, her voice weak and wobbly, "that I might faint."

"Don't you move!" Gambrielli hissed.

But Alex had looked straight into her eyes—and saw the calm conviction, and absolute lack of fear. Then, incredibly, she flashed him a tiny smile; she was contriving to provide him with the opportunity for which he'd been waiting, was his little Highland warrior!

Alex steeled himself. *Forgive me*, he prayed.

Eve moaned, then sagged, her knees buckling. Gambrielli turned his head toward her with another hissing curse. Eve whirled around and butted him with her head.

"You little—!" Gambrielli staggered back, his arm lifting. The lantern light caught the point of the knife, and as he plunged it down toward Eve's neck, Alex shot him through the heart.

The deafening report of the revolver exploded through the car, slamming Dante backward. As Gambrielli fell, a look of enraged disbelief distorting his features, Alex leaped for Eve and thrust her into an open compartment behind them. The knife clattered against the wall, then fell harmlessly to the floor.

Keeping the gun leveled, Alex kicked the knife away, then knelt beside the fallen man. Dante's eyes blazed and began to lose focus. "I . . . didn't—you don't usually . . . carry a gun."

"Unfortunate for us both," Alex told him, his voice a sober, rumbling burr. "' Tis never my first choice—but to save an innocent life . . ." He stared down at the dying man, then slowly rested his hand on Gambrielli's shoulder, surprised to see that his fingers were no longer steady. "May God have mercy on your tortured soul," he whispered.

Dante's ashen lips moved. Alex bent closer. "I . . . did love . . . Rebec—" His head slumped sideways as his body relaxed.

After a second Alex stood, then turned to the compartment where Eve was struggling to roll herself into a sitting position. When she caught sight of Alex, her movements stilled. Their gazes met, and Alex pulled out his handkerchief and wrapped it about her upper arm. He used Gambrielli's knife to cut away the ropes.

"Is he dead?"

"Yes. He's dead."

"Are you all right?"

He gave her a crooked smile. "Only my lass would ask that question at a time like this." His hands were very gentle as he searched for other wounds, then began massaging her numb limbs. "Yes, love. I'll be all right—now that I have you back, safe and sound." He lifted her chin. "Are *you* all right? Did he hurt you in any other way?"

She shook her head. Two tears welled, then slipped over. "I'm . . . glad he's dead, but I'm sorry you had to be the one to kill him. Does that make sense, Alexander?"

"Perfect sense." He kissed away the tears. "Do you know that I love you, Eve Sheridan?"

Eve put her arms around his neck, then whispered in a choked voice, "I'm very glad. I love you too." After a moment, she removed her hands and rubbed the bruises on her wrists, wincing at the pain. "Those ropes hurt almost as much as the cut on my arm."

Alex leaned over and kissed her, a long and satisfying kiss. "The only kind of bond you will ever experience again," he said gently, "is the bond symbolized by a wedding band." He paused and looked at her intently. "If you'll have me, that is."

Eve nodded, tears filling her eyes. "Of *course* I'll have you!" A smile slowly spread across her face, along with a glint of mischief. "You know . . . except for a few minor discomforts, this has all been very exciting. Perhaps, Mr. MacKay, I shall apply for a job as a Pinkerton operative. Don't you think we'd make a wonderful team?"

The sound of her teasing, jubilant voice filled the car, erasing the last echoes of gunfire and Dante Gambrielli's dying words. Alex picked her up, then holding her close against his heart, carried her onto the platform, pushing open the doors with his shoulder.

Outside, the storm had dissipated. In the rapidly clearing sky, a benevolent moon shone silvery beams upon the earth. A sparkling, magical wonderland of fresh snow and clear, frost-sprinkled air filled their senses.

Alex lifted his face toward heaven and smiled. He could almost feel a loving hand brushing his face and hear a Voice whispering into his ear. He glanced down at Eve. She was looking around, an expression of amazement flooding her face.

"Alexander!" she exclaimed. "Isn't it beautiful?" She paused, as if listening, and an entrancing smile widened her mouth. "Alexander . . . you might not believe this, but I feel, well . . . healed." Her hand crept up to touch his cheek. "I feel as if . . . as if . . ."

Alex grinned down at her. "I believe it, lass," he said. "And yes, I feel God's presence too. Now . . . how about a nice moonlit stroll?"

"I thought you'd never ask. Alexander?"

"Yes, love?"

"Did you have permission to handle Giles—I mean, Dante Gambrielli—on your own?"

"What do you think?"

"I think," Eve replied, settling comfortably into his arms, "that I might enjoy very much the climate in Santa Fe."

Epilogue

Georgia
June 1894

SIMON KINCAID'S MOUTH TWITCHED when he saw the letter and small package, both addressed with the neat precision of a scholar. He didn't immediately open them, however, too mindful of the omnipresent gaze of Miss Lila Soames, Sumner's postmistress.

Sure enough, the moment he closed the door to his box, her voice piped from behind the counter, "Is that you, Mr. Kinsley?"

"Yes, ma'am." Resigned, he stepped up to the window. "Good afternoon, Miss Soames."

"I couldn't help but notice the lovely penmanship of your package and letter," she announced, her drawl thick as the sorghum molasses his landlady served with every meal. "Would that be a sweetheart, perhaps?"

"No, ma'am. Actually, she's the bride of my best friend." Simon tipped his bowler and left before the chirping little lady drew another breath.

He stepped out into the baking sun of the hot June day. Far down the tracks a train whistle sounded. Simon longed to fling the bowler hat into the field and hop aboard the approaching train.

Instead, he tucked the letter and package inside the

leather tool bag mounted on the bicycle handlebars and pedaled down the packed dirt street.

An hour later, underneath the drooping branches of a pecan tree, he opened the package. A small book, bound in handsome green leather, tumbled into his hands. The embossed gold letters of the title shimmered in the late afternoon sunlight.

"*Birds of the New Testament: A Study by Eve Sheridan MacKay.*" The line of Simon's firm mouth softened. "Good for you, redbird." He laid the book aside and opened the letter, his expression relaxed for the first time in months. For a few minutes, he thought, he could forget the world of deceit, greed, and tyranny. The story of his friend Alex, and Eve Sheridan, almost produced a smile. Almost.

The letter was short. *I know you think you've no use for a book such as this,* Eve wrote, *but Alexander and I wanted you to have a copy. Take particular note, if you please, of my reference to sparrows. That one has helped me tremendously, and I feel certain there is a lesson there for you, Mr. Kin—* Here a blob of ink betrayed Eve's absentmindedness at forgetting his current alias—and her quick recovery. *Kinsley. Alexander, you see, has shared a bit of your background. (I do hope you won't be mightily vexed with me.) We've both struggled over much of our lives, in different ways. I hope someday—like me—you'll be able to accept the truth of these verses.*

Not likely, Simon thought bleakly.

I also wanted to tell you the exciting news: Alexander has been transferred—but not to Santa Fe. By the time you receive this, we should be on our way to Atlanta! It seems that Mr. Paxton has begun building a new empire down there, and (after considerable badgering!) Alexander convinced Mr. Hostler that Atlanta was almost as far from Richmond as Santa Fe. Mr. Hostler, I'm given to understand, is writing a very long letter to the superintendent there. Alexander just smiles.

From down the road Simon heard the sound of an approaching carriage. He glanced up, verifying the identity of the occupants, then hurriedly finished Eve's letter.

I do hope we will be able to see you someday soon. My parents, as well as Alexander, asked that I extend their cordial greetings. Everyone, you see, is most grateful to you for being my shadow for a time. I must go now, and show our new gardener the proper way to fill the bird feeders, before Alexander and I drive out to say goodbye to his family. Did you ever meet his grandfather? He carves the most intriguing wooden puzzles, and gave me one for a wedding gift. I had to let Alexander figure it out—it turned into a blue jay. Most appropriate for us both, don't you agree?

Take care, Mr. Kinsley. And . . . don't forget, please, while you're living your life in shadows, that (no matter how you feel about the matter!) you will always be safe, in the shadow of His wings. With much affection,
Eve MacKay

Simon folded the letter, tucked it inside the book, and nonchalantly rose to greet the buggy drawing to a halt at the edge of the pecan orchard. Two heavyset men climbed down, their faces red and perspiring, their suits coated with red Georgia dust. Simon leaned back against the rough bark of the tree and crossed his arms, his expression bleak.

He was about to return to a world of shadows where telling the truth meant death, and deceit was the only weapon he possessed to stay alive. It was not a lifestyle Eve's and Alex's God would condone, and Simon did not delude himself with the hope for divine protection.

He shouldered away from the tree, and walked across to meet the two approaching men.

". . . they shall mount up with wings as eagles . . ."